A fascinating story of sci … rnal fights for recognition and pow… …sts which shows science as it reall… … the people credible. "Catalysed Fus… …hat can be highly recommended both for scientists and laymen. A guaranteed page-turner!

Jan Kjellman, physicist

Thought-provoking science-fiction, very readable, the style excellent. The fact that the author is an eminent scientist is evident. A well constructed work that puts over life at CERN realistically. The character of Viktor is well portrayed and is one of the strong points of the book: a well drawn villain, and his subsequent come-uppance and redemption is good writing. The open-ended conclusion is quite natural. I read it over about a week and found myself trying to make it last; the sign of a good book.

Frank Beck, physicist

An explosive mixture of romance and murder in Geneva. Young ambitious Jeremy looks for a new source of energy but falls in love with dazzling Avelyn who becomes his mistress. Accidental death becomes murder. One of Jeremy's colleagues is accused and sent to prison, but saved by one of the clever twists in the plot. Excellent and believable physics explained in a clear and easy way. The realism of flying gliders in Switzerland. An exciting, gripping and adventurous story with romance and passion . It speeds along to high drama in Stockholm; in another of Farley's romantic twists, the hero finally understands the value of true love.

Barry Hibbit, writer

CATALYSED FUSION

Francis Farley

Love, discovery and adventure
around the particle accelerators in Geneva

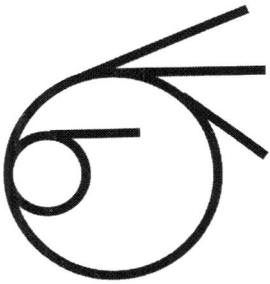

This book is a work of fiction. Any resemblance to people living or dead is entirely coincidental

Published by Francis Farley 2012
Printed by CreateSpace

ISBN 978-1481018494

About the author

Francis Farley lived in Geneva. He worked at CERN for 20 years and later with particle accelerators in the U.S.A. The Royal Society awarded him a medal for his precise measurements on the muon. He is a Fellow of the Royal Society, a Fellow of the Institute of Physics and an honorary Fellow of Trinity College Dublin. He is an experienced skier and glider pilot with international C-certificate, gold plus diamond. He lives in France.

CONTENTS

In memoriam

To the memory of

Patrick Mollet

Chief of the translation service at CERN for many years;
a good friend, wine connaisseur and ski companion.
He saw it all, knew it all but was not involved.

and to the memory of

John Bell

another good friend with his red beard, tricky puzzles, deep understanding, and enigmatic smile.

Thanks

Warm thanks to

Barry Hibbit and Neville Moray for their help and useful comments

and to my lovely wife

Irina

for everything

Preface

This is a love story, a true-to-life fantasy, woven around particle physics in Geneva. Competition, rivalry, distraction, skill and skulduggery; fun and fury at the frontiers of science. Switzerland in the eighties. Romance, science and adventure, in the city where nations meet. In those intoxicating early days, CERN was young, discoveries came thick and fast and a small group could make an impact; anything seemed possible. How science works at the frontiers of knowledge, how scientists operate around those big machines and how they relax, skiing or soaring in the Alps, on the beach or at hot spots in town. In a large establishment there are people of all tastes. Most will go home to read stories to the children: but the characters in this story were more adventurous. This is how it was, and how it still is. Then as now, the challenges were the same. Who leads? Who follows? Who succeeds? Who gets the credit? Who gets the girls, or the men? In those days computers were new, the internet was being invented; and no one had a mobile phone.

1 Love birds in Geneva

The telephone warbled! Dawn chorus on the Zambezi, tropical birds quavering for their mates. It was a new one, the latest offering of the Swiss PTT; Clare had picked it up a few weeks ago, special model, monthly rental 14 francs and 10 centimes, tax included. According to the prospectus, it had a wide choice of 'alarming calls'. By pressing the right keys you could have a Jodlerabend in Appenzell, a concatenation of cuckoo clocks, Beethoven's ninth symphony (luckily only in part), the Swiss national anthem, or the discreet burr-burr of a Swiss banker buzzing his mistress on a rainy afternoon. The instruction book (in four languages) had already gone for a stroll, so they were stuck with the amorous tropical birds. The bird called again. Clare said

"Better answer it, before it wakes the kids. It's bound to be for you." Simon and Julie could sleep through the fire of London, but her second point made sense.

Jeremy rolled out of bed, and stumbled along the corridor. As usual the bulb had gone, and no one thought of changing it while he was away. He would have to climb up and unscrew the plastic dome again. Clare never had the proper bulbs in stock, so they would end up with a religious 25 watt or a laser sharp 150 watt, when everyone knew that 40 watts gave the right warmth for reading the telephone numbers, but not enough to show the sticky smears made by four palms on the tacky Swiss wall paper.

Who would ring at this time of night? Some cretin at the lab had got his cables crossed! If the apparatus failed he would have to go in, find out why; trace the faulty connection, or change a module. He tried to remember who was on shift tonight; that bastard Bexler probably, with Marion. "Woodilly-doo woodilly-doo!" The birds chortled shamelessly and in the darkness Jeremy groped for the receiver.

"Hullo darling! You do sound cross. I thought you were never going to answer. . . . . Did you have a good trip?"

The quintessential voice of Eve. Eve the beautiful, Eve the temptress, Eve the perfect companion, Eve the presumptive mother of mankind. He could picture her broad round face and attentive smile, waiting for his reaction.

"Oh, hullo. Yes. . . . . no. . . . . hang on." He spoke quietly, hoping that Clare was asleep. Then he edged his way along the corridor, round the corner into the spare room, carrying the receiver in one hand, and the rest of the apparatus in the other. The wire was just long enough.

Tropical bird knew the score. She kept quiet. She was clever. If Clare answered she would just say 'wrong number' in one of her many languages, which gets you off the hook, so to speak, but leaves a lingering uncertainty at the other end, even suspicion. At last he was in the spare room with the door shut.

"Hi."

"Hi. . . . . Is it OK now?"

"Yes, I think so. Actually it's a bit awkward if you ring here - especially so late."

Oh - I'm sorry. How was the lecture?"

"It went very well - there was a big audience, and lots of interest. I mentioned the fusion thing, and they were all riveted."

"Oh good! But should you have told them that? I mean at this stage?"

"No problem, I just gave them the general idea, not the detail."

"And how is the run going?"

"Very well apparently. It's getting very exciting in fact. I'll find out more tomorrow of course."

She lowered her voice. "Jeremy. . . . . . He's away tonight . . . in Milan . . . he is giving a lecture too. You can guess what on." He guessed.

"Right first time." The voice went softer still, conspiratorial.

"So . . . . . are you coming to see me?"

"Well, I don't know, I am on shift at eight in the morning. And . . . . . . I must get some sleep." He looked at his watch; it was 10.30 .

"Oh, dear!" He could hear the disappointment. "And I've been looking forward to it all day; and last night too in fact. It's just . . . . well . . . . . . you know how it is!"

He knew how it was. The unslakeable thirst, the vibrant emptiness. And he knew how delightful she would be. But what could he do? How could he fit it in?

"Darling, I am sorry. It's really too difficult tonight. I . . . . well . . . . I've only just got in. Tomorrow would be better . . . .say about 4."

"He gets back then. He's on the T.E.E. He'll probably come straight home. And it's too cold now to go outside" She was right about that: it was a perishing November night.

"I am sorry, Darling. I really don't think I can make it this time. I'll call you tomorrow."

"Oh God! . . . . Are you sure?"

"Yes, I really can't."

"Oh well." There was a long pause. "Tomorrow then."

"Tomorrow."

"Oh Jeremy."

"What?"

"Don't forget."

"Forget what?"

"I . . . . well . . . . . . you know. . . ." She petered out, but he could guess what she was driving at.

"Thinking of you honey. I'll call you tomorrow."

"Bye then."

Jeremy hung up. He might have said 'love'. Perhaps it was the same. 'Thinking of' or 'loving', what was the difference? In practice it meant the same, but women liked to hear the word. It was all very well for her; she was unattached - except of course for her husband. But he had the kids That was a complication. He did not know whether he loved her or not. Whether he was coming or going. Going with her, or staying where he was, with the family. At the moment he was staying, but of course, he would rather be with her. One day, perhaps, it would happen, but meanwhile he was doing nothing. Just letting things take their course. If you waited the problem might solve itself. He went into the kitchen; looked out of the window. Snow already! It was a typical Geneva night.

Having said no, he realised that what he really wanted was yes. Images of her delicious hips haunted him. Satin smooth expanses of luminous skin, trembling under his caress. Perhaps he would go after all. A well constructed excuse, and in twenty minutes he could be in her arms; and why not? Man that is born of woman hath but a short time to live . . . and after that . . . .? Life was too short to waste. So he took the fatal decision. But he did not phone to say he was coming. Afterwards he wished he had.

"They are having trouble. Lost the beam. Either the magnets have dropped out, or the counters are acting up. They do not seem to know what to do. So . . . I think I'd better go in and lend a hand. With any luck I'll be back in a jiffy."

It was a blatant lie, of course, and he hated it. It was a lousy basis for any relationship. But what could you do? In an ideal world one should be able to talk openly, explain what you were doing, and why, however unconventional it might be. But the truth was sometimes unacceptable to the other party. They would be disappointed, upset, angry; they might even march out in fury. So one wrapped it up, trotted out something more palatable. But of course this could not go on for ever. The wave would eventually break. It was a short term fix, the coward's way.

It would have been better to have it out in the open; to say simply, "I am going off to see her, to make love, in two hours I will be back with you and the family, all nice and cosy." But with Clare he dared not try it; she was too conventional; she would be offended, hurt, annihilated. In fact he underestimated her. Meanwhile the lies, the inability to talk about what was always on his mind, were slowly poisoning the relationship. Their conversation, once so fascinating to both, had deteriorated into a sequence of trivia.

Two years earlier their life had been totally different, and looking back, through the rosy haze of distance, all seemed to have been sweetness and light. Clare was thrilled to move to Geneva, and Jeremy felt lucky to have landed a three year job at CERN, world renowned in particle physics, and a laboratory that seemed to have almost unlimited resources. Up to now he had existed on various research grants and fellowships; this was his first real job. His salary, inflated by a series of special allowances to compensate for the misery of leaving home, was double what he had got in England and tax free as well!

They settled in, but Clare soon had second thoughts. She had given up her job in England, and her veterinary qualification was not valid in Geneva. She expected to spend much more time with Jeremy, but he was never there. The huge accelerators ran continuously, day and night, so physicists using the beams had to be on site. They worked in shifts with irregular hours. Even when not on shift, the work was so enthralling that they would often drift home late. CERN wives were 'physics widows'.

To cap it all, even when Jeremy was home his mind was in another place, worrying about unsolved problems, so complex that explanations would be a waste of time. Apparently he was there with you, but in reality he was somewhere else. There and not there at the same time. So in spite of the manifold joys of Switzerland, Clare often wished that they were back in England.

Now he was off to CERN again and Clare was sympathetic but not upset. "Do be careful, it's a filthy night. And come back soon." She turned over. He pulled on some clothes; snow boots, overcoat, gloves. Wipe the windscreen. A few centimetres had fallen. It was unusual in Geneva to have it this early, but it would clear up fairly quickly. Was he crazy to go out, when he could be tucked up safely at home?

He got into the car and reached out his right hand. A gentle touch in the right place, and she was throbbing, ready to go. Then the hand on the knob and slip it in. One, two, three, four. Forward and back, forward and back, with a delicate synchronous motion of the knees. The well modulated clutch. Then you were in top and motoring.

The snowflakes fluttered under the street lamps, making bright cones of white. The country roads skirting round Geneva were deserted, white and silent. A few cars had passed, leaving crisp tracks. Snow had its special way of creating silence, deadening the noise of the wheels and letting no sound come through from a distance. The flakes danced towards him, streaked over the bonnet and divided in front of his eyes, rushing away to left, right and over the roof.

In this lonely cocoon, swishing through the night, he wondered what he was doing and why. Two years ago life had been simple, straightforward, normal; the nuclear family, happy with each other and the growing children, going out into the adventure of life. How had he got into this mess? And how would he get out of it? It could not go on for ever, that was obvious. Yet there was no way out. How would it ever end? In theory he could choose. But how could he, when the future was unpredictable, and either way might lead to disaster? So, you just drive on into the blackness, following the road ahead; it must lead somewhere.

The car almost knew the way. He got to her flat, and now he knew what he was doing. He parked discreetly at the back. Turn off the lights, lock it, pad through the snow, stamp your feet on the mat, then inside and up in the lift. They were on the top floor, of course, the most expensive. The building was quiet as a ghost.

He rang the bell. Ding - pause - ding-ding! His special signal. He could imagine her surprise, her joy. As usual his imagination went ahead of him, and he figured out what he would do with her. This time she would be on her knees, upright, with her hands against the wall. For a long time he would just run his fingers over her lovely skin, tickling, teasing, visiting every millimetre. Keep her waiting, tingling, trembling. And then what? Perhaps, the order of the wooden spoon? Yes, that would be fun, and it would make her quiver some more. Maybe a mild protest at first; but she would enjoy it. She enjoyed everything.

The erotic images came in out of the blue, one after the other in an endless series, vague at first then gradually getting clearer, each one slowly taking shape, acquiring detail, like planes coming in to land at Cointrin. He rang again; perhaps she was asleep. Ding, ding-ding! And again ding, ding-ding! That would tell her that this was not some mad intruder, a maniac with his mind full of rape, pillage and wild sexual fantasies.

2 Ivan and Juliet

On the nudist Mediterranean island, Ile du Levant, Ivan Eckerdovsky basked naked in the morning sun: rising golden from the sea it glowed on his reddish beard and well bronzed body, moist from a long swim and the glow of exercise. A beautiful day was starting, and he felt terrific. How lucky he was to work on this quiet island with a small beach just below the apartment. He had a new laboratory with good buildings contoured into the hillside, and a small staff, who were both competent and cheerful. In a way he deserved it, because as director of the deuterium project he had set it up this way. But he still recognised his good fortune, and was grateful for it.

The lithe and lovely Juliet had given him a delicious night, and would now be laying up a sizzling breakfast. She was a wonderful find, warm, sexy, intelligent, but never jealous.

"I am leaving you today," she said across the table. "Dancing class tomorrow, and your daughter needs me." Half her time was spent in Geneva looking after Liliane, and teaching young women to dance in the Rue du Grand Pré.

"The DG is coming down next week," he answered. "It would be good if you could be here."

He was referring to Michel Augier, the Director-General of CERN, who had steered the organisation towards more useful applications of particle physics, and in particular had started the new energy projects.

"He wants to see how the lab is shaping up. But I think we might get him to stay an extra day and relax a little. What's the point of being in these beautiful surroundings, if you cannot enjoy it?"

"Mais, oui, chéri!" French was easier for her. She could get by in English, but when they were at home she prattled away in her native tongue.

"A nice dinner party, perhaps; good French food; he could meet your senior staff, and a few nice girls from the lab to warm the pot - why not?" She thought for a moment; then added.

"He can stay the night. Then next day I will take him to relax on the beach. You are a clever man to think up a project that needs the sun and the sea." He smiled at his perfect wife.

"But what made you think of a fish that preferred heavy water?" Not a fish, of course, but a monocellular organism: Juliet could never grasp the details, and she did not need to.

"Nature is very supple," he answered. "Organisms adapt to their environment. For normal creatures heavy water is poisonous, but the difference in chemistry is very slight. Surely given time, and sufficient generations, they could evolve to live in heavy water instead of ordinary water. Then we could put them in the sea, and they would select the heavy hydrogen for their bodies in place of the ordinary light hydrogen. We would have something that grows, and concentrates deuterium into itself. We fish them out, and press the water from their bodies, and there you have it! Cheap and plentiful heavy water!"

"I am so confused. Heavy hydrogen . . . . heavy water . . . . . . deuterium? Are they all the same thing?"

"Near enough."

"And CERN needs deuterium for the fusion system! It's Michel's dream. But how did you know that this animal breeding would work?"

"I don't know! It's research, an experiment, an inspired guess. It may work, and it may not; but you have to try. Nature is like that too. Many seeds are thrown on the ground, but only a few grow into beautiful plants. You cannot tell by having a committee look at the seeds. Just let them run, and pick the winners."

"But you convinced them to let you try!"

"It was luck really. I got a computer trace on 'algae plus deuterium', and there were quite a lot of papers on the subject. Some suggested that the creatures could adapt. Then the genetic engineering people in Paris and Genoa offered to help with a bit of gene manipulation. That was enough to sell the idea to CERN. Oil is running out, energy is in fashion and the politicians all want research to be more applied. It fitted in with Michel's ideas."

"And only three years ago, we were living in that old house in Paris. I remember the day the CERN Council adopted your project - how we celebrated - and then two months later they offered you the job!" The memories made her radiant.

"Anyway, it's better than swimming the Danube to get out of Hungary."

Juliet was petite with a stunning smile and a lovely figure, and only 19 when Ivan first met her, but she was already well-known in the music halls of Paris. A small group of impecunious students, celebrating a birthday, had decided after dinner to sample the offerings of 'The Flaming Red Cockerel' in Montmartre. Juliet was the star attraction, and her presentation of Leda and the swan totally captivating. A more faithful embodiment of Leonardo's Leda could not be imagined, for this was exactly her figure and demeanour. Her pale body was truly voluptuous, and her shyness, nobly conquered, came across as virginal modesty. To enhance the effect she kept herself smooth and hairless; so her plump juvenile mound, folded like a ripe peach, was quite openly offered to view and as freely appreciated. Puffy puppy fat! Sweet virginal innocence, combined with an expectation of divine lubricity!

Her other talent was truly exceptional. Blushing is usually an involuntary reaction to strong and unexpected emotion, and is interpreted as such by the observer. But she could switch it on and off at will. So at the climax of her act, her mouth would quiver, her eyes widen, and a pink glow would gradually suffuse her cheeks, down even to her neck and chest, conveying a strong message of timidity and bewilderment. The fragile female automatically attracts the male, and red cheeks are for some reason a strong positive switch.

Oh how she was admired! In the capitals of Europe liquid money flowed from one plump purse to another, just for the privilege of contemplating these marvels. Engagements poured in, and she became a popular star of the cabaret circuit, moving month by month to a new night spot. Middlemen took their slice, but Juliet's pocket was pleasantly and regularly enriched. To earn her bread and butter she became the toast of Europe.

Those who frequent such establishments will know that the artists are expected when off-stage to mingle with the customers, and tactfully encourage the consumption of expensive if not always vintage champagne. By convention an entertainer never touches any other drink. Consumption is catalysed by the rule that the girls must remain in the establishment until a deadline fixed by the management. Those who thirst for deeper pleasures are obliged to keep the glasses filled, long after all desire to drink has vanished. But after closing time anything goes, and terms for entertainment in another place may be negotiated on a personal basis. Some do, some don't. Juliet always insisted that she did not.

All the same, those who knew that she had been a dancer, and it was no secret, tended to assume, probably unjustly, that her public performance had been only the tip of a rather lucrative private iceberg. What was publicly displayed one evening, could well be available for private enjoyment on another. But was it for fun or funding? Pleasure or treasure? That is the crucial question, impossible to answer. Who can penetrate the secrets of the female mind? Since time immemorial, gifts have been a talisman of love, sharing a sign of caring; and the female response has been, in part at least, triggered by the memory or anticipation of benefits in kind. Do we have to put a name to it or delineate the boundaries of social acceptability? Whether or not she lined her pocket in this way, it was clearly of no concern to Ivan.

He was enraptured by her performance and the first at her side when she reappeared. He pressed her to join them, wincing at the price of the champagne, which generously she did not touch but shared around the group. When he discovered that her parents were Polish they had lots to talk about. Intelligently he did not endeavour to prolong the evening, but instead invited her to join the group again for lunch. It was not long before she fell in love with this vigorous and impetuous compatriot, and they were soon spending all their spare time together.

3 Lake Como, Varenna

When Jeremy recalled those weeks in Varenna, the first image was of clear still water in the bright Italian light, with mountains shimmering in the morning mist. He was on the ferry watching its sharp black ripples rolling away along the crystal surface. Somehow the silence was not broken by the steady thrum of the engines, and as the boat pointed north into the quiet upper reaches of the lake a magic future seemed to lie ahead. They were enclosed in their own tiny trajectory, isolated by the silence, and the rest of the world at this moment did not exist: only the glorious creature at his side and the day unravelling before them.

Meanwhile the CERN summer school on 'New Energy Systems' was still in full swing. Antimatter, created by the huge accelerators, might become a new source of power. If only they could learn how to handle it. Not blooming likely, thought Jeremy. But the muons, they were another story; just pour them into hydrogen and you get fusions. It had been seen, measured; it worked. The only question was how well. Would it become a useful process? Could you push up the yield and make it fly? Rumour said you could; but for the old and wise it was a lemon. Jeremy was intrigued by the challenge and was racking his brains to find a new angle.

The Villa Monastero was a beautiful old aristocratic home right on the shore of Lake Como with ripples lapping softly against the balustrades. It now belonged to the Italian Physical Society who ran it as a conference centre. As usual in any lectures at CERN there was a lot of argument.

The DG had kicked off, explaining why he wanted to include some applied work to improve the public image. But many voices were raised against prostituting science on the hot bed of materialism. Like art and poetry, they argued, science should be valued for its beauty and intrinsic interest. Animals might live to eat, sleep and copulate. To be fully human Man should be more than this. It was not enough to open the refrigerator and get out your tin of frozen dog food, flavoured with beef, mutton, chicken or rabbit. Man should have poetry, gaze at the stars, reach out to understand Nature and the Universe.

Yes, said the DG, that was indeed the main task of CERN; but something useful on the side would not come amiss. "Most of you will choose the fundamental search for the whys and hows. But if we can find an application we will get more support. Each can make his own choice."

A voice was raised. “There are plenty of applications of nuclear physics; all that medical stuff, magnetic resonance imaging, PET scanners, X-ray tomography. They all use nuclear techniques.”

“And what about isotopes?” asked Jeremy, “They are used in medicine and industry as well. It's been going on for years; even the politicians have heard of them!”

“But none of those involve subatomic particles,” said Michel. “Of course they are much newer, and applications may come later, by accident so to speak. But I have to get you the money, and if I can point to something useful it will be much easier.”

Then it was Chang-Singh's turn. He was head of theory, one of those super-bright characters from Singapore, half Chinese and half Indian. He had somehow got a British passport by being in Hongkong and this qualified him for a job in CERN. A short round man with an infectious smile. Like most theorists Chang’s conversation was liberally peppered with incomprehensibles that only the initiated could follow. But Jeremy found that he was quite good at coming down to earth to explain things to the experimentalists.

“Can elementary particles be useful? At first sight no, because they all disappear in millionths of a second. We put our heads together and came up with two angles worth exploring: antimatter was no longer science fiction, and cold fusion catalysed by muons.”

One evening at the Albergo dei Pescatori, Clare found herself sitting next to the DG. He was a tall man, with aquiline patrician features, and a strong rasping voice. It was late and the pale bristles on his chin were beginning to show. He exuded quiet confidence and authority and she felt drawn to him by an invisible field. In England, she thought, someone like this would never take an interest in a young married woman; but this was Europe where the rules could be different. She was tall and slim, even if she was not a beauty. But she did have a mind, so use it!

“If you are asking for useful fallout from CERN, what about the Internet, and the World Wide Web? That is something that I believe was invented in the lab, and now everyone is using it.” There was a surprised silence. “Well, I have even used it myself,” Clare spluttered, “Yes, to do a search on leishmaniasis in dogs. The Web came up with a whole list of useful references."

Michel smiled at her. "You're quite right. The Internet actually came from America, but we are very proud of the Web. It was invented so that experimenters could easily share their data. And as you say, now the whole world is using it."

"Isn't that typical?" said Clare, "The really useful inventions appear unexpectedly, unplanned, by chance! So why don't you publicise the Web as a huge contribution of CERN to the world?"

"I have," said Michel. "But it doesn't get any credit. The administrators say it was not our mission, and anyway it was an unplanned fluke. What I need to sell them, paradoxically, is a planned useful application of elementary particles. I could get money for that." He beamed her his aquiline smile, and she felt an empty longing inside her.

This was the first time Clare had been exposed to the multilingual chatter so prevalent in the new Europe. Everybody dropped back into his own language when possible, typically within the family or with members of the same tribe. But even then the conversation was so laced with English words and Italian place names that she could often tell what they were saying. What amused her was the way they switched languages if someone from another country came along; just like zapping channels on the TV.

Another night over the insalata di mare and vitello tonnato she was sitting opposite Chang-Singh. She had picked up enough from Jeremy to ask a question. "Can you tell me, Doctor? If you put muons into liquid hydrogen, I gather you get fusions. How does it work?" Jeremy looked alarmed and gave her the red light. This was a complicated business, and he was only beginning to follow the details. But Chang was undeterred.

"Very briefly, Clare. The muon is just like an electron, but 200 times heavier. So if you put a negative muon, mu-minus, into hydrogen it goes into a tiny orbit close to the nucleus and the combination is neutral. It can drift right through the other atoms and get near another nucleus. Then the two nuclei can interact. They fuse with an enormous release of energy, and the muon is liberated, no longer wanted. It finds another nucleus and does the same thing again."

“You see the muon is not used up,” said Dribble enthusiastically.” Clare nodded. “So one muon can trigger 20,000 fusions before it dies its natural death.”

“But that's not enough,” said Jeremy. “To break even you need ten times as many.”

“So it doesn't work,” said Hans. “This is old hat, it's been known for years, carefully studied, and the numbers just don't add up. So why are we talking about it?”

Jeremy felt obliged to defend the party line. “Some of those numbers are wrong, that's the point. There is some new Russian work with oxygen-free tritium. Much more hopeful.”

In bed that night Jeremy was gently disapproving. “You were pushing your luck a bit with the muon. But you got away with it. Of course the real story is much more complicated, and I am struggling to follow it.”

“Sure, but I can't let my brain rot away completely. The wretched muon has hijacked my husband, so I want to know something about it. I gave up being a vet to come here, and I don't want to be just a domestic appendage while you have all the fun.”

“Look you are having a beautiful holiday in the Italian lakes.”

“Pouf to that! I am bored stiff filling in time until you appear. Let's do something together.”

“It doesn’t work with ordinary hydrogen, by the way.”

“Oh really?”

“No, you need two heavier varieties mixed together, deuterium and tritium.”

Clare tried to remember something. “Arthur says the muon dies after 2 microseconds, isn't that the problem. I don't suppose it would do many fusions in that time.”

“It does pretty well considering. If it lived longer we would be laughing.”

“Well,” said Clare, “Why can't you clever people find another particle which lives a hundred times longer?"

“Yes of course. But the muon lasts longer than any other particle. What you are asking for simply doesn't exist.”

"Maybe you could find one. Then you would be famous!" Jeremy shook his head, but the seed was sown. It would germinate later.

At the weekend they rented a little Fiat, and puttered over to the Lago di Garda. Clare was enchanted by Sirmione with their little hotel room right on the lake. It felt worthwhile at last to have moved from England. Their early morning swim in the limpid water she would remember for ever. It was the last time she felt totally happy and content.

4 Bexler calls

Viktor Bexler was a large man with a bristly brown moustache and a habit of standing too close for comfort. He habitually spoke with his mouth only nine inches from your nose. His frequent lectures on the muon were peppered with snide remarks, witticisms and polemic. By pulling the right strings he had somehow participated in many of the great measurements, and now he wrote endless reviews in Physics Reports, the Annual Reviews of Nuclear Science, Contemporary Physics, and so on. Every article was peppered with references to his own work: Bexler et al (1978), as shown by Bexler et al, for further information see the review by V.A. Bexler (1981) and so on. By convention authors are normally cited in alphabetical order, so in the published papers his name came first: even when his role had been peripheral he liked to claim the credit. Of course he made bright suggestions, but his colleagues felt cheated. So instead of being loved and revered, he left a trail of bitterness and resentment which he could not understand. In his turn he felt that his own nodal contribution had not been appreciated; the resentment became mutual, his character increasingly paranoid. He was always on the move.

When CERN started to explore nuclear fusion catalysed by muons, Viktor at his computer terminal in Virginia heard about it immediately. It was an old idea of course, mentioned in his reviews, but not practical. So why was CERN discussing it? There had been a conference talk by some incomprehensible Russian character, querying some of the fundamental numbers. Was there something in it after all? If it could be done, limitless energy would be available; and Viktor Bexler should be at the centre of action.

He checked his watch. It would be 3.30 pm in Geneva. He opened the top drawer of his desk and took out the yellow printed sheets that listed all the high energy physics labs in the world. Then he dialled a number and asked for Michel Augier.

Beyond the airport, between the city of Geneva and the Jura mountains lies a broad rolling plain with fertile ridges left by the Rhône glacier. The grass grows greener and more luscious thanks to the meticulous Swiss habit of fermenting the winter's hoard of cow manure in huge tanks, and spraying the resulting liquid over the fields in spring, a nauseating mixture known to the locals as 'purain'. Visibly efficacious, and economically fruitful, the resulting pong has repelled many an unsuspecting tourist. In May a yellow quilting of mustard splashes the landscape, and before long the grapes start to ripen around the villages of Bourdigny, Satigny and Dardagny. The light white wine of the 'Coteau de Genève', hardly known outside the canton, is pleasant and refreshing.

In the midst of all this beauty stands the European Organisation for Nuclear Research, called CERN: a vast complex of circular ring accelerators, buried in tunnels, and interspersed with a maze of laboratories. Above it all, in the one high building on the site, sits the Director-General and his staff. Plate glass windows on the sixth floor look out in all directions, giving a panoramic view, south across the airport to the lake of Geneva and the Alps, and on a good day, the majestic image of Mont Blanc floating white and serene above it all. From there the eye runs westward along the Salève to the Bellegarde gap where the Rhône runs through a cleft in the mountains; then further right the long line of the Jura, stretches north and east to the uplands of Switzerland, Bern, Basel, Zurich, and the incomprehensible dialect of Schwyzerdutsch.

From this high point the Director-General in his sumptuous office determines the spirit of the laboratory, the framework in which the individual scientists, theoretical and experimental, move and have their being. Michel Augier was friendly and encouraging, and these attributes of the DG filtered down through the organisation. Alone at his desk, he was in principle composing his speech for the next CERN Council. It was to be a wide-ranging review of the last three years, a tour-de-force which would carry all before it on a wave of applause, with a fat increase in the budget to follow. At least that was the idea, but it was all too easy to let one's thoughts wander. As the sun streamed through the windows he was day-dreaming about his daughter Claudine; more specifically about her thighs, moving rhythmically to music under the capable direction of Juliet Eckerdovsky. Twice a week she had her lessons in the Rue du Grand Pré, and sometimes if Monique was busy, Michel would pick her up, if possible arriving well ahead of time to sit and watch with the other dutiful parents.

Juliet had a lovely figure, which was not concealed by her thin costume: it fitted like a sheath, and to all appearances there was nothing underneath. At any rate the mounds and folds of her body were clearly discernible to the practised eye, and as she demonstrated to her pupils she would flash at him her very special candid gaze. She prescribed a similar uniform for her pupils, on the grounds that she needed to observe their muscles and that true elegance sprang from well trained limbs rather than clothing. It went deeper than that; Juliet was proud of her body, and quite unashamed: she wanted her pupils to feel the same. It also happened to be good public relations, because few fathers could resist the spectacle of a dozen mature young ladies gracefully exercising to music with such a minimum of concealment. They came when they could, ostensibly to support their daughters, but also to appreciate the manifold beauties of the female form.

In dreams images get scrambled; so in Michel's mind the recollection of Claudine's dancing mingled confusingly with Juliet's instruction. He was delighted with his daughter's progress; she was growing into a beautiful woman. He was also looking forward to his coming visit to Eckerdovsky's laboratory in the Ile du Levant. With any luck Juliet would be there, and not all the time would be spent on science. He would like to be more than a casual acquaintance.

Annette van Arnhem had taken care of the Director-General's office for longer than anyone could remember. Whatever the character of her boss, she created an atmosphere of calm deliberation. Her aides kept the files out of sight and in perfect order, and the rooms impeccably tidy. As far as possible she tried to keep his mind on one subject at a time; then clear the papers before starting on the next.

"How would you like to follow up?" she would ask, and then organise the action. Perhaps a few telephone calls, perhaps a meeting, and his notes would always reappear whenever needed. She went about her business quietly, and her staff spoke discreetly. Automatically people lowered their voices when they entered her domain on the sixth floor.

Viktor's voice on the telephone was neither lowered nor discreet. Having no secretary to set up the call he tried to compensate with a masterful manner. The mid-European accent, sharpened after ten years in north America, was now beamed by satellite directly onto Annette's tympanum. He had terrified secretaries across the globe; but her well established telephone protocol was equal to the occasion. Her principles were clear; never interrupt a meeting unless the call was relevant, get the maximum of information from the caller, give nothing away yourself, and if necessary call back as soon as possible.

"This is Professor Bexler calling from Virginia, good afternoon," said the voice, and Annette moved the receiver away from her ear. She knew it was still morning in the USA, so Bexler was clearly tuning in to European time. She decided to return the compliment.

"Good morning, Professor. What can I do for you?" The clear precise, rather fruity voice with a slight Dutch intonation.

"May I speak with Michel please?" Familiar, authoritative, Viktor knew how to get through.

"I am afraid he is busy at the moment. . . . . . No, I am sorry, I may not interrupt. Perhaps I can help? . . . . .You would like to speak to him personally? Yes, yes, of course. That could be arranged, I think, in about two hours time. Could we fix a time for you to call again? What subject shall I say?"

Viktor thought he knew all there was to know about muon catalysed fusion. The established doctrine held that it was interesting but useless. Now came the rumour that CERN was starting a big programme; he was curious, excited, impatient to know more. Perhaps he could find out from Annette.

"The subject is catalysed fusion," he said ponderously, trying to impress her. How would she react? Let the cat out of the bag? Annette waited, and he was forced to prattle on.

"I hear you are starting a programme . . . . I have studied the subject over some years . . . . . I would like to discuss . . ." She encouraged him to continue. "Very interesting, Professor. Oh yes! I am sure the DG would like to have your views. Expert on the muon? Of course, Professor. You are well known."

He was flattered; even the secretaries knew him. "So I will call again in two hours time. If I could be of help . . . . I would be very pleased . . . .until then." He rang off and he felt a fool. He had blurted out his intentions, feebly, but achieved nothing, lost the initiative. His macho image for a moment deflated, he had let himself appear as a suppliant rather than an authority whose views would automatically be sought; and he had found out nothing.

At lunch in the cafeteria Michel was sitting with Hans Issinger, head of the Division for Nuclear Applications (DNA for short), Chang-Singh the head of Theory and a few others.

"Bexler's interested in catalysed fusion."

"You bet," cried Chang. "That's typical! He wants a slice of the action, before we are even rolling."

“He’s a big name,” said Petros, “We need him on our side. Otherwise he might torpedo the project. But will he really help us or try to take control?”

"He is very bright of course," said Hans, "But he always seems to stir up trouble. I think we should keep him out of it."

"On the other hand," said Michel, "He could be a good influence, but we don't want him to steal the limelight. This must be seen as a European initiative; otherwise we will not get the money. I'll tell him to wait until we have a group established. Then he can have someone to work with and he won’t be the leader."

Secretly, if the project was a success, both Michel and Chang wanted to get some of the credit.

5 On the lake

The third and final week of the Varenna summer school turned out to be far the most interesting for Jeremy. He had hesitated about staying as Clare had to go back to Geneva; her parents had nobly offered to mind the children for two weeks, but now they were leaving. On Sunday morning Jeremy took her on the ferry to Como and saw her onto the train: the stazione was only a short walk from the dock. By a pleasant chance Arthur Dribble was on the same boat. He had been lecturing on muon catalysed fusion and was taking the late train to Milano en route to Oxford; he would dump his luggage and spend the day looking round Como and Jeremy was happy to join him.

They wandered round the water front and discovered the Palladian Temple of Volta, built in memory of Count Alessandro Volta who made the first electric battery. Inside were a few large stacks of tarnished metal discs, said to be a 200 year old battery used for getting frogs to twitch their legs. "What a shocking experiment!" said Arthur. There were also some glass flasks used for studying the chemistry of gases. They lingered on the roof terrace watching the boats on the lake and then decided to take the funicular up to Brunate; lunch in the Ristorante at the top lasted two hours. After a while Arthur said,

"Listen. I am taking a year's sabbatical starting in September. I am setting up a group to run some fusion experiments on the booster. Would you like to join? I will only be there for a year, so after that you could probably run the show, and I will come out on regular visits."

Who works with who, in high energy physics? How are groups formed? Teams are essential because no one can do a complicated experiment by himself. Management long ago learned not to dictate from above who will work on which problem. Physicists assigned to a job lack enthusiasm. But working on their own idea they will slave day and night to prove it was good. So at CERN, as in most big laboratories, people were left to form their own groups: management just offered to support certain themes.

In this situation Smith and Brown both suggest experiments. Smith soon collects a team of willing assistants, while Brown languishes on his own. Brown may even end up helping Smith, thus contributing to his success and glory. Who wins this covert battle for the hearts and minds of their colleagues, and why? Why would Brown join his rival Smith, thus helping him to advance? To be the leader you need good ideas, plus the ability to sell them to the management and also to your friends. If people feel that Smith is onto a winner, a beautiful experiment that will be fun, bring new insights and even take him to Stockholm, then they will want to climb on board and have a share of the excitement. It is better to join an express, even if you are not the driver, than to drive your own slow train going nowhere.

In Jeremy's case the answer was clear. He was a new boy, Arthur was an established performer, selected to teach at Varenna and with the prestige of a permanent position at Oxford. He had been on Chang's committee, and clearly had the ear of the management. Arthur needed Jeremy to take care of the donkey work and provide continuity while he was away, but Jeremy would be number two in a dynamic group. But Arthur was not looking for a snap decision.

"Think about it. And let me know when you get back to Geneva." They drank to that, swilling down the last of the Ruffino. "To Geneva then!" "Geneva!"

Back at the hotel, sans Clare and sans Arthur, Jeremy felt that the evening would hang heavily. But uncommitted can sometimes mean unconstrained, and therefore open to new adventures. In fact there were several new arrivals at the Albergo dei Pescatori, and not one of them was interested in fishing. A major theme of the following week was nuclear applications in medicine, and this had attracted a new crop of students and some special lecturers.

At dinner that night Jeremy was seated at one of the long tables, when a tall angular man appeared, impeccably but casually dressed, accompanied by a dazzling girl. He hesitated, then made his way tentatively to the chair opposite.

"May we sit on this table? Perhaps it is reserved?" The drawling Swedish accent. Jeremy stood up.

"No problem. Make yourself at home," Introductions were called for. The stranger was quiet but definite.

"I am Jan Olbers from Sweden." (He pronounced the Swedish J like a Y, Yan).

"This is my wive Avelyn. She is from Denmark. Actually this is not quite correct, because at present we are both from Geneva."

They all shook hands and Jan took the chair opposite with the girl next to him. She beamed briefly at Jeremy across the table and then looked down. Jeremy stuttered; one flash from those laser blue eyes had reduced him to a jelly. Copper gold hair down to her shoulders, a pale round face, a broad red mouth and gleaming teeth; her skin radiated a glowing ripeness. But Jan was rambling on.

He was a doctor, more or less permanently attached to the University of Geneva. He was to lecture on proton therapy, which CERN's division of nuclear applications was supporting. In brief a special accelerator would produce beams of protons which went into the body without spreading sideways and stopped dead at a certain depth. They could burn out deep tumours without affecting the surrounding healthy tissues. It was the therapy of the future, but expensive. As he spoke, the thought flickered through Jan's mind. All the best things in life are expensive, including his wife Avelyn; but she was worth it. Luckily his mother was a Carlsberg, so for him money was no problem.

Jeremy managed to regain his composure. Fortunately the laser beams were switched off concentrating on the menu; she looked serene, happy, questioning her husband vivaciously about the dishes in incomprehensible Svensk or Dansk. Suddenly she looked across at Jeremy, wide-eyed, serious,

"Scusi molto, non parlo Italiano!" She giggled, "That is all I know. Perhaps you can help us with the menu."

After two weeks in the hotel, Jeremy knew the bill of fare more or less thoroughly. They changed the selection from day to day but it tended to repeat after a week, so he could help them out. They swapped notes about the region, Geneva, Switzerland. The Olbers had been there for about three years, living near Satigny. The Swiss were very friendly and helpful at work, but socially they were zero; never invited you to their homes unless you had some family connection. Seduce a man's daughter and he will have you to dinner; otherwise it was no fondu!

That evening Jeremy talked to Clare on the phone. All was well with the children, she was delighted with her holiday, and he told her about Arthur's offer which was something to celebrate; the usual farewells, love, see you soon. He slept fitfully, dreaming about blue laser beams.

Is life decided by chance or choice, fate or virtue? Why do some people have all the luck, while others never get a break? Statistically everyone should get his share of double sixes. The difference must be in how they react when the joker comes up. Some seize their opportunities, while others let them pass on the other side, never to come up again. Do you jump, or don't you? Move out of the predictable daily round, turn over new leaves, follow corridors, and suffer the consequences; or stay within the narrow crib? Fate opens doors; but she does not push you through.

Jeremy woke early, with no wife to distract him, he would attack the week with renewed vigour. He slipped on his swim suit and headed for the lake. The water was like glass; he swam quietly far out into the mist, watching his bow wave rippling in front of him, the water lapping silently. But he was not alone. A shape was gliding towards him from the shore, the steady purposeful crawl of the expert swimmer. It stopped in front of him and a green bathing cap emerged, then the face breathless, the wide blue eyes.

"Hullo, " a pause for breath, "You are up early . . . . . isn't it lovely!"

Gasp. She jack-knifed into the vertical, feet in the air, plunged down deep, turned and came up again facing him, a porpoise playing in the water. She came up grinning, took a breath.

"Can you do that? . . . See you later!" And she was off, steaming further out, disappearing into the mist. There was no point in following, he would never keep up.

Back on the shore he towelled off, Avelyn was just visible in the distance, but she was soon heading back at high speed. Should he wait or wander back? There was no hurry; he took the critical decision, and jogged along the beach to fill in time. As she came out of the water he picked up her towel, stretching it out flat, his arms extended in a Gaullist gesture, a subconscious offer to embrace? She moved beautifully, long legs, slender waist, quite heavy above, the white one-piece with criss-cross straps. She took the towel and swung it over her head; then wrapped it round modestly concealing her body.

"Thank you . . . . . gasp . . . . . I love . . . . " Gulp. She was breathless after the fast swim. "I love . . . . . swimming in the morning . . . . . when . . . . there is no one around . . . . . to disturb the peace."

"So, I am disturbing you. I am sorry about that."

"Oh no! Not at all." She smiled shyly. "At least, not in that way. Jan is busy reading over his lecture, otherwise he would be here too."

They chatted as she dried herself, unselfconsciously. She had all day to fill, she would take the car and drive around. He gave her an idea of what there was to see.

"We are here for three days," she said, "Are you staying?"

"Oh yes, all the week."

"Then perhaps tonight . . . . we will see us again?"

"Yes . . . . OK."

In a way he was being dismissed; but it was time to go anyway; breakfast and work were calling. Breakfast and work all day were punctuated by images, impossible dreams. More about the muon, all about proton therapy, graphs, diagrams, arguments, all overlaid with snapshots offered up gratuitously by his memory bank. Snapshots of her, smiling, looking down, a kaleidoscope of waist, legs, eyes, teeth and copper hair. Funnily enough the images were low key, in shades of grey.

He saw a bit of Jan during the day, and they talked about the new medical cyclotron that CERN would be helping to build. Jan said he was looking for people to join the team. Jeremy did not mention the lake. The ice had been broken, and by the evening they were getting along like old friends. Jan invited him for a drink and they had dinner together again. Avelyn was very lively and full of stories about Geneva. Jan was more taciturn but with a nice streak of humour, but under this Jeremy felt an underlying sadness. Perhaps seeing so many cancer patients takes away some of the joy of life.

The following morning he was down at the beach again, same time, same place. Perhaps she would swim again. He pottered around for ages, but there was no sign of anyone. Had he been too late? Would she be at breakfast? What did it matter anyway? He dried himself and started to trudge back to the hotel.

Suddenly she appeared on the edge of the beach, carrying her green cap, and out of breath.

"Oh, hullo," she panted. "Are you going?" They walked back to the lake in silence.

"I mustn't keep you," she said, "but I . . . . ." She hesitated, looking straight at him, open, questioning, uncertain. Jeremy felt himself melting. "There is nothing to do here . . . so I am taking the boat round the lake.

The Villa Carlotta opposite . . . . it's very famous . . . . I want to see it. And then go further up perhaps. So . . . . ", she paused; looked down for a while. Then looked up again. "I was wondering. . . . . if perhaps . . . . . you might be interested . . . . . to see something different?"

She looked down, blushing, confused. Jeremy was flabbergasted, his mind racing, what could he say? Fantastic, of course, any day, just give the word and I'll be there? But what about Jan, the lectures, Clare, everything else? Life was full of constraints. His mouth opened and shut convulsively, but nothing came out.

"The boat goes at ten past nine," she said, moving towards the water.

"I'll have to think about it," he spluttered. "Er, I would love to, but . . . . I'll see if I can."

He watched her wade slowly into the water, as electrifying from that angle as from any other, tall, fragile, vulnerable. At the last minute she turned her head. Then she dived in.

Wow! Jeremy quickly checked the lecture programme. What would he miss? Not much, and after more than two weeks in the classroom he could do with a break, see some Italian villages, take in a little culture. Not a cloud was in the sky, and it promised to be a glorious day. He would think it out, over breakfast. At the table a Dutchman buttonholed him; how was he, what was the Italian for scrambled egg, could he follow Lorenzo's lectures? He prattled on and it was hard to reply: he needed time to think.

The lectures started at nine; he normally left at ten to. Somehow the dead line had passed, the hotel was quiet, but in principle he could still make it to the class. The eyes have it, he thought, and rushed up to his room, quickly found a clean pair of slacks, sun hat, stuffed a hotel towel and his costume into a plastic bag, and walked down to the quay. A small boy playing truant, trying to look casual but churning inside. Not hurrying of course but when he turned the corner the boat was in.

There was no need to go far. He bought a ticket to the Villa Carlotta, the second stop, and went up the gangway. It was early in the season and a weekday; the boat was empty. No sign of Avelyn.

He walked round the deck, then kept his eyes on the wharf, watching the men untie the gangway. She could still make it. Then the gangway was pulled up, a few hoots of the whistle, and the ferry turned out into the mist.

Jeremy, leaning over the forward railing, watched the water in front and cursed himself for a fool. Suddenly all his rationalisations were revealed as a hollow sham. He felt angry, angry with himself, and with her. The Villa Carlotta might be interesting though, but not much fun on his own. Relax, have lunch, get back on an early boat. The sun was coming through the haze in bright streaks and there were duck sitting on the water, each doubled by its upside down reflection.

He felt a rustle, warmth at his elbow. She was leaning over the balustrade, close to him. Without looking her presence was unmistakable. Relief flooded through him. The flip-flap of the ripples against the bow, clean white sheets of water like glass. A heron skimming low, its feet still dripping, leaving a trail on the glass.

The husky voice. "I was down below. Keep out of sight. There is always someone watching."

He understood; a beautiful woman is never alone, people notice, are interested, keep track, sometimes talk. He did not have that problem.

"It's OK now," she said, turning to him. "I am glad you made it."

"Yes, but I thought you hadn't."

"You shouldn't have worried. Avelyn always comes!" A quick flash, a rueful smile and she turned away, back to the water.

How good was her English? Did she mean it? Both ways? The phrase would stick in his mind, come back again and again. It summed her up; her constancy, her total reliability . . . . and of course the other.

"Shall I take your things?" She had noticed his plastic sack, and took charge of it, stowing it away out of sight in her white canvas bag. "That will be easier. We may not find a beach, but you never know."

She was wearing pale blue slacks flared from the knee, and a blue jersey matching her eyes. Her face and hair were stunning. How does one operate with a very beautiful woman? Jeremy felt out of his depth. How to resist the magnetism, keep his hands to himself, not think about kissing her? He decided to ignore it as much as possible; pretend she was ordinary, this was just a day like any other, casual acquaintances passing a few hours together politely, and then diverging.

He had never been to Denmark, so he got her going on Copenhagen, the Viking remains in the Royal Museum, hundreds of solid gold ornaments.

"This is a replica," she said turning to show her breast with the brooch. "You can get them in the museum; it's real gold, but not old of course ." He liked the brooch: he liked what was underneath even more.

"Then there's this gold chariot, incredible, a ceremonial model, but nearly a metre high with golden wheels. You must see it! Gold is easier to work than bronze, and of course lasts for ever."

"About the only thing that does!"

"And the Viking ships. They dug them out of the peat; very large, like a lifeboat. When you see one you know in your bones that the Vikings discovered America. It was warm in the year 1200. Greenland was really green - it was a Danish settlement. You must know about the layers in the ice; how we have bored down and found out about the climate thousands of years ago."

She was vivacious now, unselfconscious, chattering on with her story, and very beautiful. He watched her mesmerised. No not beautiful, he said to himself, just another girl, and forced himself to look out across the water.

"There is a town coming up," he said. It was just appearing through the mist half a mile away. "And there is Bellagio on our left; have you been there? There is a fabulous hotel on the point, the Villa Serbolloni. We looked round it. Upstairs there are two incredible suites, all panelled and with 18th century furniture. But hidden behind a secret door in the panelling is a sumptuous modern bathroom. Great for a honeymoon!"

"I've had mine, " she said.

"Me too."

"You never know though," she answered. "There could be another one. Life is full of uncertainty." He could agree with that.

The boat docked at Cadenabbia and they got off. He carried her bag.

"I think it's this way," she said, steering him with a touch. "It's a short walk to the Villa. I read about it yesterday. Along an avenue of . . . . . it's 'platanes' in French . . . . is it plane trees?" They were there all right, large, impressive, a straight mile. At the beginning was a little placard, 'Via del Paradiso'.

'Let's look round the village first," she said. "Then we can get the boat from the Villa and on to the next place. A trip to paradise should be one way only, don't you think?"

The village was quaint. She was perceptive and he enjoyed sharing her impressions. Peering into shop windows together, he could smell her hair. They sat side by side outside a café, looking across the square, sharing a menu.

"Non parlo,' she said grinning at him. "Will you help me out?" He ordered coffee, she had a luscious chocolate sundae.

"You must taste it," passing him her spoon to share without a second thought. She insisted on paying. "This is my treat."

The Villa Carlotta was quite small, but very elegant with checkerboard marble floors, and surrounded by immaculate terraces full of flowers. In the main room Canova's 'Cupid and Psyche' was breathtaking. The white translucent marble delicately patterned evoked resonances of real flesh. The girl semi-reclining with her head back and hands raised to caress Cupid's head as they gaze rapturously into each other's eyes. He supporting her back so tenderly, bending over her face, his hands near her offered breasts. It was a hymn to love, perfect and unalloyed: he full of attention, she offering herself completely.

"That's how it should be," she said. "He's captured the perfect moment, before the first kiss, and frozen it for eternity. The moment of truth. But in reality life moves on, one can't stay on the peak. All the best things in life have to end. It's a snapshot, ... very moving, ... and totally romantic!"

There was a portrait of Marie Antoinette. Avelyn gave him a bird's eye view of her life; a guileless girl caught up in great events. In one sense her behaviour helped to spark the revolution; but in another she was just an innocent victim.

"In any case," she added, "she was good in bed."

"You seem to know a lot."

"My father is professor of history. I studied it at the university. He is a great admirer of the English, and often talks about the war. If it hadn't been for you people life would be very different now. For four years you were our only hope. The Americans could never have invaded Europe on their own. So I studied English too. I don't know any Englishmen, though. Except you, of course."

"You hardly know me at all!"

"Well, I have to start somewhere."

Continuing down the avenue, the sun shone and the sweater came off revealing a white sleeveless blouse. She gave him the look women give when they take off a garment, as if to say, do you approve? He smiled back to show that he did: luscious globular bait.

They came to a white painted bench, a perfect place to rest in the sun, and there was no one around. After a while she leaned over backwards, raising her arms to imitate Psyche.

"Could we manage that beautiful pose? I want to know what it feels like. Come behind the bench and lean over."

Her fingers were on his head delicately.

"Closer. Your hand should be on my waist. Yes. And the other . . . . near my breast . . . . that's it . . . . .the beautiful moment of truth."

Their faces were only inches apart. He could smell the slightly acrid perfume from her arms warmed by the walking, see the faint ginger down. She was a genuine redhead then. Was this an invitation to the kiss? Or was she just posing, as she said?

There was one important difference from the statue. Cupid's cock had been totally unaffected by the procedure. The little fellow could caress as many ladies as he wished, with never an embarrassing flick of the prick; which was just as well if he was to appear naked in polite society and decorate the villas of the aristocracy. That way love remained pure, and childish, and the girl's virtue would never be endangered. It was a brilliant romantic abstraction.

Slowly he moved closer, he could feel her warm breath across his nostrils, and it smelled good. An upside down kiss would be funny. He was just going to try it, when footsteps crunched on the gravel.

"I don't think we were very elegant. You were too high and the bench was in the way. I banged my knee on the wood."

"I felt divinely elegant!" She turned to him brightly, eyes twinkling. "We could try it again without the bench."

"Not here, I think."

Was she crazy? Or just fooling around? Either way he did not know how to react. He was more and more tempted to fall in with her mood, and to hell with the consequences. He took her arm tentatively. She smiled, squeezed his hand with her elbow, walking closer.

At lunch in Tremezzo she chose a bench seat with a view and made him sit next to her, her bag on the other side. His right hand kept wandering away towards her thigh only inches from him; he put it on his own leg, then back on the table, but a powerful magnet was dragging it sideways.

"The female femur is longer than the male, but I don't know why."

She was puzzled. "Femur? What is that? Ah! Oh! You mean my leg?"

"Yes," he said, "women's thighs are often longer than men's. Sit a bit closer and we can measure."

Their thighs were touching, he ran his hand down to her knee, there was just an inch in it.

"You're as tall as I am," she said. "But there is a difference."

"I can't see any reason for it, being longer I mean. Probably it's attractive to the opposite sex, so it gets selected by evolution, without giving any biological benefit. You know, rather like the stag's antlers; they are completely useless, but the females go for them, so over the years they get larger and larger, and even more of a handicap."

She thought about it, got the drift. "Oh, I hope you are not right. But you are in a way. Having long legs is quite a nuisance. I have terrible trouble getting stockings that are long enough."

"Stockings! I thought everyone wore tights these days."

"Oh, they are so boring, and clammy too. I much prefer the other. I like them up to here." (Her hand was just below her hips). "Instead of down here. Do you realise what happens when you sit down? Your suspenders go like this." She put her forearm in a straight line sloping from waist to knee. "So if they are tight they lift your skirt up, which is rather uncomfortable. You need long stockings, and very short suspenders to here. You should try it some time, then you would understand our problems."

What would she get onto next? Luckily at this point the waiter came to take their order, and sharing a bottle of Orvieto he learned to skol.

"You must look the person in the eyes, clink your glass, and then say 'Skol'." She pronounced it with a long vowel to rhyme with shoal. "Then you must look down and drink slowly and thoughtfully, perhaps making a wish for your friend. Then hold up your glass and look again deeply, into his eyes . . . . like this. . . . . . .Now you can try it."

They skolled. "Not bad. Now again. You need more practice."

He held her gaze for longer this time, and she seemed satisfied. But her eyes kept flicking over him, and he looked back. They were large eyes, deep blue with a lot of white showing at the sides. He remembered reading that large eyes went with a generous libido; something to do with the thyroid.

"You have the advantage of me," he said, "speaking such good English, while I don't know a single word of Danish."

"You do - skol! But I'll teach you some Danish words. Would you like a lesson?" He nodded. "Listen carefully." She looked at him intently, finger raised like a teacher. It sounded like "yo er hya die" but she seemed to swallow her tongue halfway through. He tried to imitate it and she giggled uncontrollably. After about the tenth try he had it more or less to her approval.

"What does it mean anyway?" She looked at him intently.

"I love you," she said, and he was totally confused.

"It's . . . . it's . . . . it's just is not possible!" Her eyes were laughing.

"But that's what it means. . . . I love you. You have told me about ten times now; and you are getting better at it!"

"It's a lousy trick! It is unfair! It doesn't count anyway, if I didn't know what I was saying."

"But it counts for me." She was teasing him. "Now you understand it, how about saying it again?"

"No!" he said vehemently. "One should never say such things! It is too powerful and the consequences are unpredictable. Then it comes back to haunt you . . . . .with a claim 'you said you loved me'. I would rather not talk about it. There is no need to anyway. If the other person can't tell, can't feel it, then it's no good, is it? Why is a little word so important?"

"I can always tell anyway," she said. "But don't take me seriously, I was only fooling. At least now you can say it in Danish, if you ever want to ..... but then perhaps you never will. Let's go back to the skol: that was more fun!"

After the skol, he put his hand tentatively on her thigh. She did not appear to notice, so he left it there. "I am so glad you came," she said "I like sharing things. It's so dull on one's own, lonely even."

In spite of her protests, he insisted on paying the bill. "It is my turn, and my pleasure."

"Well, I will make it up to you some time in Geneva."

After lunch they were walking by the lake. She stopped abruptly, turned to him.

"One should always be in love, don't you think? It is like a bright light. It sharpens the senses. Everything is crystal clear, sharp . You see more, and you see better. Because you want to share, you look more intently. When I'm not in love, I'm half asleep; it's boring. But when I'm in love, I'm alive, tingling, receptive. Even if I'm by myself. Luckily I usually am."

What did she mean? Usually in love, or usually by herself? Either way would be significant. She was looking out across the water. Suddenly she turned.

"Don't you agree?"

"It's too big a word, ambiguous, confusing. Four letters which mean something different to each person. So if you say it, you conjure up a whole train of images, associations, assumptions, which you are not even dreaming of. Uncontrollable consequences. Therefore never say it. It's far too dangerous."

But the word lay between them waiting, like the ace of hearts on the table; waiting for the trick to be completed, to win outright, or perhaps be swept aside by some nondescript trump? He had been too negative, so he took her arm to compensate.

"I agree of course with what you said about sharpening the perception. Do you see the way the light shimmers on the water?"

"Of course." She squeezed his arm, then turned quietly and kissed him. It lasted a long time.

"That's better," she said laughing. "Better than talking." Then they started again with all the enthusiasm of beginners. It was true, the water now shimmered more sharply, and the duck winging from left to right were crystalline black silhouettes.

When Jeremy met Jan at the bar before dinner he was not sure how to play it. But luckily it was not a problem. Jan was positively affable.

"Ah, Yeremy! A drink? We are wanting to thank you for looking over, looking for, how do you say it, looking after my wive today." The deep drawling voice. "So kind of you to take the day of. We are so grateful."

Was it the royal we? Or the collective? And how Swedish can you get? Husband thanks you for spending a torrid afternoon dallying with his gorgeous bride! That was a new one for Jeremy. But how much had she told him?

"She is so magnetising! When by herself the men are coming all around, and this is annoying her. I am sure you would not want to pinch."

Pinch, steal? What was he driving at? Is she up for grabs then? If only I could. Don't count on it mate. Jeremy tried to splutter a reply. "Well, I . . . . I don't know . . . " But there was no need. Jan was burbling on.

"You know . . . . the Italians . . . . her bor-tom!" He drawled it out as two separate words. "It seems to make an electric distraction." Jeremy nodded; she was electric and magnetic now! Electromagnetism, what more could you want?

"They are unable to resist. They are obliged to pinch. When she was in Rome . . . . . one day she comes in . . . . and it was all covered with so many bruises! Can you imagine it?"

Jeremy found that he could. The thin blue slacks, voluptuously modulated. A hand moving, caressing, finding the best place. And then, suddenly, the cheeky nip. Then the whole process repeated, again and again. In his mind the jeans blurred, dissolved, revealing a tender expanse of pale shimmering flesh, tastefully decorated with a pattern of blue and purple patches. It was mind-boggling. Suddenly he realised that Jan was staring at him, expecting him to say something.

"Oh, sorry! " He groped for words. "Sorry. My mind was boggling!"

"Boggling? What is that?"

Jan's attention zoomed in; he was tracking a new word. Jeremy tried to explain, without explaining; turn it into a lesson in English. To his relief, Jan was apparently not possessive. Irate husbands! Wild boars snorting over their harems tend to spoil the picnic.

"I am sorry I missed your lecture though."

"No worry, I can send you a report. It is a good project, very hopeful for curing more cancers. Maybe you could join us, we need some good physicists. There are so many interesting questions."

Another job offer! People were always trying to add to their teams, build up the momentum; it made the project more credible if lots of minds were working on it. So an invitation to join did not mean much. On the other hand, if people wanted to join your project, that was different; it meant that you had arrived.

"It is building in Nizza. It is a Nice place, you would like it."

Jeremy could see the corny pun, and was groping for a witty answer. But before he could reply Jan leaned forward, his finger digging confidentially into Jeremy's ribs.

"It is a yoke!"

"A yoke! Oh ha ha."

Avelyn appeared looking resplendent, her face glowing with health and happiness. The eyes seemed if anything larger, and the long-suffering bottom was discreetly sheathed in green. Someone ought to be consoling it. She greeted Jeremy with a quick blue flash and shook his hand, but then stationed herself the other side of Jan and gave him all her attention.

Jeremy tried to re-evaluate his position. He was just an escort for the day, invited to keep off the marauders: she the body, he the bodyguard. Now, having served his purpose, he would have to reset his emotions. But what about the events of the afternoon? She certainly paid off her protectors in tangible currency! Was that meant to be the end of it? Her telephone number on a scrap of paper, even now burning a hole in his pocket, suggested otherwise.

"Ring me when you get back. I owe you a lunch. Mid-week would be best."

The blue eyes so sincere and friendly, looking straight at him. But did she mean it? Did she even know what she was doing? Or was he being manipulated? Nothing apparently was what it seemed.

They were leaving the following day. He swam as usual, but she did not appear, and he did not see her at breakfast. He tried to pull his mind back on track, but the images kept returning. Probably they would meet again, but when and how? The ball was in his court. Should he return it with a penetrating drive, deep to the base line? Liven up a bit, rally, play the game, score one, score two, score as often as you can? Or should he just let it drop, walk off, leave the ball lying like a dead fish-eye, mournfully watching him, a pathetic witness to his inadequacy?

He remembered hearing about a governor-general of New Zealand, some distinguished hero, addressing the new graduates at a university. According to the story, he finished up,

"Honour all men. Do right. Beware all women. Don't write."

Jeremy decided not to call, but he kept the telephone number! He called Clare and told her about his new friends.

"You would like them. A pleasant contact. And so good to know someone outside CERN."

Julie needed new glasses. Simon wanted a wind surfer for his birthday, and the telephone would be cut off unless they paid the bill. Family life! It was another world.

6 Gliding in the Alps

While so much physics was being resurrected and dissected in Varenna, Ivan Eckerdovsky was enjoying himself in the Swiss Alps. Between the two highest mountain massifs in Europe lies the broad alluvial valley of the Rhône, known to the locals as the Canton du Valais or Wallis, half French speaking and half German if that is a fair name for this guttural local dialect. To the north lies the Bernese Oberland with the craggy peaks of the Eiger, Monch and Jungfrau; to the south many deep valleys, separated by great ridges run up to the pinnacles of the Alps along the Italian frontier, Monte Rosa, the Matterhorn, the Grand Combin and further west Mont Blanc. In the clear skies of the Valais warm air is trapped between the mountains in a wide natural oven, and the sun ripens the fruit all the way from Brig to Martigny.

Right in the centre of this abundance and the chief beneficiary of the surrounding plenty lies the bustling commercial city of Sion. From its airport miniature airliners fly to Geneva, and the helicopters of Rhonair and Air Glacier take off with skiers, too rich or too weak to climb the mountains on foot. They carry supplies to the mountain huts and return if necessary with bodies to be mended, or sometimes buried: the unexpected happens all too often in the mountains. The helicopter has transformed the mountain huts for climbers. In the old days, wood for warmth and all the food was carried up in the summer by man-pack or pony, a day's march for a small load. It is worth paying Air Glacier to deliver hundreds of kilos to your hut with only twenty minutes flying. The caretakers are no longer wizened old hermits but young men and women, happy to earn their money in the snow and chopper back to civilisation to spend it.

Sharing the airfield with all this activity is the Sion Gliding Club. On a fine day a dozen streamlined sailplanes are lined up for take off, the pilots discussing the weather as they wait their turn to be launched. That means being towed behind an elderly but efficient biplane, gradually gaining height until, at a suitable place where thermals are expected, the glider pilot pulls the release. The tow rope drops away and, if he is lucky and skilled, he can catch the lift and soar around the Alps for hours on end, quietly munching his sandwiches and pissing, if need be, into an empty hot water bottle carried for the purpose.

If he is unlucky he runs out of lift and lands back at the airfield twenty minutes later. To keep within gliding range of the field is the cardinal rule, so very few pilots ever fall short. If they do, the conditions are inhospitable; under the network of overhead cables carrying power from the dams down to Lausanne and Geneva, lie orchards full of fruit and vineyards with long lines of massive stakes.

Scattered among these obstacles, and known to the experts, is the occasional large field and country airport: so a good pilot can roam freely across the valleys and mountains. Given a clear approach he should be able to land his ship in a space 100 metres, and from the normal cruising height, one thousand metres above the valley, he can glide 40 kilometres before he hits the deck: a modern sailplane has a long reach. Now Ivan was sitting in his spanking new ASW-15, waiting for the signal to go.

Thick set, immensely strong, and a dedicated sportsman, swimming and judo had been his main pursuits, but gliding had always appealed to his sense of adventure. He had learnt to fly as a student in Poland, under a government subsidised scheme, but then let it drop. Now as director of a CERN division, with its own auxiliary laboratory, he had the means to indulge his fancies. He joined the Geneva gliding club, operating from Montricher in the Jura, and quickly passed the test for his Swiss licence. The club had an excellent fleet, but Ivan found that sharing a glider could be irksome. The chief instructor of the day was typically a humble tradesman; but here he had power and he enjoyed using it. It was he who decided who could fly, when and in what. So after hanging around all day helping others to launch and retrieving them when they landed, Ivan often lost his place at the last moment to some Swiss crony. In the end he borrowed from the bank, and lashed out on a sleek new ship of his own.

Now it was approaching midday. The sun was pouring its energy onto the sloping pastures and rocky crags above. Even the glaciers were beginning to melt, and if you walked up there you could hear the water rustling under the ice on its long journey to the sea. Several gliders had already launched, and were being watched critically from the ground as they beat to and fro close to the mountain two miles away. Were they finding lift? Or inevitably losing height? The radio crackled. "Ca monte un metre,' called Jean Fulleman from the blue and white Zephyr; he was going up according to the vario at one metre per second. The cautious pilots would wait a little longer for the thermals to develop, not wanting to risk their 40 Swiss francs on an abortive launch. Ivan decided to take the next tow. With a little help from his friends he pushed his plane out onto the runway and clambered in.

Everything in the ship had been meticulously checked. Certificate of air worthiness in order, insurance, cables from pedals to rudder with safety clips securing every bolt, wings locked in position with both joints pinned, instruments and battery OK, radio working. Safety was the first priority in aviation, and Ivan followed his training and the practice of the best clubs; check everything in sight every day, and look elsewhere on a regular cycle of inspections. There were bold pilots and there were old pilots; but old bold pilots ...... they were not around.

The tow plane came in and dropped the cable. In the cockpit Ivan made his final checks, mentally reciting the standard mnemonic, CB-sit-CB. Controls and ballast had been checked, now fasten the seat belt, check the instruments, trim fully forward, now the canopy - yes, the plastic bubble above his head was firmly shut and locked - and the brakes; the air brakes were closed and the wheel brake was off, under carriage locked down. He nodded to the young man with the cable: it was OK to clip on. Another held the wing tip level and waved his hand below the waist, telling the tow to take up slack. As the cable tightened and the glider began to inch forward, Ivan waved his left hand forwards, vigorous overhead waves by the others told the pilot to open the throttle, and with a roar from the tug they surged smoothly forwards. The wing man ran as fast as he could to keep the glider level. By the time he let go they had sufficient speed for Ivan to balance the ship on its one wheel as they bounced along the grass.

Soon he was in the air, but the tow plane needed more speed and was still on the ground. If the glider rose too fast it would pull the tail of the plane upwards and they would never get off the runway; one of the classic accidents. So Ivan pushed the stick forward and kept the glider skimming two feet above the field as the speed gathered, watching, concentrating. Suddenly the plane rose and he reacted quickly to go up with it, keeping exactly on the same level. A wide turn to the left over the cement factory and the glider had to follow exactly the same curve; if he cut the corner the rope would go slack and then tighten again with a bang, and probably break. He did not fancy a forced landing on top of the chimneys, so he kept the nose pointing at the outer wing-tip of the plane in front, to make the ideal smooth turn. Now he had time to pull back the lever with his left hand, tucking the landing wheel into the fuselage, and at the same time correcting the small change in trim with his right hand on the stick. They circled the field to gain height, and then headed off the join the other ships on the mountain.

Max in the tow plane knew where to find the lift, and soon they were flying along the hill, just below the little village of Veysonnaz, 1000 metres above the field. Ivan checked the vario; two metres per second climb. That was normal on tow so the air outside was flat. There was some buffeting and the vario dropped to one, then down to zero; no joy, the air was sinking. Suddenly the plane in front of him bounced upwards and Ivan eased the stick back to follow it, keeping his correct station. Four up, they were in lift. He waited a few seconds to make sure it was not an isolated bubble, then pulled the release. There was a loud bang from the nose and he saw the cable dropping away. Immediately the tow plane rolled to the right and dived back towards the field. Ivan climbed turning the excess speed into height and circled to stay in the lift; move the trim back to take the pressure off the stick, flick the switch on the electric vario to on. It squealed momentarily and then fell silent; they were not in lift after all, and the gauges showed half a metre down.

Ivan took stock of the situation. He knew where he was, there were two other gliders visible above him and a third somewhere on the slope. He headed back towards the village, tucking in close to the hill, altitude 1070, speed 65 kph, just the value at which the glider dropped most slowly, 'minimum sink'; only the quiet hiss of air outside the canopy, and to his right a peasant scything the long grass in the gently sloping meadows. Push up the speed slightly for safety as he got close to the slope. Suddenly he felt a surge, the electric vario groaned then whistled, the higher the pitch the faster they were rising. The morning thermal was strong, but probably quite small in area. Ivan turned steeply away from the hill to stay in it. It was working. He weaved to and fro in a figure of eight to stay more or less in the same place, turning always away from the slope; if you turned inwards you might miscalculate and hit a tree. The lift held, 1150, 1200, 1250 metres. Now Ivan could relax, he was far enough away from the hill to circle continuously, and the thermal was getting stronger. He would squeeze this lemon to the full, and then tuck into mountain again and fly further along.

The village was well below him now, with its church tower and people like Dresden dolls moving about. He had time to look around and enjoy the view. Ahead he saw the blue and white Zephyr coming towards him at the same height; both pilots edged slightly to the right, obeying the rules of the air, and he waved to Jean as he shot past at a relative speed of 100 miles per hour. Things happen fast in the air, and you cannot afford to get it wrong. The new ship was working beautifully, the controls finger-light, and the response smooth and immediate, as though he just had to think and automatically the machine would respond to his intention. Now far below he could see the same peasant, in the same field, still cutting his hay.

For the moment this tiny cockpit was his whole universe As the landscape unravelled before him the rest of the world was not really there. He was on his own, isolated, borne up by the marvels of science and technics, driven forward by the power of the sun and the wind, which had always been and would be forever. He appreciated it all the more because of his own humble beginnings and he gave thanks for his good fortune.

Later in the day he had worked his way up to 2100 metres and, following the main massif, he came to a side valley running down from the peaks. He could either follow round it, or cut across. The slopes on the opposite side were in sun, and looked promising; there might be some sink in the valley, but it would pay to go straight for the warmth. He aimed for the crags on the other side, and much to his surprise the air in the valley was rising nicely. This was great, he was running through a nice thermal. Then he noticed a dark blob directly in front of him, and it was getting larger. It had thin horizontal lines on either side, which could be wings. Another sailplane perhaps. Yes, definitely, and it was coming straight towards him!

The rules say turn away to the right, but Ivan was reluctant to do so: he might turn out of the lift, and keeping in lift is the first priority for a glider pilot. Also he wanted to keep an eye on the other plane. So Ivan decided to let the other chap take the avoiding action. To his surprise the other glider did not turn but just came straight on towards him. Perhaps he had his eyes on the vario.

The two ships were now converging at a combined speed of 160 kph, and things started to happen rather quickly. By the time Ivan realised that there was going to be a head on collision, it was too late to turn. If he banked, his left wing would go up, and that would make things worse! Quickly he pushed the stick forward to send his glider downwards. The other plane was tearing towards him, expanding in front of his eyes! Would it pass over his head? Would it clip his tail fin? A moment later . . . PHITT!!!! There was only ten feet in it, and the sudden sharp crack as the other glider whipped over his head gave Ivan a fright.

If you are still conscious after such an event, it clears the mind remarkably. Ivan was amazed how quickly it had all happened, and resolved not to rely on the other chap next time. Later in the day after he had landed, a large stranger with a bristly moustache came up to him.

“Oh hi! We were both in the same thermal. I should have turned off to the right but I didn’t want to. Then it was too late to turn but I saw your nose go down, so I knew it would be OK."

“I had the mountain on my right, so it was my priority,” said Ivan. "Lucky we didn’t both make the same move!” Then he added, "Who are you anyway?”

"Call me Viktor ," he held out his hand. "I am a visitor from the U.S. Just having a look around. Checking out the clubs."

"Keep your eyes open then. And let's hope we don't meet again . . . . . anyway not like that!"

7 Catalysed fusion

Back at CERN Arthur Dribble quickly followed up his invitation. When Jeremy returned to his office he found a note suggesting they meet for lunch at 12. Arthur drove to a restaurant in Satigny, ten minutes from the lab, still largely patronised by the local Swiss, where they served platefuls of crisp 'filet de perche' with chips. It was a mystery how they did it, as the once plentiful perch in the Lac Leman had been wiped out by pollution and overeating. There were too many people everywhere. The fish probably came from a secret source in the mountains, but the proprietor would never tell.

"It's my livelihood, a trade secret. If I told you I would soon be out of business."

Over the meal Arthur started to expound his ideas for a new research programme. "I didn't mention it in my lectures," he explained. "If you have a good idea keep quiet about it until you have a reasonable lead. There are copycats everywhere. No one else is working on this yet, as far as I know, muons stopping in plasma."

"Plasma!" said Jeremy. "You mean ionised gas, as in a fluorescent tube or a neon sign?"

"Exactly. But those domestic gadgets have only a small electric current, and the gas is only partly ionised. If you give it a big shot, or hit it with a laser, then you get a fully ionised plasma, and the electrons are completely separated from the nuclei. The positive ions and the negative electrons move around independently."

"The fourth state of matter," said Jeremy remembering his university lectures. The four states were solid, liquid, gas, and then plasma. The fusion people had been studying this for ages, trying to heat up a gas to ten million degrees to get controlled nuclear fusion as in the hydrogen bomb; but that was a different story. What was the relevance of all this to muons?

"The muon is supposed to be a catalyst," he said. "That is to produce fusion in the cold. So why mess about with a hot plasma? Aren't you defeating the object?"

Arthur smiled knowingly and poured some more Fendant du Valais into Jeremy's glass. "Let us first drink to muon catalysis in a plasma; then I will tell you how it works."

They raised their glasses and clinked. It was a seductive wine, tasting as mild and innocent as fruit juice, but all unperceived it loosened the mind, relaxed the body and opened the lips. Into this fertile ground Arthur now inserted the key idea.

"In normal heavy hydrogen, solid, liquid or gas, every deuteron is surrounded by its negative electron. They repel each other and keep the atoms apart. If you put in a negative muon, it first has to get through this repulsive shield of electrons before it can find a nucleus. Now in a plasma the deuterons are free. The electrons do not come into it. If you put in a mu-minus it will go straight into the nucleus, and then very rapidly pick up another, and do the fusion. There are no electrons to get in the way."

Jeremy could see the point, and it was exciting. "So the whole process might go faster, much faster. Then each mu can make more fusions before it dies, and there is a better chance of getting a positive energy balance. But is there any evidence?"

"None at all," said Arthur. "It is just a hunch, but I want to try it." He touched his brow in an imaginary salute. "Hans Issinger, our division leader is in favour, and he thinks it will get through the committees. It is new, timely, not expensive, will give a lot of data, and there is a risk of a major discovery. That is what they like. Always run the risk of making a discovery: if there's no risk, you're wasting your time ..... that's where a lot of people go wrong."

The dessert was the usual offering of a small Swiss restaurant: ananas au kirsch, crème caramel or cassata. Arthur chose the ananas (pineapple), and Jeremy followed suit. Was a group feeling already being expressed in their choice? Finally Arthur got round to the million dollar question.

"So what do you think? Are we going to work together?" It was tactfully phrased, and Jeremy appreciated this approach. Arthur was clearly a reasonable guy.

"I would like to very much. But I know nothing about plasma."

"That is not important. There are plenty of plasma experts in CERN. We just have to talk to them." So it was agreed.

Having an idea is easy. Making it actually happen is hard work. They first had to sell the project to the management, get support and get a team together. Arthur quickly found two young physicists who were keen to help; Marion was a research student from Oxford, and Chris, with had a junior post at CERN, was hot on electronics. Erik from Sweden joined soon afterwards.

The apparatus looked simple enough on paper, but in practice it soon became complicated. There were huge electromagnets for steering the muon beam from the booster, a gas handling system for the high pressure hydrogen, deuterium and tritium. Tritium was expensive and on top of that radioactive. If you inhaled some accidentally it would exchange with the hydrogen in your body and stick around inside, releasing its radioactive rays for years. So it was quite dangerous, special precautions were needed, and the safety officer had to be consulted. Jeremy wondered what would happen to Clare and the kids if something went wrong. However careful you were, accidents did happen and they were always unexpected.

Then there were all the detectors which measured what was happening; counters to monitor the muons coming in, neutron counters to detect the fusions, electron counters which indicated how many muons were left as the microseconds ticked by, and they all sent their information to racks of high speed electronics which measured time in nanoseconds. All this kit had been assembled from standard modules, some from Oxford, some begged from colleagues and the rest borrowed from the CERN electronics pool. Jeremy and Chris spent many weeks joining up the units with a maze of tiny cables. Each circuit had to be tested and carefully adjusted; the length of each cable was critical, otherwise the signals would arrive too early or too late at the next stage, and each had to be labelled at both ends, else it would be impossible to trace through the bird's nest of wires.

Assembling all this kit was rather boring, hard work, but every worthwhile endeavour includes a lot of drudgery. Solving their problems together, the team felt united in a common purpose. Just before the run started they had a final meeting to allocate shifts and make sure that everyone understood and agreed the programme of tests. They all went out to lunch together in a restaurant off site, and everything seemed to be running smoothly. But over coffee Arthur announced a new development that was destined to shatter their cosy world.

"By the way," he said "I was talking to the DG yesterday. Viktor Bexler is coming to spend a year in CERN. And he wants to join our group."

8 Heavy water

The Ile de Levant is well known as a free living nudist island. The best way to get there from Geneva is to take the overnight sleeper which leaves the Gare Cornavin at 23.10 on the dot. The CERN car took Michel to the station, he boarded in good time and was fast asleep when the train moved off. The gentle hum of the wheels and the rhythmic rocking of the carriages gave him wild dreams, but he awoke refreshed to the brilliant morning light of Aix-en-Provence. A quick cup of coffee brought by the ever watchful attendant, and at 7 am he stepped off at the Gare de Toulon. He made straight for the station buffet and ordered bacon and eggs sizzling in a heavy Creuzot dish, followed by crisp croissants with honey.

A taxi to the port of Hyères, and then a ferry to the island. On his previous visit to investigate the site with Eckerdovsky they were whisked across in a naval helicopter, but this time it would be more fun to take the tourist route.

Ivan's project was way out, a dream. Organisms that would concentrate deuterium from the sea? It might work, more probably it would not. It was a long shot, but if it came off the rewards would be unbelievable. Heavy water was wanted for power generating reactors as well as fusion, and the customers were willing to pay. Up to now the main source was electrolysis, which was very expensive, and the Norwegians with their cheap hydro power were the only suppliers. Biotechnology was in fashion, so the CERN Council had bought the idea for an experimental period of five years: after all the budget was quite modest. What had tipped the balance had been Michel's contacts with the French Marine. The naval station on the Ile de Levant occupied most of the island, but with all the defence cuts its activities had been running down. With a bit of persuasion they offered free use of several buildings and an area for setting up the fish tanks. There was plenty of sun and sea water for growing the algae, and freedom from intruders. The small nudist village on the west side, complete with shops and the small hotel 'la Brise Marine', was packed with tourists in the summer, but well fenced off. Michel could hardly admit that this was part of the attraction, but here he was taking the tourist route to Heliopolis.

What surprised him were his fellow passengers. There was nothing remarkable about them! Just a motley collection of ordinary people such as you would see on any seaside ferry. Did they realise that they were heading for a nudist colony? Some, already bronzed, were obviously regular sun worshippers; but the rest? Pale faced, pudgy, middle aged couples, dowdy pillars of society complete with suitcases and a dog; and groups of carefree hikers with their rucksacks. Someone ought to warn them! Tell them that when they arrive they will have to strip off completely.

The reality was that two hours later you could recognise the same faces, totally at ease, mingling unremarked among all the other naked people; and in this atmosphere of blue sky and hot rocks it seemed totally appropriate.

On his last visit they had landed in the naval area, but Ivan had a key to the fence and they had slipped through to the public area for an afternoon in the sun. The main beach was a small cove surrounded by bushes with smooth slabs of rock to lie on. The bushes were festooned with lengths of photographic film. Unwelcome voyeurs from the mainland were often snooping with their telephotos. Their presence is not appreciated by the natives, particularly when the interlopers do not even adopt the local costume but prowl around in blue shorts. The time honoured remedy was exceedingly simple; seize the camera, strip out the film, and hang it on a tree. Bang go all those holiday snaps! The French are never at a loss for words, so typically the incident would be followed by interminable argument.

"I was only taking a photo of my girl friend."

"Fine, but in that case why do it here?"

Michel had overheard one of these discussions, and they went round and round, making the same points over and over, for hours on end.

The girls were mostly lovely. You do not stare, you do not even look, but all the same you see. And like other parts of the body, male or female, they come in all shapes and sizes, some ugly, mostly average, and a few stunningly attractive. Ivan was a hot operator at under water fishing, so he had his fins, mask and snorkel which Michel could use. There were not many fish about, but mermaids in abundance, and the goggles encouraged a more leisurely inspection. Because of refraction, everything under water looked thirty per cent larger. The skin was goose-pimpled by the cold, but the breasts, weightless under water and relieved of any tendency to sag, looked universally firm and tight. It was a shock to come to the surface and find that they were attached to a rather ordinary face.

Soon the ferry reached the quay and the tourists poured off purposefully; apparently they knew where to go. A few locals met the boat, usually wearing 'le minimum', a tiny triangle required by local decree in the shopping and commercial areas. But a group of maidens, stark but unabashed, stood on the dock chatting to the fully dressed sailors a few feet below them. They seemed to be on familiar terms, so Michel supposed that this was a daily pastime, a little thrill for the girls and a tantalising eyeful for the crew.

Ivan met him in smart white slacks, white shirt and a wide blue belt, his hairy arms looking deeply bronzed. They boarded a fast naval launch and were whisked round the island to the naval area. As they came ashore the local commander saluted and then stepped forward to shake hands.

"Capitaine Laveran. Welcome aboard! So happy that you can visit our little domain. I will leave you in the capable hands of my good friend, but I understand that we may be meeting tonight. That will give me an opportunity to fill you in on our activities."

"First we look around the facilities," said Ivan, "see how it is set up, and meet everybody. We are only 15 as you know and they all want to meet you. Then we can see the various organisms we are cultivating. After that lunch with the team, and then if you like, a session on the scientific arguments and the results so far. You are staying in our house of course and we have a little dinner party, a few members of staff and Capitaine Laveran and his wife. Then in the morning Juliet can take you to the beach. It's a good chance to unwind.

It was an ideal programme and Michel was impressed. He also liked the way the labs were equipped: closed circuit systems for heavy water, temperature controlled growing tanks in the sun, a basic chemistry lab with a mass spectrometer for assessing the amount of deuterium in the samples, rapid computer links to CERN and other laboratories world wide. The stock of heavy water was in a sealed stainless steel tank with a large label,

D_2O Gift of the Norwegian Government

The scientists were alert, active and cheerful. Was isolation a problem, he asked, but most seemed content. It was possible to commute from the mainland every day and still do a good day's work. Alternatively if you lived on the island, Ivan had set up a special arrangement with a small hotel in Le Lavandou, so it was easy to spend one's weekends on the mainland. Dress in the lab was decorous, but adapted to the heat. Most wore short shorts and lightweight tops, so if you appreciated the feminine thigh you were in your element. Judging by the points on some of the blouses, bras were not in fashion, and for these young ladies not really necessary.

"Let's go over the plan again, said Michel.

"We are trying two different algae, fast growers, natural to this area."

"And you want to modify them, so that they only metabolise heavy water?"

"Yes, exactly, using natural evolution with extra mutations triggered by a strong gamma source."

Michel looked sceptical, but Ivan went on. "In the sea 1 part in 5000 is heavy water; so they are used to that. If you put them in pure heavy, they all die. Somewhere in between the two extremes we must get some that survive, and we breed from them."

"So you get a strain that is more adapted to heavy water."

"And then repeat the process. At some point the algae are going to switch sides, and go for heavy instead of light."

"Fine, I can see that it might happen. But when you put them back into the normal sea, they will all die off. So you get nowhere!"

"Not necessarily. Remember how plants work. They pick up what they need from very dilute solutions in the soil. Salts, fertiliser, trace elements even, they are all there in tiny amounts, but the organism gets them and concentrates them into itself. So why shouldn't they do that for deuterium?"

"Maybe. I remember the argument. You sold it to the biologists and the CERN Council. But will it work?"

Ivan, like any good salesman had to believe his own spiel. But with the DG he tried to be honest. He gave a graphic central European shrug. "I don't know. But the only way to find out is to try it. And if it works, the sky is the limit!"

"I agree with that. Just harvest the bugs from the sea, and distil off the heavy water. Now how far have you got?"

"Have a look at this." Michel glanced at the microscope slide; with his naked eye he could see a lot of black dots the size of pin-heads. Under the magnifier they looked like small green flowers on stalks.

"Acetabularia mediterranea," said Ivan. "It's the largest known single celled organism, we call it TAB for short. It grows wild all around here on the sea shore. And here's another, englena viridis: grows like mad in fresh water if there are enough nutrients."

"Why these two? There are millions of plants you could try."

"Sure, but we can't afford to, so I have to make a choice; simple plants, fast growers and easy to handle. The faster they grow the more chance of mutations. Now have a look at these." Michel peered through a glass window into a sealed tank, full of dirty green bubbling sea water. "These are TAB growing in 50% heavy water. They have adapted, and the genetic code has already changed a little."

"Fabulous!"

"Actually not. The mass spectrometer shows that the water inside the cell is still light water. So these chaps are sticking to their old habits and ignoring the heavy water."

"Oh, I see."

"But wait for the next step. We are going to shock them by putting them into 90% heavy. Most will die, but those that remain will be more adapted. We will breed from them. And then move to 99% heavy."

Ivan's eyes gleamed. "At some stage they will either all die off, or they will start building the heavy water into their structure."

A long languid swim in delicious warm water was what they needed next, so Ivan grabbed a couple of towels from his office and they scrambled down a steep path through the perfumed scrub, alive with large black and yellow swallow tails, to reach a private beach reserved for the lab. No one wore costumes, Ivan explained; once you got used to it, it was so much easier; many of them brought picnics to have lunch together on the beach, and of course swam together after work. What effect does that have on the social interactions, Michel wanted to know. Very positive. You got to know people as they are, and all prurient curiosity was eliminated. So paradoxically the effect was if anything anti-erotic.

They were like a big happy family. There were amorous liaisons, of course, but no different from anywhere else.

The small dinner party was lively. Juliet had done wonders with the rather insipid Mediterranean langouste. With a discreet sprinkling of angostura bitters, and cooked with fennel, she made it taste like lobster, a trick she had learned in Paris. Puff pastry and thermidor sauce completed the illusion.

There were two Norwegians on the staff and they were both invited. Kirsten, a blonde marine biologist, had the day to day responsibility for the TABs. "They seem very happy here." she said. "I think we have found the best gamma dose for maximum mutations, and the shock treatment seems to work. Who knows what we will find next?" She was not very brown, but had freckles instead. How far did they go? Michel found himself hoping to see her on the beach. Then he realised that once this curiosity was satisfied he might not feel so attracted.

At breakfast next day Michel asked about the other Norwegian. "This guy who looks after the heavy water, on loan from Bergen, what's his name, Ogg is it? He's really a bit of a spy, isn't he?"

"Well, yes . . . . . . and no. The heavy water really belongs to them, and you have to look after it. It can easily pick up ordinary water from the air, or damp containers, and that would spoil it. So we need the expert, their man, to make sure it stays OK."

"Right. But if this idea works, then their business will be ruined; so they must be worried."

"No, they're not. Because if it works they get 50% of the action."

"Oh yes," said Michel with a wry smile, "But I reckon our friend Ogg is keeping an eye on you, and reporting back, to make sure that we don't double-cross them."

"That's OK by me," said Ivan, "I am not the double-crossing type. Who gets the other 50% by the way, is it the member states of CERN?"

"No way," said Michel expansively, "CERN holds the patents, so it all goes to us. We will be as rich as Croesus. We will rule the world!" Ivan's eyebrows shot up and he looked carefully at his boss. Was this urbane intelligent man hiding a streak of madness?

After breakfast Ivan went back to the lab, and Juliet took Michel to the beach. They scrambled down another way this time and Juliet needed a steadying hand. "Ivan and I discovered this cove, no one else comes here."

She soon stripped off her clothes and flexed her limbs, moving gracefully on the sand. She was petite, but perfectly formed, and Michel could only join the long list of admirers Her breasts were prettily pointed with upstanding areolae; they had tantalised audiences from Reykjavik to Istanbul, and now for the first time he was exposed to their attraction. Her puffy little mound was as smooth as a ripe plum. Tightly convolved and sweetly slashed, it had all the appearance of untrammelled virginity. Not that it wanted for use. For Ivan saw to it that she was regularly and thoughtfully exercised; yet afterwards, like a well kissed mouth, it resumed at once its enigmatic smile of childish innocence.

In spite of Ivan's theories, anti-erotic was not really the word for it. Being French, Juliet found him easy to talk to, and prone upon the rug she told him about her life in Paris, carefully mentioning also the landmarks in Ivan's career, and underlining how clever he was and how hard-working.

It is always relaxing for a man to contemplate the naked female form; in the flesh is better than stone or paint, and more than one, if you are so lucky, doubles the pleasure. Michel felt himself palpably unwinding. He felt at home with Juliet, and recounted some of his inner thoughts and experiences. She responded with increasing interest, her gaze more candid, her smile more open.

"It is getting warmer. I think I need some more sun lotion - would you mind?" He did not mind at all, and with her encouragement he made a thorough job of it. She enjoyed the feel of his palm travelling slowly over her skin.

"What about you?" He nodded. There was no need for haste, elegant fingers gently lingering. Deftly she screwed the round top back into the tube, put an arm around his neck and kissed him. It was not just a perfunctory peck. When Juliet did something, she did it whole-heartedly. The mouth open, moist and mobile, the tongue flickering, and she was in no hurry to finish. It was a kiss full of promise, which left him in no doubt as to her intention. It was an open invitation, and it elicited a notable erection. Juliet reacted spontaneously with a single word, intending to show appreciation and encouragement. But the result was not what she expected.

"Magnifique!" she said, and in one word tilted the relationship, which had been teetering precariously between indecision and commitment, tilted it onto the side of the angels. For this short phrase had convinced Michel, rightly or wrongly we cannot say, but he was convinced in spite of her habitual protestations, that she had been . . . . . . well, what shall we say, 'une poule', or to put her in the highest category, 'une poule de grande luxe'. The realisation shocked him, shook him back to reality. He was well paid as Director-General; paid to stand high, commanding respect and authority. He had long ago determined not to meddle with his staff or their dependants; and here he was on a public beach!

"I think it's time for a swim." His condition apparently offered no impediment to a rapid crawl which carried him some hundred metres out to sea.

"Come on in!" he cried, re-establishing his leadership and mastery.

Juliet followed, but she was not a strong swimmer, and the spell was broken. But he was grateful for the offer and a warm relationship had begun. When a man has once resisted temptation, he feels that he can expose himself again with impunity. The Eckerdovsky's and the Augier's would see a good deal more of each other, with no detriment to Ivan's career.

As Michel bade farewell to Ivan that afternoon his palm was still tingling from the touch of her skin. "Thank you for a very pleasant visit. What I have seen has been most impressive, and . . . . . . you are a lucky man!" "Ah, thank you! Let us hope that it lasts."

The chopper took him to Marignane, where a naval officer met him, drove him to the gangway of the Air France jet and handed him his boarding card, seat 2F, a window on the right: he would get a perfect view of Mont Blanc as they skimmed close to the summit on the way into Cointrin. He got home in time for an elegant supper with Monique. Although just into her fifties, Madame Augier still enjoyed the pleasures of the double bed; and this evening, invigorated by the sea breezes, he filled her more substantially and copiously than usual.

9 Rats

Meanwhile something strange was happening around the CERN proton synchrotron, usually called the PS. Bill Reed, on a boring night shift, decided to look at the background rate in his counters. The bursts of particles from the synchrotron came every 2.1 seconds: between bursts the counters were idle, clocking up only a few counts per second from cosmic rays and background radioactivity. Bill was casually watching the flashing lights on the scalers. Every time the PS put out its beams the lights would sparkle like crazy; in between the pulses virtually nothing happened. Suddenly he noticed a burst of counts in one scaler at the wrong moment. He watched for a while, and decided that something funny was happening. He asked for the beam to be turned off. There were no counts for a while; then suddenly it started; then nothing. It is a dud counter, he thought, firing off at random, better change it or it will foul up the experiment. But then to his surprise he noticed two counters had bursts at the same time; this would not happen by accident, there must be something real.

This went on for weeks without any explanation, and the disease spread to other experiments. Perhaps it was always there but no one had bothered to look. Random bursts of counts were occurring all over the PS experimental area. Some said it did not matter. In fact it would not affect the real results which depended on complex patterns involving many detectors firing together.

"It's a gremlin," said others. Years ago Maxwell had postulated a demon, an imaginary being who could systematically switch molecules one way or the other and arrange for the laws of physics to be violated. "Perhaps it's a radioactive gremlin, little green men running round the hall." Another theory was a computer virus, programmed by some joker to put numbers into the registers in a random way, and slowly spreading through the site, infecting everyone's apparatus. The peculiar thing was that it only happened at night.

Jeremy got into a discussion at lunch. "Let's suppose that there is a real gremlin What could we do to discover it?" Asking the right question is the first step to making progress.

"TV," said Bill. "We can rig up a camera and video recorder. Then record the picture only when the burst of counts comes on, you know automatic."

"Infra-red, thermal imaging," said Jeremy, "so as not to frighten them away. They have these scanners that give you a picture using the heat that comes off an object. It shows anything living, and trees as well. I think I know where I can borrow one." He was thinking of the hospital, because he had read that thermal imaging was used to detect cancer.

"But suppose the little green men aren't warm. Low light TV would be better."

"OK, see if you can find one, and I will look for the infra-red. We could try both."

So Jeremy rang Jan Olbers at the hospital. "Jeremy Partridge, do you remember? We met at Varenna."

The slow drawly Swedish voice. "Yeas . . . Ah, yeas . . . .let me see . . . Partridge, the English game bird, is it not? Yeas, we met at dinner, you helped us with the menoo. We had a good time in Varenna, I think." Glad you think so, thought Jeremy, but Jan had not finished his recollections.

"Yeas, Yeremy. Or should I say Sir Yeremy. . . . . It is a yoke of course. You must come round and see us some time . . . .bring your wive. She is charming I am sure. All wifes are charming. Ah, you would like some help? Any time, any time, what can I do for you?"

"I thought perhaps, in the hospital, you might have a thermal imager."

"Not that I know of."

"Aren't they used to search for hot spots on the breasts? You know, as a sign of cancer."

"Ah, the breasts. Hot spots! Yeas, that sounds like a good idea. But no, we are not doing it here. Perhaps it is just a research study. Thermal imaging is used in Sweden, of course, for looking at houses, to see where the heat is being lost. Maybe they are doing that also in Switzerland. It is a cold country, as you know, but not so grey as Sweden."

It was a good suggestion. The people in the purchasing office would know; they had all the catalogues and contacts. Jeremy found them tucked away on the ground floor among a maze of corridors with no view. There was a young man in charge, Marc Florian.

"We are putting all the information into a database; then we will be able to answer any question without searching through piles of catalogues."

There were about 20 girls in the office, and they were all busy typing data from the catalogues into the computer. "The only trouble is we need more girls to keep up," said Marc. He was building a miniature empire, and Jeremy wondered how he got away with it. A whole army of girls would not be able to manage.

"Surely you can buy this information on a compact disc. There must be an organisation somewhere that sells it to everyone who needs it."

"I don't think we could afford that. And anyway, we make the selection that will be of most relevance to CERN."

"OK. I am interested in thermal imaging. Who makes it, and are there any agents in Geneva?"

Marc operated the database, and they hung around for a response. Half a minute later the screen said "No information on thermal imaging."

"Sorry about that. It is not what we usually get asked."

They found an old retainer who had been there for years; he was no good on computers but he understood the catalogues. With his help they looked through an old fashioned card index. There was nothing on thermal imaging, but plenty of firms who supplied insulation for roofs. Jeremy took some phone numbers. As he left Marc said,

"Sorry it wasn't in the database. All we need is more people, and then we could serve you better."

"I'll tell the DG." Marc's face lit up. "The DG! That would be wonderful." Jeremy had apparently made his day. If the DG heard about it, heads would probably roll. But Jeremy had his own business to mind, and back in his office he rang a few firms. No one had a thermal imager. Then he had an inspiration, the Ministry of Defence: infrared vision was one of the main tools of night warfare.

Jeremy got the number from directory inquiries, 0171-218-2111, and dialled through.

"Could you put me through to thermal imaging please."

"Do you know the extension?"

"No, I am afraid not."

"I cannot connect you unless you have the extension." It looked like an impasse, MOD security rules and all that.

"This is the Swiss Federal Army in Bern. We have a requirement for a new thermal night vision system, and anticipate placing a substantial order. We would appreciate some advice. As this is our first contact I do not have the extension. Can you connect me to someone who could help?"

"Yes sir. Just a minute please."

The phone switched to martial music: massed bands of the Grenadier Guards rolling down Whitehall. Tum, tum, tetum tetum tetum, tralala tralala BOOM BOOM! The rhythm was repeated again and again, until Jeremy figured they had been up to Parliament Square and back about five times. These guardsmen had plenty of puff and they even broke into a new brisker rhythm: tum, tum, tiara tara, tumtiddy-um-tum-tum! The minutes were ticking away. Suddenly a voice came on the line.

"Surveillance, Major Spiffing speaking." Young brisk and keen, perhaps just out of staff college, his first HQ appointment. Jeremy took the bull by the horns. Might as well be hung for a sheep as a lamb. He decided to pull rank.

"Colonel Schumacher, Swiss Federal Army, good morning, I wonder if you can help. We have a requirement for 5000 thermal imaging systems of the latest specification. Could you give me the address of a British manufacturer?"

"Yes Sir! I think Barr and Stroud would be your best bet. Would you like their number?"

"Many thanks! " He wrote it down. "And do you have a name I should ask for?"

"Yessir! Peter Breadman, he's the chap."

"Breadman? You don't mean Baker, do you?"

"Baker? No, no, Breadman." The voice was puzzled.

"It is a yoke."

"A yoke? Oh, I see. Oh, ha ha!"

The disease was contagious. He had better watch it, find an antidote, or it would be impossible to stop. The joke had an unfortunate consequence; it transferred the conversation into Spiffing's long term memory, and he started telling his friends about this queer foreigner He decided to check up and during his lunch break dropped into the library. There were only a small number of colonels in the Swiss Federal Army, and Schumacher was not one of them. Oh God, he thought, have I dropped a clanger? He should have checked first and rung the man back. Reviewing the conversation he reckoned that he had not given away anything secret; but it was a bad show. Better keep quiet about it.

Jeremy got through to Barr and Stroud without further difficulty. Yes, they had an agent in Geneva, Sigrist S.A. in Charmilles. He found that they had a demonstration model; if CERN wanted to buy one delivery would take three months, which probably meant six. He went round to see it and persuaded the man to let him have it on trial for a week. Bill had not managed to find the low light TV.

It took a day to fix up the electronics. There was a time-gate, synchronised to the PS. It was shut when the PS was giving out its particles, but between bursts it opened to let through the background counts. If there were more than 200 counts between bursts, then the recorder would register the thermal image and it kept going for 15 seconds after the extra counts had disappeared. In the morning they could see if the tape had been running and look at the picture. No one had to stay on shift waiting for the gremlins. They tested the system with a radioactive source on a stick; as soon as they put it near a counter, the tape started running, and the thermal picture gave a general view of the area around the apparatus.

For several nights nothing happened: there were no extra counts, but nothing was lost as Bill's main experiment was running normally. The next night they had several bursts of counts and the video revealed everything. A nice fat rat was running about on the equipment.

"But why the counts? Rats don't make the counters fire!"

"Unless they're radioactive!"

"We must catch him and find out."

The next evening the radioactive-rat trap, baited with non-radioactive cheese, went into action. It was an old fashioned wire mesh cage with a one way door, designed to let Robert in but not out. As before they could record the proceedings automatically if there were any counts. They also rigged up an alarm. Bill had a little cuckoo adapted from parts of a Swiss clock, but triggered electronically. Much more fun than a boring old buzzer.

In the middle of the night the cuckoo started to chirp and the tape came on. Sure enough there was Robert cavorting round the beam line.

He was a bit suspicious of the cage but clearly attracted to the cheese. After sniffing around hesitantly he suddenly decided to go for it.

"Hurray!" cried everyone in the counting room. They switched off the beam and scampered down the metal stairways and long corridors to the protective gate that keeps people out of the dangerous area. Each person took a key from the control panel and the PS operator opened the access door by remote control. The personal key was your protection if you were accidentally left inside. The beam could not come on unless every key was back in the panel. The operator watched them via his TV monitor, and if anyone forgot his key he would call out on the intercom, "Take a key!"

Inside they found Robert alive and well. He was a nice fat specimen, well nourished, with unusually long fur. They brought him back to the counting room and fed him cheese through the grill.

"Is he radioactive? Let's get a monitor."

They went to the operator's control room to fetch a radiation detector and put it up to the cage. The needle read full scale.

"Wow! 100 millirem per hour! Keep clear. That is 20 times tolerance!"

They put him in another room with some cheese and water, and a big notice on the door:

'KEEP OUT - RADIOACTIVE RAT'

CERN's involvement with rats had started long before. The Swiss winter is not recommended for sleeping rough. So when autumn comes and the harvest is in, the rats look for a cosy refuge; if it is centrally heated and full of junk so much the better. CERN with its endless interconnecting tunnels and cable runs at various levels makes an ideal retreat. Unfortunately the rats make mayhem, stripping pipes of thermal cladding to build their nests and turning the whole place into a filthy warren.

Every year the chief operator of the cyclotron put in his standard order for rat poison, the tasty Swiss granules called Raticide. Then there was an economy drive and an enthusiastic young man in purchasing changed the order to the much cheaper Rat-a-tat-tat, made in the People's Republic of China. He was careful to bring this initiative to the attention of his chief. Three weeks later the corridors around the accelerator gave out an intolerable stench.

When they dug up the floors at great expense they found them in abundance. Raticide, based on the anticoagulant warfarin, makes the rats thirsty, so they go outside looking for water. The cyanide in Rat-a-tat-tat just made them curl up on the spot.

Thereafter the suppliers of Raticide were given a permanent contract, but that was not the end of the story. Rats can adapt to warfarin; either they learn to avoid it, or they develop a tolerance. Vitamin K is an antidote and is produced by intestinal bacteria.

Then there are mutations caused by radiation. Right next to the targets of the big accelerators the radiation levels are enormous; anyone in there when the machines were running would soon be dead. Outside the heavy concrete shielding, of course, it is completely safe. Inside the labyrinths of tunnels, cable-ways and ventilation shafts, forbidden to humans but readily accessible to the rats, almost any level of radiation can be found.

Radiation is used by plant breeders to develop new varieties, and small doses may even be beneficial to the health. So rats which lived in the right places would mutate and evolve rapidly. Natural selection would take care of the rest. It was not surprising that after 20 years of operation the tunnels had developed their own strain of rat, well adapted to living in this environment, fairly resistant to radiation and immune to warfarin. On the whole they kept a low profile, not wishing to come to the attention of the management.

When Bill and Jeremy captured a radioactive rat, the management were in it up to their ears. Obviously there was more than one. If they could get into the tunnels, they could also get out, and were running happily round the granaries and cheese factories of the Canton de Genève. Just imagine the headlines; Swiss cheese radioactive! The local chauvinists would throw out the dangerous foreigners, and CERN might even have to close.

The news was quickly relayed to the highest level and Michel Augier set up a committee with Hans Issinger in the chair. Bill and Jeremy as the discoverers were inevitably members. Ivan Eckerdovsky was brought in for his biological expertise, and the medicine man Jan Olbers from the Geneva hospital. As a radiotherapist he would understand the effect of various radiation levels, anyway on humans and perhaps also on rats. There were several others pulled in to contribute ideas and everyone was sworn to absolute secrecy.

Hans was a thin nervous Austrian who was always scratching his nose and wiggling his fingers. He started by explaining the seriousness of the situation. The DG was very concerned and had given him three days to come up with some recommendations. There were plenty of questions, how did the rats get there, how did they become radioactive, why did they not die of it, what were the risks, and above all, what could they do about it? There were also plenty of answers.

The French can never forget that Madame Curie discovered radium in Paris, and her son-in-law Joliot-Curie discovered artificial radioactivity created by neutrons. For the French physicist, Louis Santis, it was all quite simple.

"There are lots of neutrons in the tunnels; the rats get irradiated with neutrons and of course they become radioactive."

"That won't work," said Jan. "We are treating cancer with fast neutrons and we know that a lethal dose does not leave the patient radioactive. I reckon he is eating radioactive food."

"Sandwiches," said Luigi, "and salami. Perhaps the rats clear up the mess when people leave, take it into the tunnels, it gets activated, and then they eat it." He was improvising as he went along, and it did not make much sense.

"Then we should forbid people to bring food into the experimental areas."

"We must put up posters," said Jan. "There would be a big picture of Madonna, smiling of course, and underneath we write NO CHEESE by order of the DG." This suggestion was received with a polite silence.

"It is a yoke," said Jan. Jeremy sniggered: the man was ridiculous. Jan gave a grateful glance. "At least someone can see my yoke."

Eckerdovsky was more thoughtful. "I reckon the rats collect food from outside, grain, nuts, maybe cheese from the cheese factories, and store it in the tunnels for the winter. They may by chance be putting it where the radiation is quite strong, and this kills the bacteria so the food is preserved. You see the food in that area will last longer, while the other will go bad. So they will tend to eat more irradiated food. They may even have learned to put it in the radiation belt, and here the radiation will include neutrons which will make the food active."

It was a good hypothesis and Jan agreed. "Rats are not stupid."

"In that case," said Bill, "there must be a cache of radioactive food somewhere. Could we turn off the machines and then search the tunnels with radiation monitors?"

"Fooey!" said the others. "It might be anywhere. The whole area is active: the monitor would be confused." Anyway it would take too long.

"The main thing," said Hans waving his hands for emphasis, "is first to get rid of the rats, and then make sure that they never come back. Does anyone have a practical suggestion?"

Jeremy had phoned Jan soon after the discovery and asked him to take care of the rat. The hospital did experiments with mice, so they must have an animal house somewhere. Jan was interested, picked up the rat and examined him carefully. Now it was his turn to hold the floor.

"Before we decide to exterminate the rats we should try to understand what is happening. We seem to be confronted with an incredible scientific phenomenon, of great relevance to medicine. The rat that you have caught is quite different from the ordinary farm rat that we have in the area. His body is smaller, but he has long bushy fur with a speckled grey and brown colour. His head is broader than usual and the eyes set a bit more forward; it makes him look more intelligent. Where has he come from?"

"Now I come to the most surprising part of the story. The rat is quite radioactive, but apparently in good health. He shows no sign of radiation sickness. This is a medical paradox. According to the books his hair should be falling out, his gums bleeding, his blood count low and he should be very lethargic. Instead he is, how do you say it, full of the beans."

"Evolution," said Eckerdovsky. He was mentally kicking himself. There he was on the Ile du Levant trying to breed Acetabularia that would metabolise heavy water, and all the time evolution at an incredible rate was going on in the PS tunnels. But verbally he was more cautious.

"Could it be that the rats in the tunnel are evolving more rapidly because of the radiation?"

"And if so," said Jan, "have they developed some new repair mechanisms that make them radiation resistant?" His eyes glowed. "This could be a fantastic discovery. We might learn how to protect patients when we treat the tumours, how to protect the population from radioactive fall out, the military would be interested . . . . it is endless. We must find out how it all works."

Hans Issinger was getting impatient. "Meanwhile these radioactive rats are running round the countryside, the population are not resistant and there may be cases of radiation sickness, leukaemia or birth defects. We cannot run that risk. The rats must be killed."

"No," cried Jan. "You would be destroying valuable scientific evidence. This could be the most important discovery that CERN has ever made. We must take it further."

"Gas them," said someone. "No," cried the PS coordinator, "We cannot have them dying in the tunnels, the smell would be disgusting."

"Biological control," said Ivan. "Take a natural predator, such as the cat. We could flood the area with hungry cats."

"And then what?" asked Hans. "The cats would become radioactive. Not being resistant they would die in the tunnels, in the fields, and maybe go into peoples homes. We would have sick cats everywhere."

By now Jan had it all worked out. "The essential trouble is that the rat cohabits to some extent with Man; that is the danger. To move the radioactivity to the cat is worse, because the cat and Man are much closer. So we need to go the other way; find a predator that stays away from Man."

Many suggestions were raised: foxes, snakes, buzzards - all impractical. And underneath was the fundamental disagreement between the exterminators who wanted to get rid of the rats as fast as possible, and the preservers who wanted to study the biology of the new strain.

Hans Jorgens had a suggestion. "I know an old man who might be able to help us. He lives in Hamelin."

"The Pied Piper! " they all cried. It was just the ticket.

Jan was confused. "Is that a yoke?" he asked in the end.

"It is a yoke!" they all shouted in unison.

Then Wally Scorer's rasping voice was heard over the din; he was one of the few Aussie's in CERN, and he had a strong accent.

"Ah'll tellyer one thing about the Piper - 'e wasn't pied enough!"

It took a little time to work this out, and then the English were rolling off their chairs. "He wasn't pied enough. It is a yoke ..... it is a yoke" they all shouted again, but the continentals were baffled.

Hans Issinger became furious. The meeting was getting out of control. Purple with anger he banged the table. "Gentlemen, this is not a joking matter. We take a break. We meet again tomorrow morning at nine o'clock sharp and then we will have a serious discussion."

Still laughing, Jeremy took Ivan back home for a drink and they went over the debate again with Clare. The rats were wanted for research by Jan, they were not really a problem for the accelerator or the experiments around it; the only question was to keep them from contaminating the surrounding farms. Then Clare had a suggestion.

"I tell you what. Why not build a luxurious rat house, with comfortable beds and succulent non-radioactive breakfasts? Then the rats would have no need to forage for food, but would come to the house instead."

The others took her up enthusiastically. "Connection to the tunnels could be by a one way door."

"Yes, and it would be a highly moral order. The rats should be segregated to prevent fornication"

"They have enough of that already!"

Electric fans would spread the smell of good food and randy frustrated rats down the tunnels to attract the others in. Once a rat had dried out, that is lost his radioactivity, he or she could be released into the environment.

"The point is," said Clare, "The house will provide a base for Jan's research on the new strain. When the situation is under control, the public can be informed about CERN's new research project on radiation resistance and scientific papers can be published. We can have a major press release."

Next day in the meeting the idea was warmly welcomed. They would need money, which was no problem as the DG was desperate to find a solution, and someone to supervise the animals. When Jeremy mentioned that his wife was a vet, Hans jumped at the opportunity. She was interviewed next day, and started work under Jan's supervision to design the facility. The carpenters soon knocked it together in the form of a diminutive Swiss chalet. Inside were hygienic cages with remote controls for handling the radioactive animals and their effluent, plus a small laboratory for analysis. The main work on samples and autopsies would be done in the hospital. For safety, ventilators pulled the air away from the humans, in towards the rats, and then out along the tunnels.

On top of the chalet they put a scroll, inscribed in elegant gothic script,

Rathaus

The Germans were amused by this: for them Rat meant advice or council, the word for the animal being spelled with two t's. The Swiss however were a bit miffed: they took their council chambers seriously! But the name stuck.

As an extra precaution Clare released a battery of hungry cats to scavenge for stray rats in the fields every day. At the end of the day she rounded them up and checked them for radioactivity. In fact, no cat ever became active, so it seemed that the danger to the public had been grossly exaggerated. But she kept quiet about it, not wanting to lose an interesting part time job.

When the Rathaus was ready there was a party to celebrate. Quite a few rats were already in residence, all with splendid speckled grey fur. They were admired through the lead glass windows. Michel made a speech congratulating Bill and Jeremy on finding them, and Jan and Ivan for the scientific studies they were planning. This was an important new development for CERN, and of great international importance. He welcomed Clare as the keeper of the Rathaus; how lucky they were to find a ready made expert on their doorstep.

Many wives were present and people were laughing and joking. No one except Jan, and maybe Ivan and the DG, could really take the rats seriously. To most it was just an amusing diversion from their daily routine. Avelyn was there with Jan, as dazzling as ever, and of course the centre of attention. Ivan had her pinned down with his talk about accelerated evolution, so Jeremy decided to chat up a sweet young thing who was looking confused. In one hand she was balancing a small handbag and a fork, while the other held a glass of champagne and a plate of prawn salad. The chord of the bag had somehow caught round a button on her skirt, so every time the fork lifted to shovel a prawn into the luscious little mouth there were glimpses of long white thigh. Her efforts to unhook the bag were revealing, but ineffective.

"Hullo! Can I help? You seem to have too much on your hands."

She nodded vigorously, the mouth full of prawn. Smears of mayonnaise on the red lips, he thought, enhanced her beauty. She gestured simultaneously with the fork, bag and one finger, to indicate her inability just at that moment to speak, and the skirt jagged open again.

"Shall I take the glass?"

The eyes looked grateful. More nodding. He took the plate too, and waited while she unravelled herself.

"Do you work here?"

"No . . . . my 'usband . . . . 'ee works . . . . . solly, I am not speaking very well zee English."

Jeremy picked up the accent, and tried to continue in his halting French. The usual small talk; it was uphill work, but the girl was lively, and full of smiles.

Ivan appeared. "Ah, Juliet . . . Jeremy. . . . Ah, you have met? I was going to introduce you. Juliet this is Jeremy, I have told you about him. The Rathaus, it was our idea, was it not?" He looked to Jeremy for confirmation. Jeremy nodded. "Ah, Jeremy this is Juliet. But I see that you are talking already. Where is Clare?"

"I think she is inside with Jan, showing people round."

"I have been thinking," Ivan went on, "after this party is over maybe we could all get together and eat somewhere. What do you think? Perhaps near the airport? The Café de l'Aviation is still very good I believe."

Jan and Avelyn came too, so there were six of them. It was a celebration of the new project, of which the three men had been the prime movers, though Jan assisted by Clare would now have the running of it. In another way they were meeting as couples for the first time, and tentatively getting acquainted.

There are not many ways of arranging a table with three on each side. Ivan as the initiator put himself in the centre with Avelyn opposite, leaving the others to take the corners. Inevitably Jeremy had to sit next to Avelyn and it was exactly as the two of them had sat side by side sharing a menu at the restaurant in Tremezzo. She flashed him a quick smile, which said ‘do you remember?’. He had forgotten how beautiful she was, but now he was again intoxicated by her radiance. Faint but pervasive, her haunting acrid odour triggered a replay, and long-buried images streaked across his mind.

Soft light on the Lago di Como. After lunch they had wandered further round the shore; she held his hand. Down on the little shingle beach they were leaning against a wall. She had turned quietly and kissed him. It lasted a long time. Afterwards her eyes were dancing. Her mouth tasted of warm fresh milk, the tongue soft and active.

“I am married,” he said. It sounded wooden, stupid, unromantic, but he had to say it.

“I know. Everyone is married. It doesn't matter.”

But it did matter; vows, commitment, the fabric of society.

“What about fidelity?” he asked. “Doesn’t that count for something?”

“Of course! When you are young you reach out for contact. When you find it, or think you have found it, you magnify it. Fidelity is a lovely idea, a new dimension to explore. What will it bring? Then later another human being comes along; you want to reach out again, make contact, explore some more. Fidelity then seems less important, and it opens up a new possibility - infidelity. That is exciting too!”

She paused, giving him a long candid look, then more kisses.

“Of course if you find a new one, you want to be faithful to him too - for a while. It is like looping the loop in a plane. You dive down, faster and faster, then up up up and over the top; it all goes quiet. Then dive down again, and . . . . . into the next loop.”

Her hands gestured, palm up, palm down, over and over. “Do you see what I mean? Fidelity, infidelity, fidelity, infidelity, it’s a loop, over and over, and over again!”

Jeremy nodded. He could see what she meant, but whether he agreed with it was another matter. There was no time to think; the kisses were annihilating any form of rationality. She was either totally cynical, playing a game; or she had a completely different set of values. Either way spelt danger. What about the trail of broken hearts?

A sheep path meandered up a small knoll with close cropped dry grass. They sat in the sun and watched the boats lazily going about their business, and the traffic winding round the shore. Then she lay back, hands above her head, her breasts straining the white sleeveless blouse. They felt good. After a while the blouse slipped out of her waist band, and he eased it up. Two lace capped mountains.

"Shall we let them out of their prison?" She nodded and he reached under her and flicked the clip. Perky little things they were, and not so little either. He did what one usually does with breasts, and for good measure a few other things as well. Avelyn raised no objection. When it came to the point, she seemed to appreciate his efforts. That is what it's all about. Solitary pleasures are not much fun, sharing is everything. It was a form of communication and, as she said, better than talking. Though the range of sentiments you could express was pretty limited. You needed both he supposed. As he discovered in the cradle, you cannot say much with a nipple in your mouth.

"Do you mind?" She asked, grinning at him mischievously. "Being married, I mean, and all that?"

"Not as long as you know." Deception was not his line, or so he thought.

She was a feast, exhilarating and relaxing at the same time, and he felt at home with her, peaceful and at ease. Back on the ferry she had her arm round him, standing close. His arm caressed her hips, and just for fun he gave her a playful pinch.

"Ouch! . . . . You naughty man!" She wriggled, but pressed closer and kissed him again. Before they landed she had written down her number, and promised him a return lunch. He still had it somewhere but up to now he had decided not call.

Now Ivan was in full flood, telling her about wave clouds over the Jura. When the wind comes from the north-west, blowing strongly over the crest, it follows the contours of the land down the steep slope onto the flat plain around the lake. You can see the clouds following the slope down and then dissolving. But paradoxically, higher up the air is rising in a wide expanse of smooth lift.

"It only happens a few times a year, but I got into it once. Amazing, completely quiet, you sit there facing into the wind, just keeping position and going up, up, up, smoothly up. I got to 5000 metres, then flew along to Bern and back at 140 kph. And when I got back I was still at 4000 metres. The sky was full of wave clouds, saucer shaped lenticulars. They kept moving about, coming and going. Mont Blanc was completely clear, and seemed quite close. There were more wave clouds beyond it, over Italy."

He turned to Jeremy. "In front of every lenticular there is lift. If you had the courage, you could turn down wind and race to Mont Blanc in 30 minutes. In front of the mountain there must be tremendous lift. You would go up like a rocket to 6000 metres, more perhaps, then over the top and with the wind behind you whiz down into Italy. You could go 500 kilometres, which gets you a diamond on your gliding badge."

His eyes lit up. "The only thing is, I have no idea what's behind Mont Blanc. If it was cloudy and you dropped into it, there might be mountains. You know the saying, mountains and clouds go together, or planes and mountains, and so do planes and clouds. But planes, mountains and clouds - no good at all." He rolled his eyes expressively.

"Can you take passengers?" asked Jeremy.

"Sure . . . . in the two seater . . . . would you like to try it?"

"Er . . . . yes . . . . very much. That is . . . . if it's not too dangerous!"

"No problem. Next weekend, if you like . . . . or the one after . . . . . Bring Clare as well."

Avelyn was vexed. Why was she not included? A flight with this strong bearded man would be quite amusing and, while he and Clare were in the air, Jeremy could do with some company. She gave Ivan a baleful look across the table but, in spite of her beauty, he did not respond: two passengers would be plenty for a day floating on the Jura. He could catch up with Avelyn some other time, at his leisure . . . . . maybe.

The wine flowed freely and glasses clinked, toasts to the rats, gliding, the Ile du Levant, cancer research, catalysed fusion and so on. On his right Jeremy felt a toe, delicately pressing against his ankle. He moved his foot across, and they were interlaced, calf against calf, ankle against ankle. There was no need to look. Meanwhile Juliet was telling Clare and Jan about her dancing classes. She had found a small gymnasium in the Rue du Grand Pré, and had about a dozen young ladies twice a week.

Had she danced in Paris? Oh yes, many times, she had been one of the 'rats of the Opera', the young pupils who elicit thunderous applause. "But zer is more work in cabaret. So later I am dancing in zee Cray Ziorse." "You should have seen her," said Ivan, "So beautiful. That is where we met of course."

Jan was suddenly alert. “My goodness! Did you mean . . .? Did you say?” he spluttered. “Yes, it must be the Crazy Horse. That is the famous stripping club, is it not? Where they are showing everything!”

Juliet inclined her head in confirmation, a knowing smile, a little fluttering of the eyelids.

“She was the big star,” said Ivan.

“I don’t think I could do that,” said Clare, “it must be so embarrassing.”

“But I am not zinking about it,” answered Juliet. “I am dancing in front of zee people since I am 7 years. Sometimes it is one costume, sometimes anozzer, eet is no matter. It is zee way you move, zat is beautiful. I am not being afraid of my body. If eet makes someone ’appy, I am ’appy to show eet. And why not? I am losing nossing.”

Does the flower feel pleasure, thought Jeremy, as it unfolds in the sun? Does it enjoy the visit of the bee? But Jan’s eyes were gleaming, looking at him.

“We should go there one day. . . . . . But Ivan is the expert.”

“Have you not been?” said Ivan in surprise. He moved his head dreamily from side to side. “So elegant, so romantic . . . Ah, when I was in Paris in my bachelor days . . . then when I found Juliet, of course, I went many times.”

It was a lively evening, much enjoyed by all, and they dispersed in good spirits, resolving to meet each other more often. Who could have guessed that in a year’s time two of them would be dead: and another in gaol?

10 Bexler arrives

Back in the counting room Jeremy drummed his fingers impatiently on the table. "When the hell do we get some beam? I've been here since eight and absolutely nothing has happened."

Arthur was more philosophical. "It's always like this. The experiment looks easy on paper; then it takes six months to put the kit together, and as soon as you're ready the accelerator breaks down. Don't expect anything else."

He called the operators. "They have a leak in the cooling water; they reckon it will be fixed by twelve."

Jeremy was fretting. He normally took Julie to school on the way to work. This morning he had come in early, and after some discussion Clare had agreed to do it. As it turned out he could easily have taken her. So he was one down with the family with nothing to show for it.

"That safety officer is so pernickety. He delayed us by three weeks at least."

"Would you rather have hydrogen exploding in your face, or tritium in your bones? I think he does a good job. Let's hope it's good enough, because we rely on him completely."

Marion, Arthur's research student from Oxford, came in with three cups of coffee. "Here, this will make you even more on edge!" She was short and dumpy with straight dark hair down to her ears and glasses with thin gold rims, but she had a bright smile. She always wore a neat white blouse, with a dark blue skirt and matching tights or stockings.

"While we are waiting, could we go over the programme again?" she asked turning to Arthur.

"Well, first we put the beam straight through all the detectors and get them timed in. Remember, one foot of cable can spoil the coincidence."

"OK."

"Then adjust the range to get muons stopping in the chamber. There should be three blips from the counters in front where the particles come in, and nothing coming out at the back. Chris has set the logic to pick out these events."

"OK. And I change the range with the copper wedge. Green button for in, and red button for out."

"Sure, and you read the thickness on this dial."

"You mean we have to read dials! Doesn't it all go into the computer?"

"Not yet," said Jeremy sheepishly, "We have not had time for that. Anyway, it's more reliable this way. You can see what you are doing."

Marion gave him a sidelong glance, meaning - how old fashioned can you get?

Arthur looked at his watch. "I think Jeremy and I might have an early lunch; then when the beam comes on we'll be all bright and shiny. Marion, would you mind holding the fort, in case something happens?"

When they got back an hour later, Marion had already covered several pages of the thick ledger with notes. Onto some pages she had pasted in graphs and printed slips with numbers.

"Everything seems to work. I have 100,000 mu per second stopping in the gas. I varied the range and plotted through the peak."

"Great," said Arthur. "What's the pressure in the chamber?"

Jeremy looked at the gauge. "This 'ere dial says 10 atmospheres, but maybe Marion has it in the computer by now." He was trying to rile her but it did not work: she just gave him a conspiratorial smile.

"Right, the muons are supposed to be stopping in the gas. So let's pump it off, and see what changes."

They did this and started to count again. Meanwhile out came the pocket calculators. "Let's see. The density of hydrogen gas is one fifteenth of air, which of course is one over eight hundred. Then it's at ten atmospheres. But the metal walls are titanium, one millimetre thick, and the density is . . . . . let's see, have you got a copy of the bible?" He was referring to the little pocket book called 'Particle Properties' which everyone carried with them; it was tiny, but had all the basic data in it.

Marion got one out and thumbed through the pages. "Yes, here we are, titanium density is 4.5; stopping power 1.26 MeV per gram."

Arthur pressed the keys. "So I find that only three mu's in a thousand will stop in the hydrogen: the other 997 just persons who need no repentance will end up in the titanium walls. Then there are the counters and other junk. So I guess that only 200 out of our 100,000 will be stopping in the gas. Now let's see the result."

"Without the gas it's the same as before: actually slightly more!"

"No worry, the fluctuations on 100,000 will be 320 either way typically, and that will drown the effect. The only thing is to run for longer."

So they ran again for 10 minutes with the gas, and 10 minutes without, and they got a clear difference. "Great, so we have muons stopping in the gas. No big deal; it's been done many times, but quite a lot of things must work before we see it: not bad for the first day."

Jeremy's shift was now ending and he was due in again early next morning. If he went home he could spend some time with the kids and get to bed early. Clare would like that. Then wake up refreshed at 6 the next morning. But it was tempting to stay on, and see what happened next.

"If the muon stops in the hydrogen," said Arthur, "it will decay to an electron, after 2.2 microseconds on the average. So if we detect a delayed electron, and make it part of the signature, then we can be sure that a muon was really there. That should get rid of most of the junk."

"Yes," said Chris, "and any muon stopping in the metal walls will be captured rapidly and disappear. So it couldn't give a late electron."

"Good thinking," said Jeremy. "Let's only accept electrons that come half a microsecond or more after the muon arrives. They must come from mu's stopping in the gas. We eliminate all the other rubbish."

"Of course we will lose some events," said Arthur. "but those we select will be a clean sample and that's what we need."

So now the delayed electron counters had to be set up and checked. It was a long and laborious process, but there are no short cuts if you want to be sure the equipment is working. Those who optimistically cut corners would end up in total confusion, not knowing which part of their kit was working and which was not.

When Jeremy came in next morning, they had a good signal from mu's stopping in the hydrogen and giving a detected decay electron, about 75 per second. Not many, but it would be enough to use for the fusion tests. The electronic logic for picking out these events had been set up and seemed to work well. Now if they pumped out the hydrogen four-fifths of the rate disappeared. The remaining one fifth was 'background'; it would be nice to understand where it came from, but for the moment they pressed on.

At last they could put in the deuterium-tritium mixture and look for fusions. They would still be following the other labs who had seen catalysed fusion, but at too low a rate to be useful. Arthur believed in first doing what the others had done: once that was established they could try to do something better.

"How do we detect the fusions?" asked Marion.

"Easy," said Arthur. "DT fusion gives an alpha and a fast neutron. That will fly right through the walls of the pressure vessel, and we pick it up with our neutron detector. I calibrated it in Oxford last week. So let's pump off the hydrogen and put in the DT mixture."

"No hang on, " said Jeremy. "We should first measure the background in the neutron counter with ordinary hydrogen. Then when we change over we will see the difference."

"Good thinking, " said Arthur.

"And the other snag, is that Erik is not here. He is the only one who understands the tritium circuit, and it's fairly dangerous."

"Oh yes. He is on the evening shift. Could you call him, and get him to come in. Meanwhile we will get the background."

But Erik was not at home, and did not seem to be in CERN. So Arthur and Jeremy went down to the floor to twiddle the taps themselves.

"I reckon we can figure out what to do."

There were big red notices all around the equipment saying

'DANGER - HYDROGEN'

'DANGER TRITIUM' 'DANGER RADIOACTIVE GAS'

and so on.

"The first thing is to check for leaks," said Arthur. "The equipment has been tested many times, but a leak of tritium would be much more dangerous."

So they left the ordinary hydrogen in the chamber, and got a 'sniffer'. This was a special probe that could pick up small amounts of unusual gases. They tried it all around the system, and it seemed to be OK.

"Now we check the tritium alarm." This was a detector of radioactive gas, and it would trigger if any tritium leaked out. For test purposes there were sealed gas capsules with a tiny amount of tritium. Arthur nicked the end of one of these and waved it near the detector. Immediately a bell started clanging and lights flashed. In half a minute the booster operator appeared, rather out of breath.

"Something has gone wrong," he said in French. Then a moment later the fire brigade rushed in, with hatchets raised.

"It was only a test, " said Arthur, and managed to calm down the excited crowd. They went off grumbling.

"We forgot to switch the detector to 'TEST MODE'. Then it would have showed a red light, but not sounded the alarm. 'TEST MODE' showed a warning yellow light, instead of green for safe; this was supposed to stop you leaving it on test mode by mistake. Not totally fool proof, thought Jeremy; with so many complicated things to handle it would be easy to forget, then the alarm would not go off when it was needed, and someone would get poisoned.

"I am obliged to make a report to the safety officer," said the booster operator. He must inspect before you can continue. It took and hour to find him, and Jeremy felt irritated. He was dying to do the next test, and all the time his shift was passing with nothing to show for it: valuable machine time was being wasted.

In the end he appeared, listened to what had happened, checked the equipment again (in TEST MODE) with another phial of tritium, and gave them the all clear to carry on. It was now midday and just as they were going to start on the difficult bit, Erik turned up.

"Sorry, I was out shopping with Kara. I rang the counting room, just for interest, and got your message. So I came straight here."

Together they pumped off the normal hydrogen and flushed the system with a small amount of deuterium. Then they put in 5 atmospheres of tritium, and topped it up to 10 atmospheres with more deuterium.

"That should give the 50:50 mixture we want." The tritium alarm was set to "RUN", and everything looked OK.

They walked back up the corridors to the counting room in great excitement. This would be the first sighting of catalysed fusion in western Europe. In the room they found a stranger, sitting at the table and going through the log book in some detail with Marion. He had clearly been there some time. He was a large man with a bristly brown moustache. Somehow he seemed to take up a lot of space. The man stood up, and said

"Oh hullo! Viktor Bexler." He held out a hand. Aromas of stale tobacco effused from his crumpled striped shirt and old grey sports jacket. They introduced themselves, and he closed in on Arthur.

"The DG says I can join your group. If that's OK with you." He did not leave much space for anyone to disagree, but went straight on with his moustache twitching. "I was just looking through the log book to get up to date. I gather you are just at the beginning."

"Well, I suppose that is more or less right," said Arthur reluctantly. Bexler had a remarkable talent for making people feel uneasy. Whether it was done deliberately, or through an intrinsic insensitivity, no one really knew.

"Marion here has given me a good idea of what we are doing. Now can I see the apparatus?"

"Well, not now," said Arthur. "We have been down there for two hours and have just shut the gates. I think it is time to get some data."

"So what's the next step?" asked Bexler. He obviously wanted to be right in the middle of the action, if not in control. But Arthur rose to the occasion.

"Jeremy's in charge of this shift. I think the next step is for us to have a chat in my office. Then I will put you completely in the picture. Meanwhile we can let Jeremy and Marion get on with the experiment. What about a spot of lunch?"

"I don't take lunch. But I will come with you and have a coffee."

"Maybe you could join the midnight shift, we only have two people on that and I am sure they could do with your help. Do you feel up to it after the flight?"

They went out, and Jeremy could not understand why he felt such a wave of relief. "Phew," he said, "What a phenomenon!"

"He seemed OK to me," said Marion "He was very complimentary and gave me a lot of background on what happens in other places. He seems to know a lot." Viktor was already weaving his spell - butter up the young, divide and rule.

The next step was to run the beam into the DT mixture; they got the same number of stopping muons. Then they turned on the neutron counter and looked for neutrons coming out just after a muon stopped.

They were there all right, and there were two components. Muons stopping in the walls would get captured rapidly and give neutrons from the titanium with a fast decay; those stopping in the gas should give the fusion neutrons with a much longer lifetime, 2.2 microseconds to be precise. It took an hour or more to get the picture, but it agreed well with the expectations.

The crucial test was to find the energy of the neutrons. The detector had been specially chosen with this in mind; the size of the pulse would measure the neutron energy. So they set up some electronic time gates to let the counter signals through only if they came somewhere on the slow tail of the decays, and then they fed them into a pulse height analyser. Sure enough the energy checked out at 14 MeV, the text book figure for neutrons from DT fusion.

The only trouble with the neutron counter was that it only detected a small fraction of the neutrons. The fraction was known from the calibration, but it meant that it took a long time to get the data. Jeremy had more or less set up the electronics during his shift, Arthur had finished it off and got some results, then Bexler and the night shift had collected a lot more.

When Jeremy came in the following morning, a slightly bearded and rather smelly Bexler gave him a summary of the results. To give him his due he had written meticulous notes in the log book, and had carefully pasted in the graphs showing the results. It was all rather encouraging.

"Of course we are relying on the calibration of the counter, first for the energy, and also for the number," said Viktor. "If that is all right, we definitely have 14 MeV neutrons, and they must come from the DT reaction. If I set the time gate earlier to look at the neutrons from the walls, I get a much broader spread of energy from 1 to 10 MeV roughly. Again that is what you would expect."

"How many fusions are we getting?" asked Jeremy.

"Ah, that is what I am just calculating. Can you confirm? I look back at the log book for April 25 when you were calibrating. Efficiency for DT neutrons is given as 1.07 % - is that correct? Then we have to put in the duration of the run, the total number of neutrons counted, and compare with the number of muon stops. Also there are the angle factors depending on how far away the counter is. So I do all that, and I get only

4450 fusions per muon. That is rather low. From the Chicago data I would expect rather more."

"Are we not asking for a muon decay electron to be registered after the neutron, as part of the signature?" asked Jeremy.

That was the way he thought he had set it up. It was one of the tricks for killing the background. Bexler was not sure how it was arranged. So Jeremy started to trace the tiny cables from unit to unit in the electronics to see how the selection was made.

"Why not switch off the electron counters?" said Bexler, "If the electron is part of the signature then we will get nothing." It was a good idea. They tried it and the counts dropped to zero.

"Right, the electron requirement is in, which means we must compare with the much smaller number of muons which stop and give a detectable decay," said Jeremy. He made a quick calculation, "So that means we are getting about 20,000 fusions per mu. Isn't that more like it?"

"Right, that is close to the expected number. So everything is working OK."

There were some more corrections to put in, because they could only process one neutron signal at a time, and sometimes several would come close together, which meant that some would be lost. Jeremy reckoned he would think this through when Bexler had gone. Viktor, however, seemed happy to continue the chase.

"So we now have the classical muon fusion apparatus working. That is already progress," he pontificated. "But everyone knows that 20,000 fusions per mu is not enough. The total energy released is about 360,000 MeV as heat; only about one third of it could be turned into electricity, say 100,000. On the other side, to make one muon in the booster takes quite a few high energy protons, and only a fraction of them can stop in the DT mixture. On top of that, the booster uses lots of energy which is just wasted. On the standard calculation you are about a factor of ten out of balance."

"We are just beginning, of course," said Jeremy hesitantly. "But the idea is to see what happens in a plasma. As far as we know that hasn't been tried before, and we are almost ready to give it a whirl. Why don't we switch on the plasma and see what happens?"

He felt excited; there was chance that they would find something good. Some people spent their lives making careful measurements in known areas, and nothing new turned up. It was better to stick your neck out: the result might be zero, but at least you ran the risk of making a discovery. If there was no risk of failure, there would be no innovation. If you don't play, you can't win.

The beam was on, muons were stopping in the target, the timing gates were set and neutrons from catalysed fusion were being detected: and in the right numbers. Jeremy switched the power supply for the plasma arc to ON, and checked the filament current, six amps. Then he turned up the high voltage; 2200 volts they should run at, and this normally gave a plasma current of 100 milliamps. The meter showed nothing.

"Oh dear! It's not working. I think we must cut the beam and go down to check."

Still full of hope, he and Bexler trudged along the corridors. Marion stayed in the counting room to switch the voltage on or off; they kept in touch with the intercom. They both took safety keys and went down to the experimental floor.

"Probably a bad connection," said Jeremy. "Let's see if the voltage is getting through. Marion, could you switch it off."

The answer over the intercom was rather thick and muffled. "Plasma HT is off."

2000 volts, with 100 milliamps behind it, is quite lethal, so it was best to take precautions. Jeremy had long ago learned that you only put one hand into the electronics. Keep the other behind your back and do not touch anything else; then if you are wearing rubber soles any shock will just pass through one hand, unpleasant but not serious. He clipped the voltmeter negative lead to earth, and gingerly reached in with the positive; the clip was sheathed in rubber, but you never know. He got it onto the wire to the pressure vessel.

"Switch her on, Marion." The meter showed 2000 volts, so that connection was OK.

"What about the other side?" said Bexler.

"It should go through the meter in the counting room and then to earth." "Switch her off again, could you Marion." A moment later the answer came back. "It's off."

Jeremy moved the switches on the meter to make a measurement of resistance, and clipped on to the other lead. The needle flicked up.

"Marion, you should have a current reading on the power supply."

"No go," said Marion, "I don't see nuffing."

Now there were several possibilities. Maybe the plasma was A1, but the meter upstairs was duff; or the meter was OK but there was a lose connection; or it could be a short to earth.

"Maybe we have plasma all the time. Unfortunately the bottle is made of metal so we can't see inside. I think I'll put this meter in the earth lead and we can see if there is any current."

With a few more careful manoeuvres he got the meter in circuit and set it to show 200 milliamps full scale.

"Can we have it on again, Marion?" The meter kicked up to half scale. So the plasma current was flowing after all.

"Leave it on, Marion, everything is OK. The meter upstairs is not reading, that's all. We are coming up; get the beam on as soon as you can."

Probably the plasma had been there all along. The last half hour had been time wasted. As they walked back to the counting room Jeremy was looking forward to seeing the neutron counts with the plasma on; would they be higher than before?

"I left the meter down there; it reads OK; I think the one up here must be faulty. So now let's get some data."

He was a bit taken aback when Marion answered. "What about hydrogen safety? Remember no naked wires, all high voltage connections must be gas tight, if there is a leak and a spark we could have an explosion!"

"Hell! I forgot all about it."

Jeremy suddenly realised that he had been running a risk by fiddling with the connections while there was hydrogen around. He did not fancy going up in a ball of flame.

"Luckily there is tritium in there, and the tritium detector says there is no leak. So, we are OK."

"All the same, it might be wise to take the meter out again," said Bexler. "If the safety officer saw it he would have a fit. The plasma will still be there, even if there is no meter to confirm. Anyway, we can't read the meter from here."

So off went the beam again, and Jeremy trudged down the long corridor, this time by himself. More time wasted. Take the key, wait for the door to open.

"Marion, just make sure it's off, will you."

"Plasma HT is off."

He put the leads back the way they were. Shut the door, key back, and he called into the intercom. "Beam on, let's get some data. I am coming up."

When he got back to the counting room Bexler had gone. What a relief! But the scalers did not seem to be counting.

"What cooks?"

"The beam is off," said Marion. "Some fault on the accelerator."

Jeremy cursed. But there was nothing to be done. Bexler came back with three cups of coffee. At least he was earning his keep. His moustache was twitching as he thought out his next pronouncement. "The first thing to learn on these accelerators is to keep calm. It's no good getting uptight. Something is always going wrong, but you get there in the end." Then he added,

"I reckon the plasma will make no difference. The nuclei on the average will not be any closer together. After all, there are only so many in the bottle, plasma or no plasma."

"Oh, but in a normal gas the electrons keep the nuclei apart. In the plasma, although the average spacing is the same, there will be some very small distances."

"Yes, but that will be compensated by a number of larger distances so it will cancel out."

"I think the few very small distances will make all the difference," said Jeremy.

"Then you say that the muon is kept away from the nucleus by the electron," Bexler went on. "As the muon is 200 times heavier I reckon it will just elbow the electron aside."

Jeremy sighed. "It is not a question of mass, but kinetic energy. The muon does not have any more energy that the other particles, one half KT and all that which is less that 0.1 electron volts. On the other hand the potential in the electron cloud around the deuteron is about 2 electron volts; so most of the time it will keep the muon out."

“Ah, but the electron cannot be everywhere at once. When it’s on the other side of the deuteron, the muon can sneak through!” Jeremy was stupefied by this remark.

“What are you dreaming about? Everyone knows that the electron is spread out, Schroedinger’s equation, the quantum S-state, it’s just a blur.” Just to show that he understood what he was saying he trotted out the equation. “Psi equals one over R, E to the minus KR. No theta or phi dependence.” That should settle it.

“Fine,” answered Viktor. “But is it really spread out, or does the blur really represent our ignorance. It could in fact be localised, but you and I do not know where. So we treat it as a blur.”

It was an old conundrum, at the very heart of quantum mechanics, and it was very irritating of Viktor to raise it here. Hundreds of books had been written on the subject, the philosophers had philosophised, but the average physicist remained confused. One just knew that if you worked with the blurred wave functions you always got the right answers; the model worked, so go ahead and use it. In the same way we use Newton’s Laws of motion, without worrying about the philosophical origins of mass. But Viktor pressed on.

“What about the Einstein-Padolvsky paradox?”

Jeremy had heard the odd lecture on this puzzle, John Bell at CERN was the leading expert. Jeremy had even formed a view, but he had forgotten what it was. He suspected that Viktor could be rusty on the subject too.

“What about it?”

“We have to take it into account.”

“Sure, but I don’t think it is relevant here.” One to me, now change the subject. “The other thing about the plasma is that it pushes up the electron temperature to thousands of degrees. That will give the mu more energy also. So it is bound to be different.”

“Do you want to bet? I’ll lay 500 Swiss francs on it making no difference!”

He flourished a large sepia coloured note, the one with the naked girls on it. You did not see them very often. It showed the so-called Well of Youth, named after some Saint or other. According to the legend old crones could go into the well, and come out young and luscious. Nicely illustrated too; they had long slender thighs and smooth plump crotches.

Obviously it did not work too well, or there would not be any old crones in Switzerland. The same probably went for those other beauty products on which the ladies spent a fortune; not to speak of the investment advisers who promised to make you rich.

Viktor put the note on the table.

"If you believe what you say, now is your chance to get rich."

"Look Viktor, we are doing an experiment." He realised that he had called him Viktor for the first time. "Let's see what happens. It is important not to prejudice the result by taking sides in advance; we must be dispassionate, observe, then theorise later."

"On the other hand, experiment should be guided by theory."

Would he never stop? Jeremy felt exhausted. He walked over to the control room to see what was happening. The two operators were just sitting around chatting over some coffee.

"The radio frequency - he has gone out, we cannot bring him up. We call the expert. He is down under. Perhaps in one hour we have beam encore."

The amazing thing about Viktor was his stamina. Jeremy wondered how he kept going. Transatlantic flight, then the midnight shift, and now in mid-morning he was prepared to stay on and argue. Perhaps this was the secret of his success, he could just keep plugging when the others had dropped. The majority of successful people, they say, need very little sleep. Jeremy felt that he was flagging already, so he would never make the big time.

When Bexler heard of the delay he decided to go home. "If they say one hour, it will probably be three."

Jeremy opted for an early lunch, leaving Chris and Marion to hold the fort. In the cafeteria he glanced briefly at the menus, chose one of the lines, and shuffled through. It was still early so the place was fairly empty, but the mob were arriving fast. He paid and looked around for somewhere to sit. It was a good time to meet someone interesting, relax, hear what was going on, in Geneva perhaps or somewhere in CERN. Then there were the pretty secretaries and computer girls dotted about. You could not bowl up and sit next to them, of course, or even opposite. 'Hullo beautiful, what do you do here?' Sit across the table, two places sideways, a polite nod then feign disinterest. Then, after a while, 'oh, please would you mind . . . just passing the salt'. Gauge the reaction, positive smile or plain indifference; then, if the signs were favourable . . . . . After all the hassle of the morning, Jeremy thought he could do with some light distraction. But there were no obvious targets, and he moved towards his favourite table by the window, looking out peacefully across the lawns and shrubs.

Then he spotted Avelyn. She was in a corner facing away from the crowd, but that dazzling hair and fragile slender back were unmistakable; there was no one else at her table. He edged himself round to face her.

"May I have the pleasure?"

Her face lit up. "Jeremy! How nice! Are you going to join me?"

He could not contain his surprise at seeing her in CERN. "What are you doing here Avelyn?"

"Having lunch. What are you doing?"

"I am having lunch too; but I work here."

"It's OK. Jan brought me here to look at the rats. He will be coming in a minute." She gave him her deep look. "Tell me all about it. How are you? And what are you doing? . . . . . Did you have a good morning?"

"Terrible!" he launched into an account of all his troubles; it was a relief to talk about it, especially to her. Her friendly face and sympathy relaxed him. He had forgotten how marvellous she was, that sweet milky aroma. Barely discernable under the loose jumper, her breasts beckoned. Memories returned: the wide orange areolae, the taut responsive nipples; how freely he had toyed, enjoyed, handled, dandled, tickled, titivated, tantalised, snuzzled and nuzzled. Now she was smiling, prattling on about some film they had seen. Jeremy heaved himself back into the present.

"You know the rats are strange. I have been feeding them, through the hatch, just for fun, you know, something to do. And now they get so excited. Clare says they start jumping around like crazy before I even get there . . . . . somehow as though they can smell me! She says she knows I am there before I even arrive, just from the rats. It's weird!"

"Pheromones," said Jeremy. "I guess you sort of put out something that Clare doesn't. Something subliminal."

"I don't like the idea of that. Not at all."

"It must be something. May be it affects people too . . . . . subconsciously perhaps."

"Oh no! That would be awful . . . . . so embarrassing."

"Don't you believe in those perfumes then, that women spend so much on? They are supposed drive men wild without them knowing why."

"But that's different. . . . . it's deliberate, under control."

"But the other's more natural. . . . . less contrived . . . . . genuine, and therefore presumably better."

"But I can't stop it!"

Avelyn looked miserable. She fell silent. The table was filling up but people had discreetly left empty places next to them. Suddenly she looked up at him, then quickly searched left and right, a look of reproach, the open vulnerable blue eyes.

"You never called! Did you . . . . . forget me?"

"No, of course not." How could he? "I didn't think . . . . . . you . . . . . . I mean . . ." He trailed away, not knowing how to continue.

"I have not forgotten. . . . . . I owe you a lunch."

"Oh, but that was nothing, a pleasure, it doesn't matter at all."

"But it matters to me. You were so kind, and I. . . . . . I would like to . . . ." She hesitated. What was coming next? Do it again . . . pay you back . . . .even the score? She looked down confused. Then she blushed, looked up, blurted it out, almost sobbing. "I . . . . . I'd just like to see you . . . . . I . . . . . you know . . . . . talk . . . . . have some contact."

It was Jeremy's turn to look around the room. Was she making a scene? In the CERN cafeteria that would be most embarrassing. But no one seemed to have noticed; all around them tongues were busy waggling about problems in physics. It was ten months since their outing on the lake and Jeremy, having resisted temptation for so long, felt secure in his virtue. The telephone number was still in a safe place but he had no intention of using it.

Now he was alarmed and flattered at the same time. Calm her down, soft soap, finish your lunch quickly and get out. He glugged down some more cannelloni, thinking fast. Maybe a quiet lunch in some little café, at her expense; it would be a pleasant change, and he deserved a break. Avelyn got out a handkerchief and sniffed. He heard himself saying the fatal words.

"Yes, maybe, perhaps one day. It's a nice idea, very kind of you."

Avelyn brightened. “Good. Why not?” Why not indeed? Because of Clare, Jan, duty calls, and so on: but she was not stopping. “Why not soon? When are you free?”

“Let’s see. This week we are running, I am on shift. But perhaps after that.”

“Monday?” she asked.

“Monday, I think we have a meeting.” She looked sad, so he added. “The week after would be better.”

She got out a pen and scrawled her name on the paper lining the lunch tray, then the phone number; tore it off, folded it and passed it to him.

“Call me on Monday week then, in the morning. I’ll give you the details.” She was relaxed now, radiant. “I am so looking forward. I will try not to disappoint.”

A quick lunch, a friendly chat, nothing wrong with that. But in Jeremy’s mind the blue jumper was already dissolving to display her lovely breasts with the dazzling smile above. She was burbling now happily about the ballet Béjart in Lausanne, and what she was hoping to see.

Jan never showed up. Jeremy finished his lunch, took her tray as well as his own, and came back with two coffees. The action broke the ice, and suddenly he felt at home, talking to her across the table like old friends. He looked at his watch.

“I’ll stay on, if you have to go,” she said. “Call me on Monday week.” She signed off with a penetrating dart from those deep blue eyes.

Viktor was right, of course. The beam was still off when he got back. In fact it stayed off for the rest of the week. A large amplifier valve in the radio frequency system had burnt out. It took half a day to change it, and then they had to condition the filament. The accelerator could not run again on full power until the next week. What a disaster! Their shifts finished on Friday, so they would not be able to try the plasma after all.

“Let’s call the coordinator,” said Arthur. “We will try to get some extra time.” When Stefano Stromboli arrived, Arthur did his best special pleading. They were just ready to take the crucial data, another 12 hours and they would know. But the coordinator was adamant; “We cannot shop and shange.” The whole schedule for next week would be upset, and this was already fixed. Visitors had made travel arrangements to be here. But there was some possibility for the week after, and this could be discussed at the weekly schedule meeting on Monday morning.

"Perhaps you can let me have your request in writing and I will do my best. No guarantee, because . . " He gave an Italian shrug. "Well, you know how it is, everybody always wants more time. We can only give you more if the others agree to have less."

Arthur was philosophical and looked on the bright side. "We've had a good run. We know how to operate the beam. We have seen fusions at more or less the standard rate. Now we can actually use this time to fix up that meter, and make sure that the plasma is really running as it should. I think we must test it with tritium as well as with normal hydrogen. Then at ten on Monday we must all be at the schedule meeting to see what we can get."

Back home in the evening Jeremy told Clare about his frustrating day and tried to explain the inexplicable antagonism he felt for Bexler. Why did this man that made him feel so tense?

"One thing, he stands so close and puts his face right up to your nose."

"Where does he come from? Do you know?"

"Somewhere in the Balkans I believe . . . . . originally."

"Perhaps they have different ideas about personal space."

"Could be. But whatever the reason, it's unpleasant, disconcerting, threatening even. And the way he wiggles those whiskers!"

"Didn't you say he was famous?"

"Seems to be. Makes a lot of publicity anyway. Perhaps he's not really all that hot, but just good at PR."

Jeremy said nothing about Avelyn. In an ideal marriage you could share every thought. But what if your thoughts were likely to cause offence, or unhappiness? In any case he was not sure what to think. Avelyn could have invited them both of course; a quiet family evening with Jan. Conspiracy seemed to appeal to her more and, looking back, Varenna had started off as a secret tryst, though in the end it turned out that Jan knew all about it. Well, maybe 'all' was an exaggeration. Should he tell Clare? In principle it was so simple. 'Avelyn invited me to lunch.' But what would be her reaction? 'Why? What is going on?

What have you done to encourage her?' Reproaches, unhappiness. Easier to choose the coward's way and say nothing.

Anyway, he did not have to go. He could always phone and beg off. Or not even phone at all. He was a free man. Or so he thought!

11 Into Italy

When that Monday arrived it proved to be a momentous day for more than one person. Whenever Ivan was in Geneva, he kept an eye on the weather. He was waiting for a situation that occurs only a few times per year, a cold front coming from the west, bringing clearing skies, stable air and a strong wind from the north-west. The air streaming over the Jura plateau suddenly comes to the edge of a 4000 foot cliff where the Jura drops down abruptly to Lake Leman. The sharp edge acts like a giant whistle, producing a long rolling vortex right in front of the cliff with a long turbulent 'roll-cloud' that no one in their senses would get into. This vortex acts like a fixed obstacle, which the wind must somehow pass. Below the vortex the air flows steeply down onto the plain, but above it rises smoothly, surging over the top of the cloud. The disturbance continues downstream as a series of waves, like the wake behind a rock in a fast flowing river. Wherever the air is rising a sailplane can climb, but in the downward part it will drop like a stone. The tops of the waves are often marked by long thin lenticular clouds, which keep changing position as the wind varies.

Ivan got up early as usual, and when he looked out of the window he saw the cotton wool sheet of cloud streaming down the hill, hugging the slope, a sure sign of waves higher up. This could be the day for his record breaking flight into Italy! He looked at his diary; there was nothing special to keep him in the lab, so he would take the day off: maybe even two, as hopefully it would be a long journey back.

For months the glider had been ready; oxygen cylinder fitted behind the seat, (he could just reach the control valve to turn it on). The clockwork barograph which would register his height, minute by minute, and would be essential for claiming a record. The little battery which ran the radio and the artificial horizon for flying in cloud was always on charge. He opened his filing cabinet and took out the folder marked 'FLIGHT PLAN Rimini via Mont Blanc'. The maps, heights, and compass bearings were all prepared; he flicked through to make sure it was all there, but he did not need to refresh his memory. Every detail was living in his mind.

He rang Max Wenger, the power pilot, and asked him to fly the tug. Then he woke Juliet. She was excited to hear that this was the big day, but she could not keep a flicker of anxiety from crossing her face.

"Don't worry, love, I will be careful. We will keep in touch on the radio, and hopefully you will meet me in Italy. And then we will have something to celebrate!"

He was reassuring, but he knew that this flight carried an element of risk; a strong wind, and unknown mountains to cross: but that of course was the challenge. In a small bag Juliet packed some sandwiches and fruit, a bar of chocolate and a bottle of water.

By ten o'clock everything was ready and checked out, battery installed, horizon tested, turn and bank indicator working, maps and flight plan handy, dark glasses, some Italian lira, passport and glider papers, the parachute had recently been refolded by the experts and formed a comfortable cushion for his back. The barograph was running, and now the first problem was to contact the lift. The wave clouds were still there on the other side of the lake, and on the nearby slopes of the Jura the cloud was still streaming downwards.

A final check, and he was rolling along the grass, then climbing behind the tow plane at the expected rate, 2 metres per second. Max circled to gain height, then headed for the dark roll-cloud hanging in front of the Col de la Faucille, the sickle-shaped cliff facing the little town of Gex. One thousand metres above ground, and they were under the cloud, gloomy and forbidding. The vario dropped to zero, then showed 1 down; they were losing height even on tow, and there was a lot of buffeting. The cloud was quite close to the mountains, but over Gex there was a wide hole in front of the cliffs. Max steered into this, and suddenly they were climbing fast with the cloud on their left. 1200 metres above the field, and the vario showed 4 up. Ivan pulled the release and cruised along the cloud with plenty of speed in hand. If he missed the lift he could land in a field near Gex. On one side was the huge forbidding roll-cloud, craggy mountains on the other; but above his head the sky was clear. Luckily he was climbing rapidly in front of the rotor, and soon he was above it. He trimmed her back to minimum sink speed, pointed into wind, and relaxed. The vario read 2 up, but the air was completely smooth. There was nothing to do now, except keep more or less in the same place, watch the altimeter climbing, and look at the view.

He called up the control tower at Cointrin to get the pressure reading, and reset his altimeter to read height above sea level. This would correspond to the heights on the map, and would be better for crossing the mountains. He also called base to tell Juliet that everything was OK. Good time to eat an orange; the peel went out of the little sliding window. He wiped his sticky hands and studied the flight plan; refolded the map so that he could see it at a glance.

By eleven o'clock he was at 5000 metres and still climbing. The best lift was further forward now right above the Jura plateau: rather a mystery because underneath him was just a flat sheet of cloud streaming towards the cliff. How did the air know that the drop was coming? But somehow it did. Nature did what she wanted, even if you, personally, could not explain it. But you could tune in, adjust your plan and take advantage.

It was 80 kilometres to Mont Blanc. In still air his gliding angle was 1 in 40, so he could get there and lose only 2000 metres of height. With the strong wind behind him he would make it in half the time, so he should only drop 1000 metres. But there would be down draughts. To be safe Ivan decided to pick up another 1000 metres from the Jura. He got out the oxygen mask and turned it on. Apart from the smell of rubber it worked fine. The little red and white wheel on the instrument panel was turning slowly to show that the gas was flowing. He had enough for four hours, so he had to use it sparingly. A shortage of oxygen makes people drunk. You perform inefficiently but are not aware of it, and then you become woozy. Worse than alcohol, you can suddenly black out, slump over the stick, and push the glider into a steep dive. It would quickly exceed its maximum safe speed and break up, so when you woke up you would be in a steep dive yourself, if you were not already underground.

Ivan reckoned the flight could last six hours, but only a few of them would be at high altitude. Most of all he needed to be fully alert when he crossed Mont Blanc. So he turned the oxygen to 'FULL OPEN', and went on climbing. At 6000 metres above the sea he would turn and head down wind.

At this height the lift was weaker, and at 5500 metres it was flickering below 1 metre per second. He gazed down at Geneva airport two and half miles below, its toy planes parked at the terminals and another climbing off the runway heading south-west. Next door he had a clear view of CERN; its many circular ring accelerators covered with earth could be distinguished if you knew where to look. At this height he would be flying in the airways, AMBER 1 to Nice and Rome, so he called the tower. They worked with altitudes in feet, but he could do the conversion in his head; multiply by three and add 10%. It was near enough.

"H-B one nine oh seven, 17000 feet over Gex. Course 130 to Mont Blanc, Aosta, Rimini. May I proceed?"

By international convention numerical registration numbers are used for gliders, while the powered planes only have letters. The control tower knew that this was a sailplane, and they were rather startled.

"Geneva, 1 9 0 7. Confirm level and course."

He gave it to them again.

"Geneva control, can you maintain flight level?"

"9 0 7, altitude variable, but lift is good. Anticipate strong lift in front of the mountains. Emergency fields at Passy, Aosta."

There was a pause. Obviously they were discussing it. Then

"Geneva, 907, clear to Mont Blanc, will warn other traffic. We have you on the radar. Wind at Mont Blanc is 120 degrees, 50 knots. Report from Mont Blanc, and good luck."

"907, thank you, report from Mont Blanc."

It was good news, he wanted the wind, but it could be a rough ride. The altimeter read 5600 metres: it was enough. He swung the ship round in a wide arc and started his stop watch. Mont Blanc glistened clear in the distance, and he aimed straight at it. Check the compass, it should read 120 degrees, and it had better be accurate for the next leg over the Italian mountains where he might be in cloud. It was spot on. Then he called base.

"It is fantastic up here. I am 5600 metres ASL over Geneva, and I am on my way. Suggest you start off for Chamonix."

Juliet sounded excited. With some help she had the long trailer hitched up and ready to go.

"OK chéri. Et bonne chance!" She wondered if they would be the last words she would say to him: so she added, "Be careful chéri. Je t'aime beaucoup!"

Ivan realised that she was worried. Of course there was a risk, but that was part of the game. Now he had got so far there was no turning back. He picked up the mike again.

"Thank you, Julietta. I love you too!"

To get the best glide angle in this ship you flew at 80 kph. That gave you the maximum range in still air, or got you there with the least loss of height. If you had height to burn, you could push along faster and that was good for a long distance flight; but you ran more risk of hitting the deck. Now he had the wind behind him, which meant that the optimum speed would be slower. But the advantage was not much. Ivan decided on 80 kph, and with the wind behind him his ground speed would be about 160: he would get to Mont Blanc in half an hour. That was not allowing for the waves, but probably the ups and downs would average out.

As he crossed the lake the vario fell back, flickered near zero, and then the pointer moved decisively downwards to -2. He pushed the nose forward, speed up to 100 k. Down 3! Get out of this. 120 on the clock. He was covering ground rapidly now, but losing height; should he divert to look for lift off a mountain at the side? He kept going, crossed the Salève, which looked like a small ridge far below, but it had deflected the wind upwards. The river Arve was on his left, and he cruised effortlessly past Bonneville, 15 minutes out and 5000 metres up. The air was smooth, no vibration, just a quiet hiss over the canopy.

The valley now bent to the left, and he kept straight on across craggy peaks, but they were far below. On the right the lake of Annecy was in easy reach. It had been a hot dry summer; the Alps were a grey-brown sandy green, a mass of convoluted rounded crests like the sea, and higher up the jagged peaks. In the valley toy houses, surrounded by brilliant green fields watered by human hand: at a pinch he could land in one of them, 100 metres would be long enough. Small high lakes, trapped between the mountains, patches of snow. Higher up the hills became greener, and where a gash in the turbulent masses reached down to civilisation they were criss-crossed by paths and tracks. These isolated valleys were dotted with dwellings, and a stream ran down, disappearing round the corner, but presumably ending up somewhere.

Over the pointed top of the Pointe Percé, Sallanches with its factories was straight ahead, and beyond that the little aerodrome of Passy. He was dead on course. Over the centre of Saint Gervais he checked the altimeter; at 4400 metres he was below the top of Mont Blanc, but well above the other rubbish. To his left he could see Chamonix , and ahead the dark hunched back of Mont Joly. Mont Blanc loomed in front of him, a mass of rocks and ice, and he was rushing towards it at 100 miles an hour. He would turn left and approach it crab-wise.

Suddenly the craft shuddered, swayed from side to side, and he started to drop. Not enough air speed; the vario dived to -5: he had hit a down, an eddy coming off the ridge behind him. Ivan pushed the stick forward, nose down, dive, pick up speed. Now his air speed was 130 kph, he skimmed over the green fields of Les Houches aiming straight for the jagged right hand shoulder; where the ground rose smoothly the air would rise too. But in front of the cliff there could be vortices, a turbulent rotor which would force him down. He edged further to the right, where the rocks were less steep, skirting the western flank of the mountain. Still 3 down, and the ground was coming up at him fast.

Suddenly he felt a surge under him, the glider creaked as it took the strain, and he was catapulting upwards, but the crest of the mountain was just in front, and on the other side would be another down. He must keep out of that at all costs. Instinctively he banked right, pulled into a steep turn. Stay in the lift, maintain speed to keep control. He checked the vario, 9 metres per second up; that was more like it. Facing into the wind with 100 kph on the clock, he edged back towards Geneva; he must keep in front of the mountain, and now it was difficult to see how far behind it lay. He was still rocketing upwards, the altimeter needle was moving round like the second hand of a watch; back through 4000 metres again and climbing fast.

Ivan relaxed. That had been exciting. He checked the oxygen and looked around. Where was he? Saint Gervais was below, beyond that his emergency airstrip, the lake of Geneva in the distance and Chamonix on his right, half shrouded in mist. He swung the glider round and looked straight into the old crinkled face of Mont Blanc. How many climbers, how many aircraft had perished there? Then he crabbed along the ridge, moving forwards and back, looking for the best lift.

It was 40 minutes since he had left the Jura, and he had been in the air for nearly three hours. It was time for a sandwich, a drink. 5000 metres and climbing fast, but how do you eat and drink through an oxygen mask? It was a problem he had not faced before. If he waited he would be higher, still more chance of blacking out; and he needed to eat soon to keep his blood sugar up for the next few hours. He unwrapped a ham sandwich, so lovingly prepared by Juliet; looking at it made him all the more hungry. He turned off the oxygen, pulled down the mask and began to munch.

He was above the mountain now, so there was no risk, crabbing into wind to keep his position. He turned the plane, and looked over his right shoulder to see where he was going next, the Aosta valley with the plains of Liguria dimly visible beyond. Actually there were several valleys, so he had better be sure to take the right one; otherwise there would be no way out at the other end. He would climb up to 7000 metres if possible, and then race down wind to Milan and on to the Adriatic. With the wind behind him his gliding angle should be 1 in 60 at least, so he should get a 400 kilometre free ride. A few clouds had formed over the mountains, but on the whole the sky was clear. This would be an epic flight.

One of the common indications of anoxia is a feeling of anxiety, and Ivan suddenly felt uneasy. He finished the sandwich and got the mask on again, switched on the oxygen. At the back of his mind there was a niggle: something was wrong. Suddenly it hit him, the radio, air traffic, he had forgotten to report back to Geneva, and he must also call Juliet. He did not realise that the controllers in Milan knew nothing whatever about him, and he was now right in the middle of a busy airway.

He called Geneva, gave his position and altitude.

"Climbing to 20,000 feet, then vector 120 for Milano."

The answer was cheerful. "OK 9 0 7. Watch out for other traffic. Call Milano on 124.75 and good luck." Ivan acknowledged, signed off, and twiddled the dials to set the Milan tower frequency. Then over his shoulder he saw the jet. It was on his level and heading straight towards him at 10 miles a minute: he had perhaps 15 seconds to react.

For the passengers and crew of Alitalia 409 from Milan to Geneva, this was an easy run. No one had the slightest inkling of what was about to happen. The air hostesses were scampering around the cabin with coffee, suave Italian business men had their noses in 'La Stampa' and their eyes expertly assessing the potential of the female passengers nearby. It was the job of the youngest (and prettiest) air hostess to bring coffee to the pilots, and she was waiting behind the captain as he made his flight announcement.

"This is your captain speaking, we are at 5200 metres, 17,000 feet, and are starting our descent to Ginevra. If you look to your left you will see the summit of the Monte Bianco, the highest mountain in Europe. In twenty minutes we will be landing at Cointrin."

He always used the Italian name for the mountain, subtly claiming its altitude as one of the glories of Italy, though as the frontier ran along the top the honours were really divided. This was a routine flight. He usually flew low over the mountain to give the passengers a good view and had overlooked the strong north-west wind. The co-pilot called Geneva and was just getting their reply.

"Geneva - 409 clear to Papa 4000 feet." This was the turning point over Lake Leman. "Watch out for a sailplane over Mont Blanc."

In the glider Ivan was watching the jet with disbelief, trying to estimate its course and height. Was it really coming straight towards him, at the same height, and if so what should he do? It was too late to use the radio. In theory he could scoot rapidly out of the way. But which way should he go? The wrong decision might take him right into its path, so he needed to be sure before acting. The vario was still reading 4 up; perhaps he would climb above it.

The girl leaned forward, smiling her best smile, and gave the cup and saucer to the captain. He looked round into her blue-green eyes, and raised the cup in salutation. This was a promising new one, she had possibilities. At exactly that moment the Boeing slammed into the air pocket. It did not just fall, but was driven downwards by a vicious vortex swirling behind Mont Blanc. The left wing went down first, canting the plane sideways and it dropped 200 feet in a few seconds. The cup, still firmly held by the captain, was pulled down too, but the coffee stayed behind, splattered onto the switches above his head and showered down onto his white uniform. The pretty girl floated upwards, bounced off the roof and crumpled inelegantly onto the floor.

In the passenger cabin there was total chaos; the hostesses and the few passengers without belts were thrown around, overhead racks flew open, luggage rained down and food trays were all over the place. Some people screamed, thinking they were crashing, but most just held their breath, looking goggle-eyed at the oxygen masks dangling above their heads.

The captain's first thought was that the automatic pilot had gone berserk; his second was that they were going straight into the mountain in front of them. He grabbed the controls, pushed the button to take out the computer, banked steeply to the right and put on full power. As they crossed the ridge into France they passed into rising air and the jet surged upwards, throwing people to the ground and causing more luggage to leave its perch. It took the rest of the flight for the crew to sort out the mess and calm the passengers. No one in the Boeing had noticed HB-1907.

Ivan watched all this happening with astonishment. He saw the jet dip its wing and dive suddenly to the left. He thought they had seen him and were taking avoiding action. Then the plane banked to the right, climbing and apparently coming straight at him again. Finally it swept round and passed slightly below and to one side.

Quickly now he called Milano. "Aliante HB 1907 . . . " He used the Italian word for sailplane to make sure they got the message, but said nothing about the near miss; least said soonest mended. After some chit-chat they gave him clearance; no more airliners were expected for the next hour.

A moment later he had a queer sensation, an invisible hand seemed to have taken hold of his rudder and was waggling it from side to side; the movement came along the control wires to his feet. A friendly spirit of the air? In fact it was a turbulent eddy from the huge aircraft, finally catching up with the glider.

Soon it was time to go, the altimeter showed 7000 metres and he should follow his plan. Life is always a gamble, but you cannot hang around waiting; you must commit yourself for better or worse, and go for it. He called Juliet, and heard her voice.

"Hullo, chéri. I am waiting at the entrance to the Mont Blanc tunnel. I can see you, very high, just a speck. I am following."

Behind the mountain would be a strong down draught, but it should go up again on the ridge beyond. When the sink began he would dive through it. Ivan turned the glider, course 115, east-south-east. Courmayer was right below him, Aosta with its factories visible ahead. Put the nose down and go for it. He was soon soaring over Monte

Emilius, 3559 metres high, the last of the giants; then he picked up the motorway at Ivrea. Over the little Lago di Candia right on track, 95 k from Mont Blanc; he was making good time and his altitude was as expected.

Now he could see the meandering river Po, glinting in the distance; but he kept south over Alessandria to get some lift off the Apennines. The mountains came up in turn, and he headed for the peaks, working the waves and getting some lift off each: Maggiorasca, Orsaro, Cimone with the lake beyond. Bologna was clearly visible on the left with its airport about 60 k away; he could get there easily, but the Adriatic beckoned. He could see it in the distance on the left with the airfield at Ravenna just a vague smudge.

Ivan pressed on towards the last peak, Monte Falternona 1654 m high. Here he had 3500 metres in hand, 140 km to go in theory before hitting the floor. With his ruler he measured off the distance. Ancona, way down the Adriatic coast, was 150k, a little too far, but why not try for it? Or he could turn south, follow the mountains to Perugia and land at Assisi, only 110k. The coast would be safer, flat with fields to land in. He swung left, course 95 to hit the sea at Senigallia.

The air was smooth now. Ivan trimmed the ship to 80 kph, the speed for longest glide; he had an hour and a half to go, and there was nothing to do except keep on course. The ship could fly itself; so just relax and enjoy the view. He sat back, ate the apple and cracked out a bar of chocolate; it tasted fabulous. He tried calling the trailer and Juliet on the radio, but there was no reply. Probably she was too far away, and he was too low.

In the air over new country you cannot guarantee your position. No easily legible road signs with names in big letters; and superficially the towns all look alike. One is always looking for confirmation. Ivan was relieved when he finally reached the coast. Further south it swept round in a curve and that had to be Ancona on the point with its smoking factories and smog. The aerodrome was beyond his reach. Only 900 metres up; better find somewhere to land quickly. There were fields of young wheat, large flat and inviting. To his dismay Ivan noticed light reflecting up from them; they were waterlogged after weeks of rain and the glider would stick in the mud and tip up on its nose. On the map Falconara Marittima near Ancona had a small flying field; that would do well, and in theory he could get there easily. He followed the coast road, straining his eyes to see his target; and when he found it, it looked rather far away.

You cannot stretch the final glide. The optimum speed is the best, flying faster or slower will do you no good, though it is tempting to try. Ivan shut the sliding window to minimise drag, a tiny effect but it might just tip the balance. 700 metres on the altimeter looked safe enough. Aim for the field, go past it, turn into wind and land, and hope there was no other traffic to delay you.

The ground looked surprisingly close, and with a start Ivan realised that the altimeter was optimistic. He had come a long way and the air pressure was lower here, so the instrument needed resetting. He looked carefully at the field; it was still at the same angle of view, so perhaps he could just scrape in for a downwind landing. Unpopular with the locals, but he had no choice; and the wind seemed to have dropped to nothing. The next few minutes seemed a long time. He was getting closer, he could see the terminal building, but he was getting lower and lower. He skimmed over a farm about 50 feet up, but here at last was the boundary. Now he was across it. Lower the wheel, open the air brakes and get her down before you run out of space. There was a plane taking off, coming towards him, but luckily further to the right on the main runway.

Now he was skimming over the grass a few feet up; then she settled sweetly and he rolled to a halt right in front of the control tower with its little café. A man ran out gesticulating wildly in disapproval: this was not the correct way to arrive.

Stiffly Ivan clambered out, reached behind the seat for the barograph. Was it still running? Without a valid trace, the flight would have been fun but useless for a claim. Luckily it was OK. He collected his papers, and hobbled over to the buildings. Various signatures would be needed to confirm his flight. When the locals saw the Swiss markings and realised what he had done there was considerable amazement: hands were shaken, bottles cracked. It was 632 kilometres from his point of release over Gex. Certainly no one had followed this route before. He had won himself a "Gold C", the international gliding badge, with three white seagulls on a blue ground, plus a diamond for flying 500 km, and another diamond for climbing 5000 metres. Life was good, very very good.

12 A free lunch

Meanwhile back at CERN the schedule meeting had run its predictable course. The muon fusion group sat together at the end of the third and fourth rows, close enough to the front to influence the proceedings, but far enough back to observe the other groups. At 9.30, after a lot of hesitation, Jeremy had finally phoned Avelyn. Tentatively he said hullo.

"Jeremy, how nice, how is everything?" She chatted away. Then she went on, "Are you all right for today? Lunch I mean. I am expecting you."

"Yes, I can. It's very kind of you. That is if you really want."

"Of course I want."

"OK. So where do you think we could meet?"

"Well, why not here? I can cook up something. So much more pleasant. You know I hate being overlooked. Have you got a pencil? Then I will give you the address."

It was in Aire-la-Ville, in one of those new blocks of flats probably. Not too far away. He wrote down the instructions. "Come about 12 then." Jeremy hesitated, it would take a while to find the place. "Well, never mind, just come as soon as you can. I'll be waiting. And I hope you will not be disappointed. Bye!"

So the die was cast. He had not been given much option: an irresistible torrent was sweeping him along. In principle he could still opt out, ring and cancel, something had cropped up. But of course he did not want that. He was thinking of that supremely kissable mouth, the delicious body, and felt almost sick with excitement. He sat for a minute dreaming, then pulled himself together and went to find Arthur. Bexler was already there, and they were yakking away like old friends, discussing the strategy for the meeting. Arthur's policy was simple: ask for the moon, and hope to get a decent slice.

The accelerator had been off. Everyone had been delayed. They all had reasons for getting more data quickly, a conference coming up, lecturing commitments in universities, Ph.D. deadlines, decisions to be taken as to the next step, and so on. Arthur stuck his neck out, being on the verge of an important discovery; but it was counter-productive. The rest of the meeting laughed it off.

When they had all deployed their arguments the coordinator produced his tentative schedule for the next three weeks. It was pretty well balanced, and after some minor changes of a day here or there, it was accepted. Everyone felt that they had made their case, done their best, and they all adjourned to the cafeteria for coffee. The rivalries were forgotten over more important discussions, the latest physics, the new restaurants, and who was going to the Viennese ice show. Chang-Singh was a connoisseur.

"Skating develops the thighs," he announced. "We went on Saturday with some friends, and as the curtain went up we all raised our binoculars. Thirty girls and every one a winner!"

Jeremy checked his watch. 11.30, it was time to be moving. But he had to tell Arthur.

"I am going out for lunch today, if that is OK."

He almost hoped that Arthur would say no, but it was apparently not a problem. Because of the shift work, time keeping at CERN was very flexible and irregular. If you did the job, within wide limits no one cared when you did it. All Arthur said was,

"See you later then, bon appetit!"

Quickly Jeremy tidied himself up, jumped into the car and zoomed down the route de Meyrin. Did anyone see him leave? But if so, they would think he was going home to lunch like so many others. So why did he never do that? Go home, relax, chat up the children, share their sausage and mash, fraternise with the wife. The theory was that during lunch at CERN you might make some significant contacts, hear what was going on. And travelling time was in principle time wasted. So in that case what was he doing now? He recognised the inconsistency and made a resolution to have lunch with his children once a week. So at least one good thing would come out of this tryst with Avelyn!

He turned right at the lights at the bottom of the hill, and sped along towards Satigny. He was running late. Check on the paper with her address, yes it was there. He was all excited, nervous as a naughty schoolboy, his tummy churning and his palms moist on the steering wheel. Take it easy; this was not a good time to crash the car or get a speeding ticket.

Should he take her a present? Flowers? A bottle of wine? It was rather late to shop now, but he drove slowly through Satigny looking for a suitable store. There was something, a small grocery. Of course there was nowhere to park. He abandoned the car in front of someone's garage, hoping for the best, and sprinted back. There was a bottle of Malvoisie. This high class, sweet desert wine from the Valais would be just the ticket: 27 Swiss francs, but she was worth it.

"We have a bottle in the cooler, if you want to drink it immediately." The shopkeeper obviously understood the tender midday rendezvous, but he took some time to fetch the bottle and wrap it carefully. When Jeremy got back to the car the owner of a smart Mercedes was fuming on the pavement.

"Can you not see the sign?"

"I excuse myself profoundly. It was just a little minute."

"Woof, woof, woof. . . . . Next time I am calling the police. . . ." But he got away with it.

Now it was already twelve and he still had to find the right place. He took the long straight country road to Russin, turned left at Verbois and down the hill to the barrage over the Rhône. Across the river he turned right, following her guidance, and along the wooded hillside he found an impressive residence, set in its own gardens, with spacious balconies arranged in a rather free flowing modern style. The Olber's apartment was on the top floor, and faced both ways. On one side you could see Geneva, the lake and the Salève, a vertical wall of limestone with rolling pastures on top, so popular with the Genevois for their Sunday walks and picnics. On the other side was the grand sweep of the Jura.

Jeremy clutched the elegantly wrapped bottle, still cool to the touch, checked the names in the front hall and took the lift. It was dark in the corridor; he adjusted his tie and rang the bell. There was a long silence. Was she out after all? Or would Jan be there too? In a moment of panic he wondered what to say if Jan opened the door. 'Er, um, let's see. I . . ah, yes, . . . I was just passing. And I, er . . . I thought you might like to taste this little bit of wine.'

Then he heard footsteps, light and quick, definitely feminine. There was a rattling of locks, and the door opened a timid crack. He was being checked. Then the chain came off, and there she was.

"So sorry to keep you waiting."

"I am sorry to be late."

"I was in the kitchen, checking the oven."

"I stopped off for some wine."

"I have to be careful who I let in."

"And nearly got clobbered by a Swiss banker."

"There are some funny characters around."

"So that's why I'm late."

"No problem, any time is right for me."

"It is lovely here."

"You found the way then."

"No problem, your instructions were perfect."

"The main thing is that you could make it."

"So this is the wine."

"Is that for me then? Thank you! " She smiled, lent forward, touched his arm, kissed him on the cheek. "I will put it in the fridge. Come this way." She led him by the hand through the spacious sitting room into the kitchen.

"By the way, you don't have to worry. He never comes home before six. Too keen on his work."

He had expected her usual jeans and sweater, but this time it was different, a one piece jump suit with snazzily cut shorts joined to a sleeveless top, the whole thing held up by straps at the shoulders. The shorts had smart little turn-ups at the top of her legs, and the various pleats and pockets gave a decorative effect. As far as he could tell, she did not have much else underneath, no other straps anyway, and the breasts bobbed pretty freely under the square cut tunic. She dumped the bottle on the counter and turned to him.

"First we must say hullo, French style." She offered him her left cheek, then the right, then the left again.

"Now Danish style!" She grinned maliciously, then put her arms around his neck and gave him her lips. Her mouth, her tongue, her taste infiltrated his brain, annihilating the power of thought.

"Would you like a drink?" She unwrapped the Malvoisie, and complimented him on his good taste. "We will have that later. To start with let's have some fizz." She opened the fridge and swapped over the bottles. Out came some pink champagne, Breton fils, brut rosé.

"Shall I open it for you?"

"No, no, you sit down. This is my treat."

By the sofa two flutes were ready on a silver tray. She stood in front of him, unravelling the wires, long tapering legs with pointed shoes matching her outfit; they were well covered, succulent, the skin luminous. She moved freely, confidently, but her hands on the cork seemed nervous. She was young after all, and Jeremy suddenly felt more secure and relaxed. Why worry?

Bottle at the correct angle, she twisted the cork expertly, a loud pop but no spillage; then filled the glasses, lifted one demurely and offered it to him.

"This is for you, sir."

"Won't you join me?"

"If you say so."

She plopped down close to him on the sofa, stretching out her legs. She held up the cork vertically, twirling it in her fingers, the straight shaft and bobble at the end.

"This always reminds me of something."

"A mushroom?" asked Jeremy. Avelyn shook her head and giggled.

"Do you remember how to skol?" She looked at him. "The guest has to start it."

Jeremy desperately polled his memory. Had this now vital data been erased, dumped into some backup area, or been lost completely. His eyelids flickered while the circuits whirred. Then it came back. Raise the glass, look her in the eyes, say skol, clink, drink thoughtfully eyes down; then look her in the eyes again (they were blue as the Mediterranean sky), hold the glass up, do not smile. Clink, drink and wink, perhaps.

"That was great," she cried. "You are a promising pupil. Now it's my turn."

It passed the time pleasantly enough. "If you know someone very well, you can kiss afterwards." She gave him a demonstration.

In the dining room the table was elegantly laid, dark polished wood, lace mats with gleaming glasses and silverware. The whole apartment breathed luxurious relaxation, and there was plenty of space. She took his hand and led him from one side to the other to admire the views: explained how they had taken the whole of the top floor and knocked through to make one large flat. Through the sliding windows you could walk out onto a small roof garden, completely private, looking south. It was immaculately tidy.

"Do you look after it?" he asked.

"Not really. I snip a few flowers. We have a gardener who comes twice a week. Didn't I tell you? Jan's mother has lots of money, so he just doesn't think about it. Whatever we want we can have. But his tastes are rather modest, he doesn't believe in splashing it around. His work's the main thing. He wants to make a contribution." She gave him a bashful smirk, then added. "I'm his biggest luxury!"

"You could live in one of those super villas round the lake, have a swimming pool, private beach, your own sailboat."

"We could. But neither of us really wants that; it's a big hassle, organisation, maintenance, running servants. This is so much easier, and quite big enough for two."

No kids, but she did not mention it. Probably they wanted them. Some people have too many, they somehow cannot avoid it in spite of all the methods. A catholic woman can use mathematics to avoid conception, but anything physical or chemical is not allowed. Others were longing for children, but they never arrived. Life was a bastard really. So perhaps, in spite of all this wealth, they were sad at heart.

Jeremy settled back to enjoy his lunch. A cold soup was followed by hot chicken and mushroom pie, with pastry on top. It was delicious.

"I thought I would surprise you. I learnt to make the English pie when I was an au pair in Canterbury." It was just what he needed, an au pair like her. The mind boggled. Perhaps the wine was going to his head.

The table was oval, and she had laid the two places close together, not opposite in confrontation. She dodged fluidly to and fro into the kitchen, the lithe legs rippling purposefully. When she served him she stood close, the thighs a few inches from his left hand. His fingers itched to caress them, show appreciation, feel the marbled coolness. At Varenna he had fondled them, but that was in the safety of the café and they were sheathed in jeans The naked leg was more appealing, but the taboos were stronger. With difficulty he managed to keep his hands to himself, but the drink was getting to her too. Each trip to the kitchen was a little more unsteady, and each time she lingered longer by his chair.

Next came fresh peaches with syrup and cream. He felt really spoilt and the Malvoisie went with them perfectly. Under the table she stretched out a leg and their feet were touching. She put her chair closer and he caressed her arm.

"It was so nice in Tremezzo," she said. "We sat close together, you had your hand on my leg."

"Like that?"

"Yes, like that. I like it. I remember it all so well."

Her ankle came across his. She twitched the muscles under his hand, then slid the foot up, put her knee over his under the table. He moved his hand down to the soft spot inside the knee, touched her there for a while, then up the leg and across to the other one. It was naughty, her legs apart, open, but clearly she was enjoying it. He felt dizzy with pleasure, but as the hand was occupied he was not getting anywhere with the peaches. She took his spoon and fed him like a baby.

Eventually she scrambled up, cleared the sweet, and came back with cheese. She stood by his chair again.

"Can I feel your muscles?"

He put a hand on each side by the knee, pressing with his fingers and thumbs, feeling the tone, gradually moving up. She was well covered, resilient. She tautened and relaxed the extensors.

"I am keeping fit. In the summer swimming, in the winter skating and skiing. It makes life so much better."

His hands were now around her right leg, getting near the top. He inched them up another step and felt her twitch as the side of his hand touched her between the legs.

"Now the other side."

He started again at the knee, really appreciating every inch of her.

"If you're fit, everything is more enjoyable."

"Everything?" he asked.

"Yes, of course."

When he got to the shorts, she jerked again.

"Sorry. I'm rather jumpy. I . . . . . I can't help it . . . . I . . . . I like it, but . . . . . it just does that!"

He ran his hand in again, touching the shorts.

"You like that?"

A whispered throaty 'yes I do', and she was blushing. A few more times, and she started to quiver.

"Shall we have the cheese?" asked Jeremy, and she relapsed into the chair, looking drained, exhausted. It was a sharp pungent Roquefort and very refreshing.

"Come and help me make the coffee." She led him by the hand into the kitchen, started the electric kettle and lent against the counter waiting for it to boil. He stood behind her, feeling her waist, the hips, her breasts through the tunic. Then somehow the buttons were undone, and he was inside, titillating and kissing her neck. Before long all of them had been opened and he was exploring her hips, her tummy and ravelling in the hair below: and she was leaning back against him. The kettle boiled and clicked off, but they ignored it.

She turned her neck to kiss him, and his hands crept slowly upwards, paying tribute to the breasts en route, till they came to rest on her shoulders. The tunic and shorts were now entirely pendant on the two shoulder straps and if he pushed them off the whole outfit would slither to the ground.

Jeremy suddenly realised that they had passed the point of no return. She was raising no objections, and he could hardly pull back at this stage. Looking back, it would be hard to pin-point the decisive moment.

Delicately he felt her shoulders, her arms, the collarbone, her neck, making diversionary raids to the nipples. After a while he eased the straps over her arms, exposing the breasts to view: they were as glorious as ever. She did not bother to clutch at the garment and it slipped down to her feet. He caught a glimpse of ginger tuft as she turned, flung her arms around his neck and kissed him.

"You naughty boy! Fancy undressing a lady without her permission!"

She kicked off the shoes and shorts, and led him into another room, maybe a spare, undressed him and drew him onto the double bed.

She was a true redhead all right. Immediately he put his hand to her, to set the scene, tell her the time of day. She was plump and moist, but there was no hurry. He lay beside her, relaxing, exploring the rest of her body, and she allowed him to arrange her limbs in any way he wished.

"You are so absolutely lovely!" There was no compromise with this one, she was one hundred per cent beautiful.

Eventually they both knew that it was time to crown the feast. She stretched herself out, and Jeremy paused to savour the full the beauty of those entrancing seconds. Was this what Canova was driving at? The perfect moment! Cupid and Psyche frozen in perpetual anticipation. The moment of truth. The matador poised for the long straight thrust to the heart, the sword hovering in the ideal position, he leans forward balanced between the wide spread horns, waiting, making it last as long as he dares. The bull conquered, submissive, waiting patiently for the 'coup de grace'.

Then straight and true he ran her through. To be answered with a cry, a long drawn sigh. The strangled gasp. The head jerked back, hips lifted against him. It was a movement that had to be repeated, refined. He tried it again. The moment of truth, and then the long smooth thrust, . . . and again . . . . .and again . . . . . and again. And each time her long drawn cry .... ooh! ...... oooh! ..... Oooh! .... Aaaah!

Exultation surged through him, victory, mastery, achievement. The tension had melted away, and now he could really enjoy her. It lasted quite a while: she and the wine had relaxed him.

Afterwards she was glowing. Food and garments strewn everywhere, but he did not hang around. It was time to get back to duty.

"Don't worry about the clearing up. I can fix it." Still naked she embraced him in the hall.

"It was absolutely glorious."

"When can you come again? Tomorrow?"

He hesitated: tempting but crazy, he needed time to think. They settled for Friday, four days later.

"Phone me after nine. I will be waiting . . . . . . and good luck." She opened the door a crack, peeped out, and let him go.

Jeremy spent the rest of the afternoon in a daze. He had a mistress! He had arrived. Suddenly for the first time he felt truly grown up. The whole thing was completely unbelievable, and yet so real. Totally exhilarating, and rather worrying. What was he getting into, and where would it lead?

When he got back to his office it was nearly four, and his first action was to ring her number. She recognised his voice at once.

"Jeremy darling! How nice."

"I just wanted to thank you . . . . . for the delicious lunch. And see if you are OK."

"I am absolutely fine. I feel fantastic. I am full of energy. Everything is cleared up, and there are no problems. It was so good to see you. Don't worry about anything. Have some beautiful days, and. . . . . . see you soon." The soft conspiratorial whisper at the end. So at least there were no regrets on her side: she was simply incredible.

In the counting room again, Jeremy dragged his mind back to reality, which for him was unseen particles weaving a complicated dance inside a bottle of exotic gas, and his efforts to make them dance to another tune. This now seemed utterly abstract compared to the tangible reality of Avelyn's body and her bright vitality. That in its turn conflicted with the reality of family life, Clare and the children, the measured course of everyday events.

Which was real, and which was an illusion? There were so many layers of reality, all coexisting on different planes. There was the world of the theorists, full of imaginary wave functions and complicated mathematics; the other world of the laboratory with its maze of wires, pipes and machinery: numbers coming up on flickering lights. In Geneva there were the bankers with their gold, the diplomats jousting in the United Nations, the World Health and other international organisations, the film stars who lived around the lake, and the Arab sheikhs and Japanese who owned most of it; actually there were also a few Swiss. Running across all this for each person was also the world of the family, and the world of other interests, be it sport, hobbies or perhaps a mistress.

All these worlds coexisted at the same time, and in the same place; layer upon layer. The various realities interweaved like some gigantic tapestry, the threads sometimes separating, sometimes overlapping, sometimes in harmony, sometimes in conflict. Occasionally there would be an interaction, a connection, an intrusion even, from one world to another, and this made it all the more interesting and colourful. One person could play a role in many different layers.

Could he live in this polyvalent universe, aware of all of it, and somehow taking part in it? Who was he? Where was he? How did he fit in? Could he make sense of it all, and keep sane? Or would he get thoroughly confused and flip his lid?

Back in her apartment Avelyn was thinking. If this happened regularly people would gossip; the concierge discreetly observed all comings and goings in the apartment block, that was his job, but she knew how to cover her tracks. That evening she was particularly bright and cheerful, and Jan remarked on it.

"I have a new doctor," she said. He raised his eyebrows. "You know those headaches I have been getting, pains." She pointed vaguely at her body, and to be frank he had no recollection. Perhaps she had mentioned something.

"He came today, a new treatment, pressure therapy; he finds the right spot, and then very skilfully vibrates his fingers . . . . and it works . . . . the pain goes away!" She paused.

"I have to be nude on the bed."

"Nude! On the bed?" The eyebrows were working again.

"Oh yes I must be totally relaxed."

"Totally?"

"He says I need it two or three times a week."

"And how long does it take?"

"Oh an hour perhaps . . . . . maybe two . . . . I am not sure." She could see that he was calculating the cost, home visits, so long, so often! Like all the super-rich, he kept an eye on the detail.

"Don't worry, I can pay him myself. It's cash anyway." She knew he would look him up in the medical register. "He's not official, a Lithuanian refugee, Popodov, he is doing this part time."

It was a good story, and if Jan had his doubts he decided to go along with it. He would have a word with the concierge in the morning: best to avoid rumours. Meanwhile she had given him some ideas.

"Nude on the bed! I think we should see this. Maybe I can find some of these pressure points myself. After all I'm a doctor too. So let's see the colour of the skin!"

She did not mind being ordered about; like all beautiful women she had enough fawning and grovelling. He started to explore; the crystal coolness of the skin, pale soft and endlessly varying, like a landscape.

"So where are all these pressure points then?"

"Oh, all over . . . . on the back . . . . mmm, that's good . . . . . the neck . . . . behind the knee . . . . . and . . . . . yes, round there." She was face down with a pillow under her hips, the legs stretched out.

"Totally relaxed are we?"

"Oh yes . . . . . . yes . . . . . . perfectly."

Redheads had that special heady aroma. The two dimples behind her hips, making the celebrated triangle of Praxiteles, were supposed to be a talisman of beauty. He put his thumbs on them, pressed, vibrated, stretched out his palms to feel her buttocks, probing through the muscle to feel the bones underneath, finding the spots which made her react, and then exploring around them. Around . . . . and between . . . . . and for a while he toyed with her.

"I think I have a better idea."

"Yes?"

The reply was husky, barely audible, but indubitably affirmative. Avelyn knew what to expect. She waited quietly; on the pillow the raised bottom pale and round, delicately offered. He caressed it again for a while, and then it was time to spank her. He ignored her cries and struggles, and continued until it was a cheerful pink. When he turned her over, she was hot and bothered, the skin moist with sweat, her hair all mussed up, the face flushed and smouldering. This he preferred to her cool suave public image; a woman ready to be enjoyed. Then he revelled in her. It had been some time so he did it thoroughly, reaching for every corner. And she kept herself moving and took care to make all the appropriate noises. Thus, since time immemorial, has the complaisant husband been rewarded - with entertaining bedtime games. But her thoughts were far away.

He was happy with his wife; decorative, good for his image, and a competent housekeeper. He had the money to keep her in style. If he did not feel the urge these days to take her so often, she was always willing. He could enjoy her any time, day or night, which perhaps is why he did not bother so much. Afterwards in the bathroom she clung to him, her breasts bobbing against his chest.

"Was I a good doctor then?"

"Excellent." (But not as good as the one who came this afternoon.)

"So it's a case of patients rewarded." She looked at him puzzled, unable to figure out the pun. "It is a yoke!"

"Oh!" She embraced him, smiling. "Maybe you should do it more often!"

13 A diplomatic dinner

That was how it had begun. Six months later the quest for catalysed fusion seemed as unattainable as ever. Arthur's group had reproduced the standard results for muons stopping in the deuterium-tritium gas mixture, 20,000 fusions for every muon stopped, but it was not enough to break even and make a viable source of energy. If only by some trick they could get twenty times as many! The Russian suggestions had proved to be misleading.

Bexler had been right, the plasma had not helped. They had got it going in the end, tried various currents at all sorts of pressures, and diagnosed the plasma temperatures. It made a difference, but not much. Now the theorists were busy making their models with several adjustable parameters in an attempt to fit the data. If you played with enough variables you could fit anything. It had little predictive power, but gave them something to prattle about at conferences. Chris painstakingly analysed the results in terms of their latest model.

"I get a good fit if alpha equals 0.173, kappa is 4.6 and lambda is 0.531."

'So what?' thought Jeremy, 'who cares about these parameters?' One way to succeed was to convince the world that this was a vital issue; that alpha equal to 0.167 would call into question the whole fabric of science. If you could get the audience to worry about this sort of thing then you had it made.

Viktor did not show much interest in these numbers and left all the propaganda to Arthur. Instead he had thought up a new route to catalysed fusion. Everyone is mesmerised by the DT reaction, he argued, because it is used in the bomb. Muons will catalyse it all right, but perhaps there are other possibilities. We ought to explore more widely, some other reaction could be better.

Why not try lithium? It was cheap and abundant, and everybody knew the reaction first found by Cockcroft and Walton in the 1930s. Lithium, bombarded with protons, turns into two helium nuclei with plenty of energy released; and advantageously in this case there were no neutrons to share the energy, it all went locally into heat. As before, if you got a mu-minus attached to the proton, the combination would be electrically neutral and could sneak up to the lithium without feeling the normal repulsive forces and when it got close enough the two nuclei would fuse. It had to work some of the time, but no one had seen it. How well was a matter of speculation. No one knew, so we ought to find out.

Bexler knew how to play the committee game. He had written an impressive proposal, ten pages closely argued and peppered with learned references and diagrams. He emphasised the potential benefits, the large areas of unknown, and proposed a series of experiments to clarify the question.

Arthur and Jeremy thought that the chances of this working as a practical process was zilch. The data could be interesting, but the catalysis chain reaction would soon peter out. It was hardly worth wasting time on. In research you had to be selective, try to pick a winner and not lose time chasing red herrings. Choosing the right line to follow was in fact the most difficult part. It was always a jump into the unknown, and therefore a matter of intuition, guessing correctly. A minority could do it, and they had brilliant careers. Others never got it right; they worked equally hard, but no one took an interest in their results.

Viktor meanwhile, in his role of distinguished visiting scientist, had got himself appointed to a number of advisory committees; so he was convivial with the influential decision makers including the Director-General. All those who mattered received copies of his paper, and when he found them in the cafeteria he made sure that they followed his reasoning.

A committee man is often faced with proposals that he cannot totally follow; he is rusty on some of the background, and does not have time to read up the detail. As a result he feels uneasy, and rather than admit his difficulties he votes for rejection, or at best deferral. If, on the other hand, he understands the proposal he is preconditioned to say yes. Viktor, through painstaking individual lobbying, made sure that every member of the committee had grasped his arguments: as a result the programme was approved. Arthur, who had seen which way the wind was blowing, gave his support. It was better to keep the new ideas inside the group; and with two programmes they would be allocated more machine time. Then they could make their own decisions on how to use each shift.

"We are invited to dinner," said Clare. "At the Olbers, on Wednesday week. We had better dress up a bit because they are rather well off." Jeremy made no comment. He knew the sumptuous elegance of their home well enough, but better keep quiet about it.

When the day came Clare looked ravishing in a new dress. She was showing more leg than usual and Jeremy raised his eyebrows. Clare answered his unspoken question.

"Skirts are going up."

"I know," said Jeremy "And I am all in favour. But I didn't think you'd noticed!"

"I notice more that you think!" Was it a warning? Or just an innocent remark? Anyway, she was not as frowzy as he thought, and that was a good thing. Jeremy dutifully got out his best suit.

"Are you sure they are this formal?" He was thinking of Avelyn padding round the apartment in bare feet and various states of undress.

"Oh yes! Swedes are all terribly formal. The guests will have to make a speech, anyway the men, so you had better think of something to say."

Clare had organised a rather large formal bouquet all done up in transparent plastic with expensive looking florist's labels all over.

"Swedes love flowers, they are hard to grow in such a cold climate." She took his arm affectionately as they went out to the car. "I think this could be rather an exciting evening."

She was right, the party was elegant. Dagmar the Swedish representative at the United Nations was wearing a slinky black dress, her bare shoulders enhanced by a glittering diamond necklace. She was not so young, but had all the confidence of a once pretty woman. With her came a British bureaucrat, Sir Hugh Beaver from the Department of Education and Science. He was attending some chat-up about the environment and Dagmar was chairing the working group on acid rain. Sir Hugh was defending the British position that all the acid falling on Sweden came from the Ruhr. There was a Swiss doctor from Jan's hospital with his wife, a young medic from Singapore, and to Jeremy's annoyance Viktor A. Bexler. Avelyn whispered in Jeremy's ear, "Jan thinks he may be interesting. . . . . . but I don't like the smell of it."

Avelyn's outfit was a kaleidoscope of dazzling colours, mauve, blue, purple and green; a loose cloak of ribbed silk, open at the front, came just to her thighs. Underneath was a matching costume of embossed silk with microscopic legs, neatly nipped between the legs, rather like an old fashioned swimsuit. Her multi-coloured necklace and earrings had been chosen to match the dress, and her long rounded thighs under the thin patterned tights seemed to be covered with purple whorls of primitive tattoo. Sir Hugh was obviously riveted, and who wouldn't be. She was pleased with the flowers and immediately set them in water on a side table.

After the champagne and caviar snacks, Jeremy found that he was seated next to Avelyn with Sir Hugh opposite. The first course was on the table, but no one touched it until their host had spoken.

"Welkom," he said ponderously, using the Swedish pronunciation. "We are very pleased to have you all with us; a decision maker from Great Britain, two men of science (he smiled at Jeremy and Viktor), Dagmar is an old friend and my dear colleagues Fritz and Heide. And last but not least our brilliant visitor Kim Song from Singapore. A tasty appetite to all! Now I have a question which must be answered before we eat. It is very simple. What is the matter?"

They were all flabbergasted. What was wrong? They looked round, but nothing seemed to be amiss. Had they given a bad impression, or broken some subtle Swedish protocol? There was a stunned silence, followed by anxious interrogations. Avelyn kicked Jeremy secretly and gave him a wink. Jan was looking round the table.

"What is the matter?" he asked again with more emphasis. "Sir Hugh?"

"No comment."

"Jeremy? Fritz, you should know. Heide?" But no one knew what to say. Finally Dagmar broke the silence.

"I think I can guess." She had been in Switzerland a long time, and she knew how Jan's mind operated. "It's in Zermatt, the river running down to Visp, that's what it is. The Matter. It's a river! Now can I eat my sill o'dill?" Sighs of relief all round. Jan was beaming with amusement at his success in baffling the great minds.

"It is just my little yoke! Dagmar, you are the brightest. Let us all skol to Dagmar." They raised their glasses, 'Dagmar', 'Dagmar the brightest', 'To Dagmar', etc etc. Dagmar just sat there smiling. She could not drink to this one, but she was thirsty. So when it was over, she raised her glass.

"Thank you Jan. You are so kind, and so clever with your jokes in English. I am so happy to be invited to this delightful party, and to meet your distinguished friends. Let us all skol to Jan and Avelyn." She took a big gulp to make up for the last round. The wine was superb, a Chablis Grand Premier Cru, slightly smoky, slightly fruity with just the right amount of tang. The experts would have prattled on about overtones of walnut and boysenberries, balance and staying power. They might even have called it complex.

Half way through the meal Viktor decided to have a go at Sir Hugh, who had been pontificating rather needlessly about the Prime Minister and the Prince of Wales.

"I keep reading in your papers about the decline of British science. Even the President of the Royal Society is concerned. Is it really a lack of money, or is it just bad organisation?" Jeremy looked up. He expected the usual waffle with maple syrup, statistics on the fraction of GDP spent on science by various countries, numbers of Nobel prizes and so on. He was surprised when Sir Hugh answered,

"It's a major worry for us. The Government is committed in principle to cutting public expenditure, though in fact they never succeed. The public is always clamouring for lower taxes and better health care. Defence of course offers excitement and glamour. So there just is not enough money for education and science." It was a soft answer; the bull had not reacted to Viktor's prod. But Kim now chimed in.

"If you want to be an advanced country in the next century, you are obliged to spend more on science. In Singapore, twenty years ago, the government decided we should be the leaders of technology in south east Asia. So what did they do? They said, double the number of universities, and they found the money. In England you are closing universities, that will never work. Education is the key. We are a developing nation, we are investing in science. You are developed, but you are closing down. Soon you will be underdeveloped. One day perhaps our roles will be reversed!"

"I remember Harold Wilson," said Dagmar. "It was some time ago now, was it 1964? He campaigned for the 'white heat of technology', but when he was elected he just said 'Yes, but there is no money for it' !"

"I was there at the time," said Sir Hugh. "There was nothing we could do. The House of Commons decides how much money we can have, in accordance with their perception of the national will. Basically education is boring, unglamorous. Prosperity they want, but they do not connect it with education."

In the middle of all this discussion Jeremy felt a delicate caress, Avelyn's toe gently moving against his shoe. He stretched out his leg and wiggled back. Then he caught her eye and winked. She smiled back and briefly squeezed his hand under the table, then turned away to chat. Was she longing at this moment, as he was longing, for their next afternoon together? Life now seemed incomplete when they were apart. Her foot said that she was, and reassured by that he felt happy just to be in the same room with her. Sir Hugh was still in full flood.

"Years ago there was a Department of Scientific and Industrial Research. They had enough money, and their support for science was reasonably generous for the time. Then the DSIR was abolished and science was linked with education. That has been a disaster. Ever since then science has been gradually starved of funds, and the brains have been draining . . . . . and they still are!"

Kim now intervened. "So why not link science with industry, innovation and the future. Have a separate department, as they do in most countries?" Hugh nodded: it would almost certainly be better. The toe was still wiggling, but Jeremy thought it was time for him to attack the establishment.

"The worst thing is the way you divide up the money. All those committees solemnly arguing, asking for more information and usually turning down anything original because they don't understand it."

"The peer review process," answered Hugh. "It's the best way we know. It's democratic, and the department does not lay itself open to criticism."

"It may be democratic, but it's not dynamic. In fact it is stultifying. The committees seem to be largely motivated by jealousy, and in the end they just divide up the cake among themselves. Most of the members are second-raters anyway, so how can they guide the research of the country. They don't recognise a good idea unless it is dressed up in the latest shibboleths."

"Those who can, do," intoned Viktor, "those who can't, teach!" Sir Hugh completed the aphorism, "Yes, I know; and those who can't teach, teach teachers."

"Or go into administration," said Viktor aggressively. "Then the people who never had an original thought in their life have the fun of telling others that their ideas are no good."

"Yes," said Jeremy. "You can see that everywhere. The people who are good at research keep going, they have no interest or time for administration. But those who are no good at research, or have run out of ideas, go into management. So it ends up that science is run by people who are no good at science!"

The pace was getting hot for Sir Hugh, but he seemed completely unperturbed. A top civil servant keeps calm under fire. "So what else could we do?" he asked. There was a silence, and Hugh looked round triumphantly. Jeremy was busy with his footwork.

"In Sweden," said Jan, "we have a group of 'wise men' to divide up the money. Quite a small number, they are the top scientists or leaders of industry, very carefully chosen, and we keep them in the job for a long time to build up their experience. Then we trust their judgement. Sometimes they give their support to quite young researchers." That gave Jeremy an idea.

"Why not give the money to the Fellows of the Royal Society, and let them divide it up? I am sure that they would have better judgement than the typical committee."

"Not a bad idea," said Hugh, "but what would stop them giving it to their friends?"

"But that happens anyway. The difference is, they would have better friends!"

"So you want to go back to paternalism, elitism. Trust the chosen few. It would work well, but you can never sell it to the public . . . nor to the MP's. The real trouble is that Britain is too democratic. So, inevitably, that means mediocrity. The public simply will not vote for a restricted coterie of excellence, although it would do them more good in the long run. Now in Switzerland, . . . in Sweden, ...and above all in Singapore," (he looked at each of them in turn) "you have leadership by the few. And that, of course, is far more effective. That's the situation.

There is nothing that we in the Department can do!" Then he added as an afterthought, looking at Dagmar, "Please don't quote me!"

At this stage Avelyn got up to check something in the kitchen. To Jeremy's amazement her foot was still there, firmly pressed against his! Or was it her shoe? No, he could see both of them daintily tripping across the room. He looked across the table at Sir Hugh, who was looking back at him with an expression of ill-concealed disgust. Then the foot was quickly withdrawn. Two bubbles of erotic fantasy punctured by the same pin! The new owner of the oscillating shoe deflated visibly, as he added one more to his gallery of disappointed hopes.

"Meanwhile," said Viktor, "your best scientists, produced by schools and universities that are really very good, are just leaving Britain for better jobs abroad."

"Unfortunately you are right," said Hugh. "You meet them everywhere, in America, Australia, in Europe, pillars of society, holding down responsible jobs and contributing to the general good. If only they were all in England the place would be on fire.

"Talking of fire," said Avelyn, "let us have coffee in the other room. By now she had thrown off her cloak. The costume was cut more for the Croissette at Cannes than an evening in Geneva, but it was saved by the quality of the embossed, ornately printed silk and smart tights, which all suited the salon more than the beach. Jeremy had been watching the patterned legs flitting about all evening, and thinking about the broad ginger tuft at present invisible beneath the tiny shorts. Looking at her serving the coffee, he wondered why she wore such a spectacular costume.

In one way her beauty frightened her, but in another way she enjoyed the effect it had on the victims. Viktor and Hugh were both drooling over her this evening, while Jan of course took it all in his stride. She liked to display, to tantalise and he guessed that this gave her a kick of adrenaline or some other chemical euphoric. He felt no jealousy, however, knowing that he could have her whenever he wanted, and they could not. Or was she planning to give herself to one of them? Maybe he did feel jealous after all. It was impossible to guess what was in a woman's mind, especially this one. Distracted as he was, he gave no thought to what might be in the mind of his wife.

When eventually they left, Avelyn offered her cheek, French style, to the men and women alike; a kiss on the left, then on the right, and once more on the left. When Sir Hugh was leaving with Dagmar he said,

"We must meet again soon."

"I do hope so."

To Bexler she was noticeably less enthusiastic, and let him kiss her with some reluctance. But there was not much choice; if you kiss one, you have to kiss the lot. To Jeremy it was "One more for luck! Keep in touch." He was in touch, with his hand resting gently on her vibrant hip.

Clare he noticed was offering her cheeks quite freely, and also putting out a series of warm see-you-again-soons. The evening had clearly switched her on, and he had little idea what had been going on at her end of the table. Afterwards she said

"You never made your speech!"

"I wasn't the only one; I thought those two at the beginning were enough."

"I am sure Jan will be disappointed."

"Wait till we have them to dinner. I will make one then. Give me time to think up a few good yokes." Clare gave him a look which he could not readily decode, but he was soon dreaming again of Avelyn and her glorious legs. It was definitely an evening when 'the thighs had it'.

Next time he saw Avelyn, when they had fulfilled the principal object of his visit, which invariably was to be wined, dined and delicately entertained, she said

"That toad Bexler keeps ringing me up. He wants me to go out with him, lunch or something. Then he starts on these risqué remarks, so he's obviously not just interested in my conversation."

"Well you rather asked for it, wearing that daring outfit."

"Oh, didn't you like it?"

"Naturally I liked it. It was super. But it was rather a switch. Lots of leg always gives men ideas, especially long legs. And especially yours!" He took the opportunity to run his hand along her thigh and she smiled.

"Oh dear! It's the latest fashion from Milan. Jan bought it for me at Missoni's, so I had to wear it."

"Then you should get him to deal with the consequences."

"Can't you say something to Viktor? Tell him to keep clear."

"My God, no. I've got my hands full of Viktor already. If I start defending your chastity as well, I'll be in it up to my neck."

Mulling it over afterwards in the middle of the night, Jeremy saw a solution to all his problems. Jan would warn Viktor to keep away from Avelyn; they would have a quarrel and Bexler would get hurt or be disgraced, and have to leave the area. Perhaps they would have a fight and they would both be killed! Then he would have no further problems at work, and he and Avelyn could live happily ever after. Blissful thought. Too good to be true as usual.

As he woke up his mind cleared and he was horrified at the idea. How could he want Bexler to be dead? But come to think of it, maybe that would be just the ticket; natural causes maybe or perhaps he would be run over by a bus. He travelled a lot. An air crash. These things never happened when you wanted them. Wait and see. You never know your luck. The more he thought about it the more horrified he was. On the other hand, he came to realise that if Bexler were somehow to disappear, he would not be terribly sad. When he met Avelyn again he said lightly

"And how is the affair Bexler?"

"Oh that skunk. He is still pestering me. I've told him no way, but he seems to regard it as a challenge. I rang you in the lab the other day, and as usual you weren't there. She gave him a rueful look, half joking. "But HE answered, and recognised my voice. He thought I wanted to talk to him!!"

"I think you should get Jan to deal with him. Wield the big stick. Father figure stuff and all that. Or better still threaten legal action, an injunction to stop meddling with his wife. Then Viktor would be disgraced and he would have to leave Geneva . . . . .NEVER TO BE SEEN AGAIN!"

"Jan wouldn't do anything like that. He is so permissive. He'll just say 'That's your problem. If you don't like him, keep your legs together and tell him to piss off."

"What's the Swedish for piss off?" Avelyn looked surprised.

"Why do you want to know?"

"Oh, nothing. You mentioned it, and I just wondered. Chance to broaden my knowledge. You never know, it might come in useful one day." She was furious, and turned on him.

"You're so stupid! You don't take anything seriously. This is not a joking matter. I warn you, Viktor is dangerous. He frightens me."

14 Skiing in Gstaad

The winter season in Geneva was going with its usual swing. As the leaves fell, minds turned to the serious business of the city, new projects were launched and old ones pushed with increasing determination. Low cloud settled over the lake and the traffic jams on the Pont de Mont Blanc got worse every year. Petrol fumes accumulated in the cold damp air and a decree went out that engines should be switched off when the lights were red. Cars with odd numbers were only allowed into the city on Monday, Wednesday and Friday, with the other days reserved for the evens. Sunday was free for all, but most of the population drove into the mountains to ski, skate or simply walk in the crisp clear air and bright sunshine. It was so easy to climb through the layer of cloud into the pure light above. Every time it induced a feeling of euphoria and freedom; self congratulation for being in the sun, mingled with patronising commiseration for the wretched beings still trapped in the murk below: to which of course one was destined to return.

Every year Clare and Jeremy spent Christmas skiing in the Alps with the children. This year they had rented a chalet in Saanen, not far from Gstaad. If the jet set favour a resort, there is usually a good reason and Gstaad was popular because it provided a wide variety of runs, most of them easy, but a few hard enough for the experts. It was a good centre for family skiing, and usually had snow at Christmas. Saanen was two miles away and the chalet was half the fashionable price, while with a car you had access to all the facilities of Gstaad. The Egli ski lift close at hand had the best slopes for children.

The chalet was larger than they needed, but the only one available when Jeremy had booked the previous spring. One evening Clare and Juliet had been gossiping at a party and it transpired that the Eckerdovskys had no plans for Christmas.

"Why not join us in Gstaad? We have two spare bedrooms, and we would enjoy your company. Liliane would fit in well with Simon and Julie." Chalet holidays were a great break for dad and the kids, but not much of a holiday for mother. Self-catering gave her no respite from the daily chores of shopping and cooking. So it would be good to have another woman around; Juliet and Ivan agreed.

They had the place for a month, and as CERN closed its doors completely for ten days (to save electricity), Jeremy had no hesitation in taking a three week holiday: but there was no lolling around. The children were enrolled in the Saanen ski school, which assembled at 9.30 each morning. Having dropped them off Jeremy and Clare set off for a morning on their own at one of the 26 lifts spread around the area. Then they took the young to lunch in a mountain restaurant, goulash soup, pizza or cheese, and they all skied together in the afternoon.

Jeremy concentrated on the children, giving up the runs he preferred to guide them down and pass on techniques he had learned. Simon in fact was already a competent skier, getting to the 'hey dad, look at me' stage, and he was always pressing to try something more difficult. "Can we go down there, dad?" or "Why can't I try the black run?"

When the Eckerdovskys arrived they all skied together. Ivan was a stolid performer, but very steady. He was also a good teacher and very gentle with Liliane. Juliet, in spite of her dancing skills, was the least competent and most cautious of the group, but she made up for the delays with her ineffable charm.

The combined domestic life of the chalet went along with brio. Juliet provided some excellent French cuisine and Liliane showed Simon and Julie some new table games; once the kids were in bed, the four adults had some sizzling rubbers of bridge. Ivan had some bottles of Borovitska, that little known Czech liqueur, which he got from a friend in the United Nations. It tasted faintly of cherries and had a fabulous kick, but left no hangover. After a few rounds of this Jeremy started fantasising about a little wife swapping session, but he did not dare to suggest it. Although Clare seemed attracted to Ivan, he thought she would be furious. Perhaps he should come to an arrangement with Ivan to lead Clare off to a bedroom, thus leaving the way clear for him to suborn the divine Juliet: but how to broach this delicate subject? For a few days he almost forgot the glamorous Avelyn. But he had underestimated her resource.

She knew all about Jeremy's Christmas arrangements, because there were no secrets between them. Having nothing special to do, she persuaded Jan that ten days in Gstaad would make a perfect break for them both. Sweden was gloomy at this time of year, and Geneva would be slushy and dreary with everyone away. Luckily the Palace Hotel had a cancellation. It would be a beautiful surprise she thought for Jeremy; although she had no idea of his address, Saanen was a small place and she was sure that they would meet. Leave it to chance for a day or two, and if that did not work she would drop in at the children's ski school.

"How are the rats these days," asked Ivan one evening, turning to Clare as Juliet dealt the cards.

"Oh, I've been meaning to tell you. You know they have very long whiskers. Well I've been wondering if it's genetic, or is it because they're older than we think?"

"Ah . . . . really," said Ivan. "How can you tell? I know that the hairs keep growing all their life."

"Yes, so I dyed the whiskers on some of the rats and now I can see how fast they grow out from the roots."

"Oh brilliant," said Jeremy, picking up the message. "Then if you divide the present length by the rate of growth, you can get the age of the rat."

"Exactly. And the results are rather surprising. By all the usual signs the rats are quite young, one or two years only; they are lively, the eyes are bright, there are no signs of arthritis and they're sexy. But the whiskers say they are 4 to 7 years old!"

"What!" cried Ivan "Rats normally live only 2 or 3 years."

"Yes. So it's very surprising."

"Maybe they are born with long whiskers," said Ivan.

"No, that's not it," answered Clare. "We've got a litter that's just been born, in captivity so to speak, and they have quite short whiskers. I am checking on their rate of growth of course."

"So there is something about these rats that makes them stay young," mused Ivan. "We need some independent checks on their age. But that's not easy, as all the usual signs of ageing have to be discounted."

"Wow," said Jeremy. "If they've found the secret of eternal youth . . . . . then you've really got a winner."

"My bid," said Clare, "and I will open two hearts!"

The Olbers were both good skiers so Jan could not understand why Avelyn wanted to stay on the easy slopes. "We must warm up gently for the first days, it's so much safer that way." Ignoring the formidable Wassengrat, they bashed up and down all the red and blue runs, but drew a blank. Sunday followed, with no ski school. They stopped for coffee in the Grueblihutte half way down the Egli run. It was hot inside, and coming in from the crisp mountain air their goggles immediately misted over. Ripping them off, together with a few layers of clothing, they clumped through the crowded café picking their way over a jumble of legs, boots and sticks to get to the counter. Suddenly there was a shout,

"Look who's here! Jan, Avelyn, come and join us."

It was Ivan, looking more bulky than ever and rather scruffy in his woolly hat, striped jersey and ginger beard. They were all there together and soon squeezed up to make a place for the newcomers. It was a convivial meeting. Clare and Jan, who were working together on the rats, were soon deep in conversation; Avelyn's eyes were shining, but Jeremy tried to keep his excitement under control in front of the others. Avelyn's brand new green salopets were a snug fit and narrowly cinched at the waist. An almost imperceptible lilt to her movements broadcast the message, come and get me, and Jeremy was not the only one to pick up the vibes. But this was subliminal. On the surface she was giving all her attention to the children, vivaciously drawing them out, and when this succeeded glancing quickly at Jeremy to see if he approved.

They spent the rest of the day skiing together in one big group. Jeremy tried not to show too much interest in Avelyn, but somehow they were always close to each other, and on one occasion a collision sent them both sprawling on the snow. Some of the time she led the children down, giving them a useful lesson. Eventually, by the luck of the draw, Avelyn and Jeremy were side by side on the same chair lift. Immediately she slipped a gloved hand into his, drawing it over to her lap. "Darling, how are you. I am missing you so!" She twisted round to look behind: no one they knew was in the next chair. "It's OK," she said, and kissed him.

Jeremy realised immediately that this was going to be a frustrating combination that would spoil the family fun. He would love to be on holiday with Avelyn, but here she would get him all excited and they would be unable to do anything about it. On top of that, how could he keep his mind on the children when she was around?

"Why did you come?" he asked. "It is going to be very tricky and the others will guess."

"Oh dear," she answered, taken aback, "I wanted to give you a nice surprise. Can't we all be good friends? Your children are sweet. Jan was quite keen on meeting you all."

At the top of the lift she squeezed his hand before racing off with her elegant parallel turns to catch up with the others. Soon afterwards the Olbers decided to call it a day, but by general acclaim they arranged to meet again the next day. Schoenried was an excellent run according to Avelyn, so they agreed to try it.

"There is dancing in the Palace every night," said Jan. "Why don't you all come over after dinner and we could have some fun?" It seemed a great idea, apart from the baby sitting.

"You go," said Ivan. "We will be happy to look after the chalet. Then another night, if you like, we could swap." Swap! Swap wives? Jeremy's mind was boggling again.

"Swap what?" he asked naively.

"It's quite simple, it will be your turn to mind the chalet, and Juliet and I can dance."

"Great idea!"

So after supper they put on their smartest après ski kit, Clare making herself quite glamorous and smelling like a scent factory. They held hands in the car. "This should be rather good fun," she said.

The Palace hotel was an old fashioned gothic wedding cake with large rooms and ornate chandeliers. In one corner a five-piece band was playing with an irresistible rhythm. Posh people floated about, chatting to each other, and looking very much at home. Apart from their money they were no more attractive than the average, but the quality of their clothes and relaxed demeanour showed they had oodles in the bank.

"Come on, let's dance, " said Jeremy, picking up the beat. "We can find a table later." Clare somehow hugged her bag as well as Jeremy, and they made a few circuits. Jeremy was enjoying the scent factory. Clare was smiling: "We should do more of this, it's quite like old times."

Then they spotted Jan and Avelyn. They had a table and the champagne was lined up. A waiter filled their glasses and Jan proposed a toast. "Here's to us, then!" It was a happy thought, somehow meaning everything at the same time. They skolled silently, clinking glasses, and looking at each other in pairs. Jeremy remembered his lessons, and sent a silent message of friendship to each one.

"May I have the honour?" said Jan to Clare, and whisked her away to the floor. Avelyn and Jeremy sat for a while talking. The tension of the afternoon was past now; they were old friends. By mutual understanding they were putting off the pleasure of dancing together, knowing how delightful it would be. In fact, Clare and Jan came back before they had started.

"Aren't you two dancing?" he said in amazement.

"We are just about to," said Jeremy, and this got them going. She was as light as a cloud, and followed perfectly, sometimes adding some special decorative steps of her own. She kept herself close, touching his chest, their cheeks often in contact, and when they turned to speak their lips were almost touching.

"This is divine," she said. "I love you so much."

Jeremy had trouble with his trousers, and she could feel it.

"I know a place," she said. "I will take you there tomorrow. Then you won't be mad at me."

Ivan and Juliet were asleep when they got back to the chalet. Clare went to fluff up the cushions on the sofa, and found a bra. "Well, at least some of us have not been wasting time." Jeremy spent a restless night, pursued by erotic images and the tension of desire, and wondering what would happen next day. Where could they go, and how could they manage it?

The following day was sunny with an inch of new snow. They left the children at the ski school, and drove up the main road to Schoenried, where Jan and Avelyn met them. ~~This~~ was a more interesting run than the Egli, steeper and longer, with several ways down. They paired off for the chair lift, Clare and Jan, Jeremy and Avelyn, with the Eckerdovskys skiing together. For a couple of circuits they all kept together, but then Avelyn proposed going down to the left of the lift, instead of right as usual. Very few tracks went that way, so Clare and Juliet were too nervous to risk it, and the other men gallantly agreed to keep them company.

"See you at the bottom," she called out as they started. "But don't wait." She led him down the piste, and it was only slightly more difficult than the standard descent. She was full of energy, swooping about exuberantly in front of him, and then waiting with a broad smile. Half way down she said,

"Can you manage the trees?" She pointed to an untracked area dotted with clumps of bushes. "I think we could cut through here and get back to the lift. It will be more interesting."

"Do you know the way?"

"Sure, no problem, just follow me."

But Jeremy was nervous. Off the piste you might hit some crusted snow, soft underneath with a layer of ice on top. If your skis slice through they can be trapped, so it is impossible to turn; then you cross your skis and break a leg. Apart from that you may get lost, go over a small precipice or simply prang into a tree. They were living dangerously, but it is better than not living at all. In fact the trees were fairly far apart and the snow was excellent.

She led him down, and he found he could turn easily in the silky fresh snow. Once they were well into the woods she stopped and kicked off her skis. They found a flat area behind a tree and stripped off their anoraks to make a bed. The sun was shining, and although the air was cold they were both glowing from the exertion. He soon had her salopets unzipped and down around her ankles. He pushed her jersey and bra up to her shoulders, loosened his own clothes and tried to do the deed. But it was not so easy.

It would have made a comic sight for any hidden spectator; both with their trousers round their feet, pink bodies thrashing about on the ground, but they were not getting anywhere.

"Come on get you knees apart!"

"I can't," she cried out in frustration. "It's these damnable salopets around my ankles. I'm imprisoned." In the end they had to stop while she got her boots off and then her trousers, tucking them under her bottom.

"It's all very well for you! It's damn cold down here. Why don't you try lying in the snow?" But his next action made her gasp. Perhaps it was worth it after all.

"That's better! " he said, "I have been missing you so much."

They kept quiet for a moment, but nothing could be heard except the rustle of the trees and an occasional plop, as lumps of snow heated by the sun dropped off to the ground. Then they settled into some strenuous action.

"I think it's quite unfair," she said afterwards, as she watched him adjusting his zip. He was almost ready to go and she was still semi-naked, searching around for her kit. "You kept your boots on, and I had to strip off almost everything! And I was the one who had to lie in the snow." All she got in reply was a smug smirk of male superiority.

Filled with post-coital euphoria, they got back to the lift without difficulty and joined the queue. Soon the others turned up, and the waiting skiers let them crash the line to be with their friends.

"How was it?"

"Fantastic!" said Jeremy, and turning to Avelyn. "Can we try it again some time?" Then he realised that he had been far too positive; he was not a good diplomat.

"Perhaps I could come too," said Ivan. That would be an undesirable complication: had he guessed? Avelyn answered,

"Why not, if you know how to handle the bushes." Did she flash Ivan a quick wink? Perhaps she fancied him. Jeremy ended up thoroughly confused. Only later did he realise that Avelyn fancied everyone; but she usually kept it under control.

At lunch over the rolls and goulash Ivan tackled Jan about the rats. "Apparently they are radiation resistant and they live longer. Do you think the two could be connected?"

"Well . . . . . yeas . . . . . I think they might be."

"You see ageing is due to random mutations gradually piling up in the body. And rats age more quickly than humans because the DNA repair mechanism is less developed. So these fellows must either have less spontaneous mutations or a better repair system."

"Well . . . . yeas . . . I see . . . . yeas . . . . . so if the DNA is more stable, that will protect them against radiation as well."

"Exactly. The two are linked." Ivan gave Jan a penetrating look.

"Yeas . . . . . that's very interesting."

"But what's the secret?" asked Clare. "If only we could find it, we could help people to stay young. And that's far more important than resisting radiation!"

"Just as a matter of interest," said Ivan, "Perhaps you could let me have some samples of rat tissue. We could run a few analyses down in my lab. You never know, we might come up with something."

That evening it was Juliet and Ivan's turn to go dancing, with Clare and Jeremy minding the children. Clare was moving about the chalet in a lively manner, and kept bumping into him accidentally: the day's skiing had clearly zipped her up. They played a few games with the kids; when they were tucked up she turned down the lights and produced a bottle of fizz, Kriter brut, extra sec, nicely chilled.

"What are we celebrating?"

"Oh, just us! And a nice holiday. Happy Christmas and all that!" They clinked their glasses, English style.

"Here's to us! I've enjoyed this year. Since you discovered those rats I have been using my skills again. And working with Jan has been a pleasure. He's got a good mind, knows what he wants, but he's always so quiet and courteous."

"His yokes are pretty corny."

"Well, yes, in a way; but it's quite amusing. And better than saying nothing!"

Jeremy raised his glass. "I am sorry, Clare. I know I'm a bit taciturn. I have so many problems whirling in my brain."

"Can't we share our thoughts? We used to talk about everything."

"The trouble is, you wouldn't like my thoughts." He took a deep breath. Where to start? "For example, I am attracted to Juliet, but I am not supposed to be. So I can hardly tell you about her charms."

"It would be better if you did. Then we could both enjoy them, and maybe I see her in a more balanced way. I guess Avelyn bends your mind a bit, too."

Jeremy would not be drawn on that one. Instead he said,

"It's the arrangements. All those practicalities. Life is so complicated and we are always wrestling with problems: housing, the kids, taxes, immunisation, insurance. There's no poetry in that, no romance, no fun, no jokes." He smiled at her and refilled her glass.

"Perhaps loving, and living together are incompatible."

"Some people seem to manage it," she said.

"But it's pretty rare!"

"Yet love is what everyone wants. To give and to get, to love and be loved." She put her arms round him, but Jeremy was still tense and distant.

"The trouble is I don't know which way to go. I don't even know what I want any more!"

"Well, I know what I want. Being with Jan on the slopes is stimulating, and skiing makes me randy. So if those two girls are getting you all hipped up, come to bed and give me the benefit." She poured some more wine for both of them, came close, and for a short while made him forget his troubles.

The rapprochement oiled the wheels of the family holiday, but Jeremy still spent most of his time dreaming and on edge. Where was Avelyn now? Would she appear today, and if so would they be able to sneak off to the woods again? Was she with Jan? Or Ivan? And if so what were they doing to her? Whenever she appeared their divine symbiosis was as warm and wonderful as ever. They glowed for each other, while trying to keep their light under a bushel. But when she was not there, unable to communicate by telephone, he was torn with jealousy.

Luckily after a week the Olbers went back to Geneva. In a way Jeremy felt relieved, and found that he could now concentrate on skiing with the children, and attending to his reawakened wife. What had stimulated her need to be repeatedly ravished did not enter his thoughts.

In spite of all these distractions, Jeremy managed to make some progress in the lab. He kept the experiment going, but it was bogged down, getting nowhere. So when he could evade Viktor, Arthur and Chris he spent some time in the library, reading papers and reports, and trying to think of a better way. In the end he found one.

15 Chemical warfare

The return dinner for the Olbers went off quite well. It was a smaller affair; Ivan and Juliet were invited so it was almost a repeat of their skiing party.

"Do I really have to make a speech?" Jeremy asked Clare. "It is not really in the English tradition, and this is our party."

"Yes, but they would love it. I think we should try to make them happy. And it will give Jan an opportunity to make a speech in return: you know how he would enjoy that."

So a speech there was. Later in the meal someone broached the question of chemical warfare; it was in everyone's thoughts given the happenings in the Middle East, and the use of CS gas for crowd control in Zurich. It boiled down to the projection of power, how to control a hostile group while you imposed your will. The will could be good or bad, a dictator's iron rule, or a new world order based on peace and justice, the 'will of God' or the latest sectarian bigotry. In any conflict both sides thought they were right, but leaving aside that fundamental debate, how could power be projected? The bullet, they all agreed was rather crude and unnecessarily violent, but it had a sporting element. If luck was on your side it would miss, and you would be all right. Chemicals did not miss, so there was no element of chance; perhaps this is why everyone thinks they are unfair. Definitely not cricket! The current generation of chemicals were even more awful than the bullet, crude weapons of terror with horrific effects. But why not a milder form of chemistry, a gentle anaesthetic that would make the population drowsy, with no long term effects? Wasn't there a harmless nerve gas that would paralyse or hallucinate, but only temporarily?

"Biology can do better than that," said Jan. "A nice cocktail of entero-bacteria that makes you vomit and gives you the runs. Just as you recover from the first bug, the second starts to work, and then after that, the third. After five days on the run nobody cares what happens to them. Then you come in with the antidote, and the population welcomes you with open arms." Ivan agreed.

"And it's easy to distribute, you just spray it from a plane, or get it into the water or food. Bacteria multiply and pass from person to person. It's not hard to start an epidemic."

"But difficult to limit the effects to something reasonable. All the same, would you rather be sick for a week, or have a bullet in your guts? One day this will be regarded as a more civilised form of warfare or, if you like, crowd control."

"What a horrid subject for a dinner party," said Clare. "You nasty people are quite putting me off my food." She turned to Avelyn, "Tell us about your trip to Lisbon."

They changed the subject, but it had given Jeremy an idea. How to dominate the enemy, control the situation, without fuss or confrontation; that was his problem with Viktor. A little biological cocktail would be perfect, keep him away from the lab during the tests and perhaps a little bit subdued afterwards. Those lecture tours would be much less fun on a runny tummy. He determined to have a quiet word with Jan when the opportunity arose.

It did so, a few days later when he saw Jan in the cafeteria. Apart from a cup of coffee, he was all alone.

"You know that biological cocktail you were talking about."

"What's that?"

"You know, it makes you sick for a week, and then no after effects. You were talking about it at dinner."

"Oh that! Not a very nice subject for dinner, was it. Are you all right? No bugs in the food I hope."

"No, of course not. No, we're both fine."

"It was a very nice dinner, by the way. I would like to thank you again."

"Oh thank you, we enjoyed having you." Jeremy hesitated, then took the plunge. "The thing is . . . .I was wondering . . . . is it possible to get hold of this stuff?"

"What stuff?"

"You know the biological cocktail."

"My God no. It's lethal. Anyway, it's just an idea. I don't know if anyone's working on it." Suddenly Jan caught on. He looked across at Jeremy with a sharp interest.

"Why? Do you want to make someone sick?"

"Well yes, in a way. You see I am having a lot of trouble at work, with . . . . you guess who. If he wasn't there . . . . sometimes . . . . on important occasions, it would be . . . . . well, an advantage."

"I see . . . I see . . . I know what you mean," said Jan slowly and ponderously. He started to think it over. Bexler was a shit. A little extra time sitting on the bucket would be quite appropriate.

"So you want me to help?"

"No, no . . . . . . well, in a way, yes. I am really just asking for advice, some guidance."

"It is difficult. First of all, these bugs, if you could get them, I have some friends in Sweden, but they are very dangerous, infectious. You could start an epidemic. Who knows where it would end?" He looked gloomy. "Then there is the Hippocratic oath. I am a doctor. I must not give anyone something that makes him sick. It is a sacred obligation."

"I thought you would say that."

"Well . . . . that is how it is then. But it is an interesting idea."

Jan could see some mileage in this one. If Bexler's libido could be deflated, he might leave Avelyn alone; and then she would stop asking her husband to beat him up. Chemical warfare would be far more civilised. Then another thought struck him. If Viktor were poisoned, and it transpired that Jeremy had given him the fatal dose, then he would be locked up for 20 years: thus two birds would be eliminated with one pill and he would be free to enjoy his wife in peace; or even to pursue the unattainable Clare. Jan quickly dismissed the concept as unthinkable, and leaned across the table.

"You could try phenolphthalein."

"Phenolphthalein! You mean the indicator. Alkali turns it pink. We had some in Simon's chemistry set."

"Yes, that's the one," said Jan. "It's the basis of that clever trick, turning the water into the wine? But you'd better not drink it!"

"Why not?"

"Peristalsis!" said Jan darkly. "Makes the gut contract. That will keep him moving."

"Have you got some?"

"Nej, leave me out of it. We don't have chemistry sets in the hospital. You could try the toy shop 'Jouet Weber', or a pharmacy."

"How much do I give? I don't want to kill the bugger."

"Are you sure? " Jan was grinning. "It is a yoke of course! I am not sure of the dose; but I can look it up, and let you know."

As so often happens, what starts as a vague inquiry, completely open-ended with no intention to proceed, suddenly takes on a life of its own. You are looking at houses, out of curiosity to see what is on the market; then unexpectedly you are buying one. You are flirting with a woman, then taking her out, then seducing her. Without any real attachment you find yourself in court as a co-respondent.

Jeremy asked the chemists at CERN who were separating radioactive isotopes. Phenolphthalein! They had not seen it for years. These days everything is done with electrometers. The pharmacist was more forthcoming; he looked it up.

'Yes, I can get some. Conjuring tricks is it, something for the kids?"

"Yes, yes certainly. But what happens if someone drinks it?" The good Swiss chemist looked at him severely.

"It is not recommended!" For him there was nothing more to know. Don't ask questions, do as you're told. Follow the instructions, if you want to grow old.

Jeremy collected it the following week; a small bottle of white powder, carefully labelled 'POISON Not To Be Swallowed' in four languages.

Jan rang him at home a few days later. He beat about the bush for a bit, then came to the point.

"You remember that stuff we talked about, the indicator."

"Yes, naturally."

"Did you get some?"

"Yes at the chemist, no problem."

"Ten milligrams!"

"Are you sure?"

"Yes, give it a go. And oh, by the way, let's keep this to ourselves."

"You bet!"

"Good luck then." He rang off.

Jeremy did not tell Clare. He did not tell anyone; but he wrestled with his conscience. It was not a nice thing to do. On the other hand Viktor was full of dirty tricks himself; it would serve him right. But what if something terrible happened?

Ten milligrams, he needed to weigh it out; cannot afford to make a mistake. The chemists at CERN luckily still used balances. He measured out ten doses while he was at it, and folded them up neatly in crisp white paper. It looked like salt, so he carefully labelled each one 'PH' to avoid confusion.

Better get some practice! At home he tipped a dose into a glass of water. It dissolved quickly, but the water went pink! Tap water must be slightly alkaline. He tipped it away, and washed the glass ten times. The next experiment was coffee; that looked good. If it was pink, you could not see it. Very gingerly he tasted a little: there was nothing to notice. Then he spat it out and rinsed his mouth. For the rest of the day he was expecting an attack of indigestion, but nothing happened. He kept the packets in his office at CERN, locked in a drawer. Perhaps he would never use them.

It was a sultry day on the Mediterranean. Fair-haired Kirsten was wearing a thin pair of shorts over her freckled thighs and a light blouse, but she was still too hot. The door of Ivan's office was open as usual, but she knocked anyway out of politeness.

"Can I have a word? I feel as though I am losing my grip, going mad or something." She perched on the edge of a stool with her legs stretched out and frowned.

"You know those rat samples you gave me. They are radioactive of course, so I am handling them in the airtight cupboards. And . . . . well . . . . I was not too sure what tests to make, so I mashed up some of the tissue and put it through the usual mass spectrometer analysis we use for the TABS. I just thought we would get an overall composition to start with, maybe pick out some major molecules and so on." Ivan nodded to show he agreed.

"Well, this is the part I can't believe. The deuterium content came up as a by-product, I wasn't looking for it, but it's two and a half times normal. I mean why? It just does not make sense. Or am I making some stupid mistake?" She wiped her hand across her brow. "Or am I going off my rocker?"

"Kirsten, take it easy. This could be important. But there is a lot of heavy water round the lab. So your sample could have got contaminated."

"Sure. So I've done the tests several times, and it's always the same."

"OK. I think I'd like to see this myself. Could we do the whole thing again together?"

"Yes, of course. That's just what I'd like. There is still some tissue in the safe that I haven't touched."

"Why don't we check first with an ordinary rat?"

"Yes. But I don't have any ordinary rat!"

"No. But there are plenty around. Let's nip across to Heliopolis and pick up a trap."

Ivan could see that Kirsten needed a break, so they might as well go shopping together. He reached up and unhooked the key to the interconnecting gate and together they strolled into the nudist village. Joe who ran the old-fashioned general store had everything for the camping tourist and as usual the place was crowded with sweating semi-naked shoppers, all jabbering away in French.

"We'll catch one tonight, chop him up and run the test tomorrow."

"It might be a her," said Kirsten.

"True." The thought of a female victim made Ivan feel sad. So he added, "Anyway, it's all in the name of science. Meanwhile I suggest you get back to the TABs and cheer yourself up."

"I'm worried about them too. The TABs in the 90% D2O are looking a bit sick; I think they may have some disease."

"Oh no That's the last thing we want. But adapting to the heavy water may have made them weaker. Let's put some samples under the microscope and see if there are any parasites or bacteria. Algae can get cholera if there's pollution in the water, I hope it's not that."

They caught two rats from the island and put them through the tests. Their composition was normal, which verified that their procedures were correct. Then they repeated the test with a clean sample from Jan, so there was no chance of contamination. Sure enough the deuterium content was 1 in 2000, instead of the usual 1 in 5000, two and a half times more as Kirsten had claimed.

Now she was beaming and relaxed; her results were confirmed, and her sanity as well! "I've been thinking about this," she said. "These rats age more slowly. Do you think that deuterium in the cell could be responsible? You see the chemistry is exactly the same as for ordinary hydrogen, but because of the greater mass the atoms would be less subject to thermal agitation and random knocks. So the molecules would be more stable. That means fewer mutations!"

"Ah yes. Good thinking Kirsten. But the deuterium would have to be in the genetic code, the DNA, that is in the cell nucleus." He thought for a moment. "Of course the nucleus is much smaller. So if the deuterium is only there the concentration will be much larger, nearly all the hydrogen could be heavy."

"Exactly. So we have to extract the DNA and test that."

"Right, but how do we do it?"

"It's easy. There's a standard procedure. We did it in the lab in Oslo."

"So you say the rats living near the accelerators have evolved to become resistant to radiation; and they do that by using deuterium in their genetic code which makes it more stable. And that makes them stay younger as well. It's only a hypothesis. But a good one. Let's try to confirm it. Meanwhile I must telephone Jan and give him the news."

16 Annecy

During the summer holidays Clare decided to take the children to England, visit her parents and look up old friends. Jeremy was too involved with the experiment to take a break; he could not contemplate cooling his heels for two weeks while there was so much to play for in Geneva. Having someone to play with was also a factor.

"Darling, how marvellous! Jan will be away too, he is going to Stockholm for a few days, so . . . . .I can look after you."

She looked down shyly, put her hand on his.

"Will you come and stay with me?"

The frank blue eyes; it was impossible to refuse, and why should he? It was a lovely prospect, and he was looking forward to it already. It would be the first night they had spent together, and hopefully not the last.

When the time came he presented himself at her apartment complete with a small suitcase. Although he had been there countless times before, it somehow felt strange.

'Lovely to see you. So pleased you could come." She had dressed herself up. A soft short-sleeved jumper, pale green, it made her eyes look greener, and went well with her red hair which was piled up on top of her head in a mass of bouncy curls. Below that a gorgeous smile. She looked tall, high heels to match the jumper, stockings and round the waist an apron with frilly lace edges covered everything. She bowed him in, holding the door, and followed him to the spare room.

"Put your things in here, unpack if you like. When you're ready we will have a drink. Make yourself at home." Kiss, kiss, and she backed out.

It did not take him long, and he found her in the kitchen. He held her close, his fingers on her waist, and below . . . .the jersey ended half way down her hips, and below that was bare, satin-cool skin. It felt good. She turned around to show him, leaning forward, one hand on the wall to steady herself. The long stockings completely encased her thighs, but apart from some thin suspenders there was nothing else, no skirt, no shorts, no panties!

"You are wicked."

“Do you like it?” She turned back, threw her arms round his neck and kissed him avidly. “It’s so good that you’re here. I am really going to enjoy this.”

“Me too. It’s totally marvellous. And you look so gorgeous.”

“Do you think I’m naughty?”

“Yes, I do, very naughty!”

She wriggled against him. “Do you think . . . . naughty girls . . . . need to be . . . . well . . . educated?” Jeremy raised his eyebrows. It was a new concept; he tried to figure out what she could be driving at. But she soon made it more specific. “You know . . . . corrected . . . . . chastised?”

“Well . . . . maybe.” She was young, but hardly a child, and he had no complaints about her behaviour.

“My bottom’s been bothering me all day. You know . . . . tingling and wiggling. Its very naughty ..... it needs to be spanked.” She looked at him coyly. “So would you mind?” What could he say? It was embarrassing. Not the normal way to treat a generous hostess. Jeremy thought it over.

“Well, I suppose so . . . . . if that's what you want.” Avelyn brightened, flounced over to the drawer and got out a flat wooden spatula.

“Here you are then. How would you like me? . . . . like this?” She spread herself out over the kitchen table, feet on the floor, the long legs and hollowed back. He held the instrument in his left hand; it seemed a shame to attack the smooth pale skin, so tender round and globular. So he took his time to run a hand around her, feeling, caressing, exploring. The flesh smooth and soft, simultaneously firm and wobbly. He tested the vibrations with his finger, trying the response in various places.

"Mmm! " she said, "That's nice. It likes being wobbled. It needs a lot of attention."

"Well you've come to the right department. They are a little presumptuous, I must say. Perhaps they need something to think about." He pinched her, working his way along. A row of pink patches. "Aaah,"

“So now for the little lesson .... to teach them to be good girls in future.” He gave her a sharp resounding crack. “Ow!” Then two more. Then three on the other side. That ought to do the trick. Avelyn did not move.

“Why are you stopping?”

"Six of the best! That's the standard ration in the English boys' schools."

"Girls are tougher than boys. They need more . . . . lots more." Jeremy did not want to appear inadequate, so he gave her what she was asking for; another ten on each side, thoughtfully spreading it around. Then another ten. There was something in this; it was actually quite stimulating: the bright red marks, sharp edged at first, slowly diffusing and joining up, and after that being reinforced. It was a pretty picture. Avelyn waited.

"Ten more, each side! Then you can get up." To finish her off he made them a bit harder. "Ouch!" she said, but stayed still on the table.

"Aren't you getting up? We could have that drink." She was flushed, the eyes moist, the half open mouth seemed a bit swollen, but she looked at him lovingly, glowing with happiness. And kissed him passionately

"Thank you, thank you! Thank you so much. You are a wicked master." Jeremy was hot now to take her to bed, but she would not let him.

"Let's wait, I must finish the dinner." He watched her working; the rosy behind apparently was no impediment, though she passed her hand across it occasionally, and kept turning to give him adoring looks. When the time came she sat down rather cautiously.

She kept him waiting until bedtime, talking, playing dominoes; it was an easy game, in principle, but she was cunning and usually managed to win. When he finally got her to bed, she was not cooperative, lying face down with her legs together.

"Open up!"

"No, I want to be like this." Jeremy was getting desperate.

"Come on, I can't get at you."

"Silly man, don't you understand. My bottom! I'm giving you a special present. It's a treat to celebrate our first night together." Jeremy was totally confused. It made no sense to him at all. He could not even get his hand to her.

"Try it the other way. Greek if you like. There's some cream on the bedside table. Shall I lift it up a bit?" Jeremy got the message at last, and it was surprisingly easy. Also rather pleasant. They lay quietly together, savouring the new sensations.

“It’s rather beautiful.” he said.

“Lovely, more intimate. I’m enjoying it.” Afterwards she said,

“Now you know me completely. And I am completely yours.”

It was beautiful to sleep together, wake up together and make love again with all the time in the world ahead of them. In the morning he asked her,

“Have you done that before?”

“Oh yes. Why not, if you enjoy it? Juliet and Ivan do it a lot.”

“How do you know?”

“She told me of course. It’s good for contraception. If you’re afraid of the pill, and you don’t like the other things.” It was a new concept for Jeremy. Then she added, “Always supposing you don’t want children.”

They took off for the day in her red Mercedes with the top down. It was a perfect car for two, zooming over the Salève and down to the lake. They stayed at the quiet luxurious hotel called ‘Le Cottage’ at Talloires on the shores of the lake. Their room was on the ground floor with a wide French window leading out to a green garden with large trees and chattering birds. From there a little gate let to a private beach. Avelyn was in raptures, “This is really heavenly!”

They swam, windsurfed and settled down for a gourmet meal.

“How’s the bottom, by the way. I have been meaning to ask.”

“Oh fine thanks. No problem at all. Why? Do you want to spank it again?”

“I don’t think so.” But it was an intriguing thought.

“You can if you like. Anything you like, any time. I am here for your pleasure, so take advantage while you can. It may not last forever.”

“Thank you.” It was unbelievable! She took his breath away, and his reply seemed inadequate, so he added,

“I will.”

“That’s a nice phrase! Perhaps, one day, I will say it to you, ‘I will’, in front of . . . . well, some official. Then you can say it back to me, and we will both have our second honeymoons, together. Why not the Villa Serbolloni?”

It was a fascinating idea. The train was waiting at the station, the guard was blowing his whistle, green flags were waving; all he had to do was to get on board and they would be off. To travel with her, on the most romantic journey in the world. But was he ready to leave? He kissed her, and snuggled up in bed. But said nothing.

"Goodnight Darling," she said. "It's been a most beautiful day. And happy dreams."

"You too sweetheart."

Avelyn woke early, the summer dawn was just breaking. Jeremy was deeply asleep, dreaming perhaps of difficulties and discoveries. So she wrapped a towel round her body and crept out quietly into the garden. It was so beautiful with the dew under her bare feet and the mild clean air. She opened the gate and wandered along the beach looking at the reddening sky. The water was lapping against the sand; it looked so inviting. There was no one around, so she threw off the towel and gently waded into the lake. Half way in she paused, opened her legs and let the ripples flap between her thighs. It felt good. If only Jeremy were here, they could enjoy the dawn together. She was tempted to go back and wake him, but better to let him dream on and wake up fresh when he was ready.

Way out on the water was a lone fisherman trying his luck in the dawn. She swam out to the boat without difficulty and the man waved. "Morning!" he said in French and beckoned to her. She came closer and he realised that she was naked; this would be a better catch. "Aren't you tired? Come on board and have a rest." But Avelyn would not be hooked by this grey haired peasant. "Bye-bye! And good luck with the fish!" She turned to go back but the man got out his oars to follow her. Luckily the boat was heavy and he was old, so by putting on a spurt she quickly got out of range and he gave up.

Another little adventure to share with Jeremy. Why was he always in her mind? Their souls were in perfect tune; the only one who could truly share her thoughts. With him she could always speak frankly, openly and with no inhibitions. Did he feel the same? It was hard to tell. Quite rightly he felt a loyalty to the children. That was as it should be. She was longing for a child too. If it were his, so much the better; then they would have something to share and perhaps it would tip the balance. But that they could not talk about: not yet anyway. He wasn't ready for it.

17 A new idea

Back in CERN Jeremy decided to consult Chang-Singh; was there any sense in his new idea? Along the corridors to the theory division, he found his office. It was empty. There was no outer office: Chang was head of the division, but he did not believe in protocol; the theorists are democratic because the youngest guy can come up with the best idea. The general office, which served the whole division, had four girls to do all the typing and administration. There was a new one on the right, long dark hair, red blouse, fruity with large specs, a ripe plum. She gave Jeremy the works, but he already had enough women on his plate to last a life time. Instead he addressed the lady in charge.

"Chang? He's here . . . . . somewhere. If he's not in his office, he'll be in the corridors. Try one floor up. He may be talking to Demetri." She was always vague: it was no good trying to do better, because the theorists were all vague themselves, it was impossible to keep track of them.

He went upstairs and heard Chang's voice. "OK, I think it's a good idea. I'll have a word with the DG." How much time did he spend on physics, and how much on internal politics?

"Could I have a word?" Chang was friendly, affable, approachable, which was why he had become division leader. They went down to his office.

"It's probably a mad idea, but I would like to sound you out on something that might be possible?" Chang nodded, and relaxed into his armchair to listen. "Can you imagine a particle with roughly the mass of the muon, but having high spin, say five halves; 5 over 2, perhaps 7 over 2, or more?"

"Yes, I can. The new theories of 'super-symmetry' even predict such things. But it's all very vague, no specific masses or anything like that. Why? Have you seen something?"

"No, no, no. It's just an idea - for catalysed fusion of course."

"Oh yes, such a thing would be a wonderful catalyst."

"How would it decay? It would live for much longer than the muon, wouldn't it?"

"Well, let's see. If there was another lepton with spin 5/2, but smaller mass, then your particle . . . . .what shall we call it? How about 'hijaon', because it has high angular momentum." Everyone used the letter J for angular momentum, or spin, which for all practical purposes was the same thing.

"OK, hijaon," Chang continued, "Well lets call it 'jaon' for short? So, if there was another lepton of the same spin, but lighter, then the jaon could decay into it, and that would be rather fast. The lifetime would depend on the energy released, that is the mass difference between the two particles, and it goes as the fifth power. So it could easily be a factor of fifty either way, either shorter or longer than the muon life.

"But . . . . .ah ha!" Chang raised a significant finger. "If it were the lightest member of the family, it could not decay at all! If the transformation is a point interaction, (and that is all we know about at present), then the spins of the final particles must add up to the spin of the parent. That is necessary to balance angular momentum, which as you know is a sacred principle. Therefore it could not decay in the usual way to three ordinary leptons, which just have spin 1/2. They could add up at the most to 3/2, which is not enough." He thought for a moment.

"Ah, yes. It could, in principle, decay into 5 leptons of spin 1/2. But we have no theory of that. We could make one up, of course. Let's see . . . . .we would need a 'jaon-neutrino', an electron and an electron-neutrino, and then add two more particles, they could be two more neutrinos, or an e-plus and an e-minus. Then . . . . .we would need a five-particle point interaction to couple them all together. We could do that with the intermediate bosons, like this." He scribbled on the blackboard. "Yes, that would do it. But you can see that we have four vertices and two intermediate bosons, so it's second order weak. Then the lifetime would be . . . . of order . . . . let's see . . . . well, it's a guess, depending on the masses . . . . say ten to the power ten seconds." He looked up.

"That is 300 years." said Jeremy. "You would never see it! "

"Exactly, " answered Chang. "YOU WOULD NEVER SEE IT. It would just look like an ordinary track, stopping, and then doing nothing. You could mistake it for a mu-minus which gets captured at the end of its range, giving a neutron plus a neutrino - you see nothing. Or you might mistake it for a proton. They are a dime a dozen."

"So that's the point," said Jeremy. "They could be around all the time, but we DON'T KNOW THEY ARE THERE."

Chang raised his eyebrows; he was getting interested. "How would you make them?"

"Well, in the normal way, you cannot make them, not in the ordinary proton-proton collisions that we always use. Two spin half can never give spin five halves."

"Quite right," cried Chang. "So you can't make them, and you can't see them. . . . .so . . . . . what's the use??"

"But they could be there," said Jeremy. "A whole new family of spin 5/2 particles; if only we could contact them."

"It is conceivable," said Chang. "I've heard crazier ideas. How could we get in touch?"

"Well I think we should collide two nuclei with large spins. Then there is a chance of making a high spin particle. For example aluminium has spin 5/2. If we collided two aluminiums together at high energy we might have a chance."

"It's not quite so easy," said Chang. "Usually the collision is just between two of the individual nucleons. To get a high spin state you would need the whole nucleus to participate." He paused. "Yes . . . . but there is evidence in pion production by nuclei of cooperative effects, in which several nucleons participate. It might work." Chang relapsed into thought.

"Bizarre things happen inside the nucleus, and we do not by any means understand them. One might imagine that some of the nucleons exist momentarily in higher spin states; thermodynamic spin fluctuations. There would be a Boltzmann factor. Then if the nucleons that were temporarily in high spin states collided you would get what you want. We could easily invent a theory like that." His eyes danced. "Then if your experiment worked, we could explain it; better still we could have 'predicted' it!"

Chang was now in his element, and started to lyricize. "Just give us a new fact, and we can easily invent some theoretical model to explain it. The funny thing is that in the end people remember the theory, and the original fact and its discoverer are soon forgotten."

"It is actually better without any facts at all. Experimental facts can be rather awkward; they limit the fantasy of theorists. In an ideal world there would be no experiments, and we could all speculate to our hearts content!" He flickered his eyebrows wryly. "How many angels can coexist on the point of a pin? Those mediaeval philosophers had a great time; there were no experimental facts to limit their imagination! But of course we have to deal with the world as it is . . . . . and that is where you come in." He smiled broadly, and patted Jeremy on the arm.

"So what's the verdict?" asked Jeremy.

"I think it's a great idea. There could be a new world of high-spin, long-lived particles, perhaps linked with the theory of super-symmetry. It would be useful to look for them. It is new, it is interesting, it is timely; it might even work! I think you should put up a proposal. I will speak in favour. Meanwhile we will find one or two theorists to work out a bit more about their properties, make 'predictions'. You know what I mean!" He winked at Jeremy.

It was unbelievably encouraging. Jeremy reeled down the corridor back to his office in a drunken dream. Was this true? Was he really originating a new line of research inside this great international laboratory, and getting support from high places? High spin particles! Did they exist? Could you make them? It was a way out idea, but Chang was in favour. Was there a high spin nucleus which could be accelerated, preferably a gas to make the ion source easy; and a high spin target nucleus, preferably a solid to bang them into? Perhaps that would do the trick. And a long lived particle would catalyse more fusions! At least there was a chance of finding something new.

Dig where there might be treasure; probably you would draw a blank, in which case do not complain, that is the way the cookie crumbles. But if Fortune smiles, the sky should be the limit: if not, you are wasting your time. Always run the risk of finding gold.

The first step was to find the right nuclei, if there were any! The CERN library was superb, centrally located, and set up meticulously by the first librarian. He had been a bit of a niggler, but the result was worth it, and the tradition of tidiness and completeness had been continued. Everything you could possibly want on nuclear physics, particles and related subjects was there. And it was quiet inside.

Jeremy went to the reference section. Encyclopaedias, Who's Who, the World of Learning, University calendars, European Scientists, each with endless lists of names, catalogued like fossils. One day, perhaps, he would be in these books, but by then he would be a fossil too. Anyway, this was not what he had come to find. That was the trouble with libraries, they were full of diversions, all interesting, and you could end up mentally exhausted, forgetting why you came.

At the desk was a rather florid Dutch woman with cow's eyes, deep brown and friendly. She was shuffling cards, loan slips or whatever, but Jeremy decided to enlist her help rather than wander aimlessly through the labyrinths of books. Usually people at desks are bored out of their minds with their anonymous bits of paper. They will gladly procrastinate in favour of a real human customer, and they enjoy demonstrating their usefulness: so never hesitate to ask.

Anneke was no exception. "A Table of Isotopes?" She brightened up at once. "I am sure we can help. Every book is in the computer, so let's try a search. I will show you how to work it, and then another time you can do it yourself." She looked at him archly and waddled over to the machine. Born to teach, she was in her element and enjoying it.

"Press this key to start. Then you have a list of options. Do you know the author? Well, then we can do a search by subject, or title. Press key 1. It asks you for the subject, so I type in 'isotope*'. Put a star to show that it might be plural or it might not, we do not know. Don't worry if you get it wrong, the machine is very forgiving. Just put it in and see what happens, you can always try your luck!" The calm brown eyes holding his for a little longer than necessary. She turned back to the screen.

"Now type 'and', and add 'table*' to show that we are looking for a combination of the words isotope and table. Press 'return', and away we go!" Anneke looked at him in triumph, and the screen obediently blinked its message 'searching'. It soon came back with a reply, '12 items found' and a list. The first was 'An Atlas of Cosmic Ray Spectra', which did not seem relevant, but there were several 'Tables of Isotopes' with their shelf references.

"Now you can look at each in further detail, if you like. Or shall we just print the list?" She turned to him smiling, happy to be of service, to be appreciated. She was one of Geneva's stranded spinsters. Girls flock to Geneva in the hope of finding a mate, attracted by the fat salaries and easy living. But the men usually come with a partner, so there is a serious mismatch; lots of lonely ladies, making the best of it.

"Nice work," said Jeremy. "Let's print the lot, then I can look on the shelves." The printer rasped to and fro like a cicada with tonsillitis, then chugged with self-congratulation, spewing out the paper. Anneke took the sheet.

"Which ones do you want? I'll show you where they are."

He followed the trail of Diorama, which could have been erotic on a younger player. Eventually on shelf QD 466.T2 they found a huge tome, several inches thick, in which some German character had collected every published fact about the 523 isotopes known to Man. He probably had a whole army of students to help him.

Anneke had strong arms, with pale orange freckles. The skin looked soft and silky. Before he could intervene she had lugged the tome off the shelf and laid it on a nearby table. Jeremy beamed his thanks and set to work. At first he was discouraged. There were charts for every isotope, with fine horizontal lines showing every known energy level, and diagonals connecting them with measured transitions; references to who had reported what, beta rays, gamma rays, alphas. Somewhere, hidden in all this mass of data, he might find the nuclear spin, but he would have to leaf through the whole book to find the few isotopes with the highest spin. It would take days.

Then he looked again at the list of contents. There it was in small print, appendix III, pages 943 to 987, table of nuclear moments. He guessed that with the magnetic moments the spins would also be listed, and sure enough they were; all the known isotopes with their spins in forty pages. It started with the proton, spin value 1/2 in some fundamental unit of measure. He ran his eye down the column to pick out the larger values. Neon-21 spin 3/2, aluminium-27 5/2. That would be good because natural aluminium only has one isotope, while many elements were a mixture. You could get separated isotopes from Amersham, but they were expensive.

As he went down the table there was the occasional larger value; he should have started at the other end. Calcium-43 7/2, titanium-49 7/2, cobalt 7/2. What next? Krypton-83 9/2. Whoopee! Krypton was a gas, which would be easy to put into the accelerator, but it was a mixture of isotopes, only 11.5% of it was krypton-83, but perhaps that would not matter. The accelerator could be tuned to select one isotope only .

Wow! Niobium-93 also had spin 9/2, and it had only one isotope. That would make a perfect target. It was a rare metal, probably more expensive than gold, but he would not need much of it. Jeremy reckoned he had a viable proposal.

Which of the CERN accelerators could speed up krypton-83? The proton synchrotron was being used for experiments with heavy ions, so it would probably do the trick. The PS coordinator was a Swiss who came from Bern. He spoke French in the singsong manner of the Vaudois, but broke into incomprehensible Swiss-German dialect whenever a fellow countryman appeared: very proud of their nationality the Swiss. Jeremy did not know him too well, and found him rather stiff and forbidding. Perhaps it would be better to find an engineer who knew the accelerator. Arthur would almost certainly know someone, and anyway it was time to put him in the picture. One cannot launch a new experiment by oneself and what better ally than one's group leader. On the other hand Jeremy wanted to get the credit if the idea worked out. It was a fine line to tread, but hopefully Arthur was an honest man.

The office door was ajar and Arthur was peering at the computer screen.

"Blue movies? What did the butler see?"

"Oh hi! I am trying to simulate our next experiment, but it keeps saying 'accumulator overflow'. . . . . some stupid glitch in the programme."

"Arthur, how about lunch in Tortella's. I've got a crazy idea I want to try on you."

"Not again! But any excuse for a good meal."

Tortella was an enterprising Spaniard, who years ago had semi-illegally set up a lunch hut for workmen on the CERN site. He got up at 4 am to buy fresh produce in the markets and his dishes were unusual, delicious and good value. The hut was soon patronised by the senior staff, and when the time came to open a second restaurant on the French part of the site Tortella got the contract. The restaurant was now under a new management, but the name had stuck and the tradition for exotic dishes continued. Tortella retired and was last seen at Nice airport where a Rolls Royce was meeting him: a man who knew how to operate. The food was excellent, and there was a small section with a set menu and waiter service, a good place for a leisurely chat.

It was early and they found a secluded table. "The wine's on me," said Jeremy, and launched into a description of his project. Arthur looked dubious.

"It's a very long shot. You would probably see just the usual junk, pions, muons, kaons and all that. But any new particle would be a sensation."

When Arthur heard that Chang was interested, he brightened up a bit, but then became even more reflective. He had to figure out whether to support the idea, which meant giving it his time and reputation. Jeremy had less to lose and obviously had the bit between his teeth. If he did not support it, Jeremy could go off and work with someone else. Then if it succeeded Arthur would look a fool. Choosing how to spend your effort was the most critical decision in research; you could waste a lot of energy on the wrong track. So to buy time Arthur said,

"OK, let us go and talk to the PS people, and find out what they can do. I think we might try Jean-Marc Métereau, he is chief of operations and knows every wrinkle. Well, talk of the devil!" Jean-Marc had just walked in, with another PS engineer. Arthur beckoned them over and more wine was poured.

"We want to ask you a question." Arthur gave Jeremy the nod: it was his idea, so let him do the talking.

"Can you accelerate krypton?"

"Well," Jean-Marc was feeling his way. "We have not done it, up to now. But I can see no reason why not. We have done argon, and many times we are running with xenon. Even with lead we have been making a test. What energy are you wanting?" Jeremy looked across at Arthur; he had not worried about this detail.

"Oh, not too much, 5 GeV per nucleon perhaps. It's not critical."

Jean-Marc had now made up his mind. "It is not a problem. A bit of the cake, do you say? When do you want them?"

"When can you do it?"

"Oh let me see. In two weeks time we have machine development." He looked at his colleague for confirmation. "I think we have no special plans, we might do a quick test." Mario nodded.

"There is an extra complication," said Jeremy. "Krypton is a mixture of isotopes, 82, 83, 84 and maybe others; ideally we only want one."

"You will only get one anyway? The machine is only accelerating one at a time. Which one do you prefer?"

"83. It is only 11% abundant."

"No problem, you will get slightly less beam, that's all."

"What is it for anyway," asked Mario. It was a natural question, and if you want cooperation it is best to give out the background: but Arthur stalled skilfully, glancing at Jeremy.

"Oh, it's just an idea at present. There is no proposal yet, and we would like to check the feasibility before we put it in. Jeremy thinks krypton might have a special effect."

They seemed satisfied; everyone at CERN knew that it was better to keep things to yourself initially. When the time was ripe, the ground prepared, then you could go public.

"Officially," said Jean-Marc, "we need the coordinator's approval, but as this will be machine development we can do what we like; I think we can fit it in." Mario nodded.

"Have a refill." Jeremy caught the waiter's eye and ordered another bottle. Arthur raised his glass with a conspiratorial wink.

"To the krypton factor! I heard a good analogy from a wise old German professor. The history of physics is like the exploration of the world. There are three stages. First come the explorers. After them the pirates. Then finally the civil servants!" They all laughed.

"We know plenty of pirates," said Jeremy. CERN had its share, people who jump on the bandwagon, lay claim to ideas, and even publish things they have gleaned from others. He was thinking especially of Bexler.

"We are needing the civil servants," said Mario. "They are writing the books, classifying the results and publishing the tables of data which we all use."

The unspoken assumption was that each thought of himself as an explorer.

After lunch Arthur encouraged Jeremy to write up the proposal in a form suitable for the committees and to figure out what equipment they would need to search for new particles. This was quite easy, as there were standard techniques for measuring the masses of particles as they streamed away from the targets. Meanwhile they would keep the idea to themselves.

In a few days Jeremy had the paper ready. He typed it up himself using his terminal linked to the main computers, and made sure to collect the result from the print room as soon as it was ready. As he did so, he realised that nothing on the computers was really secret. In principle other users could not see his files, but this protection was easily circumvented. You just needed to log in as the 'system manager' with a special password, and then you could read what everybody was doing. That meant that a 'system manager' could read all the memos that were being secretly prepared for discussion within a limited group of friends. There were lots of system managers, working in shifts, and they all knew the passwords, so it would be easy for some pirate to log in and read Jeremy's file. Not a bad way to get ahead of the game! If you knew where to look, and if you had the time, and the inclination. But probably no one had all three.

So Jeremy thought about deleting his memo from the computer, after it had been printed. Then he realised that he would need it again, if Arthur approved, to make some modifications and print more copies for the committee. Also, he recalled, even deleted files could be recovered by a systems expert; they would still be there somewhere. The only thing to do was to leave it, and run the risk.

Risk seemed to loom large in his life these days. He thought of his escapades with Avelyn and the danger of being found out, the icy roads, the ski slopes where a false move could put you on the rocks, his sailplane ride with Ivan, radiation and high voltages and explosive gases at CERN, and the risk of making a discovery. It was a dangerous world, but Jeremy decided that he could live with it. All you could do was to take reasonable precautions and hope for the best. If you worried about every danger you would, as likely as not, end up in the madhouse.

By the time Jeremy had finished his paper, Arthur had figured out what to do. True to his promise he had kept the scheme to himself, but he had not been idle. He had looked up a few things in the library, and had a quiet discussion with Chang who was already in the know. Arthur was faced with a dilemma. The proposal might be ridiculed; it was offbeat and would probably lead to nothing, so if he was part of it he could lose credibility and become an object of derision.

On the other hand, if it came off, and he had not given his support, he would have no share in the glory and would look a fool as well.

Furthermore there was the danger that Jeremy would take the idea to another group and carry it off successfully; then Arthur would look even more of a fool. So often in science people are motivated more by the fear of failure or of missing the boat, than by a genuine expectation of success! In this climate, the few true believers who are confident of their path succeed in their persuasions, even when they are wrong!

Arthur read the proposal carefully and called Jeremy for a discussion.

"It is good. I think we should give it a whirl. I am all in favour, but the question is what is the best procedure? You have very kindly put my name on the paper as an author, but it's really your idea. So I think it would be better to put it to the committee under your own name. I will put in a note saying that the group will support it. That way you will get the credit from the start." Also, of course, if the idea was a flop Arthur would not get the blame; this way he reckoned to have the best of both worlds.

"Probably it will be best to wait until Jean-Marc has made his test with the krypton-83, and then you can report this in the proposal." Jeremy agreed, but he had another suggestion.

"We might keep it out of the committees for a while. Keep it to ourselves, and get some data on the side, perhaps using the test beam. It already has equipment for labelling particles according to their masses, and if we add a silicon detector to measure the energy loss in a thin layer we should get a confirmatory signal from anything new. Then there would be no doubt. If we use a niobium target when the PS team are testing the krypton, we might see something. Officially of course we would just be calibrating the silicon counter! What do you think?"

"Brilliant," said Arthur. "Much better to keep it quiet. These committee proposals get copied to labs all around the world. But it will need a lot of string pulling to get them to use a special target, and have time in the test beam at just the right moment."

"That is where you come in," said Jeremy, "with a few more bottles of bubbly."

"I'll see what I can do. You get hold of a counter and test it out. I have already put in an order for some niobium foils!" Arthur was pleased with the outcome. This way he would share in the spoils if it worked, but he would not look stupid if it failed.

"By the way," said Jeremy, "Let's keep this away from Bexler. We don't want him sticking his nose in and trying to claim the credit."

"Agreed. If only he were away from the lab . . . . on holiday . . . . or lecturing . . . . or something. Then it would be much easier."

18 Coffee anyone

While they were waiting for the krypton beam to look for high spin particles Jeremy and Arthur kept the idea to themselves. There were more tests to do with the muon fusion apparatus; one of the theorists had calculated that the 50:50 mixture of tritium and deuterium was not the optimum, it would be better with 30:70, so they wanted to try it. The beam came on at 8.50 and they started taking data with Viktor dominating the proceedings. There was a prepared programme of tests to make, in some kind of logical order. But Viktor preferred to think as he went along, and make his own order. It was not wrong, but rather irritating. Jeremy felt for the little piece of folded paper in his shirt pocket; a few grains of white powder. It was good to know it was there, but using it would be a jump into the unknown; over the precipice in a hang-glider, to land you know not where. On the other hand, this was a good occasion to try it, and he had to be out of the way for the big new test. It was now or never.

"Coffee everyone? I'll get it. How do you want it? Milk? Sugar?" He went along the corridor, put the money into the machine. Nobody was around. He slid the powder into the first cup and stirred it with an old spoon. Do not mix them up! Bexler liked it black, Marion white. He took the cups to the counting room; there was lump sugar in a jar, each one separately wrapped, collected over the years from various restaurants. He went back for his own cup.

"Your health," said Bexler; though a dominant man he believed in the common courtesies.

"And yours too," said Jeremy raising his cup. Bexler wiped his moustache and went on writing in the logbook. He drew little graphs on the squared paper with cogent remarks: 'good beam', 'unreliable point', 'accelerator unstable', and so on with arrows pointing to the corresponding data. Jeremy watched him carefully, but nothing particular happened. Perhaps it was innocuous: one of Jan's little yokes.

The range changer stopped working, so Jeremy went down to the floor to check it. Beam off, open the door, lights on, all that palaver. It was trivial, a dead fly had got jammed in the microswitch, he scraped it off with a screwdriver and called up Marion to test the drive again. When he got back to the counting room Viktor was not there, but he did not dare ask why. They took some more data.

After a quarter of an hour Bexler came in, walking slowly and looking rather green. Jeremy could see sweat on his forehead.

"I don't feel too bright . . . . Gastric attack! Phee . . . . phee . . . . phee . . . " he spluttered. Jeremy was terrified. Phenolphthalein, had he guessed it already?! "Phee . . . . phee . . . . .feels like phee . . . . phee . . . . fever."

"Sit down, take it easy, shall I call the infirmary?"

"No, no. No need for that." He sagged into a chair. "But I think I had better go home. I have been sick as a cow, and my stomach is all knotted up. I don't want to pass it on." That was decent of him. Viktor rummaged in his pocket for his keys, then got up.

"Terribly sorry." Then he shuffled off.

It was a worry. Would he make it to his car? Get home safely? He was living on his own, as far as they knew, so who would look after him? If he called a doctor, would he find out? The only thing to do was to get on with the experiment and hope for the best, but all day the anxiety kept coming back. Should he phone to see how he was? Or would that be suspicious? He did not usually take an interest in Bexler's personal problems. Was this different? In the evening he decided to call. The numbers of all members of the group were listed, in case they were needed in an emergency, and he had a copy at home. It rang for a long time. Perhaps he was OK, gone out to eat, or perhaps he was there but could not answer, because . . . . . because . . . . some of the possibilities were too awful to contemplate.

"Oui." The voice was cold and weak.

"It's Jeremy. How are you? I just thought I ought to call, after this morning I mean. Do you need any help?"

"Oh Jeremy. . . . . thank you. . . . no help. . . . the doctor came . . . . lots of pills, but they aren't doing any good . . . . feel like death . . . . thank you for calling." He rang off. It was not very encouraging. Or was it? This was presumably what he wanted? Should he contact Jan?

The next day, and the day after, there was no sign of Viktor, and he did not phone. Just no news at all. Perhaps the worst had happened, but Jeremy did not have the courage to call again. Keep a low profile, do not act suspicious. People often get sick, if they are not there the others just carry on. He reckoned that if Bexler was dead, someone at CERN would hear about it. If not, the longer he was away the better. Forget about it, and get on with the run. In fact the experiment was going well, and the group was in good spirits.

A week later Chris and Jeremy were sitting in the counting room waiting for the beam to start, at the same time tingling with anticipation and bored with hanging around. Jean-Marc was finally ready to try out the krypton. Test beams were available whenever the accelerator was running, and they had managed to borrow a silicon detector which would give signals of different heights for particles of different masses. They also had an ADC, the slang name for an electronic box that sorted the pulses according to their height and counted them into a computer memory. The whole outfit was connected to a PC, programmed to show a picture of the results. They had checked it all out a few days before under normal conditions.

The screen showed the expected sharp peaks at various masses, corresponding to the standard particles in the beam. Protons of mass 938 on the physicist's scale gave the largest pulses, and were by far the most numerous. They were the original protons from the accelerator, which had got scattered into the beam. Lower down came the kaons, pions and muons, and the smallest pulse of all came from electrons in the beam. This group was rather blurred due to a number of well-understood effects. Higher up they had seen a small bump at twice the proton mass, presumably due to deuterons, and further up still there were a few tritium and helium nuclei, fragments knocked off the tungsten target.

It all made sense, the gear was calibrated, and now they were waiting to see whether a krypton-83 beam hitting niobium would make any difference. Officially this was 'machine development': they had no control but just had to wait hopefully for a beam to come through.

Arthur had pulled the strings quite well. The krypton source had been tested the previous week. For the next development period he had persuaded them to mount two targets that could be interchanged, one the standard tungsten foil and the other niobium. It was lucky that this high spin element also had a high melting point; otherwise the intense heat liberated by the main beam could liquefy it and contaminate the accelerator.

The rest of the group knew what was going on, but so far they had not told Bexler. He was still away sick, or giving lectures in various places or generally enjoying Europe; nobody knew exactly and no one really cared. Except Jeremy. He worried about the outcome, but at the same time hoped he would not show. Ideally Viktor would be incapacitated, but not permanently! Now Arthur came into the counting room with Marion.

"How is it going? Got anything interesting?"

"Nix! No beam so far, but we are ready to go." Jeremy showed them the calibration curves.

"They are beautiful," said Arthur. "Nice sharp peaks." Then it was Chris.

"The proton is the marker, it checks the scale. I have programmed the PC to calculate the mass of anything else." He pushed a few keys, and messages came up on the computer screen asking for the data. "Enter the beam momentum," it ordered.

"It is 3.24 GeV/c," he said, and keyed in the figures. "Now it asks for the channel number for the protons, it's channel 496 as you can see. Now the channel for the particle you want to know. Let's take this peak at channel 241. I put that in, and press 'return' . . . . . and it gives you the mass in MeV . . . . as you see it is 105.6. That's the mass of the muon . . . .so it works."

Suddenly the loudspeaker blared. "Hullo T3, the beam is on. Niobium target, Krypton-83." They recognised the voice of Jean-Marc, who seemed to be taking a personal interest.

"Get back to the ADC program and press start," said Jeremy. He was excited, but there was no need to give the order; Chris was already doing the right things.

"I have cleared off the old junk, and made a fresh start." It was running, and they could see the data coming in fast.

"Are you on positive or negative beam," asked Arthur. "We want negative particles for catalysed fusion."

"Yes, but we thought we would start with positive to get the calibration protons; that is the only way to be sure."

"How long do we run for?"

"Ten minutes, usually. But you can watch the spectrum building up on the screen."

"Can we change the scale Chris? It is all completely flat." Chris attacked the keyboard again. Arthur sighed. Oh for one of those old fashioned 'kicksorters' where you just turned a knob to set the scale. So much quicker and easier. These days everything is done through the keyboard, and you have to be an expert to drive the thing.

Now they could see the counts building up in the different channels, the spots slowly moving upwards in irregular spurts, every 1.4 seconds there was a burst of activity as the accelerator spewed out its particles; then paused to pick up a new mouthful.

"Here are the protons," said Chris, "still in channel 496. And there is something coming in lower down."

"Ka's, pi's and mu's I expect," said Arthur. "What channels should they be in?"

"241, 265 and 372. The pi's and mu's are there all right, but I can't see many ka's."

"I think we ought to mark these channels," said Arthur. "Then we will know what we are looking at."

"If we stop a moment, I can get the computer to mark them," Chris offered.

"Don't stop for Christ's sake," cried Jeremy. "We need the data, and any moment the accelerator may crash."

"Let it run on," said Arthur. "It's not a problem." He got out a felt pen and drew little vertical marks on the glass screen, coinciding with the peaks. Then he wrote p for protons, and marked the others mu, pi, k. The peaks were all very narrow, only a few channels wide, which showed that the apparatus was working well. They scanned the screen hopefully for something else, and there seemed to be another bump a little above the kaons.

Just then Bexler walked in! So he was not dead, but he looked weak, thinner and a bit chastened.

"I was sick as hell. It was awful. I'm still on medication, and that doesn't do you any good."

"Geneva tummy," said Jeremy. "There's a lot of it about."

(In fact there are seven more packets in my drawer). Jeremy felt enormously relieved. Viktor was still alive, though a little run down, which was not a bad thing. He seemed to have no suspicions. So he had got away with it! Which meant . . . . he could do it again. Now in a sense he had Viktor under control, in his power even. But he had better be careful; once too often and the victim might catch on. On the other hand, if the first dose had been successful, maybe a double portion would keep him away for longer. He would only use it when really necessary, and he decided not to mention it to Jan. Out loud he added, "Better take it easy for a few days." But that was not on Viktor's agenda.

"I am bored with being at home. Work does me good. So what are you all up to?"

"We are just checking out a solid state detector," said Arthur. Bexler looked puzzled. "Help to label the muons in the next run." It was a feeble excuse: they both knew that the counting rates were far too high for that to work. Just then the ten minute run came to an end, and the computer beeped.

"I think we had better print the numbers," said Jeremy, "and get a graph as well." The printer rasped away, filling the pages with figures, ten channels to a line. Then it printed out an enlarged version of the picture on the screen. This time the channel numbers were printed underneath. Chris and Jeremy spread out the chart on a long table, and examined it critically, all the time looking for signs of a new bump.

"There is nothing much," said Jeremy, "except for this small bump at 372."

"That is where the kaons should be," said Chris. "At least they were there last week."

"In which case what is this large peak at 340?"

"Holy Cow!" said Chris. "Something must have changed. The calibration? No, the protons are OK! It could be a reflection in the electronics . . . . if a terminator has dropped off we could get a repeat of the proton pulse, but smaller and later." He thought it over. "I can check with the scope."

He peered into the hood on the fast oscilloscope. What the butler saw again? "It looks OK, but if I move this switch I get a reflection. Perhaps we should run again like this and see what it gives."

"No, no." Jeremy answered. "If we start putting in deliberate faults we will never finish, there are so many possibilities. Let's run again, and see if it is still there." They did and it was. Meanwhile they had got out the similar chart from the week before to see if Chris had made a mistake. Then the big peak had been at 372, and now it was at 340.

"The only thing that's supposed to have changed is the PS beam," said Jeremy, "and the target. So let's go back to where we were."

Arthur said, "It will take hours to go back to protons instead of krypton, but we can easily change the target." He called up the control room.

"Hullo, T3 here. Can we have the tungsten target in, instead of niobium?" Jean-Marc came back at once.

"Bien sur." And a moment later, "Niobium is out, now you have krypton-83 on tungsten." They started a new run, leaving everything else unchanged.

All this had a riveting effect on Viktor. "What's the idea?" he asked. It was tricky. Bexler would find out sooner or later what they were up to, and accuse them of being devious. Also if he spotted a new particle on the trace he would claim the discovery for his own. It would be better to tell him honestly. By now Arthur had this figured out.

"You will probably think we are crazy! Promise not to laugh." Viktor nodded, and Arthur went on. "There might be a family of high spin particles which can only be produced by colliding two high spin nuclei. So . . . . . we are just having a quick look."

"Krypton-83 and niobium both have high spin," added Jeremy, pleased to tell the maestro something he did not know. "Tungsten has spin zero, of course, apart from one isotope which has spin a half." Bexler said nothing, but they could see that his mind was whirling.

Meanwhile the new data were coming in. They could see at once that the peak at channel 340 that Arthur had marked on the screen and labelled 'k' was no longer there. Instead there was a strong peak at channel 372, where the kaons had been the week before. They printed the data and compared the two charts, one with the tungsten target, and the other with niobium. There was an obvious difference. Was the signal at 340 due to a new particle? None of them could really believe it; they were stunned. It was what they were looking for ..... but so unexpected.

"Shall I work out the masses?" asked Chris.

"No, keep the computer running. We must get more data."

"I think we should plot a graph," suggested Bexler. He looked round hopefully to see if anyone wanted to collaborate. Marion produced some graph paper, and they set out the known points, mass on one axis and channel number on the other. There were four points to plot, and then

Viktor rather skilfully with a pencil sketched in a smooth curve between them.

"There," he said, expecting instant admiration. "Now we can read off the mass corresponding to the peak at channel 340. It is . . . . . . 320 to 330 MeV. Incredible! That is three times as heavy as the mu and there is absolutely nothing known in this region." He threw down the pencil and leaned back, looking round for applause. If this was a discovery he clearly thought that he had made it himself.

"It could be an artefact! Two particles going through the counter at the same time would give the larger pulse. Say two mu's, or a mu and a pi. We could get that just by chance."

"No way. The rate is too low to give us two particles at a time. Not as often as that."

"Or we could get it from kaon decay near the counter, into a pi and a mu for example."

"There are not enough k's for that," said Jeremy. "And why should it only happen with the niobium target?" It was clear that this made all the difference and that was the clinching argument.

Bexler's mind was now in overdrive. "The crucial question is, are they there with a negative beam? Is it a hadron like the pion, or a lepton like the muon? And what is the lifetime?" They could guess that he wanted to use it for catalysed fusion, but he did not say so.

"OK let's go to negative beam," said Arthur. "We can do that ourselves, as we have control of the magnets.

"Right," said Chris. He and Marion twiddled the knobs on the magnet control panels, old-fashioned style. They got similar data, except that the proton peak had almost disappeared. There were just a few antiprotons in the negative beam in the corresponding channel. With the niobium target the peak at 340 was still there. Chris marked it 'JA' in large letters.

"I have an idea," said Jeremy. "Let's suppose it is a new particle, a jaon. We must find out more about it. For example, is it strongly interacting? If it is, then one or two metres of polythene will kill it. But if it goes through, then it's not absorbed by nuclei and it's the one we want."

"Brilliant suggestion!" Arthur looked at Marion. "Your French is pretty good. Would you mind going to the stores and see if they can cut off a bar of plexy or polythene. I guess we need about 10 centimetres diameter, and say one and a half metres long, two metres if you like. Give us a ring if there are any queries. Also here is the reference number for our experiment; you will have to put that on the stores slip." He scrawled on a scrap of paper, and smiled at her. "Many thanks!"

"Where are we going to put it?"

"Anywhere in the beam, but as far away from the counters as possible." They decided to slide it into the quadrupole lenses, where the beam came through the concrete wall.

"All the peaks will move of course," said Chris, "because of the energy loss in the bar. We will have to recalculate everything, maybe calibrate again with the tungsten target."

In the end Marion returned with more or less the right thing. They asked for the beam to be turned off, and went into the radiation area. The bar was propped up on wooden boxes, and they put a few lead bricks around it to stop particles sneaking past the edge. It was all rather makeshift. After another hour of running under various conditions, they had the data. The pions and the remaining kaons had been killed, but the muons and the new particles, (if they were particles), came through loud and clear. Bexler drew another graph showing the calibration of mass for the new conditions, and the mass of the newcomer came out the same as before. It was very encouraging. Best of all it behaved like a muon, so it would be good for fusion.

"Congratulations! An incredible idea!" Arthur offered his hand to Jeremy and shook it warmly. Everyone exchanged handshakes; Marion even got a kiss. They were all unbelievably excited, eyes shining with wonder; but at the same time they could not quite believe it. Surely there must be some snag. Jeremy looked at his watch, it was 5.30 pm.

"I think we might call Chang. He has been so encouraging. There is a good chance he will still be there."

Arthur said, "Good idea! But in that case we had better get to Hans Issinger; as the division leader he ought to hear it first. It is still not certain, of course, but very interesting." So Arthur called Hans, and Jeremy phoned Chang. Luckily they were both in, and said they would come over.

"How about trying a lower beam momentum," suggested Bexler. "If it is a particle it should still be there. We might also get an idea of the lifetime, because slower particles would have more time to decay." They halved the magnet currents, and tried again, with and without the plexy absorber. The five peaks were all there, mu, pi, k, protons and the 'new particles', all in the right places. Chris wrote JA against the new peak again, and added a large tick. Arthur called the control room.

"Is Jean-Marc there?"

"No, he has gone home."

"Do you have his home number?" They had of course, and Arthur dialled it: he wanted to put him in the picture as well.

A female French accent, "No, 'ee eez not 'ere. 'ee eez working late tonight." Something did not add up, but it was not for Arthur to pursue it. "It is not important," he said, and hung up politely. The last thing he wanted was to screw up Jean-Marc's personal life after he had been so helpful.

Chang and Hans arrived and were admiring the charts spread out on the table. Chris had run his computer program to calculate the masses and written them in against the peaks. It was all quite consistent, and with the tungsten target the new peak disappeared. Chang was explaining to Hans how the high spin particles were hard to make, and why they could have remained undiscovered for so long. "Also," he added, "the lifetime will be long."

"Are you going to publish?" he asked, and they started to discuss the possibilities.

"Isn't it a bit early?" said Arthur. "We do not want to make fools of ourselves!"

Publish and be damned, thought Jeremy. On the other hand, he had noticed that many people became famous by publishing wrong results, which they withdrew later. There is no bad publicity.

"You could make a tentative announcement," said Hans. "Just give the facts."

"Preliminary indications of a new leptonic particle," suggested Bexler.

Then there was the question of where to publish and in what form. Years ago everyone read 'Nature' which came out every week. A short letter to the editor would be printed immediately with no questions asked. You just said 'we have done this and seen that.' Now 'Nature' had gone out of fashion with physicists, nobody read it. Instead they sent letters to the 'Physical Review', but this had proved too slow and too ponderous: the editors wanted to referee the letters, check their quality, and this took time. Various 'letter journals' had been started for short communications (not more than four pages), but these had turned into papers in their own right, complete with abstract, references and acknowledgements; it still took two or three weeks to appear.

So for really hot news people had turned to press releases, typically if you were American, in the New York Times. It was not really professional, but it was important to register your priority, and how or where you did it was not that vital. Rumours would soon be flying round the world, and there were several labs in which the experiment could be duplicated rapidly. In the end they decided on a short paper to 'Physics Letters', a European journal published in Amsterdam.

"There is an editor in CERN," said Chang. "I am sure you could get into the next issue."

"At the same time," suggested Jeremy, "we might get a news item in the 'New Scientist'. That comes out every week, and there is a woman at CERN who writes for them."

"Whatever you do, be careful," said Hans. "As soon as this breaks there will be an enormous hobbob." It was a new word he had just learned, ('hubbub' would have been better), and he was proud of it. "I should like to see the paper first."

"Of course," said Arthur. He knew the CERN rule that every publication must be approved by the division leader, to make sure it was well founded, and to check the authorship. For anything sensational this was even more important.

"Let's pack it in," said Arthur. They were all tired, and they could have the beam again in the morning. "It's time for a drink." They went across to the cafeteria, Arthur and Hans ordered bottles of champagne, and they all celebrated.

True to form, Bexler tried to hog the limelight. He explained to Hans in great detail how to produce a high spin particle. Eventually Jeremy was provoked. "Look Viktor! This was not your idea, you did nothing to prepare the experiment, and you only turned up halfway through. So why don't you dry up?" Bexler looked daggers, but said nothing.

"It has been a great day," said Arthur. "We will think it over, and work on the paper tomorrow. Meanwhile I suggest we all keep this strictly confidential. Do not say a word to anyone!" On the way out Jeremy buttonholed him. "Do we have to share this with bombast Bexler? He only came in at the end."

"It's pretty tricky. He is a member of the group. But I'll see what I can do." They both realised that if Viktor had his name on the paper, he would claim most of the credit. It would be another case of 'Bexler et al.'

Before leaving CERN Jeremy rang Avelyn to tell her the news.

"Darling, how wonderful! Come round and we can celebrate."

"It's too late. I 'm sorry but I must get home. I just wanted you to know. I am so excited."

"It is marvellous, darling. Thank you. Congratulations, and . . . . lots of kisses."

Back with the family more bottles were opened, Clare was thrilled, perhaps all her loneliness would be worth it in the end, and the children were goggle-eyed. He tried to explain it to them.

"Will you be famous Daddy?"

"Who knows? Anyway, it's not sure yet. We may find some snag. And don't tell anyone! This is supposed to be a big secret until we decide to tell." But nothing can be kept secret for long!

In bed Jeremy started to wonder what to call the new object. If you discover a particle you have the right to name it. 'Jaon' was an obvious possibility, and it had the advantage of beginning with his initial. But there was already a meson called J, so it would be somewhat confusing, and therefore unacceptable to the mob. He would like to name it after his lovely mistress . . . . why not the 'Avelon'? But that would not make any kind of sense to the others and it would give the game away; Clare would be furious, and he would look uxorious. What was the corresponding word if you were not married? Besotted perhaps. Even if he was, it would be better not to parade his frailty in public.

19 The JAV

Next morning Jeremy got in early, but Chris was already there turning on the equipment.

"By the way," he said, "this new particle, what are you going to call it?"

Jeremy was looking at the charts from yesterday. The JA, with a big tick after it, caught his eye. JAV Jeremy-Avelyn!

"Why not JAVELIN?" It was perfect. Dynamic, forceful, and a tribute to them both.

"Yes, Ja. Let's see. We can call it 'Jav' for short," said Chris. "I like it. And we can think of it as Jeremy-Arthur. Yes, it's a good name." So 'Javelin' it became. Only later did they realise that V could stand for Viktor, and this would confirm his part in it. The semi-informed might think that it stood for Jeremy-Arthur-Viktor.

"I think we should try to stop the particles, and measure their range. And if that works we can watch them decay, measure the lifetime."

"OK," said Chris. In the little pocket book of data there were graphs showing range versus momentum for particles of different masses; the charts were rather tiny, but good enough.

"How low can we go in momentum with this beam?" asked Jeremy. "The lowest possible will make it easier." They figured that out, then looked up the range. It would be about one metre of aluminium. To measure the range in the standard way would need more counters, but they decided they could make do with what they had. If a particle stopped in the silicon detector it would give an extra large pulse, so this would be the signature they needed. All they had to do was vary the amount of aluminium in front until they got lots of large pulses. But how to vary the thickness of aluminium? If they stopped the beam each time and ran in and out with metal blocks, it would take forever; they needed some kind of remote control.

"We can easily borrow a beam scanner and put a metal wedge on it and drive it sideways, so that the beam goes through different thicknesses."

In fact there was a scanner in the adjoining area. They went and talked to the people there, and that was easy. Chris and Marion started to shift it, while Jeremy went to the workshop to get a wedge cut. He took with him a rough sketch.

"When do you want it?"

"Well, now . . . . . as soon as possible."

"First come, first served; that's our policy, saves argument." He looked at his lists. "You can have it in two weeks time."

"But . . . . that is useless. Can't you give us some priority? After all it is just a simple job."

"Not so simple. Machining that from a solid block will take half a day. If you want priority you will have to go to the division leader."

"Can I phone him from here?" Jeremy got through. Hans was still on a high over the discovery.

"Fantastic experiment! Are you writing the paper?"

"I am in the workshop trying to get a wedge cut, to measure the range. Nicoletti says it will take two weeks."

"Put him on the line." Dark bushy eyebrows were raised, Nicoletti was getting ready to protest; he held the receiver loosely and Jeremy could hear everything.

"Buon giorno, Nicoletti! Monsieur Partridge has top priority. Anything he wants, do it at once. If necessary drop everything else. Let me know if there is any difficulty." Contradicting his last phrase, he rang off: there was to be no discussion. Nicoletti gulped in amazement. Who was this young guy anyway?

"All right, we will start it right away. It will still take five hours to machine."

When Jeremy got back to the test beam, he found that Chris already had the scanner in place.

"We do not need the wedge. We have a stack of aluminium plates one centimetre thick, to make a staircase. We can use the drive to put different thicknesses in the beam. Friedl is just screwing it all together."

It was a better concept anyway, as the beam was rather wide; with the staircase all the particles would go through the same thickness. Jeremy rang Nicoletti to cancel the order. He tried to smooth ruffled feathers, but felt rather stupid.

"Chris, do you mind carrying on with Marion. You know what to do. I think I had better start drafting the paper; you'll both be authors of course. If we get some range information we can tack it on later." He went back to his office, not knowing that Bexler would turn up half an hour later, and participate in the tests.

Meanwhile Arthur was working on the difficult question of authorship. Viktor would want to sign. The only way he could think of keeping him out was for Jeremy to write the paper on his own; after all it was his idea. But that would be tough on the younger members of the group who had helped to set up the tests, especially Chris. In any case, it was Arthur's group, and he wanted some of the limelight too. Why not appeal to Bexler's sense of decency. He knocked on his door. Viktor was on the phone as usual.

"I am just cancelling my lecture in Antwerp on Friday, this is much more important." It was a pity; he was also giving up an amorous weekend with an entertaining Dutch girl, but Viktor had a well-developed sense of priorities and the Flemish frolic was not at the top of his list. The new particle would be the route to fusion, and he had to be at the centre of action. "We have made a wonderful discovery!" Arthur was a good diplomat, but he could see that the going would be tough.

"Can we discuss the authorship of the paper? First a matter of principle, not everyone in the group has to sign every paper, but only those who contribute to the particular piece of work. Now in this case you have just come back after two weeks away." He gave Viktor a copy of Jeremy's proposal document which had not yet gone to the committees. It would have been easier if it had but fortunately it was dated. He explained how they had discussed the scheme with Chang, and got the PS people to run with krypton. Then the idea of the niobium target, and setting up the silicon detector.

"All this happened while you were away, so we feel that you have not been a contributor to this work."

"Oh, but I have. I plotted the graphs, worked out the mass. Without me . ." He stopped, realising that 'without me you would never have done it' would not sound convincing this time.

"Then there is another important factor," Arthur continued. "You are already world famous; one more paper to your name will make no difference to your standing." Bexler shook his head. "Furthermore, because you are famous, if your name is on the paper, you will get the credit. People will think it was primarily your work. On the other hand, Jeremy and the others, including me, we are almost unknown. We need to publish and get our names before the public. So I guess I am saying, why not do the decent thing, stand down on this one, and let us take the credit?"

It was a tactical mistake. Viktor did not have a sense of decency; his whole career had been built on its absence. Letting Jeremy take the credit was totally unacceptable. Viktor thought for a minute calculating the pros and cons. Then he said firmly,

"I am a member of the group. I participated in the run. I plotted the data. I should sign the paper."

"Well, I don't think that's right. We will put the paper to Hans without your name."

Bexler looked furious. As a precaution Arthur went to see Hans immediately. The division leader was beaming.

"Excellent work! Excellent work! I have just told Nicoletti to give you top priority in the workshop. Now we must see what else you need, a better beam, more time, reschedule the PS, I will talk to the coordinator."

"Thank you, thank you. We will need a little time to work out how to proceed. I think the first thing is to get out a quick publication." Hans nodded.

"Yes, definitely."

"But we have a slight problem."

"Problem? The results are still OK, I hope."

"Oh yes, it is still looking good. The problem is the authorship. Who is going to sign? The difficulty is Viktor: he was not really in on it."

"I saw him there."

"Yes, but he had only just arrived, and now he wants to sign." Arthur carefully went through the whole story, and handed him a copy of Jeremy's proposal.

"I know you were not in the picture. Sorry about that. The idea seemed so way-out. We just thought we could make a rough test before bringing it to the committee."

Hans nodded. "This must be seen as a CERN discovery, another first for Europe. As Bexler is well known, people will tend to give him the credit. If his contribution was small, it would be better to leave him out. How much time did he spend on the experiment?"

"He was not involved in the planning. He did not help with the apparatus. He turned up half-way through the tests, just after we had seen the new bump."

"I agree," said Hans. "Send me the paper without him. I will approve. No doubt Viktor will scream, but what's new about that? We must keep the credit."

"Do you realise that this might lead to catalysed fusion?" Hans clearly had not thought about it. "It is a massive negative particle, probably of high spin and therefore long-lived."

"Mein Gott! It is very big then. Let's get the paper off as soon as possible."

Arthur went to tell Jeremy of Hans' decision. But they had no conception of Bexler's cunning. Jeremy had already made some progress with the report. 'Physics Letters' would prefer a page or two, so he took the opportunity to set out the thinking that had led to the experiment. He had already given the arguments and references in his draft proposal. On the computer it was only a matter of moments to cut and paste all this into a new document. Then he added a description of the apparatus, not forgetting the krypton-83 beam and the interchangeable niobium-tungsten target for which he gave credit to the accelerator team. They were warmly thanked at the end. Finally the graphs of the peaks taken in various conditions, with the tungsten and niobium targets compared on the same figure. This was followed with a discussion of the interpretation, various ifs and buts, a tentative suggestion that it might be high spin and therefore long-lived. He suggested the name, javelin.

The title was "Evidence for a new particle of mass 320 MeV" and he put all the group except Viktor as authors. Bexler got thanked for useful discussions of the data, and Chang and Hans (the latter really out of politeness) for their warm encouragement. By early afternoon it was all finished bar the figures; he ripped off a copy and gave it to Arthur. Arthur approved except for the speculations at the end.

"You have already mentioned high spin in the introduction, so this has been covered, no one can come in with that suggestion as their own idea. Better not to claim anything that we do not know. Stick to the facts, and we will be on safe ground. And leave out the authors for the moment, we will put them in later."

After making the changes, they went down to the test beam to show the others. They found Viktor, Chris and Marion beavering away at some new data in perfect harmony.

"We have got the range, and it checks out perfectly," said Chris with elation. "Quite a high rate of stops in the detector."

"Here is the range curve." Bexler held up his latest graph with an impressive peak. "Your wedge idea was not very good; Chris has set up an aluminium staircase with a few sheets, very simple, and it works perfectly." It was typical Bexler; in one move he put down his perceived rival, and buttered up the juniors.

"Then instead of using several counters we are just looking for large pulses in the silicon." He had a knack of giving you back your own ideas, as if he had thought of them himself; worse still he explained them as something new, which you were supposed to admire. Perhaps he was just naively carried away by his enthusiasm for science, but Jeremy always felt that he was being got at. It was hard to control his reactions. Yet anything he could say would only appear childish and egocentric. He tried to ignore the darts, but could not help glowering.

"Nice work," said Arthur. "This is an important confirmation. Now I think we can publish with confidence."

They wanted to discuss the paper, but it was awkward with Viktor there. He was entrenched, taking data, making friends with the young. They could hardly go away and leave him in charge, so the only thing to do was to stay and join in. Arthur kept the draft in his pocket, and Chris took them through the day's data.

"It's enough I think," said Arthur. "Do we need any more?" He meant for the paper, but it was a mistake.

"The next step is to look for the decay, measure the lifetime. We have about 500 stops per minute. We need to set up some delayed time gates and see if the particle breaks up into anything detectable." Viktor was telling them what to do, and how to do it, though it was obvious anyway. Luckily, although he was quick on the principles, he had no competence in electronics. Someone else would have to set up the gear.

"Perhaps we should take a break," said Arthur. "How about some coffee or tea in the snack room. Then we can relax and make some plans. Also we want to discuss the paper."

The PS coffee bar was a favourite afternoon rendezvous, where a rather jolly lady dispensed cups of not too poisonous liquid (don't call it coffee, just a drink) and a succulent choice of pastries. The warm fluid and gelatinous carbohydrate perfused them with bonhomie. Arthur decided to pass out copies of the draft paper, without the authors' names, and they all read it quietly and with apparent satisfaction. Suddenly Bexler went into orbit.

"What's this at the end? Why do I get an acknowledgement?" Arthur replied calmly,

"We want to thank you for your help, plotting graphs and so on."

"But you cannot acknowledge an author!"

"As I have already explained, you did not contribute to the design, planning or setting up. So you are not an author. Hans agrees." Bexler went purple.

"Then why am I wasting my time helping you characters? This is outrageous. I have been slaving away analysing the data, and all you offer me is an acknowledgement. It's monstrous!" Then he added calmly and with sinister emphasis, "I am going to protest!" and stalked out.

The juniors looked embarrassed. They got on well with the visitor who, feeling no rivalry, treated them courteously; and they enjoyed his ready flow of anecdote. They did not know which side to take in this argument.

Jeremy and Arthur breathed sighs of relief, and got down to discussing the paper with the group. They made a few changes, and added a new paragraph about the range measurement. It all hung together rather well. At the end they decided to mention the possible application to catalysed fusion. 'If this new particle turns out to be long-lived, it may play a role in catalysed fusion'. The main point was to show that they were aware of it, so that no one else could claim the credit. Arthur asked Chris and Marion to get the diagrams drawn and printed up nicely; they could do that on the Mac. By tomorrow morning the paper would be ready.

There were no further problems. Hans Issinger called all the authors into his office, and asked if they were sure of the results. "No problem with the authorship? I see that Viktor has a warm acknowledgement. Let us hope that satisfies him." He looked round, but there was no comment. "Have you showed it to Blattman?" Arthur shook his head. "Then let us get him round." He was referring to the CERN representative on the editorial board of 'Physics Letters'; the easy way to get the paper accepted was through him.

When Blattman read the paper his eyes were rolling in amazement. "This is incredible. How is it possible we missed it for so long? High spin, you say, and heavy nuclei as target and projectile may be essential. Why didn't we think of that before?"

"How soon can you get it published?" asked Hans.

"Right away. This is so important. Catalysed fusion! My goodness, we are setting the world on fire with this paper." Everybody looked happy. Blattman was thinking.

"Let's see. The next issue goes to print tomorrow. I will phone Groezinger. If he agrees I could fax the paper to North-Holland, and it will be published next week." Then he added, "Much better than the New York Times. We are a real journal."

"Do you have some copies?" asked Hans. "As this is so important I think I should give a copy to the DG. And you will give one to Chang, of course. Then we should arrange a seminar; I will speak to the organiser."

Over lunch they discussed the next step; to detect the decay products of the javelin. If this could be done, the distribution of decays in time would show how long it lived. If it lasted long enough the fusion would certainly work. They were off-site, eating in a little restaurant in Satigny, and putting away an appropriate amount of Fendant du Valais. It was a time to relax, celebrate, toast the talents of the team and generally appreciate each other.

The afternoon was well advanced when Arthur got back to his office. He found a note from Hans. It was brief. "The DG want to see us, please call when you come in."

In Michel's office they sat in easy chairs around a circular glass topped coffee table. The DG came across from his desk with the paper in his hand. He smiled warmly.

"If this is true . . . . many congratulations!" Then he looked at Arthur intently. "Are you sure? We do not want to make fools of ourselves!"

"Look at the data," said Arthur. "It speaks for itself."

"These are genuine results? You have not cooked the figures?"

"Absolutely not! We have plotted the points automatically, as they came out of the memory. I do not want to look a fool either. It is all quite consistent and reproducible." Michel seemed satisfied.

"Now, what about Bexler? He wants his name on the paper. He claims he helped with the work. Why is he not an author?"

They went through the whole story again, and Michel listened sympathetically. Then he said,

"I know what Bexler is like. But the trouble is, he has a lot of influence. He is an important figure in America, and he is lecturing all over Europe at present. We do not want to antagonise him." It is blackmail, thought Arthur.

"I understand that it was not his idea, and he did not help with the preparation. But he did participate in the data collection and analysis?"

"Yes, but he only came in half way through. By then we had already seen the particle."

"But he did participate, some of the time?" Arthur nodded. "Then I think he has a case. It is normal to include those who have helped with the data, even if only partly." The DG looked at Hans and then back at Arthur.

"We are in the middle of some important negotiations with the States to get money for the big accelerator. It would be bad if they turned sour. I would appreciate it if you would include him as an author."

He had put it politely, but they both knew that there was no point in arguing. At CERN only a fool crosses swords with the DG. But Arthur tried to save something from the ruins.

"The trouble is that his name will come first. Then this great discovery will always be referred to as Bexler et al. CERN will not get its proper amount of credit, people will think we could only do it if he was helping." Michel nodded.

"It was Jeremy's idea, and he pushed it through. If Viktor has to be an author, then I think we should put his name at the end; and Jeremy should come first. If that is agreed, then I will accept it."

"D'accord!" said Michel. For him the matter was closed. "Let me know if there are any problems."

Outside the DG's office Arthur said to Hans,

"With any luck it will be too late."

"Fred said they go to press tomorrow," answered Hans, "I will have to call him." Blattman was not pleased. He had already pulled strings to get the paper out quickly, and now more hassle would be needed to change the authors. But, yes, they could do it. So that was how it turned out.

Once Viktor had his name on the paper he was free to refer to the discovery as 'our experiment'. He already had many lecturing engagements, and as usual he spoke of the latest work on the frontiers of physics; indeed he was expected to do so. The titles were neutral in their attribution, 'New heavy particle', 'New long-lived lepton', 'High spin long-lived particle', 'New particle, possibilities for catalysed fusion'. But he showed himself prominent among the list of authors, in alphabetical order, why not, and his phrases were all of the form: we thought, we tried, we did, we found. The speculations on future use for catalysed fusion came across as the profound thoughts of Viktor A. Bexler.

It was all very natural, understandable and inevitable, given the circumstance of a famous man visiting a little known group, and given his character. But Viktor's strong emotions and personal animosities subconsciously twisted his objectivity. He always appeared to be leaning over backwards to acknowledge the role of the CERN team and to give credit where credit was due: Arthur as group leader was mentioned a good deal more than Jeremy. But the general impression was that Bexler had been a key player.

There is a universal rule of group dynamics, when two or three are gathered together to discuss a problem. The group, if it is working well, is greater than the sum of its parts. One idea triggers another, and from the dynamic interaction of several enthusiasts a new concept is born. The group arrives at a destination which no participant would have reached on his own. That is how it should be, and frequently is. But so often afterwards, each member thinks that he had the key idea. The egocentric "I" puffs itself up. "I asked the essential question. I found the solution." Or to put it more crudely, "IT WAS MY IDEA!" So when the excitement has died down, the members of a once friendly and dynamic group fall out with each other, as each one claims the essential insight. In reality the group is greater than the sum of its parts and the credit should go to the group. Bexler was just an extreme example of a common phenomenon

Viktor's recovery was rapid and he was soon phoning Avelyn again. He tried for her sympathy, but got no dice.

"How is the beautiful Fru Olbers? I have been sick, very sick; some Geneva tummy bug. It was awful."

"It's probably Aids. That's one of the first symptoms, a gastric attack. It means that the virus is getting into an active phase. So you had better keep clear of me. I don't want to get it!"

Afterwards she mentioned the conversation to Jan.

"What rubbish! The whole point of Aids is that you get an infection, but the body doesn't react, the immune system isn't working. An acute gastric attack is just the reverse."

"I only said it to tease him! Don't you appreciate my jokes?" So Jan now realised that Jeremy had carried out his plan, and he wondered how much further it would go.

20 Javelin fever

Jeremy gave a talk in the large CERN auditorium the following week. It was packed out, and they gave him a standing ovation. The news hit the Geneva papers, and then the big international dailies; Christine wrote a column for the 'New Scientist', so CERN's discovery was soon well known.

The announcement of the new particle was greeted with universal amazement and excitement. If it had come from a small university it might have been treated with scepticism, but CERN had a reputation which carried authority. Furthermore, the evidence presented was convincing, and the case nicely understated. Everyone scrambled to confirm the discovery and find out more about the new object; but not many laboratories had the equipment for accelerating heavy atoms. In any case it took some time to set up the krypton source, the niobium target and the appropriate detectors. Brookhaven National Laboratory on Long Island got there first, closely followed by the Gesellschaft für Schwerionenforschungen near Darmstadt.

The catalysed fusion experts immediately recognised the potential, and tried to get in on the act. But they were in other laboratories where no heavy ions were available. Only in CERN was the equipment for catalysed fusion coexisting with the means for making the long-lived lepton.

In CERN itself several groups jumped on the escalator. Within two days of Jeremy's lecture, proposals for follow-up experiments had landed on Hans' desk, with copies to Arthur, Jeremy and the appropriate committee. Ironically Arthur and Jeremy's proposal had still not been tabled officially. Rather than have a mad scramble, Hans Issinger organised a day's discussion on the way ahead. Theorists speculated on the properties and significance and came out with a string of possible scenarios; and the experimentalists put forward ways of adapting their existing equipment to understand how the javelin was produced, to measure its spin, lifetime, decay, mass and all the other imaginable attributes. Others, primarily Arthur and Jeremy, proposed to put it to work as a fusion catalyst.

As usual everyone claimed, 'My idea is best', but on the whole the atmosphere was friendly and constructive. They all realised that CERN was ahead on this one, and they wanted to go fast and stay ahead. This meant working together in collaboration. Inside CERN Jeremy and Arthur's role as originators was clearly acknowledged, and Viktor was seen as peripheral. The meeting ended with fairly general agreement to promote three fundamental experiments on the properties of the javelin, while Arthur's team would pursue catalysed fusion with all speed.

The PS now ran most of the time with the krypton beam and the results came in thick and fast. The javelin turned out to be only the lightest of a whole family of high spin particles, and there was plenty of work in unravelling their relationships. The lifetime was measured, and turned out to be 4.2 milliseconds, 2000 times longer than the muon. The decays were analysed in detail, and this led to a mass determination of 317 MeV, an ideal value for the fusion process. The theorists argued about how many fusions there would be per javelin, and how fast they would go, but they all agreed that it would be far more efficient than the muon.

The events of the next few months were burned indelibly into Jeremy's brain. It was all very well to discover a new particle, perfect for catalysing fusion, but you still had to show that it worked. Other teams in other countries would be racing for the same goal.

"We have a head start," said Arthur. "But if we goof up, make some silly mistake, have an accident, or take too long to set it up, then the others will get there first."

So it needed careful planning and attention to detail. They had to find some space near the PS, design an intense beam of javelins, move the equipment, set up the hydrogen safety systems, and so on. It was easy to make the list, but it added up to a lot of sheer drudgery. Fortunately they had the full support of the management, and many new people were volunteering to help. Unfortunately one of them was Bexler who wanted to call the shots himself. At the same time Jeremy was trying to see Avelyn as often as possible, keep Clare happy, make publicity for his new discovery and occasionally have a conversation with his children. To crown it all, in October Arthur had to move back to Oxford. He would keep in close touch, and come back to CERN on visits as much as possible; but duty calls, students had to be taught and his salary came from the university.

Hans ruled that they must have a group leader who was full time in CERN, especially for this experiment which was now in the international limelight. Bexler lobbied with Hans and Michel to take over the leadership himself; after all he had the experience and trotted out a long list of Jeremy's failings. There was a good deal of string pulling and discussion behind the scenes with Arthur and others. Luckily the directors had some perception of Viktor's talent for creating discord; they appreciated Jeremy's contribution and wanted to keep the group firmly European.

So Jeremy got the job and a rise in pay. With it came customs privileges, diplomatic status, quarter price petrol, duty free grog from a special supplier in Basel, and best of all, immunity from fines for small peccadilloes such as parking offences. Now instead of a ticket, he would find a polite note on his car asking him to kindly park somewhere else in future. It was intoxicating, and for the first time Jeremy felt important; but it did not speed the experiment.

Viktor was not pleased, and made life difficult for the new group leader. On the other hand he was as keen as any to press ahead with the work. Sabotaging the preparations was not in his interest; trying to show his superiority was. He had lots of useful suggestions, but instead of talking them over quietly with Jeremy, he would wait until the weekly planning meeting, and then raise them as red herrings to the current discussion. When Arthur was present he would suavely control Viktor with a

"Great idea Viktor! I am sure we need time to think about it. Perhaps at the end of the meeting you could explain it in more detail." But by the end of the meeting it would almost be time for lunch, and no one wanted to hang around. With Jeremy in the chair, Viktor was more argumentative.

The old bubble chamber building near the PS was allocated to the experiment. A beam line already existed, and could easily be renovated. The hall had all the installations needed for hydrogen safety, and massive concrete shielding. Access was through a huge concrete sliding door, which slowly creaked across on rollers, the 'nutcracker' Chris called it. Inside the cavern was a false floor made of metal grills on which they had to walk. You saw through it to the empty cellar below. In this eerie chamber metal clanked disconcertingly whenever one moved, and the semi-transparent floor was frightening. But after a few minutes you realised that it was safe and walked on it quite normally, ignoring the echoes rattling round the room.

They were shown round the building by a PS engineer. Power points, connector boxes for high current magnets, plug boards taking signals up to the control room, intercom to talk to the PS operators or your own group, and so on. There was a panic button, always illuminated, which would cut the beam; if anyone accidentally got stuck in the room with the door shut, all they had to do was press it. A display panel showed whether the PS was running and whether the beam stopper was open; a red light meant that the beam was on, but you should never see it as sharing a room with the particles would endanger your health. The same display was duplicated in the counting room where it was more useful.

"Now safety procedures." said Karl. "The light switch is inside the door. The convention we all use is that the last person out turns off the light. (That is a clear warning to anybody who might be left inside; he should shout). Then come out and shut the concrete door. It won't shut if the light is on." He demonstrated.

"Also you have to keep your finger on the button while the door is moving; then if anyone tries to come through the crack you will see him . . . . or her, of course, it might be a her." He glanced at Marion. Then he drew attention to a gadget in the ceiling, half way along the narrow corridor between the moving door and the wall.

"A final safety feature. Up there is an infrared photocell. It detects the warmth of the body; so if anyone is in the way the door will stop. I'll show you. It's a good idea to test it occasionally." He asked Marion to keep her finger on the button so that the door slowly, slowly creaked towards the wall. When there was about one metre space Karl boldly walked into the shrinking corridor, and the movement stopped at once.

"Double safety! First someone has to keep the button pressed, and they are assumed to be watching. Secondly, if anyone tries to come through, the heat of the body will be picked up by the sensor and stop the motion.

The particles from the niobium target sprayed out in all directions. In the test beam no special arrangements were made for collecting them, so the number of particles reaching the apparatus was quite low. Now they had powerful lenses to gather up the javelins and focus them onto their equipment. As a result they should have millions per second, and would be able to see in much more detail exactly what happened when they were stopped in the hydrogen.

Jeremy was keen to make the big leap forward in one gigantic stride. Pour javelins into the deuterium-tritium mixture, and look immediately for evidence of fusion; a large flux of 14 MeV neutrons would prove that it was working. If they got a signal they could publish, and then go back to clear up the detail. Other groups in the States would be trying to catch up, and might get there first; this was the way to keep ahead.

Others in the group were more cautious. Bexler, in particular with his greater experience, argued that they must proceed step-by-step, making sure that they understood what was happening at each stage. Perhaps the great stride forward would work, but probably they would flounder and would not know what had gone wrong. The slow way could be faster in the end, and would give lots of scientific data en route. First they had to check out the new beam, find out how many javelins they had, re-measure the range, optimise the stopping rate and tune up the detectors. Then they could put in the hydrogen bottle, and go from there.

21 The concrete door

Setting up the experiment invariably meant many trips to the experimental floor. Each time something had to be changed they had to turn off the beam, go down the stairs, follow the long corridors, then push the button to open the concrete door. This was heavy and it moved very slowly. When the crack was wide enough to get through you could stop the motion, go in and do your work. Coming back you remembered to turn off the light, squeeze through the door, then keep your finger on the 'close' button while it slowly crawled shut. Once this was accomplished you could shout into the intercom, 'OK, beam on, I am coming up', or some such message. When the door was shut the beam could come on, but you still wasted a couple of minutes walking back to the counting room. Often you would only need the beam for a minute before going down again, so it was all rather time consuming. Viktor, in particular, found these delays irritating, especially when he was on shift in the middle of the night.

"It's crazy, waiting here with my hand on the button. There's no one around. If only the door could be set to close itself, we could get back to the counting room and get ready to start. Then as soon as we have beam we take the data. These goddamn bureaucratic rules! They make me sick."

One morning Bexler got hold of Chris. "Bring a few tools. I would like you to help me do some research on this door." He had found a metal plate let into the wall near the door, and guessed that this might cover the control circuits. Chris took out the four screws to reveal several plug-in modules and a maze of wires. There were a few switches and knobs on the panels.

"This must be it," said Viktor. "What do you think?"

"Pretty baffling. I don't think we should play around with the settings: it might screw up completely."

"If it does we just call up maintenance."

Chris peered inside the box, and found a folded piece of paper tucked into a corner. They spread out the diagram and tried to follow the wiring. It was a challenge, a puzzle to be solved.

“There is a relay here,” said Chris, “which looks as if it would keep the door moving. But this switch stops it. Maybe if SW3 was moved to ‘ON’ it would do the trick.” They looked again at the panels.

“This looks like SW3, and it seems to be off.”

“Flick it over,” said Bexler. “Let’s see what happens.”

“I don’t think we should. Why not call the engineer and ask him to do it.”

“Nah, give it a go. It’s just an experiment.” Viktor slid the switch across, then pushed the red ‘close’ button on the door. He took his finger off, and the door kept moving.

“There you are!”

“Careful, will it ever stop?” yelled Chris. Viktor calmly pressed the green ‘stop’ button.

“It’s OK.”

They made a few more checks; the end contact still switched the motor off when the door was closed, and the infra-red detector still stopped it moving.

“It makes more sense this way; and it’s still perfectly safe. I think we should leave it like this.”

Chris was more doubtful. Bexler looked at him steadily for a while: then picked up the screwdriver and put the cover back. He spat on the crack and rubbed some dirt around it.

“We'll tell the team that the door has been modified.”

“What about other people who might use the room?”

“They can keep their fingers on the button if they want. Anyway, it’s perfectly safe.” Viktor pushed the ‘close’ button, waited until the gap was quite narrow, and walked into it. The door stopped.

“I am hot, you see. Even the stones recognise it!” He slapped the concrete in a gesture of camaraderie. He was grinning like a small boy who has just learned to ride a bicycle.

Rumours about the extra deuterium in rats and its possible connection with longevity were soon flying around CERN. Viktor always had his ear to the ground and soon got to hear of it.

“We can make money out of this,” he said to Jeremy.

“How come?”

"Heavy water, the elixir of youth! We can sell it in tins and get rich."

"Easier said than done."

The grinning face came right up to Jeremy's nose with the whiskers twitching. "Just wait and see."

Viktor had his contacts in Wall Street and Chicago. The internet and the transatlantic phone lines were soon alive with messages. His associates raised capital and set up the "Viktoria Water Company", which owned a number of patents and trademarks on all conceivable permutations of deuterium, heavy water, deuterated water, etcetera. Before long the TV hype began, with stories about the long-living rats, interviews with scientists and slogans such as 'heavy water keeps you young', 'deuterium for your health' and so on. The bottles and tins of water were soon available everywhere, sportsmen were suborned to drink it and they all carried the message in prominent letters 'Contains HEAVY water'. The American FDA were not interested in water; it was beyond their scope.

22 Ginger

One evening Jeremy felt restless; he needed some distraction. Clare was working with her rats, and Avelyn was not available. The children seemed settled, so he left a note and drove into town; just to wander round and see the sights. The river on a late summer's night was beautiful, quietly reflecting the many coloured lights. One of the glories of Geneva was that no flashing signs were allowed. The 'jet d'eau' was still running, the floodlit white plume reaching up far into the sky. Happy people wandered about, going nowhere in particular, and he was happy to be part of it.

Jeremy crossed the narrow pedestrian bridge over the Rhône, and cut through the old arched tower to Grand Passage and Place Molard. Then, just for fun, he strolled along the Rue Neuve towards Place Longemalle. He did not need a tart, far from it, but it was amusing to see what was on offer, and pleasant to be ogled by long-thighed damsels in block heels whispering words of love. The selection was not particularly appealing, he thought, until his eye fell upon something totally unexpected. Leaning nervously against a doorway was an attractive pair of bare legs, the hands on the hips were drawing the short skirt even shorter, but the face was unmistakably familiar. He crossed the street and went up to her.

"Ginger, whatever are you doing here?" It was the young Canadian wife of his division leader! She had no need to 'round out the end of the month' as the Swiss so euphemistically put it, so what on earth was going on? Ginger blushed scarlet, gulped, and gave him a wild look.

"Oh hullo Jeremy! Are you looking for action?"

"No, not really, just going for a stroll."

"To admire the view?"

"Yes. Well, no." He hesitated. "Ginger, you shouldn't really be in this street. I mean, not standing around like that. Someone might think . . . . I mean . . . . get the wrong idea." She looked at him straight, wide eyed.

"You mean someone might pick me up?"

"Yes . . . . well . . . . worse than that. They might think you were one of them." He jerked his head along the street. "You know, for sale!"

"Jeremy, perhaps that's what I want." He looked round alarmed. This was not the place to be observed chatting to a blond. Suppose someone from CERN was passing by. He should move on, but he could hardly leave Ginger here, especially in this crazy mood. Sir Galahad to the rescue, maidens in distress, Saint George and the Dragon. So much the better if they were young, lissom and lightly clad. The familiar archetypes raced across his mind, and subconsciously oriented his behaviour.

"Come on, let's have a coffee or something?"

"I might prefer the something."

"Come on. Let's get moving." He led her by the hand along the street, through Place Longemalle, past the floral clock and into the park by the lake. Once they were out of that area, Jeremy felt more relaxed.

There was a steamer tied up, with music and refreshments. She sat opposite him, ordered a whisky and reached a hand across the table.

"Ginger, I am not picking you up. I am rescuing you! You just can't stand around in that gear, especially on that street. What if someone saw you?"

"Shut up Jeremy, and listen to me." She fixed him with her large hazel eyes. "Hans has gone off for the weekend. Officially he is mountaineering, so conveniently I have to stay behind. But I happen to know that he is taking a girl, Annabelle! She just gives herself to anyone who comes along . . . . the CERN whore! So . . . . . I thought I'd get my own back . . . . by doing the same. I feel like a delicious session in bed with someone, and if they want to pay me for it so much the better! How much do you think I should charge?"

"It's a difficult question. I am afraid I don't know the going rate. If you charge too little you get the riff-raff. But if you are too high, then you won't get any action. It must depend on how desperate you feel. Anyway, you are not going back there, the other girls could beat you up, they all have their territory. And someone might see you, I mean someone you know."

In fact, she had already been noticed. And not only her, but also Jeremy. He was not the only physicist passing along the Rue Neuve that evening. What the spectator was looking for in this area is quite irrelevant. As a scientist he would draw conclusions from his observations, but he could easily misinterpret the facts. An unscrupulous observer might even distort the information to his own advantage, and in the long run the consequences would be grave.

"I don't need to go back there do I, because I've found you?" Ginger smiled at him enthusiastically and took his hand. This was rather embarrassing. Ginger was a nice girl, lovely really, and this evening, with her theatrical make up, she looked particularly attractive. She had cleared the decks for action, and it could be amusing. But making it with his boss's wife was not on Jeremy's agenda. What happened after Saint George had slain the dragon? The books never said. He could play for time, cool her down and get her to go home.

"I don't think I could afford it."

"Oh nonsense, Jeremy. I think in your case we might negotiate an introductory offer. A free ride shall we say? Let's dance!" The music on the open deck was dreamy in the night air. She clung to him, moving expertly.

"I will make it good for you. The apartment is just up the road, by the Parc des Eaux Vives. Or do you want me to go back on the street?" It was a dilemma. What should he do? What would Hans think? They had another drink, then another dance, in the middle of which a familiar voice greeted them. It was Ivan, dancing with Juliet, and looking more tanned and vigorous than ever. They joined them at the same table, and did not seem at all surprised to find Jeremy and Ginger together. They danced in various combinations, and drank some more. Then Ginger dropped hints about going home and Jeremy hesitated, unsure what was involved. Ivan gallantly chimed in.

"If it's out of your way, Jeremy, we could easily see Ginger home. It's no problem, what do you think Juliet?" His wife agreed.

"Oui, avec nous. Bonne idée!" Yes, come with us, good idea. So Jeremy had missed the boat, a golden opportunity to enjoy a new experience. Suddenly he felt curious. How would she have been? How would she kiss? How would she feel, and above all how would she react? Everyone was different, inside as well as out, and as the opportunity receded so did his inhibitions. Ivan escorted Ginger off the boat and Jeremy could picture him giving her the full treatment, with Juliet no doubt participating in some ecstatic trilogy. He cursed himself for a fool, but it was impossible to backtrack. Then Juliet said,

"Why don't we all come back to our place? I have a bottle always in the frigo. Some music, we could have a good time, yes?" Juliet clearly knew the score, and probably found a quartet more exciting than a trio. In the apartment she produced a box of chocolates.

"I think we need some resuscitation, how do you say it, bouche à bouche?" She took a chocolate in her teeth and passed it to Jeremy, mouth to mouth.

"Now you pass it on to Ginger. She took it, gingerly, but seemed eager to pass it on to Ivan. After a few rounds of this, the sweets became less important than the sweet receptacles, but Juliet asked Ginger to help her get the glasses from the kitchen. There was a good deal of giggling and whispering, and when they returned with the drink they were bare footed. Ivan and Jeremy were relaxing, but the girls stayed on their feet popping the cork, serving the wine, smiling and passing round the niblets.

Juliet turned up the music, turned down the lights, and switched on a projector which threw changing coloured patterns across the room. Then they started to dance, twirling about in front of the men, flicking their skirts about and generally going wild. It soon became apparent that they had removed their underwear, as first a bare hip was revealed, then a buttock and finally flickering glances of the whole thing. In the end they were whirling around, more or less bare from the waist down, but in the half light of flickering patterns projected on their bodies it was hard to see what was what.

The music stopped, and Ginger had to top up the men's glasses. Ivan had his hand up her skirt and there was no objection. When his turn came, Jeremy thought he should follow suit, why not? A dreamy foxtrot, and Juliet was inviting him to dance. Needless to say she was a beautiful dancer. She held herself close, and Jeremy moved his hand down to appreciate the roundness of her hips, her muscles moving under his fingers. In the semi-darkness he noticed Ivan and Ginger obviously enjoying each other.

"Wait," cried Juliet. "We have not finished the entertainment." She made the men sit down, and under the dim flickering lights the girls slowly removed the rest of their garments. Juliet certainly had a harmonious body, petite but in perfect proportion, an ultra-slim waist and round swelling haunches; Leonardo's Leda would be the nearest thing, and for a moment Jeremy could see some merit in being a swan. Take me to your Leda! She was bronzed all over without a line anywhere. In contrast the Canadian girl was taller with long coltish legs, and under the brown waist she was a pale tender white. That in its way was attractive too; more vulnerable and feminine.

Now Juliet was standing in front of him, holding out her arms, pulling him to his feet, to dance again? Instead he kissed her; it was something he had always wanted. Her mouth was soft and mobile and tasted of angostura: she was in no hurry to stop. After some time she took him by the hand, held a finger to her mouth in a conspiratorial gesture and whispered "Come with me."

When he left it was late, very late, and he had a long walk back to his car; no taxis were in sight. He had asked about taking Ginger home, but Juliet said not to worry, she would probably stay the night. The idea did not seem to worry her a bit.

"I am glad we met tonight," she whispered, tiptoeing him to the door and turning for a voluptuous farewell kiss. Then sotto voce, "Until the next time!" But Jeremy knew there would be no next time. This was not an affair, but a passing whimsy. She had been lovely.

His mind turned to the slippery fish that might have been; the one that got away always evokes more dreams than the one that is, or was. What a good thing he had rescued her from that crazy project; if he had played his cards more freely, he could even now be rolling in her arms on a double bed. But being with her had led, curiously, to an amusing evening with Juliet. Set a girl to catch a girl. No doubt Ivan would think he was plying Ginger regularly, instead of hardly knowing her at all. An opportunity wasted, and after his negative response she would not give him another chance. Or would she? Perhaps he should call her up.

Ivan was lucky: having the delicious Juliet always at hand, ready no doubt at any moment to be enjoyed, but willing also to be passed across the table as a token, bartered for some alternative amorous fancy. No doubt he deserved his good fortune. At any rate he had the sense to pick a wife who fitted his tastes and objectives. The lovely Juliet! If anything should ever happen to Ivan, Jeremy might offer his services. But of course she would have hundreds of invitations.

When he finally crept home, Clare was deeply asleep. He did not tell her about his adventures; she would have been furious. But he did tell Avelyn at the next opportunity, and she was much amused.

"You're like a small boy, floundering out of your depth in a grown up pool! But I hope you won't change. That's what I like about you, your perpetual innocence." He tweaked her bottom playfully.

"Ouch!"

"Sorry."

"It doesn't matter." She was in his arms again, forgiving.

"You got it pinched pretty thoroughly in Rome. Jan told me. I guess that was after our day on the boat."

"Oh that! Did he tell you about that?" She thought for a moment. "It wasn't pinching actually; I told him a bit of a story. You see, I went with this guy and he beat me with his belt. That's what made the marks. So I had to make up something."

"How awful for you!"

"Not a bit. I enjoyed it."

"But how could you?"

"It's hard to explain. I . . . . . it's really exciting. I feel . . . . . well really exposed . . . . kind of super-naked."

"And you like that?"

"Of course! I thought you understood me."

"I guess I am beginning to." They kissed again for a long time, while he gently caressed this vulnerable area.

"You are amazing. And so loveable . . . . and tender . . . . . and so fragile."

23 Dynamite

Theorists all over the world were churning out speculations about the new particle. They took their pet bits of theory, the mathematics that they had learned to handle, and applied it to the javelin. It was all based on hypothesis. If this plausible theory was relevant, then so and so would follow. Even if the theory was implausible, it did not matter: a few days of calculation and you could give a seminar. Papers were rushed off to the journals, with 'preprints' circulated to everyone who might be interested. They all sent copies to Jeremy, so he was soon inundated with reports and only had time to read the abstracts. They piled up on his desk: how the javelin might decay, how long it should live, negative javelins in orbit round a nucleus and what X-rays would be emitted, negative javelins captured by nuclei, and inevitably javelin-catalysed-fusion. JCF had become the fashionable subject. It was Jeremy's idea, but they were all writing about it. He had no time to write, because he was trying to make it work. Experiments took much more effort. Somehow Bexler managed to get his name on a few of these theoretical offerings.

What Jeremy did have time for was discussion with Lars Svensson who was working out the details of javelin fusion. He started by reworking all the standard stuff on fusion with muons, but putting in the new mass of the javelin and its much longer lifetime. It was not surprising that he got a big increase in the number of fusions.

"The molecule is three times smaller, so the overlap of the nuclear volumes is greater by a factor of 27. Therefore it goes much faster. On the other hand the lifetime is 2000 times longer. You are bound to get a huge effect." Then Lars discovered some new angles.

"It's very interesting," he said, "The javelin mass is almost exactly one sixth of the mass of the deuteron, but the force on each of them is of course the same - action and reaction are equal and opposite. This means that the javelin whirling round in the D-T molecule can excite a resonant vibration of the nuclei, in and out like this." He waved his hands, making a concertina motion.

"So the nuclei are regularly coming closer together, and guess what?"

"More fusions?"

"Exactly! I have worked out the resonance condition in the D-T molecule, and, would you believe it, we hit it dead on." Jeremy looked sceptical; it was too good to be true.

"I have shown it to Chang, and he thinks it's OK."

Jeremy was trying to figure it out. "Are you coupling the orbital motion of the jav to the in-and-out vibrations of the nuclei?"

"Exactly. But there is something more I want to tell you. The helium trapping. As you know, that is what limits the muon fusion. The mu gets stuck on helium produced in the fusion. Then it is not free to wander off and catalyse another reaction; the chain comes to an end. With the muon this limits the number of fusions to about 20,000 for every muon, and that is not enough."

"I know," said Jeremy, "and presumably with the javelin the same thing will happen. That is my main worry."

"No, no, that's the whole point of my new result. The resonant motion of the nuclei makes the fusion happen just when the nuclei are closest together, and then javelin is farthest away. So when the helium is created, the jav is nowhere near. Trapping is strongly reduced. Depending on the phase of the resonance, it might not occur at all! It is very sensitive to the phase and there will be some small corrections, so I cannot be sure. Also we really need a more accurate value of the javelin mass. Anyway, you might get quite a large number of fusions per jav." Lars looked at him, proud of his discovery.

"How many?" said Jeremy. "I mean roughly . . . . what is the ball park?"

"Fifty million! Maybe more. It's hard to say exactly. We have to do some more work."

"This is dynamite!" A new power source would be in the bag. "Are you going to publish?" He was wishing that he could do the experiment first, rather than have the theorists get the kudos; but they could always work so much faster on paper. Grappling with the real world was more difficult.

"I think we have to publish," said Lars, "before someone else gets the same idea. But I am planning to give you the credit for starting the whole thing. How about this?" He opened a drawer, pulled out a piece of paper covered in scrawl and started to read.

"Following suggestions of J. Partridge in April this year, and the subsequent discovery of a new long-lived particle, the javelin. . . . .reference to your paper of course," he looked up. "I think that states the position pretty clearly." The date given was a month before the discovery, so it gave the credit for the idea quite firmly to Jeremy. Needless to say, he was amazed.

"This is how I go on . . . . catalysed fusion was from the beginning an objective of this search . . . . and then I develop the new arguments. What do you think?"

"Fantastic!" Jeremy shook Lars by the hand. "Thank you very much. If you publish in those terms, I shall be delighted . . . .of course! Thank goodness there are still a few honest men in the business."

"It is only fair," said Lars.

The northern Europeans knew what fairness meant. What a pity the idea had not spread more widely.

"The rats are looking sick," said Clare over dinner. "I don't know what's wrong."

"Do you think it's the food?"

"No, they get a super diet, rich in vitamins and full of tasty goodies."

"Perhaps they're just bored . . . . . don't like being in captivity . . . . . even the most luxurious hotels pall after a few months. Do they have anything to do? You know sports, like running through mazes, treadmills, problems to solve, electric shocks . . . . . . all the things that make life interesting."

"One of the problems is they're segregated . . . . . you know, male and female. That was the idea from the beginning, though I am not sure why. Obviously that's unnatural, and it may be getting them down."

"I think the idea was that they would get randy, and generate odours that would attract the other rats into the chalet."

"Maybe. But a sexually active rat may be more attractive than a frustrated bachelor. Anyway I'm worried."

"Why not mix them up then . . . . . and let them have some fun?"

"I suggested that to Jan. He just said he would think about it . . . . men can never take decisions!"

"Perhaps there's something they need. You know, special food or something. Or maybe radiation! They've adapted to it, so perhaps now they need a shot every once in a while . . . . . . to keep them tuned up."

"Well, could be . . . . . I might try that. Give them a few gammas or something."

The following day Jeremy bumped into Jan at lunch. "I hear the rats are getting sick," he said.

"Yeas. And they are not the only ones apparently! A bit more alkali might put them in the pink." He winked, but Jeremy did not want to pursue this subject.

"Talking about the rats, what do you think of this Viktoria Water stuff that Bexler is selling?"

"Even for the rats, we have no evidence that drinking heavy water has any effect. It would take years to do a proper test, especially on humans. The rats seem to have changed their genetic code by evolution to build deuterium into their system. That's something totally different."

"So there is nothing in it!"

"It's just a trick."

"Also if there's heavy water in those tins, I don't see where he gets so much of it; and how he can sell it so cheap. It is rare and expensive; that's the whole point of Ivan's project."

"So why don't you ask him?"

24 Blackmail

The following day Jeremy happened to be alone with Viktor going over tactics for the next run. Unexpectedly Bexler changed the subject.

"Oh by the way, Jeremy, how did you make out with Ginger the other night?" Like a good diplomat he paused to observe the effect of his remark. Jeremy was startled and gulped involuntarily.

"Ginger! What do you mean?"

"You know very well what I mean. I saw her waiting for you in the Rue Neuve, all done up with bright make-up. She looked very attractive. It's not a good place to meet you know, that street is quite notorious." His moustache was twitching from side to side. "Let me give you some advice: it would be wise to be more discreet."

"Viktor, I just happened to bump into her by chance."

"Some chance! Don't tell me she would be hanging around there just for fun. And then you walked off hand in hand, like old friends. She is attractive of course, I can quite understand, and I am sure you had an enjoyable evening."

Viktor naturally had jumped to the worst conclusions, but Jeremy decided not to be drawn into more indiscretions. Explanations would be futile. He looked straight into Viktor's repulsive face.

"It's none of your business."

"Agreed, agreed. The only thing is, you should be more careful. If Hans should hear of this, it could be curtains for your brilliant career at CERN. He is a possessive man, and I don't think he would like another finger in his little plum pie."

"I haven't gone anywhere near the girl!" cried Jeremy.

"That is not the point, old boy; it doesn't matter what you actually did, it's what it looks like that counts. If this gets out, Hans would lose face."

"Then he should not go waltzing up the mountains with Annabelle!" Jeremy kicked himself; why say it, why give out more information?

"That's his privilege. You should keep yourself out of trouble. Haven't you got enough on your plate already?" Was he referring to Avelyn, Jeremy wondered? What would he get to next? Then Bexler added,

"Anyway, don't worry. Your little secret will be safe with me. But someone else might have seen you too."

Was it a threat, as well as a warning? Arthur had gone back to Oxford and Viktor would like to run the group himself; now he had a ready made lever and just when the experiment was coming to the crucial point! It could be a disaster.

"About this heavy water you are selling. Is there any evidence that it makes people live longer?"

"None at all, old boy. But we don't claim that. We are just advertising the longevity of the rats, and that it seems to be due to deuterium."

"And where does it all come from? Deuterium is expensive, and you must need an awful lot."

"Quite simple, it just comes out of the tap. And cheap at the price."

"But that's just ordinary water!" Jeremy said in amazement.

"Quite so. We just say it 'contains heavy water'. As you know natural water is 1 part in 5000 heavy. So we are in the clear. No one can trip us up."

"Then it's a complete con," cried Jeremy.

"Of course . . . . . . but it's selling like hot cakes."

"If the public realised it's just normal water, they would stop buying it!"

"Sure, but luckily they don't. Not yet anyway. We are just about to licence some brewers to use our trademark, 'Contains heavy water' "

Jeremy shook his head slowly from side to side, trying to digest this information. Bexler's face came right up to Jeremy's nose. "We don't want this to get out, of course. In the circumstances I am sure you will keep it to yourself."

Thinking it over later, Jeremy could only see two alternatives; either he had to keep Viktor sweet, but at what cost? Or he must get the correct story to Hans in advance, explain how he had rescued Ginger from her madcap scheme. But how can you tell a man that his wife was planning to prostitute herself in the Rue Neuve, just to get even with her husband? He would love you for that! Perhaps he should phone Ginger, and get her to explain to Hans. But there was no mileage in that: after what had happened she would not regard him as her dearest friend. Why should she risk a quarrel with Hans, just to save his bacon? Paradoxically, if he had gone to bed with Ginger and given her a good time, she would probably have told Hans some story to cover her tracks and there would be no difficulty.

On the other hand he could blow the gaffe on Viktor over the heavy water; (though how to do it effectively was not so obvious). In which case he would immediately run to Hans with his story about Ginger. And vice versa! Whoever struck first could be sure of an immediate riposte, and they would both be damaged. So it would be better if they both held their fire in a sort of nuclear stalemate? The truth about 'Viktoria Water' would come out eventually; so there was no need to be involved. But could Viktor be trusted?

Jeremy ducked talking to Hans or Ginger, and started to calculate what it would take to keep Viktor sweet. It would be sufficient to string him along for a few months until they got some results. What Bexler wanted in exchange for his silence came out a little later.

Jeremy made the schedule for running the experiment, three shifts of eight hours each. They found it best to change over at 8 am, 4 pm and midnight. To get the ball rolling he put himself and Viktor together on the morning shift; that way they could at least thrash out any differences of approach, and Bexler would have less chance of spreading dissension covertly. This time they had a new more intense beam of javelins, and they were going to set up the momentum and range so that as many as possible stopped in the hydrogen bottle. The focusing and bending magnets also had to be checked. The first question was whether to start with hydrogen in the bottle; if they did then all the hydrogen safety procedures would apply, and they would be less free to go in and make changes. The group meeting had decided to start without hydrogen, using a 'dummy target' of plastic with the same equivalent thickness. But at the beginning of the shift Bexler was still arguing. Luckily the dummy target was already in place, and Jeremy persuaded him to start by setting up the magnets which would be needed whichever strategy was finally chosen. Viktor sat himself at the keyboard and asked Marion to read out the desired currents.

"Just key them in," she said, "and press 'return'. Then wait for the computer to run up the magnet. When it is ready, it stops flashing and displays the value." After a few of these Viktor got tired of waiting.

"We could have put all these numbers into memory in advance; then it could all have been done automatically." There was always another way of doing things.

"Yes," said Marion. "We can and we will. But Jean-Paul has only just given us the data."

Well, thought Jeremy, do we really have to put up with this? He had another packet of the magic powder in his pocket, so perhaps this was a good time to use it. Then there would be no more talk about Ginger, at least for a while. He went out to the machine and brewed up, taking care to keep the cups separate. No problem, it all went off as before and in twenty minutes Bexler had sloped off. It was all too easy.

By the end of the run they were stopping plenty of javelins in the liquid hydrogen. They would be ready to put in tritium and try for fusions next time. That meant setting up some more detectors to look for the neutrons and getting the tritium system installed. All the tritium safety precautions would have to be put in place.

Jeremy spent some time working out what would happen if Lars was right and each javelin gave its fifty million fusions. They planned to stop a million per second in the liquid hydrogen, so that would give 5 times 10 to the power 13 fusions. Quite a large flux of neutrons would be produced; easy to detect, but would there be a health hazard outside the building? He got some figures from the shielding experts. According to the rules, the three metre thick wall around the room was just about sufficient, but the roof was much thinner. There might be some 'sky shine', that is neutrons going upwards, being scattered by the air and coming back to earth outside the building: back to where he was sitting for example. It looked rather dicey, but Jeremy decided to keep quiet about it. The chance of Lars being correct seemed small. If the flux was one hundred times less than he predicted it would still be a record. All the same, they would monitor the number of neutrons in various places, and if the flux got too high they would cut the beam.

Next Jeremy looked at the heat produced by all these fusions. It was an easy calculation, and the result was 160 watts. That would warm up the liquid hydrogen, and probably make it boil. Once it had turned into gas, the reaction would stop, so it should be self-limiting. Again it would be prudent to stop well before they reached that stage, and the neutron counters would tell them what was happening. He arranged for a thermocouple to be installed to keep track of the hydrogen temperature.

Just for fun he estimated how many javelins were produced in total by the accelerator. Most of them missed the beam lines and buried themselves in the concrete shielding. If somehow you could collect them all and put them into the liquid deuterium-tritium mixture you would get megawatts out: more than enough to run the accelerator and have power to spare for cooking lunch. Perhaps catalysed fusion would be useful one day, but for the present it was the chase that mattered. Would anyone ever get there? And if so, who would be the first?

25 The Matterhorn

Ivan was having a great time soaring over the mountains. It was a beautiful October day with a cold front from the north turning the sky deep blue. But there was still heat in the sun and the warm air, sliding up the bare rocks, was peeling away in vigorous thermals each marked by a puffy cumulus cloud. The air was dry, so cloud base was at 4800 metres, well above the highest peaks, and under one of these clouds Ivan was weaving lazily, floating steadily upwards. He had taken off from Sion and worked his way southwards, following the mountain ridges. Now he was circling in front of the Dent Blanche, 4357 m ASL. Below him the mountain swept majestically down to the sprawling village of Zermatt, and beyond rose the great black shadowed face of the Matterhorn. To its side he could see down into Italy and the Po valley, misty with heat haze trapped by a strong inversion. It reminded him of his epic flight over Mont Blanc to Rimini and beyond. The altimeter read 4100 metres, the vario was showing 2 up, it was a glorious day and there were no problems.

This was just a pleasure cruise, with no ambitious flight plan. So often in soaring you are guided by where the lift is and its strength, and you improvise en route as the day develops. The only airway was further south, Blue 4, running from Milano to Mont Blanc. He would keep out of that, but the best lift would be on the Italian side. It would be fun to get south of the Matterhorn and then cruise along the peaks, Breithorn, Castor and Pollux, Lyskamm, Monte Rosa. Then he might glide down the Monte Rosa glacier, pick up some lift on the Gornergrat and sneak back home across the mountains. If the lift gave out, there were aerodromes at Aosta on the Italian side, and at Zermatt.

This thermal was a good one and he was soon above the Dent Blanche, still climbing. No oxygen today, he had not expected such good lift, so he should not go too high. 4000 to 4500 metres would be fine, he was quite used to that, but for safety he would stay below 5000. He looked at his fingernails; if they were blue he could be short of oxygen, but they were bright pink. At 4400 m he broke off the climb and set course for the Matterhorn only 4 kilometres away, and the visibility was perfect: he got there in three minutes. The enormous cliffs rising from far below were quite frightening, so he kept well away, edged round to the south face and came in tangentially. It is hard to estimate distance at this level, because there are no familiar objects to set the scale. Then he saw a party of climbers, roped up; they looked tiny, so he decided to go closer on the next pass and give them a wave. He swooped down in the rising air, diving just over their heads to say hullo. Climbing or flying is a lonely business, perfect for those who want to get away from it all, but paradoxically when you see someone you want to give a greeting. Loneliness balanced by camaraderie. The climbers waved back.

Soon he was above the Matterhorn. There was a crowd of mountaineers at the top. He circled a few times, admiring the world's most spectacular mountain. Then east across the Theodule Pass. On the Breithorn late summer skiers were still using the drag lift and running down the wide open slopes. Just for fun Ivan joined them. He kept well away from the pylons and followed the ski run in a gentle dive, 20 m above the snow, aiming straight at the line of sportsmen waiting for a ride. He whirred over their heads at 200 kph, then pulled up in a steep climbing turn. He could see their faces, goggle-eyed, turned up to watch him. The variometer whistled, showing lift, and with a few deft turns he centred on the thermal; within minutes he was back at the peak of the Breithorn, ready for another ski run. He thought the better of it and cruised on eastwards. Lago di Maggiore only 50 km away was within easy reach, but it was in an airway.

Ivan looked at his watch, 3 pm: it was time to turn back. With the shortening days, the lift would die early and the wind was northerly. Perhaps he had already lingered too long. Soon he was over Zermatt again and heading for home, 4000 metres on the clock; in still air he could cover 120 kilometres before he reached the valley floor, and as the crow flies the field was only 40 km away. But the crow could not fly that road, there were mountains in the way and the wind was freshening.

He picked up some height on the side of the Gabelhorn and looked down its shoulder onto a vast open snowfield running northwest towards Sion. There was another ridge ahead, but there was a low saddle. Once over that he would be in the Evolene valley which led straight back to the airfield. Mentally he judged the angle to the next pass, he had plenty of height to make it in a straight glide. Soaring is about assessing the risk and taking decisions. He thought about it carefully, and then moved across the ridge, into the vast bowl of snow and glaciers; set the speed at

80 kph for optimum glide and aimed direct at the low point perhaps 3 kilometres away.

Down below he could see a mountain hut and two characters waving at him; they looked like girls but from this height it was hard to be sure. As he approached the saddle, Ivan expected the line of sight to the ridge to move gradually downwards, eventually to disappear under the nose of the glider as he passed over it. It was not! Instead it stayed obstinately ahead of him at the same angle. Wow! The vario was reading 2 down and falling. He pushed the nose forward to pick up speed and get out of the downdraught; the vario dropped to -3, then -4.

This was no good, he was running into a major area of falling air, and losing height rapidly. He swung the ship sharply to the right and headed for the edge of the bowl, which was still in the sun. The air could not go down everywhere, so somewhere he had to find lift. Stick forward, 120 kph, a shallow dive to get out of trouble. He could not go back the way he had come, and ahead of him now the mountain was still higher, a forbidding face of ice; but the sun was on it. He swung left to follow the face, and over a dark crag the vario beeped. He pulled her up, slowed down and started to climb. Phew! That had been a nasty moment. At a pinch he could have landed in the snow near the mountain hut, spent the night with the girls, but it would need a chopper to lift the glider out.

He cursed himself now for taking this route; he should have skirted the outside of the bowl, and if necessary gone down the Zermatt valley to Visp: it was a longer way home, but it would have been safer. Perhaps the lack of oxygen after several hours above 4000 metres had warped his judgement, and his blood sugar could be low as well. The fingernails were still fairly pink. He must concentrate to get out of this bowl. Turn smoothly, keep in the lift, go back along the mountain, keep the speed correct. The lift was patchy, so work the good spots.

Eventually he had climbed a few hundred metres above the broad, snow covered saddle, and the lift was failing. He skirted round the bowl, keeping close to the ridge that sloped gradually down to the pass. Beyond he could see more mountains but to the right, out of sight, there would surely be a way through. A little more speed and he was diving for the pass, swinging gently right, skimming 30 m above the smooth snow saddle, and he was through! Through the pass, but to what?

To Ivan's horror, instead of the expected open valley leading down to Evolene, he was now in another smaller bowl, and the far side looked inaccessible! Nevertheless he turned right to work the sunny side, but this time there was no joy. It was too late in the day, little peeps of lift, but not enough to raise the glider. He flew anti-clockwise round this high forbidden valley, but there was no way out. He flicked on the radio to report his position just in case he had to land; but it was dead. Then he remembered. His own battery with his name on it was always on charge with the others belonging to the club. But that morning when he went to pick it up they had all disappeared! In its place was a scrawled note which said, "The club is out of batteries, so I have borrowed yours. Hope you don't mind." It was signed 'Viktor 'and had yesterday's date! The bugger had borrowed his battery and not even bothered to bring it back! Like hell he didn't mind! Typical Viktor! The Swiss were reliable. They might be boring, but at least they were honest, and they respected your property. Now with this stranger floating around anything could happen; he would give him a piece of his mind next time they met! Well, he would not be in controlled air space this time, so there was really no need for the radio so he took off without it. Now he did need it; and he needed it badly!

There was no doubt about it. He was trapped in this bowl, gradually losing height and sooner or later he would have to land. What a fiasco! But there was no choice; he would have to make the best of it. The valley seemed to have a smooth floor, covered with frozen snow with brown moraine stones at the sides. On the west side the ground rose smoothly to a pass, which presumably led somewhere. He circled a few times, trying to assess the wind, and picked a gently sloping snowfield. Unless there was a miracle, he would have to land in this valley, land but not crash: his main priority was to keep the sailplane and himself in one piece. The ground was in shadow and white everywhere; it was difficult to judge height or see bumps in the snow: but there was no escape. Better get it over. Decisively he opened the air brakes, diving, increasing speed to lose height, skimmed round the edge of the bowl, his eyes fixed on the chosen area. Then he straightened up on the approach, dive down low, lower, lower, then flare, rising parallel to the slope and hold her steady. The landing wheel was still retracted for a belly landing on the glacier. The snow sizzled beneath him as he slid along it, a few bangs, judder and a subsiding hiss; the plane veered to the right, but came safely to rest. Ivan looked around: nothing seemed to be broken.

To make a successful out landing in difficult terrain is the real test of a soaring pilot, and every time he did it a surge of exhilaration and relief swept through him. But this time it was short lived. What next?

Ivan unfastened his harness, opened the canopy and climbed out, surveying the scene. The valley was desolate, totally different and much larger than he expected. All around were glaciers and crags. It was cold and very, very quiet. The trickling of water running off the snow had already stopped as the ice refroze with the falling light. Down in Sion it had been hot, and under the perspex hood of the sailplane it was usually warm; so Ivan had been flying in a light shirt, shorts and sneakers. Luckily he had a sweater tucked behind his seat, and he put it on. There were also a few things to eat; apple, chocolate and a stale sandwich. He had only to call the field and within twenty minutes a chopper would be on its way to pick him up. Instinctively, hoping against all reason, he tried the radio again; but of course it was useless.

The situation was not encouraging, but he had got out of plenty of scrapes in his time. What was the best strategy? Eventually, as it got dark, his friends in Sion would start to worry, wait for a telephone call to say he had landed somewhere and then, failing that, gradually realise that he was missing. It would be too late to do anything until morning. If he stayed with the glider it would be a clear night, and unbelievably cold; under the canopy, wrapped in his parachute he might survive for 24 hours, but it would be miserable. If he climbed up this slope to the pass, and down the other side to civilisation, the exercise would keep him warm and with any luck he would find a friendly farmer, get help, report to the airfield and have a decent meal. Which was the best policy? Which was the safest? Ivan arranged everything in the best possible way, put a pile of snow on the wing to hold it down firmly and carefully fastened the canopy.

26 The price of silence

There was another delay in the accelerator schedule. This time the linac, in which the krypton ions picked up speed before being projected into the synchrotron, had broken down. In addition the antimatter group wanted more time. The story was that they were getting an exciting result, and they needed more data before the Fourth International Convention on Antimatter and Astronomy in Buffalo. After a lot of objections and discussions they were given two extra weeks of machine time. In late October the fusion group finally got another run. To save time they decided to move towards Jeremy's original policy of trying the ultimate deuterium-tritium mixture, short cutting some of the preliminary tests. The task of the first shift was to check out the beam again. Jeremy, Viktor and Chris were taking data and everything seemed to be going smoothly. They were full of optimism; this time they could really get some evidence of fusion catalysed by javelins, and that would be a break through. But when Chris was out of the room for a moment the atmosphere changed abruptly.

"By the way, how is Avelyn these days?" Jeremy was startled to hear Bexler's question. Little did he realise that their friendship was a popular topic for coffee table gossip and Viktor was the last person with whom he wished to discuss Avelyn's charms. He grunted, trying to indicate that he did not care to pursue the subject, but Viktor kept going.

"She's not worried about your little affair with Ginger, I hope?" The taunt had its intended effect of infuriating Jeremy and putting him off guard.

"She knows all about it, and doesn't care a pin." Then he added heavily, "I told you before, there is nothing between me and Ginger; it's all in your imagination."

"In my opinion," Viktor was always airing his opinions. "In my opinion Avelyn is very attractive; but she is rather elusive. I would like to meet her, just the two of us, somewhere. I thought you might be able to lay it on, arrange something."

"Viktor, Avelyn's social life is her own affair. Why don't you ask her yourself?" He knew very well what Avelyn thought of Viktor; 'a slimy toad' she had called him, so he was unlikely to make much progress.

"Jeremy, I think she needs a little persuasion, and in the circumstances I thought you might use your use your influence."

"I am not a pimp, Viktor!"

"No, no, of course not. I just saw your role as, what shall we say, well more of a catalyst. A catalyst, you will recall, just brings the reactive molecules into close proximity. After that their intrinsic attraction is sufficient to draw them together, they fuse and all the latent chemical energy is released." It was a revolting picture. After a pause Viktor added,

"I met Hans the other day. He obviously has no notion yet of Ginger's little escapades." No notion yet! The implication was obvious, and totally repulsive. It was also totally impractical. Knowing Avelyn's character, and her feelings for Viktor, there was no way she would accommodate his fantasies, whatever the pressure. So he would try to play for time and string Viktor along.

"OK, I will ask her. But I do not think you will have much luck."

"I am counting on you to persuade her."

Chris came back, so that was the end of the conversation. Jeremy relapsed into a morose silence; he could no longer concentrate on the experiment, and the very smell of Viktor with his tobacco and bristly moustache made him feel sick. How could he get out of this intolerable squeeze? How could he continue to work on physics with a man who was openly blackmailing him? He could go to Hans and demand that Bexler be moved to another group; but this was impossible because of Ginger. Arthur might have helped but he was in England. Jeremy decided to call him up and suggest that he came over as soon as possible.

What about Eckerdovsky? He was a straight guy, and knew all about that fatal evening and Jeremy's refusal to get involved with Ginger. Ivan might have the courage to talk to Hans and expose Bexler's dastardly tactics. Better still they might arrange to see Hans together. He went back to his office and dialled Ivan's number. There was no answer.

The helicopters of the mountain rescue service at Sion were out at first light, searching the mountains to east, west, north and south. There was a general feeling that Ivan would be south of the Rhône valley, but no one knew where he had gone that day. The two glider tugs were also scouring the area. Eventually at 11.25 one of the choppers saw the white sailplane with orange wing tips, lying in the snow, apparently undamaged. They landed beside it and opened the canopy. There was no one inside, but Ivan had left a note explaining why he had landed, and what he would do next. They followed the footsteps up the hill. After about one kilometre the track stopped by some rocks. Further on they picked it up again. Then it petered out once more.

By the time Ivan left the glider it was already well after four thirty. The sun sets early in the mountains and by six it would be getting dark. He had only a short time to climb over the pass and find a way down the other side. Unfortunately there were no tracks. Not a good sign as when there is a way through there is usually a path, or at least a trail left by mountain goats and chamois. He had no torch. Puffing a bit from the altitude, Ivan clambered up the slope and got to the edge of the ridge at its low point. From here he could see down into the next valley, and as expected there were signs of habitation; huts, the odd chalet and in the distance a visible track leading down to a village. What he had not expected was the steep rock face on the northern side, dropping sheer for a hundred feet. Usually on a cliff face there is a gully somewhere, cutting through the wall, and providing a way down. So Ivan followed the ridge upwards for a while, but there was no way through. It was tantalising: so near, and yet so far. Now he understood why this bowl was so desolate; it was virtually inaccessible, except by air.

The only thing to do was to go back to the glider, wrap himself up, somehow survive until morning and wait for help. By now dusk was falling and he was feeling the cold, but he could see the machine neatly parked about a mile below him. He decided to make straight for it, taking a short cut across the snow. Running down the hill would warm him up. He was bounding along merrily when suddenly the snow gave way and he was falling into emptiness.

The rescuers lost the trail on the rocky ridge. Had he somehow climbed down the steep northern face? Or tried that way and slipped? They looked over the precipice, but could see no signs or tracks on the ground below. Then they searched up and down the ridge and eventually saw more footsteps. They followed the trail until they came to a hole in the snow. Ivan's body was ten feet down in a small crevasse, and completely cold.

The funeral was in its way splendid. He had so many friends, for all of whom a source of joy had suddenly been switched off. Juliet had asked them not to wear black. ‘Come to say goodbye, but he would not want that.’ There was the gliding fraternity from Geneva and Sion; one of them made a speech about his abilities and helpfulness to others. Virtually everybody came from the Mediterranean laboratory, including a bevy of pretty girls, a large contingent from CERN, and friends from Geneva, Paris and other cities. Jeremy and Clare were there, Jan and Avelyn, Ginger and Hans, but Viktor was absent. It was rumoured that he was sick again.

In his valedictory address the Director-General reviewed Ivan’s life history, his contribution to science, his originality of thought. But above all he emphasised his dynamism, his positive attitude to everyone, the happiness that this strong tolerant man created around him. He lived life to the full, (did that mean he had lots of women?), and it was in following this approach that he met his unfortunate end. There should be no regrets for him, because he had been a happy man, a man fulfilled. But there was sadness for all of us who were left, because he was no longer with us. Particular sympathy for Juliet, who had always supported him so perfectly and for his daughter Liliane. Michel’s sympathy so eloquently expressed was soon to take a more concrete form.

At the reception everyone was swapping memories, and for the first time the girls were sharing their experiences and comparing notes. Juliet was in a daze; she could not believe that this was happening. Liliane was quiet and pale, but listened avidly to all the praise of her father.

Over drinks Jeremy managed to have a few quiet words with Ginger.

“How’s it going?”

“Very well thanks.”

“And Hans?”

“Oh, he’s not so bad.”

“You no longer feel the same then?”

“No, not so much. But thank you for your help.”

“Oh no trouble. . . . . someone saw us you know.”

“Does it matter?”

“It was that bastard Bexler.”

“So what?”

“He wants to make trouble . . . . . tell Hans.”

"Oh God, whatever for?" Then she added, "I don't care really. It might do him good to know that I don't just stay at home and mope."

"Yes, but what about me? He might be angry."

"That's your problem."

"Do you think we ought to tell him, I mean bring it out in the open? I mean, we didn't do anything wrong." Jeremy was just getting to the point when someone else came up.

"Want a roll? The sausages are excellent." They were interrupted, and Ginger wandered off. Her last words were

"Let him find out. It will do him good." She did not care. Worse still, she had no feeling for his predicament. She had moved away without even an encouraging smile: so there was no hope of a solution from her.

What a marvellous guy Ivan had been. He helped himself to whatever he fancied in life, paid the price, and enjoyed it. His friends enjoyed it too, so somehow he was smart enough to get away with it. He broke the rules, but in such a nice way that everyone loved him for it. Anyhow they did today. What were the rules? The old puritan ethic had been blown away, but what was left? People seemed to have principles to live by, beliefs firmly held, but what were they? It was never spelled out. Maybe 'do not toy with your boss's wife' was one of them: he did not know. It was shifting sands. Perhaps it was not what you did, but how you did it, that mattered. Some people could get away with murder. Interesting thought! But he dismissed it: he was sure to be found out. Just then Clare came into view, looking bright, stimulated by the company.

"Such a sad occasion, isn't it. Do you think we should go? The party seems to be breaking up." She took him by the hand.

27 Picnic lunch

"Have you thought about it?" The question came out of the blue. They were lying on the rug in detumescent euphoria. His right hand was caressing her rump. At the bottom of her spine, infinitesimal blond hairs glinted in the autumn sun. Was this usual? He did not know. Jeremy's chances to scrutinise the female surface had been rather limited, though now indeed he was making up for lost time. Hairiness in this region could imply a whisker or two of male hormone circulating in her blood, and that perhaps would account for her steaming sensuality.

They had accomplished the main business of the day and his thoughts turned to lunch. It was time for her to crack out the picnic. It was such a pleasant arrangement. Twice a week, the secluded meadow, wild flowers and resilient grass; she always brought him a bottle of beer, and a fancy selection of sandwiches to share. After an hour of munching and chatting he would be ready to take her again, before dragging himself reluctantly back to work. The quintessential continental siesta! And what could be better?

"Had I thought about what?" She had asked the question timidly, mumbling, face down into the rug, and he had missed her meaning. Now she turned square on, and looked at him with those big vulnerable blue eyes reflecting her uncertainty.

"You know ..... us! We talked about it before. Couldn't we ......?" She looked down, tracing circles with her finger. Then suddenly she looked up again.

"If we did, we could do this all the time . . . .instead of. . . . well. . . . . . just occasionally." She smirked ruefully and turned away.

She had opened herself completely, kept nothing back, virtually asked him directly. While before she had only hinted at it, now she had made herself totally vulnerable. He could not say no; it would hurt her too much. But he could not say yes, either. There were so many other factors in the equation. At least eight eyes would cloud over in pain, if they ran off together. And where would they run to? His job would hardly fund two households, and Avelyn had expensive tastes: with a rich husband she got everything she wanted. He could not imagine her scraping along on an ordinary salary, or more probably only half his salary: it would never work.

"Yes, I keep thinking about it. In fact I think of little else. I go round and round . . . . . but there is no answer. Yes, I would love to . . . . . of course . . . it would be paradise. But would it work? Would it last? And would it be right to break up so many relationships? You and Jan? Me and Clare? The children? It would be awful for them." Avelyn said nothing, just looked at him, watching, trying to read his thoughts and see beneath the surface.

He felt an obligation to Clare and the kids. It would be wrong to just slope off when some fabulous new creature came along. In any case he enjoyed them, watching them grow, listening to their fresh innocent chatter, playing games, showing them how to do things. Fatherhood he realised had been one of his ideals, something to strive for, an achievement in itself. Even if, amidst all the pressures, he did it rather badly, he was still a Dad! In the end, walking out on the family was simply not on the agenda. Having a mistress was another thing altogether. Anyway, it had not been planned that way, it had just happened.

The truth was that the present arrangement, in spite of its strains, suited him rather well. He kept his family, and had an adorable mistress supported by someone else. What could be better? A mistress is always randy and ready to go. Lovingly perfumed, she prepares herself for the occasion. A wife is more often submerged in the daily business of living. Why waste time dressing up for your husband?

A wife wears a nightie in bed and takes off her make up. A mistress keeps her make up on and takes off her panties. A wife is tired after a long day and wants to sleep, but a mistress is wide-awake and ready to go. He was getting the best of both worlds.

"Jan is such a decent chap. And he treats you well. I can see no reason for stealing you away. And with me, you would have none of those lovely things. We would be on the bread line. I don't think you would enjoy it at all."

"How can you talk like that? Don't you understand? I love you Jeremy. I want to be with you, all day, every day. That's what would make me happy. It doesn't matter what we do, or how we live. I don't care for all those beautiful things. They just happen to be there. But I am stuck in that apartment, day after day, all on my own. I am bored out of my mind!" There was only one possible response. He took her in his arms.

"Darling, you are so beautiful, and vulnerable and fragile! Let me think about it. I need a little time; then maybe it will become clear."

"If you want something, do it. Don't dither about!"

But he was not ready to make a choice, either yes or no. When confronted with the irreconcilable, the only option is to wait. Wait for the alternatives to clarify themselves. Wait for the situation to change, fate may intervene in the shape of someone else's decision, a new attitude, a move, even an accident. He kissed her, and she was ardent.

"I love you the way you are now. If we lived together I am afraid it would be different. So many trivial practical things would crop up. You would be disillusioned."

"Not at all," she said, but he did not believe her. They ate some sandwiches and kissed some more. Then out of the blue she said,

"Would it make a difference . . . . . if . . . . . . " She looked down, hesitating.

"If what?"

"If I were pregnant?"

"Pregnant, what do you mean pregnant?" He leapt up flabbergasted.

"You know what I mean, pregnant; having a baby! Would it make a difference?"

Jeremy was shattered. A difference? Sure it would make a difference. He would feel different. She would be different! A different kind of person, a mother to be. And he would have a new obligation; a reason perhaps to leave one family and join another. One could not leave the little bastard without a name! Yes, it would make a difference.

But wait a minute! She was married. He would not be a bastard at all, but a member of the rich family Olbers. He would have all the best things in life and inherit millions from his 'dad', drive a Mercedes, have fun. The best thing for the little chap, if there was one, was to leave things as they were!

"Yes, it would make a difference. Of course. But I don't know which way. But why are you saying this? I thought you took precautions!"

She looked at him wanly. "I do . . . . . or I did. You know I am not on the pill. Jan wants children, and so do I, but nothing ever happens.

With you I did. . . . . . at the beginning . . . . . at the critical times. But recently . . . . . you see sometimes I forget. Now I know you better, it doesn't seem important."

"I thought you looked after these things."

"I know . . . . . . I ought to. . . . . but I get carried away."

"Anyway, are you? . . . . . I mean, having one?"

"I don't know." Now she was sobbing. "I was just asking . . . . if it would make a difference. I don't want to make you angry. I would love to have one . . . . with you . . . . that is if we could. . . . . . I don't know, actually . . . . I am rather irregular anyway." She paused. Then added,

"It's not very easy, being me. I mean having my kind of body." She shook convulsively. "People are always chasing me. And of course I want them. He doesn't do it often enough." She took his hand warmly, desperately.

"But I want you more than anything. Aren't I good enough for you?"

"Of course you are! Too good in a way. I just can't believe it's true!"

"So why not then?"

"There are the others . . . . .the kids."

"Lots of men see the light and walk out on their children."

"Maybe, but I just can't see myself doing it. It's not in my script."

Perhaps that was it. You started out with a picture of how your life would unfold and develop. If the world offered you a different possibility, it would be hard to switch. In his mind he could not relinquish the role of the upright English gentleman, and turn into the typical continental cad. But . . . . . one day . . . . . perhaps . . . . . .

When Jeremy got home Clare was striding about the room, distraught.

"Something terrible has happened!"

"What?" asked Jeremy.

"We're all finished. Washed up. It's the end."

"Why?"

"The great escape! They've all gone, disappeared, vamoosed."

"What have?"

"You know. The rats, what else? They've vanished."

"No! It isn't true! How come? Where are they?"

"Who knows? And all my work will be wasted. I have been keeping records, following each one, analysing. Now it all seems pointless."

"What happened then?"

"Well, it's rather stupid really . . . . . obvious in retrospect. You know the chalet is made of wood. That was the easy way to start . . . . at the beginning . . . . and it seemed OK. We thought they would find it so attractive that they would be clamouring to get in, not out. Well they simply gnawed a hole in the one-way door and left."

"Where to?"

"Well, back into the tunnels I suppose. But from there they can get out into the fields and farms and so on. We'll have to tell the management."

"Well at least they are still around . . . . . on the site I mean . . . . I mean, probably. With any luck they will come back. Can you tell which are which?"

"Oh yes. The all have coloured rings on their wrists with identification numbers."

"We'll have rats running round the experiments again! I thought we'd seen the end of that."

"That's your main worry then? What about my work? And finding out how they tick?"

Jan took it all much more philosophically. He reckoned the rats needed some variety and after a few days they would get bored with the tunnels and come back to the cosy home. Meanwhile they could clean it up and make it more secure. That is how it turned out. After some discussions they let the animals go in and out of the accelerators much more freely, and it seemed that contamination of the surrounding farms was not a problem after all.

28 Juliet

Juliet was shattered by Ivan's sudden death. The last line especially of his note had been addressed to her: 'Juliet - Thank you for everything - I love you - Ivan'. He had been everything to her and for 8 years she had lived her life totally around him. Now suddenly she could not see him any more, talk to him, call him up, laugh or just relax together. Slowly she pulled her life together, sorted out Ivan's possessions, started to think about the future. A cause of dismay, when she found out, were the rules of the CERN pension scheme. The widow's pension would be quite generous, but only for those who had worked in the organisation for five years, or alternatively had bought in some extra years by paying a capital sum when they joined. Ivan had no capital, and although he had been a consultant for longer, his official employment had only lasted 4 years and 10 months. Therefore no widow's pension. Furthermore, now that her husband was dead, Juliet had no right to live in Geneva, or to run her dancing classes. Going to live in nearby France was an option; that way she could keep her friends and perhaps restart the dancing school over the border. It might work.

The administrators of the pension fund were very sympathetic, but they had to work to the rules. There was nothing they could do. However, it was always possible to appeal to the DG. As for everything else in CERN, he was the ultimate authority. If in his judgement it was right and good for the organisation, he could bend the rules.

"We could put your case to him. But it would be better if you called on him yourself." So Juliet made an appointment, and found herself knocking at the secretary's door. For some reason she felt like a naughty schoolgirl, summoned to the headmaster's study. She had dressed carefully, a demure but flowing silk frock with stockings and petite shoes. To the discerning eye the buckles of her suspenders might just be perceptible as small bumps in the surface of her skirt. The overall effect was fragile and delicate.

Naturally they talked in French. As on his visit to the island they used the familiar tu-toi option; once you have moved to this, you can never switch back.

"Juliet, it is a pleasure." She moved round the room admiring his beautiful office, looking out at the view.

"Michel, I am so grateful for your kind words about Ivan at the funeral; it was wonderful, really, so moving." Annette brought small cups of coffee and some patisserie. He asked about Liliane, how was she taking it? They talked easily about her problems with the apartment, her residence permit, the dancing classes. She thought she would go back to Paris where she had lived for so long. Then she came to the problem of the widow's pension.

"That is terrible," said Michel, "Ivan was an exceptional man, in charge of a new division. He was doing such important work. I think we might be able to justify an exception in his case. I will look into it." He chatted on about Ivan, how much he had enjoyed working with him, his visit to the island, and the many aspects of Paris.

She stood up to leave and as she offered her cheeks, first one side and then the other, her body trembled slightly.

"Do not worry. One way or another we will see that you are looked after. Oh, by the way, how is your cash position at present. Often after a bereavement things can be difficult for a few months."

"It is rather difficult," she answered demurely.

"The official procedures are slow. Let me give you a cheque to keep you going." He overruled her protests. "It is nothing . . . . you can pay me back when you have the money." The cheque was for 10,000 Swiss francs, not a negligible sum. Her face lit up. It would keep her going for a couple of months at least, but for him with his comfortable DG's tax-free salary it was a bagatelle.

"Je suis foudroyée (I am struck by lightning), I am so grateful. I will pay you back without fail as soon as possible." But in what currency? A warm handclasp, a significant look, and she left.

Michel still had a mental image of Juliet on the Ile de Levant, her delicious figure moving freely on the beach with its plump little juvenile cleft. In a month or two, deprived of her husband's virile membership, it would appreciate some tender care and attention. He had kept to his principle, not to meddle with his staff or their wives, but now the situation was different. Not in Geneva, he decided. He could wait until she was back in Paris. All those who had enjoyed Juliet's favours, and many who had not, were entertaining similar fantasies; but they nearly all dismissed them as impractical.

Michel's immediate concern was to arrange Juliet's pension. She deserved it, Ivan deserved it, but it should be done correctly and within the rules. The DG, though seemingly all powerful, is answerable to the Council for his actions and exceptions to the normal policy might well be noted in some annual report. He pressed the small button on his desk, requested the rules of the pension fund and studied them carefully. He looked for the names of the management committee and then asked Annette to summon the secretary, Albert Pflumli, a dour Swiss accountant in the finance division, giving him advance warning of the subject.

"Bonjour, Monsieur le Directeur."

"This case of Eckerdovsky is a little embarrassing. What do you think we should do?" Pflumli reviewed the facts. It was against the rules, but the rules did allow the committee to make exceptions, and there was also provision for appeal to the Director-General.

"On the other hand, if we make an exception in this case, there will be others similar, and we will run out of money. She is young, the widow's pension is 25% of his division leader's salary, indexed for inflation, and according to the tables we must expect to pay it for 53 years. It is an important sum."

The CERN pension fund was stuffed with assets. It had been well managed for years by a clever member of the committee and owned buildings all over Switzerland as well as substantial industrial investments. But if CERN were closed down tomorrow, they could only just meet their liabilities. CERN was still expanding, but you never know what the future may hold.

"Well," said Michel, "in my opinion this is a very rare case; a division leader, invited personally by me to help us with a new project, and dying only just before the qualifying date. In addition he had worked for us, part time, for a year before that. Such a case will not occur frequently."

"We cannot have one rule for division leaders, and another for the junior staff," objected the administrator, who was one of the juniors himself. Michel could see the force of the argument, so they were left with a rather flimsy case.

"I would like you to put it to the committee. If possible we should be gracious. I think CERN should be seen as a compassionate employer, and Eckerdovsky was a well-known and important figure. See if the committee can come up with something. Ideally they should make the decision themselves; I do not wish to intervene."

Predictably the committee was divided. Some bought the idea of the generous employer, while others trotted out the familiar objections; if this, then that, thin end of the wedge, slippery slope, where will it all end, and so on. They did not want to bend the rules. On the other hand, if they were overruled by the DG, that would really be exceptional and it would give them some protection for the future.

In the end Michel had to summon the whole committee for another meeting in his office. They went over the whole story again. Could the pension fund afford it? Then Janus Schmetterling piped up. He was a young staff representative, elected to the committee because he opened his mouth on every possible occasion.

"The main danger to the pension fund is not Madame Eckerdovsky. It is the money that was borrowed by CERN to pay for LEP, and this has only been partially repaid!" He was referring to the new collider still under construction. It was a continuing source of anxiety. If for any reason the organisation lost the support of the member states, the money might disappear forever.

The Director of Finance was a member of the committee, though not in the chair. It was late November, coming up to the end of the financial year. He knew, and the DG knew, that there would be a clear surplus in the CERN accounts that year, arising from the late delivery of some major equipment. Michel turned to him.

"Herr Schmetterling has a point. It would be good to liquidate this debt as soon as possible, perhaps before the end of the year. What do you think Bruno?"

"Naturally, Director-General, I would have to look into it. As I recall the amount outstanding, with accrued interest, is about 33 million Swiss francs. I anticipate that at the end of this year we will have a little room for manoeuvre. Very probably, but I would have to check, we could refund most of this amount to the pension fund." There was astonishment, smiles all round, faces turned to Janus in congratulation.

"That would be excellent," said Michel. "So I think this year, subject to further investigation of course, we can probably put our house in order. Thank you, Herr Schmetterling, for that very valuable remark. Now perhaps we can return to the case of Eckerdovsky. Could someone sum up your view?" The view was quite simple; taking everything into account they did not wish to make an exception in this case. It looked like a dead end. There was silence. Then Pflumli spoke up.

"Director-General, the rules do provide, as you know, for the DG to intervene in special cases, if he considers it to be in the interests of the organisation This is in fact one of the rules. Now in my opinion those who drafted the rules must have foreseen that one day they would be used. Is there any point in having a rule that is never used? Some of us, I think, feel that this is perhaps a case where the DG might quite reasonably intervene." Indisputably Michel was relieved. He looked around the meeting.

"Is this a general view? What do you all think?" There were smiles and nods. Michel had been scrawling figures on a pad in front of him. He got out his HP pocket calculator and punched in some numbers, wrote down the answer.

"If that is the general feeling, I must say I appreciate Herr Pflumli's remark, I think in this case the organisation should take a compassionate view. How would it be if we awarded Madame Eckerdovsky a reduced pension of 43.5 per cent." Smiles all around the table indicated general approval. The number was reasonable, neither too high nor too low. No one knew how it had been reached (not even Michel) and no one asked. It was a compromise, and they had got a major concession from the management.

"That seems to be agreed then. Ladies and gentlemen, I thank you for your time and trouble." Going down in the lift the committee members congratulated each other ebulliently. Conveniently forgetting their previous penny-pinching speeches, they were basking in the glory of their own generosity. The refund was a formality, but it would remove a long-standing worry.

A few days later the Director of Finance invited Juliet to his office. He might as well enjoy the pleasure of telling her himself. At Michel's suggestion he did not mention the role of the DG, but she found out anyway. Ivan had a life insurance, and prudently he had told the company about his gliding activities, and they had accepted the risk as reasonable. It could be argued however that the death arose in fact from mountaineering, which had not been mentioned, rather than aviation. It took them a few months to decide, but in the end they paid up. She sent a cheque to Michel, repaying her debt, and thanking him for all his help. She appended her new number in Paris, and ended - 'be sure to let me know when you are in town, most gratefully yours, Juliet'.

Michel had many occasions to visit the capital, either to give lectures on physics, or to keep in touch with the Minister of Research. Were his visits now a touch more regular, and did they last a trifle longer? Nothing could be more satisfying that the sensitive interplay of squamous epithelia, convoluted surfaces, delicately intertwined, exploring the deepest recesses in reciprocal rediscovery. But it would be wrong for us to probe too deeply, to speculate when we are not informed. It was apparent only that he returned each time invigorated, a new lightness in his step, his confidence deeper, his inner smile more serene.

Jeremy's problems were not so easily resolved. As he got to know her better, to like her more, Avelyn increasingly dominated his thoughts. Should he, or shouldn't he? Would he or wouldn't he? She had made it quite clear that she wanted his love, a full time relationship, and hopefully a child. As he was ceaselessly reviewing this question, his small talk was reduced to zero. He had less and less to say at home and brooded continually. One evening Clare decided to have it out, and try to clarify the air.

"Jeremy, what's on your mind? Obviously something is not right. Can't we talk about it? Maybe I can share it with you, help in some way."

Jeremy was on the spot; he had to say something, but rather than talk about Avelyn, he tried to explain his difficulties with Bexler. He described how he had found Ginger, lingering provocatively in the hottest street in town. How he had rescued her, and taken her to a café where they had bumped into Juliet and Ivan. He mentioned the drinks party afterwards. Then he explained how Bexler had seen him with Ginger, and his threats to tell Hans, probably in order to discredit him and take over as group leader. Clare's reaction was quite unexpected.

"Oh what a silly man! I am sure that Hans would not worry about such a trivial thing. Ginger can go out on the town if she wants to, and if you happen to bump into her so much the better. You are better than some unscrupulous sex maniac. At least he got her back in one piece. She might have been spirited away, or chopped up for cat meat."

"Yes, but if Viktor starts telling stories to Hans, he might see it differently." He had not told her about Juliet and Ginger's dancing, and what happened afterwards. Nor did he mention Bexler's price!

"I tell you what, we must tell Hans first. At least in general terms." Clare had taken the difficulty on board as her problem too. "Why don't you buttonhole him at coffee? Just say, 'guess who I met in town the other day'."

"I don't think I can. Anyway, not now, it's too late for that."

"I bump into Hans sometimes; he seems quite approachable, even friendly. So . . . . I tell you what . . . . . let's invite them to dinner. Then it can all come out quite naturally. Let's see, I could just ask him, as a subject of conversation, 'if Ginger and I were down in Geneva and we met a couple of guys from CERN and we all went for a cup of coffee, what would you think?' Then after that, we could move on to Ginger on her own, maybe meeting you. 'Of course I wouldn't mind', I'd say." Clare turned to Jeremy,

"What do you think? It might defuse the problem."

"Brilliant! Certainly worth a try. It would be interesting to see what he says. Bexler, of course, thinks that Hans is as jealous as a randy bull." What a relief! And what a sensible wife he had! He should talk to her about some of his other problems . . . . . if only he could. As if reading his thoughts, Clare said,

"I tell you what, let's invite Jan and Avelyn too. You like her don't you." It was the understatement of the year.

"Yes, I do," he answered carefully. Then he added, "I think she's lovely." He wondered how much Clare knew. Was she teasing him? If so it was not apparent.

"Good," she said. "I am looking forward to it already. Then we can all talk openly, and that nasty little Viktor can rot in his own garbage." She put an arm round him. "I am sorry you are having problems. Come on, there is a good film on the box, let's watch it together."

"Thank you," said Jeremy. "How good you are."

But before the dinner party could take place, events took another turn that made this little ploy unnecessary.

29 Avelyn

The snow had started already; it was early for the time of year. Avelyn looked at the flakes swirling in conical pools under the street lamps, and slowly covering the cars below. No snow on the balcony yet; it was melting as it hit the tiles. Hopefully it would soon stop and with any luck all be gone by morning. Not a soul in sight! A deathly silence everywhere. No noise in the building, and none outside. Which was not surprising. At this hour anyone with sense would be tucked up snugly with a nice warm man.

Her thoughts all day had been dominated by one subject, men; to be specific, the two men in her life. Jeremy had been away for three days, and she had not seen him for a day or two before that. And this was Jan's second night in Milan. She was weary of being by herself, rattling around the big apartment with no human contact. She had been to the ice rink, and now she could feel a warm glow suffusing her body as the well-used muscles signalled their appreciation. If only there was someone to share it with.

If Jan were here she would seduce him; that is, if he was not too tired. With Jeremy there would be no need for that; he was always up for it. Perhaps if she was with him always, he might lose interest, but it was hard to imagine.

Most of all she wanted a child. Jeremy's child would be the best. Somehow with Jan nothing ever came of it; perhaps it was him, or perhaps it was her, it was hard to guess. Which was why she had been taking risks with the other: to find out. Now perhaps she was having one, but it was too early to be sure. She should go to the doctor; but for fear of disappointment and losing face, she kept putting it off.

So Jeremy was back at last and it had been good to talk to him. But he was too tired this evening, or too busy to come round. At least that seemed to be the message. She knew he loved her, though he was taking him a long time to realise it. Maybe he would change his mind and come after all, in spite of the beastly snow. If he did, they would have some wine and talk for a bit.

Wine! Better get some ready, just in case; and she could do with a glass herself. Meursault was his favourite. She looked in the fridge, then in the cupboard; nothing really worthwhile, but there was plenty in the cellar. It would only take a moment to nip down to the basement and stock up. After her bath she had not bothered to dress, but a dressing gown would be fine. There were no signs of life anywhere as she took the lift down to the gloomy grey cellar, with its array of slatted storage cubicles; using the big key she let herself in.

In one of the spaces Jan had installed two refrigerators, specially designed to keep wine at the right temperature. Avelyn was moving to open the left hand chest, when suddenly a large cockroach jumped out from under it and barred her path, its legs spread out and antennae bristling. It was disconcerting to say the least, and in her sandals her feet felt vulnerable. She gave a little cry, stepped back and wondered what to do. There was no one to help, and no objects ready to be used for attack or defence.

A trained zoologist would have known that cockroaches are harmless. But the ordinary mortal is brought up to treat insects with respect, if not hostility. Bees, wasps and hornets sting; mosquitoes, midges and horseflies bite. Scorpions are charged with deadly venom. The cockroach in aggressive mood appears to bristle with multiple armaments. Indeed its awesome appearance may be a mechanism for discouraging attack. Avelyn knew nothing about the genus, but she wanted to get her wine. And there was another factor, cockroaches in the cellar were not in harmony with her concept of good housekeeping.

She rummaged around and found an old plastic tray. That would do as a shield, and perhaps it would scare the monster away. Then she advanced carefully, holding the tray vertically in front of her feet. The animal stood his ground. Never before in its short life had it been confronted with a tray. It gave out an interesting odour and might be edible; on the other hand the massive surface was daunting. Its small brain had not been programmed for this eventuality, so unable to decide whether to advance or retreat, it stood its ground, shuffling its legs and wiggling its whiskers.

For some time they faced each other. Then Avelyn let the tray topple forward. Too late now, the unfortunate creature tried to dodge, but the falling surface was too large. Its legs folded under the weight into unnatural positions. Relief now mingling with apprehension, Avelyn's instinct was to finish the job. She put her foot on the tray and pressed.

With a sickening crunch the exoskeleton collapsed, juices oozed out, and the poor thing was reduced in an instant to a mushy pancake.

Ugh! She was sorry for it. But hopefully this sudden death would have been relatively painless; better than being asphyxiated by a chemical spray, or slowly poisoned by powder. In the morning she would ask the femme-de-ménage to clear up the mess, and perhaps spray some insecticide around for good measure. Dismissing the incident, Avelyn selected half a dozen choice bottles, put them in a string bag, carefully locked up and went back to the lift. Going up she checked her watch; all this had taken much longer than she intended.

Jeremy meanwhile had changed his mind and was speeding along the snowy roads to Avelyn's apartment. Tingling with anticipation, he rang the bell. It was late, but she would recognise the code, ding - pause - ding-ding! In a moment she would appear, lightly dressed perhaps, and certainly with a glowing smile of surprise.

But no one answered. Standing outside her flat on this cold November night, Jeremy gradually realised that he had missed the train. He cursed inwardly. He should have phoned to say he was coming. Women are fickle. If they do not get what they need, they go elsewhere. And why not? Do not blame them; only blame yourself.

So now what? It was too early to go straight home, so he might as well drop into the lab, catch up with the news, encourage the troops. He scrawled a note, tucked it into her door, and went sadly back to the car.

A few minutes later Avelyn came up in the lift with her wine, read the note, and cursed her luck. He had been! That was marvellous. But he had gone again. They must have missed each other by moments! The note ended, 'I'll call you in an hour from CERN and hope you will be in by then.' After that came lots of X's and hearts. How lovely! But an hour was too long to wait. She ran to the window and saw fresh tracks in the snow. Perhaps she could just catch him.

She threw off her gown, grabbed the large Siberian silver fox coat from the cupboard, fur hat, gloves and bootees to match, and she was off. The lift of course took ages, but soon she was in her little sports car, the lovely red Mercedes, out of the underground garage and on her way. It had stopped snowing luckily, but better go easy as there was quite a bit on the roads.

She got to CERN without catching Jeremy, but having come so far she might as well go in and find him. The security barrier was down, but the guard recognised her and let her through. She came to the lab fairly often, sometimes with Jan, sometimes without, for an easy lunch, to feed the rats or to change a book at the recreational library. Jeremy had several times taken her to see his experiment, which was so impressive though she could never follow the detail. The security guards knew her, always let her in and usually gave her a broad smile.

This time was no different and Avelyn smiled back. She felt grateful, relieved, and without thinking she gave him one of her best. The uniformed attendant, damply going about his duty on this miserable evening, felt suddenly illuminated as a flash of pure angelic beauty lit up the night. It seemed like a vision from heaven and for hours afterwards he could think of nothing else.

The only way she knew to Jeremy's experiment led tortuously round various buildings and ended up in a dead end, just outside the experimental floor. She managed to remember it, but was puzzled that there were no other tracks in the snow. She swung the car round in a wide sweep, parked, got out and wondered what to do next. There must be another way to his control room, and probably Jeremy's car was on the other side of the building. Should she drive round, or walk through? She hesitated for a few minutes, then tried the door and it opened.

Yes, this was the correct place all right. In the corridor she saw a phone. The number of the counting room was easy to remember, 2021; she had used it a few times before. Phoning would be better than barging in, especially in the middle of the night, and in this coat. She was just dialling the number when she heard footsteps coming down the long corridor. She hung up and waited, giddy with exhilaration: it was probably him. Just for fun she flattened herself behind a pillar, half hidden, to give him a surprise. Her last words to him on the phone had been 'Don't forget' and she had wanted to add. . 'I love you', but somehow it had not come out. She was ready to say it now. But the figure that came round the corner was not Jeremy!

He had reached CERN some while ago and had already been wafted away to another plane, the abstruse world of particle physics held him in thrall with all mortal distractions for the moment suspended. In the counting room he found Marion and Viktor, and they welcomed their group leader like a long lost friend.

"Hullo! I am back. I just thought I would drop in to see how it's going."

"Fantastic, we are making marvellous progress! Come and look at the data." They turned back the pages in the thick ledger.

"In brief, it's working. But let us show you the evidence. We followed the plan."

First they had run with deuterium in the pressure vessel. The neutron detector nearby would signal whether there were any catalysed fusions. But there could be other sources of neutrons, produced by the stopping javelins, without fusion. So it was important to record the neutron energy.

"So here you have it with deuterium," said Marion. The graph had been printed out by the computer and carefully glued into the book. "This one is for 10 million stopping javelins. Here is the peak due to D-D fusion at 2.2 MeV. It fits almost exactly with the calibration. And this is the important point, the background at 14 MeV is very low. There is nothing that looks like a false D-T signal. When we get to the run with tritium, you will see the difference."

"What about the rate?" asked Jeremy. "How many D-D fusions are we getting per javelin?"

"I've worked that out from the calibrations and written all the steps into the book." Marion was not stupid. You do not get a D.Phil. from Oxford for playing around. "Each javelin gives about 15,000 D-D fusions. That is a little more than the theorists were predicting. But as you know, it's not enough for an energy source." At this point Viktor chimed in; he could not resist communicating his excitement.

"Then we took out the deuterium, and put in the 50-50 D-T mixture. Now look at the result!" They turned the pages forward, past notes like 'Machine off for two hours', or 'HT fails - replace the module', and there it was! The neutron spectra with D-T showed a really huge peak at 14 MeV.

"That's incredible," said Jeremy.

Bexler twitched his whiskers. "It's not incredible. It may be impressive, but you have to believe it. It is definitely there."

"You know what I mean. Amazing."

"It's not even amazing, because we expected it." He always had to argue, even at this moment of triumph.

"You know what I mean," answered Jeremy. "When you want something very much, and it comes along just as you have always dreamed, then I find it hard to believe that it's really true. It seems unbelievable!" At least Marion would understand. They looked at the curve more carefully.

"The D-D neutrons are still there of course, as you'd expect," said Marion. "But on this scale the signal is much smaller. And this wide low region in between, we think might be the T-T." It all made sense. Jeremy asked the million dollar question.

"So how many of the D-T do we have?"

"The calculations are different of course, because the counter is much less sensitive to the high energy neutrons. But in spite of that the peak is much higher. It comes out to about 1.2 million."

"Wow!"

"We are getting used to it," she added. "In fact it is not far out of line with Svensson's predictions. D-T has this resonance, as you know, and that is hard to calculate."

Viktor said, "We have got a bottle of champagne in the fridge. Shall we celebrate?"

"Why not! I could do with a boost."

"And I am famished," added Viktor. So they popped the cork, clinked and Bexler downed a couple of glasses. He wiped his mouth on his shirtsleeve and sighed, "That's better! Now . . . . we were just going on to the next step, which as you know is the copper cylinder."

Jeremy remembered the reasoning. Some of the javelins would be trapped on the helium nuclei produced in the fusion, and would then be unavailable for further catalysis. X-rays of the correct energy could knock the javelins free again, and so they would get even more fusions. Javelin trapping, as it was called, was the main way the chain would end. If they could get rid of that, well, it would go like a bomb.

So this was the new idea. The 14 MeV neutrons from the fusion could be put to work to generate the right kind of X-rays; then the javelins would be regenerated, and the whole process would really fizz. The more fusions, the more X-rays and the better it would go. It would be regenerative, non-linear. At low intensities, nothing much would happen;

but as you put in more javelins, after a certain point it would really take off. According to the calculations this might not happen, and anyway it would need more javelins than they had in this beam. But they might see the beginning of it, and that was all that was needed to establish the new effect.

The optimum material to absorb the neutrons and generate the correct X-rays came out to be copper. So they had a copper cylinder, 2 centimetres thick, ready to put in place around the cell containing the tritium. There was a hole at the end of course, through which the 14 MeV neutrons could get to the detector.

“So, if you agree,” said Bexler, “I think we might go down and put the copper in place. Then we can see if it makes a difference.”

“Good idea. Would you like me do it? I can easily nip down.” Jeremy felt that he ought to make himself useful.

“No, no, don’t worry. I know exactly where everything is, and a little walk will do me good. We have been cooped up in this damn counting room for hours.”

He went out and Marion with a happy smile emptied the bottle into the remaining glasses. Her eyes were shining. "This is really fun, and exciting too. I am so glad I joined this group. I've already got enough data for my thesis."

Jeremy smiled back. "So glad to have you here: you're doing a great job."

Viktor trudged down the long corridor. He was elated. What a fantastic year he was having in CERN. It had all worked out more or less as planned, but in fact unbelievably better. The discovery of the JAV (as he preferred to call it) was one thing. And now the clear demonstration of catalysed fusion! With any luck it would prove to be a viable industrial process. All this would mean fame. He would be invited to lecture, offered professorships, awarded prizes, honorary degrees. How delightful!

These last shifts with Marion had gone very well, she was a pleasure to work with, a bright cookie. When he went back to the States he would try to offer her a job, continue the partnership. If he went back. Maybe he could get a nice job in Europe. Europe was so much more rewarding, and the girls were pretty; a few of them even appreciated his attentions.

He could do with one right now. After four nights on shift he was more than ready for some fair company.

Bexler rounded the final corner, and to his amazement, there was Avelyn! She was flattened against the wall between two concrete pillars, and tricked out in rather a superb pale grey fur coat and hat. This was a perfect opportunity to chat her up.

"Oh hullo Avelyn! What a nice surprise. How very nice to see you. There is no one I would be happier to meet in these dark lonesome corridors. He pressed the button to open the huge concrete door leading to the experiment. "I have been hoping we could have a chat, and what a better time than now, while we wait for this monster to open. The mills of God grind slowly, but they grind exceeding fine."

Avelyn said nothing. She was wondering whether to ask if Jeremy was there. Or should she just walk right past him, up to the counting room, and see for herself? She was hoping not to disturb the whole crew. (In fact, there was only Marion, who would have been pleased to see her). Now Bexler came up in front of her, rather too close for comfort.

"Don't you think we could be good friends? I like you very much, and I would like to see more of you."

"Oh. . . ." Avelyn did not know what to say. "I . . . . . . I don't think . . . . . it wouldn't be easy. You see . . . . . " But Bexler interrupted. The proximity of Avelyn's body, her emanations, were warping his judgement, blowing his mind.

"There is a special reason I would like to tell you about." He leaned forward for emphasis, taking hold of her lapel, the whiskers twitching close to her face. "What a beautiful coat this is. You must have a rich admirer."

"I do . . . . . . richer than you." She backed off as far as she could into the corner.

"The other evening I was in Geneva, minding my own business as usual, and I happened to see your friend, we all know who that is. He was going along with a married woman, Ginger. Maybe he has a particular fancy for married women. Anyway, they were going along rather well, he was holding her hand and leading her into a café, for anyone to see."

"I know all about that, it's not important." Viktor took no notice.

"Of course I am a good friend of Hans, and I thought perhaps he would not be pleased if he heard about it. On the other hand, I thought that as a good friend, maybe I should put him in the picture."

"I don't suppose he'd care."

"Oh, I am sure he would, very much."

"Just going into a café, what's wrong with that?"

"That is for him to decide, I would say." Viktor now took the high moral ground. "It is question of friendship. Out of loyalty, I ought to tell him. It would be bad for Jeremy, of course, but probably I should. On the other hand, if you and I were good friends too, then it could be different. I am your friend, you are Jeremy's friend, therefore I protect him to please you! That could be more important than my friendship with Hans. Ergo, we should be good friends. Do I make myself clear?"

"Totally!" Avelyn was furious. She wrenched herself away from him. "And the answer is NO. I am not for sale! Above all to you, you slimy old snake!"

Bexler laughed. He seemed to regard her remarks as a challenge, an obstacle to be overcome. He came close again, held her arm, leaning forward with his repulsive smell of tobacco.

"The consequences could be quite serious . . . for our mutual friend. Think about it." He slid his left hand inside her coat and discovered bare skin inside.

"Ah ha! All dressed up are we? To meet our little lover boy?" Avelyn was livid. She slashed at his face violently. Then forced him away. In the process a button flew off her coat.

"Get away!! Leave me alone, you slimy toad!" She cursed him in Danish and then in Old Norse, calling down upon him all the wrath and fury of the ancient Nordic gods, Wotan, Thor and Freya. Visibly shaken but unrepentant, Viktor turned towards the concrete door, now wide open.

"Excuse me, but some of us have work to do. I am sure you will think about it. I can't wait for ever you know." He disappeared through the long slot into the dark, then turned on the light inside.

Avelyn felt an enormous surge of relief. Thank God he had gone. While he was leering over her, she was paralysed by fear; but now she bounced back like a coiled spring. Her instinct was to get away as fast as possible, and she started up the corridor towards the counting room. Then she stopped. Bexler was a menace! Dangerous to her, physically, and dangerous to Jeremy. He would probably carry out his threat to make trouble with Hans, and Hans' reaction was unpredictable. It was time to act, do something, shut his silly mouth and preferably forever.

Her first thought was to shut the door on him, leave him in there to fry in the beam. She put her finger on the 'close' button, but nothing happened. (The light was still on inside). Then she spotted a metal bar lying in a pile of stuff on the floor. That would be better. Knock the bastard off, topple him down the stairs, so it looked like an accident. No one would suspect her, or know she had been around. (In this moment of high emotion she did not think about the guard at the gate, nor the easily recognisable tracks of her car).

She held the bar above her head in a moment of supplication, gathering her strength and determination, and then crept through the door, walking warily across the clanking metal floor. There were cables and junk everywhere, blocks of concrete, pillars of steel, contraptions of all sorts. She inched forward, peeped round a corner. Bexler was bending over the experiment, fiddling with something. Notices were all around, danger high voltage, danger hydrogen gas, danger radioactivity, do not turn, do not touch, keep away. She got close to him, raised the bar with two hands. She was just about to bring it down, when he turned and moved away to the left. But fortunately he had not seen her and she hid behind a pillar, watching.

Viktor had finished what he had to do. He made one final check, then turned and walked quickly to the entrance. There he followed the usual procedure; turn off the lights as a warning to anyone left inside, then through the door, and press the 'close' button.

In theory Avelyn should have yelled, 'Hi! I am here!' But she did not know the procedure. Outside the door, Bexler pressed the switch on the intercom.

"The copper cylinder is in place, door shutting. I am coming up." Then he looked round for Avelyn. She was not there; presumably she had gone up to the counting room to see Jeremy. He could do with some fresh air, a cigarette. He went out into the snow, took a deep relaxing breath and lit up. This was great. Then he saw the red Mercedes; Avelyn might be inside. Perhaps he had been a bit rough with her, a little sweet talk would have been better; but he could make up for it now.

In fact the car was empty, but unlocked. Viktor looked inside. He had never sat in one of these, so now was his chance. He got in. How comfortable! The keys were in the ignition, so why not give it a whirl? Try it out. Why not drive it a short distance and leave it in another place, just for a tease? Why not indeed? It was the worst decision of his life; the stolid Swiss could never believe that a famous professor of physics would play so infantile a joke on a beautiful lady. He enjoyed driving the Merc, but he did not exaggerate. Out into the main street of CERN, round a corner, and leave it in the main car park: perhaps 200 yards in all. Avelyn could follow the tracks, and find it easily enough; it would give her a pleasant walk! Subconsciously it was his way of invading her privacy and asserting his power. He parked the car, left the key in the ignition, and strolled back another way, enjoying the remains of his smoke with deep satisfaction.

In the counting room Jeremy and Marion were going over the results, but after a while he began to feel uneasy. Something was not quite normal. Viktor had been gone quite a while; was he having problems?

"I think I'll wander down and lend a hand." Then the phone rang. It was Clare.

"Oh hullo Clare, how are you in the middle of the night?"

"Jeremy, are you all right? . . . . . Oh . . . . . that's OK then. . . . Sorry . . . . it's such a filthy night, and . . . . . I just woke up from a terrible dream. I thought something might have happened. So . . . I thought I would call you . . . that's all."

"Everything is absolutely fine, as far as I know. The experiment is going rather well actually. We have solved that little problem, and we are just starting again. I will be back quite soon."

He rang off and started down towards the experimental hall. He saw no sign of Bexler, and down below the door was shut, or at least shutting. It was creaking and crackling in a strange way. A bearing might have gone, he would report it in the morning and get someone to grease the machinery. He went on a few steps and looked out into the snow. There was Avelyn's red Mercedes! Whatever could she be doing here in the middle of the night? Waiting for him perhaps! He was just about to step out to meet her, when the car moved off. Jeremy stood there, pondering.

Oh Avelyn . . . . . . .Avelyn . . . . . . Avelyn! A deep feeling of spiritual unity with this lovely being surrounded him. She was so wonderful, the perfect companion, and to be with her was life's fulfilment. Now he saw it all clearly. If you are loved, deeply loved, by a lively and beautiful girl, then you are the one-in-a-million lucky guy. Go with it. Cleave to her, cherish her, give her everything she wants. Life can have nothing better to offer. At last Jeremy knew what he had to do, but he had an uneasy feeling there was not much time left to do it. And where was she going now?

When he got back to the counting room, Bexler was not there, but Marion had started the run, the beam was very feeble but some data were coming in. Then there was a fault in the accelerator, and it went off again. Eventually Viktor turned up.

"I came back another way. Needed some fresh air." He said nothing about Avelyn, and Jeremy did not mention the scratch on his face.

Ten minutes later Jeremy decided to pack it in. He was on shift in the morning. Avelyn could be home by now, so he rang her from an empty office, but there was no answer. He had seen her driving off in the red car; but where was she now? In the end he went home, and slept fitfully.

30 Accidents

While they were waiting for the beam the next shift came in, so Viktor and Marion handed over and went home. Chris and Erik were now in charge. The big point was to see if they got more fusions with the copper cylinder in place; and if they did, whether the effect was greater at high intensity than low. In theory the bigger the beam the greater the effect. So it could be unstable and they had to go carefully; just in case it worked. Most probably it wouldn't of course. They were to start with a fairly weak beam, and slowly build it up, keeping a careful eye on the neutron counts and the hydrogen temperature, to avoid any danger. It was typical of the PS to pack up at just this moment.

Eventually the beam came on again, but it was very variable and weak. Chris got the main control room on the intercom.

"It's the linac. There is nothing we can do about it here, but they are working on it." The operator was quite calm and friendly in the circumstances. Probably groups from all around the machine were calling up, and they could get quite testy at times. If you gave up your sleep to take data, it was very irritating to sit around waiting for beam. But this was the life of particle physics; long periods of drudgery and boredom, punctuated by brief moments of high drama.

Because the beam was so weak, Chris decided to open up the slits and at least get something. It took 30 minutes to get the first point, instead of the usual 2 to 5, but the data were interesting. They looked back in the logbook for a comparison, and the fusion rate per JAV was nearly a factor two higher. Even with the weak beam there were enough X-rays to release some of the trapped particles.

"Oh boy! The copper seems to have hit the resonance bang on." Then the beam went off completely. They set the equipment ready to take the next point, made coffee and hung around. While they were waiting, they figured out how good it might get at high intensity.

"What's the best we could hope for?" asked Erik.

"Well, if the JAV is not trapped at all, then it could give say 100 million fusions, maybe more. But some other process would probably come in and cut off the chain. I've no idea what that might be."

After nearly an hour the speakers boomed. “Beam is on.” They saw at once that it was back to normal. They had full beam with all the slits open and the counts were really racing.

“Look at that! It is terrific!”

Then suddenly everything stopped. The accelerator was still going, so there must be some fault in the electronics or the detectors.

“Just our luck!”

Then the tritium alarm came on. It looked pretty serious. Lights were flashing in the counting room, and they could hear a bell clanging down on the floor. The MCR had the alarm too, and the operator called them.

“I have a tritium alarm for your area. I am shutting your beam stopper. Do you know what is happening?”

“No. We also have the alarm, but we don’t know why. There must be a leak somewhere.”

“If you do not know, I must call the safety officer, and the fire service.”

“OK.”

“Do not go down to the floor. It may be dangerous. The safety officer has the right instruments.”

To fill in time, Chris started checking the detectors one by one. There was usually a small background count in each, even with the beam off. Now most of them were completely dead, as though they had been disconnected. But two were working, and in both cases they were counting like crazy.

“It might be the tritium affecting them, but the soft beta ray should not get through the wrapping.” It was a puzzle. Erik took the count rates and wrote them in the book. Chris thought of calling Jeremy, but it was not really necessary. Better let him get some sleep.

The safety officer on duty that night was Klaus Schneebecker, a Swiss engineer. He was not particularly familiar with tritium, but he knew the procedure. Turn off the tritium supply with the obligatory remote controlled valve. Wait for the gas to clear through the ventilation system. Then enter the area, using gas masks and a portable tritium sniffer to make sure the area was clear. The amount of tritium they were using should not be a hazard to the public; it was lighter than air, and would go straight up into the clouds.

Schneebecker was a bit nervous. This was the first tritium incident at CERN, and he was not too confident; on the other hand he had to show who was in charge.

"Have you turned off the tritium source by remote control?"

"Yes, as far as I know. But there is a doubt. I pressed the 'off' button on the panel here. But these indicator lights, red for open and green for shut, are not working. So we don't know if the valve actually moved."

"Right, that means it may still be leaking. We can use the alarm above the apparatus to tell us if there is still tritium present. Where is the control box?" Luckily it was outside the experimental hall, so they could get at it.

They all trooped down the corridors, accompanied by four firemen in full rig. The bell was still clanging, and it was deafening. Klaus turned it off. Then he pushed the 'reset' button, and waited to see if the alarm would start again. It did not.

"No tritium is indicated in the room. So I think we can enter. But we take the precautions. I will be the one to enter. You will all stand back." He felt a minor hero, standing by the concrete door, all kitted up like an astronaut. With the rubber nose, large round goggle-eyes he looked like some queer insect from outer space. He held the tritium sniffer on a long rod in front of him. He moved it up and down the crack in the door, and it gave no signal.

"Now I open the door a few centimetres." His voice was muffled by the mask, his eyes on the tritium meter. He opened the door a little and then stopped it.

"All is clear!" With more confidence he opened the door further, six inches, a foot.

"Gott in Himmel! What is this?"

When Viktor left the experimental hall, Avelyn was still inside. He had turned off the lights, and the door was slowly shutting. She was very frightened, and when you are frightened you do not always do the right thing. Blind panic is worse, but Avelyn did not panic. It was not completely dark. All around her, amid the cables, magnets and concrete bric-a-brac, were yellow or red panels, each flashing a warning of some specific danger. She did not know the way around, she did not want to be stuck in here all night and most of all she did not want to be irradiated by a lethal army of undiscovered particles. If she moved, there was the danger of falling down some hole or stairway, and if she held on to something to keep her balance she might be electrocuted. There was an emergency stop button, but she was unaware of it. There was an emergency button for opening the door, which in the semi-darkness she did not see. There was even a telephone, undiscovered on the wall.

Then in the semi-darkness she heard the rats, scuffling and squeaking. There must have been four or five of them, and they came scampering up to her, climbing up her coat in great excitement. "Go away!" she screamed, kicking out with both legs, shaking her arms and pushing them away as best she could. She swung at one with the metal bar, but missed.

Impeded by the rats Avelyn retraced her steps as fast as she could manage. The blessed light from outside still shone through the door, and she stumbled to it. The gap was narrow now, and she realised that the door was slowly closing, but she had no way of stopping it. If she hesitated it would be too late; she would be cut off and the beam would come on. She reckoned she could squeeze through in time. There must be some safety device, a bar to press: doors always stopped if someone was in the way.

In this case the designers had foreseen someone standing outside, obliged to activate the motor continuously and therefore obliged to watch; but this necessity had been by-passed by impatient users. The second line of defence was the heat sensor in the roof. In the Siberian plains, winds sweep down from the North Pole at fifty degrees below zero. Across this frozen landscape the silver fox must venture forth in search of food, but he is superbly equipped for survival in the Arctic. Exquisitely designed by Nature, his fur conserves every quantum of precious heat. And now Avelyn was wrapped from head to toe in this most perfect of thermal insulators. By any criterion, the consumers' associations would have given it their highest accolade: hardly a calorie escaped. The infrared photocell registered a tiny flicker, but it was hardly above the background noise, and not sufficient to trigger the circuit. The door kept on moving remorselessly forward.

In front of the girl was a small notch in the wall, intended to close off any cracks; she could not get past it. Then she realised she could not get back. She was trapped because of her beautiful coat, like many a previous fox and stoat.

"Stop!" she screamed. "Stop! Help! Jeremy!" But nobody heard. Viktor was happily driving her car, and Jeremy was fifty yards away, walking down the corridor.

The door was a solid concrete block, 3 metres wide, 2 metres high and several metres thick, weighed about 50 tons and was carried on four steel rollers. The first priority of the designer was that the door should move. In ideal circumstances, one ton of horizontal force would be enough, maybe two. But one must cater for the unexpected, an uneven track, a tired bearing, low mains voltage, and even the debilitating effects of age. Rather than become the laughing stock of CERN he preferred to play for safety, and decided to apply a force of 5 tons. In addition, like any good engineer, for each element in the estimation he took the most conservative figure. So the machinery finally installed would, if the crunch came, deliver at least 10 tons before tripping the overload.

Human bones are miracles of engineering strength, but on a completely different scale. Athletes in training may, in short pulses judiciously applied, exert strains of 1000 pounds. As many a skier will testify, it is not recommended to exceed the specification. At one ton, even the strongest bone will shatter irretrievably. So the door moved on, unknowing and unrelenting. The micro-switches that signalled its closure operated normally, and the beam came on.

Schneebecker's first thought was that some animal had been trapped. He peered in. A pancake of long fur and clotted blood. It was weird. He forgot about the tritium and opened the door a little more. It was a gruesome sight. Then he noticed the golden hair, and an unmistakable human hand. The implications slowly sank in. He staggered back and ripped off the mask.

"Mein Gott," he said slowly. "Someone has become an accident!" Cautiously he opened the door a little more, and contemplated the awful mess.

"Do not move," he ordered. "No one must come near. Call the doctor. Call the ambulance. Call security." In spite of the contradictions a fireman ran to the phone. Then Schneebecker called the MCR on the intercom.

"Here we have a very grave incident. You must turn off the accelerator."

"Is that really necessary?"

"Yes, I order you!"

So the message went out all over the PS. "The machine will be turned off in thirty seconds. We have an emergency in the bubble chamber building. It will probably be off for some hours. We will keep you informed."

Now Schneebecker's mind was whirling. What had gone wrong? There would be an inquiry, blame would be apportioned. Would any of it land on him? He must do the right thing. Foul play could be suspected. He needed a breather, time to think. He moved to the outer door, and opened it. There were tracks in the snow; a car had come and gone. There were footsteps also. All evidence must be preserved. He detailed two firemen to block all access to the road, and another to follow the tracks in case they led somewhere.

Then he remembered the tritium. He picked up the wand again and did some more sniffing. Thank God it was clear, but no one could go inside until this accident had been investigated.

31 Prison

In the sleepy village of Bernex the telephone trilled again. Jeremy was asleep, but his mind was whirling. Slouched in his seat in a huge auditorium, he heard the grey-haired professor with gold-rimmed spectacles holding forth.

"And now we welcome the inventor of this wonderful process, our visiting lecturer Dr. Jeremy Partridge, from the European Organisation for Nuclear Research in Geneva. You will all know of him, perhaps the most famous physicist of our time, and certainly the one who has done the most for humanity. I have great pleasure now in inviting him to give his lecture."

The audience was buzzing with expectation. The professor came down from the stage and bowed; Jeremy stumbled up the steps with his brief case and got to the rostrum. There was an expectant hush, upturned faces were hanging on his every word. But Jeremy could only stammer.

"Er . . . . thank you, Professor . . . . er . . . . S-ss-Stibbening for your very kind remarks, which are quite undeserved. Now I must get out my slides and notes." He fumbled with the latches of his brief case. "Without them, I will have nothing to say, will I?"

The audience chuckled, but the case would not open. Frantically Jeremy punched the buttons on the keyboard which controlled the locks, peep-peep-peep it said, but to all to no avail. He tore a screwdriver out of his breast pocket, levered it into a crack and with a huge effort wrenched the case open. It was completely empty!

His mind went blank. He had no idea why he was there, what he should say, or even the subject of his address. He turned the case over and banged it, but nothing fell out. Then he searched his pockets for notes, but they too were empty. Blind panic. His mouth opened and shut, but nothing came out of it. The audience started to giggle, then laugh, then slow hand claps. "Blaah!" shouted someone, and the others took it up. A chorus of raucous cries, "Blaah blah! Blaah blah! Baa baa!" He looked over the auditorium, and it was full of sheep, all bleating mindlessly. Near him on the stage the old professor was wringing his hands, sheepishly. He walked across to Jeremy, and seized him by the shoulders and started to shake. Then he heard Avelyn's voice calling faintly from very far away. "Jeremy . . . . Jeremy . . . .Jeremy . . . . where are you?" When he woke up Clare was leaning over the bed.

"Jeremy . . . . Jeremy . . . . Jeremy . . . . . it's CERN again."

"What's that?"

"The phone. . . . . .CERN . . . . .they want you again. Something urgent."

He staggered along the passage: perhaps it was Avelyn at last.

"Hullo," he said hopefully. But it was Chris.

"Oh hi! There's a bit of a crisis here. I think you should come in."

"Why? What happened?"

"Well, we have a tritium alarm, and the apparatus has gone dead."

"Dead? How do you mean dead?"

"Well dead . . . . no life. No signals at all. It's just kinda . . . . disconnected . . . . .logged out. And . . . and . . . . well . . . . ." He hesitated, not sure how to put it.

"And what?"

"We cannot go in to look, because there has been an accident with the concrete door. Someone . . . . well, someone . . . . seems to have been hurt."

"Who is it?"

"We don't know."

"You don't know?! You must know who it is!"

"No we don't. You had better come and see for yourself."

The vultures soon started to gather round the kill. The calls were relayed along the chain. The doctor came: naturally he could do nothing. Security, the local police from Meyrin, then the inspectors and detectives from the Place Bourg Four. The CERN hierarchy was informed, and many came to show their concern. Everyone who arrived asked the same two questions. "Who is it?" and "What happened?" To be answered with a shrug, a shake of the head, or simply "We do not know."

Avelyn's car had been located and cordoned off, together with the route it had followed. By the time Jeremy arrived the place was seething with officials. They had found a more or less empty area to set up an incident room. In the counting room, Chris and Erik were forlornly drinking coffee and looking through the logbook.

"What on earth is going on?" asked Jeremy.

"You had better come and look for yourself." Chris took him down the corridor and Jeremy had to explain to the pickets who he was. One of them took him forward to the now half open door. Jeremy knew at once who it was. He recognised the red-gold hair, the pale fur coat, which was not completely obliterated, and the blue ring which she wore so often. But how could it be, when he had seen her driving away? He could not believe it. But nor could he disavow the unmistakable signs of identity. Suddenly he felt his inside turning over, he rushed outside and was violently sick.

He too saw the footsteps: a woman's coming, and a man's going away. It was very puzzling. He walked up the corridor in anguish. Perhaps it was not Avelyn. Desperately he found a phone; the number rang and rang. He tried it several times, but there was no answer. Was it her or not?

Coming back in a daze to the counting room his mind was full of questions. When? . . . . How? . . . . . Why? . . . . . Had the door been operated after he left? If so who by? What on earth was Avelyn doing in this area anyway? Then he bumped into the head of security.

David Duminy was a Genevois, a retired policeman, who had landed this normally pleasant job at CERN. He spoke several languages and spent a lot of time gossiping and listening to gossip in the CERN cafeteria. That was the best way to get to know people, and smell out anything funny that was going on behind the scenes.

"Ah, Jeremy. You are the group leader, I think. Maybe you can spare us a minute. Most unfortunate business, most unfortunate." He ushered him into a room where another man was sitting. He introduced him as someone from the Swiss police, Jeremy did not catch the name.

"Please . . . have a chair . . . maybe you can help us. We are trying to understand what we can about this sad affair. Who is it? How could it have happened? No one seems to know, but we must try to piece the facts together."

"I know who it is," said Jeremy. "That is almost certainly. I wish it wasn't."

"You know who it is!" They both leaned forward in surprise and expectation.

"I think it's someone I know."

"A friend of yours?" This was getting interesting; when something goes wrong, friends are the first to be suspected. They could have a motive.

"Well, yes. The wife of a friend of mine."

"What is the name?" Jeremy could hardly bring himself to say it. It would crystallise what was still only a suspicion, make the nightmare come true. They wrote it down.

"How do you know? What are the signs of identity?" He gave one only.

"Her husband must be called."

"He is not here. He is away." It was a stupid remark, but it just came out. Jeremy did not appreciate his situation.

"How do you know?"

"Oh, I am a friend of the family. He is lecturing in Milan, I think."

"When does he come back?"

"This afternoon, I believe."

"How well did you know this Madame Olbers?"

"Well, quite well." Suddenly Jeremy noticed that there was a tape recorder running on a side table.

"When did you last see her?"

"A few days ago."

"And last night, did you see her last night?"

"No, no! I spoke to her on the phone though, at about 10.30 I think. She rang . . . . . she rang us at home. I can't think what she was doing here." He shook his head in disbelief.

The inquiries went on. They registered that the door had been opened and shut, while Jeremy was in the counting room. Chris maintained that it had not moved since, and the PS operators confirmed this. Opening the door would have cut the beam automatically, and although the PS had been off part of the time, the beam stopper had not moved.

Who had been on shift when the door was opened? Bexler and Marion with Jeremy helping. And who had gone down to the floor? Bexler. And where was he now? Still presumably in his apartment in town. The inspector began to take a lively interest in the visiting professor. He called the policeman who was waiting at the door, and handed him the name on a slip of paper.

"Get him here as soon as possible. And while you are there, have a good look round his apartment." Within a few minutes a patrol car with three policemen would be on its way.

The pathologist arrived to examine the remains. He was quite used to cutting up bodies, looking for evidence of cerebral haemorrhage, cardiac arrest, rape, poisoning, shooting and other commonplace occurrences. His job was not only to pinpoint the cause and time of death, but also to indicate whether someone else had been involved. This was by far the most difficult case he had seen. Normally with a female victim one looked for bruises, fresh semen and damaged clothing. In this case none of these signs were available. Her watch was a Rolex Oyster Perpetual. To his amazement, when he picked it out of the mess it was still telling the correct time. So that did not help.

He could not say much about the time of death, except that it was several hours ago. Everything was completely cold. But he took the rings and necklace, details of the teeth. Samples of hair, blood and clothing would all help to establish identity. Her right hand, stretched out as if in supplication, was almost intact.

Viktor was still catching up with his sleep when the gendarmes rang. He shuffled to the door in pyjamas, his hair all untidy. There were two of them, but they were quite polite. They had orders to bring him to CERN, but that was all they knew, so they were unable to answer his questions. Viktor knew that there was no mileage in arguing with the Swiss police, better to play it cool. They gave him time to get dressed and collect his cigarettes, but that was about all. He wolfed down a glass of orange juice and took a book; if he knew the police, there would be a lot of hanging around.

By the time he arrived the inspector had begun to form some picture of the order of events. Jeremy, Marion and the PS operators had already told their stories. By all accounts Bexler had been the last one to shut the door, so he must be able to clarify what had happened. Viktor saw a lot of people hanging around, among them some he knew, but he could only nod a brief greeting as he was ushered into the incident room. He had no chance to find out what it was all about.

"What's the problem? What is going on?" Duminy greeted him, and introduced the inspector, who immediately took control.

"So sorry to disturb you Professor, but there has been an accident, and perhaps you can help us. Would you mind if I asked you a few questions?" Viktor was quite unperturbed.

"Of course, I would be happy to help."

They first established his general role as a visitor to CERN, and his work on shift that night. The identity of the victim had not yet been officially confirmed, but Inspector Lederle decided to take a chance. Out of the blue he said,

"Do you know Madame Olbers?" Viktor was rather surprised.

"Yes, certainly I know her."

"When did you last see her?"

"Oh well, let's see, I guess it would have been a month or so ago."

"Where was that?"

"Ah, they gave a dinner party in their flat."

"And you have not seen her since?" It was getting complicated, but Viktor thought he had better stick to his story. He nodded.

"Professor Bexler, we think Mme Olbers was in the vicinity of this experimental area some time last night; we are trying to trace her movements. Now you were around at that time. I hoped you might have seen her. It would be very helpful . . . . ." Lederle looked across at him, and waited."

"Well, let's see, yes, now that you mention it, I did see her. I am sorry, but I am only half awake. Your men woke me up, no time for coffee." Lederle made a sign to the gendarme at the door.

"Get him a coffee! Milk? Sugar?" Then he went on,

"Now this is very interesting. Can you tell us where you saw her?"

Viktor described meeting Avelyn in the corridor outside the hall, and his surprise. He assumed she had come to meet Jeremy. Yes, they had a short chat. Then he went into the hall to do his work. He described what he had to do.

"When I came out she had gone."

"Gone? Where to?"

"I have no idea. I thought she had gone up to the counting room to see Mr. Partridge. She is a friend of his, as I suppose you know. I did not think much about it."

"That's a nasty scratch you have on your face, Professor! How did you get it?" To Lederle's expert eye, it looked quite fresh, but Viktor was not aware of it. He had flopped into bed without washing, and there had been no time for that in the morning. Now he felt his cheek.

"Oh, have I? Perhaps I cut myself shaving." It was a stupid answer. Lederle could see that he had not shaved recently, but he let it go.

"Excuse me a minute. Perhaps you would not mind if I ask you to wait."

The inspector got up and left the room. He walked down the corridor and had a chat to the pathologist who was still hard at work. The doctor explained what he had found so far, and under his guidance Lederle had a careful look at the evidence. A metal bar, partly covered with blood, was on the floor near Avelyn's feet. Interesting! They both felt enormous sympathy for the victim, but apart from a sad shake of the head there was nothing they could say.

They had found the button from Avelyn's coat, lying in the corridor, and matched it with the others. Lederle took it with him.

"Can you recall, I wonder, what Madame Olbers was wearing?"

"Oh yes. A rather nice pale grey fur coat, with hat, gloves and boots to match. She looked very chic; well dressed if you like." He saw no point in mentioning that she apparently wore nothing underneath. "It was a cold night. I imagine that she had just come in. Her car was outside." Another stupid remark! Why did he let himself prattle on?

"Her car? You know her car?"

"Oh yes, the red Mercedes. Everyone at CERN knows her car." Lederle showed Bexler the pale grey button.

"Do you recognise this button?"

"No, not at all."

"It was found in the corridor, outside the concrete door. Have you any idea how it got there?" Viktor was now becoming alarmed. Something must have happened to Avelyn, but whatever could it be?

"No, I have no idea at all." He was genuinely surprised.

After many more questions, Lederle took a decision. There was much more to be found out, and it would be better if the chief suspects were kept in a quiet place.

"I am sorry to tell you, Professor, that Madame Olbers is dead. You seem to have been the last person to see her, and therefore I will have to take you into custody until the matter is clarified."

"Custody? Me? Whatever for? I need a lawyer."

"You can make some telephone calls if you wish. Sergeant Beziers will look after you." He rattled off some quick fire French to the gendarme, and that was it. Viktor Bexler was in prison.

But Jeremy was not out of the wood. As a friend of Avelyn he could have a motive, and he was there when the door was last operated. Maybe Bexler and Jeremy had somehow conspired together to do the terrible deed. As a precaution, and pending further investigation, Lederle ordered Jeremy also to be detained in Saint Antoine. This prison was conveniently close to his office in the Place du Bourg de Four in the old part of Geneva.

Even for those awaiting investigation, and possibly trial, life in the prison was rigorous. Jeremy had his own cell, and the sanitary arrangements were tolerable. They rose at 6 am, had a light breakfast at 6.30 and he had to spend the rest of the day writing a full account of his relationship with Avelyn, Jan, his family, Bexler and anything else that might be relevant; particularly the events of that dreadful evening. In a way it was therapeutic. All these questions were already tearing round his brain in a wild scramble. The writing helped to get them into some kind of order. Inspector Lederle came every day, and quizzed him for hours.

Clare visited as soon as possible, got him a lawyer, brought various creature comforts, books to read. She was very warm and sympathetic, and quite sure that he would be out soon. She clung close to him.

"Darling, this is all so terrible. But when it's over, we'll get together again, and have a happy life."

Arthur came over from Oxford, and went straight into Geneva to see Jeremy.

"So . . . an apartment in the old town! That is really up-market!" Jeremy managed a rueful smile. Arthur became more serious. "Tell me, what happened?"

"I've no idea. It's a nightmare. I just can't believe it. Bexler could have done it. He was down there for a long time. But why should he? He was mad about Avelyn, and she couldn't stand him: so perhaps they quarrelled, there was an accident, and then . . . . . " Jeremy paused, thought for a bit, then cried out,

"But why was she there in the first place? Did she come to meet him? Or me? Or what? The awful part is, we will never know. If only I had gone down with him! Then it would never have happened."

32 Explosion

Boards of inquiry were set up at CERN, and the police detectives worked in parallel. As soon as Avelyn's sad remains had been collected up, and the area cleaned, tests began on the door and its safety systems. They soon found that it would keep moving without requiring a finger continually pressing the 'close' button. All the group knew that it had been modified, and for the first time Chris explained how it had happened. Bexler could not deny that he was the one who had made the change, and the management were far from pleased.

The infrared device was working perfectly, and always stopped the motion. If someone were in the way, the door would keep moving only if the button was pressed. It seemed clear, therefore, that either Avelyn was dead and cold when she was put there; or else some incredibly cruel person had deliberately held his finger on the 'close' button while she was being crushed. Most likely she was knocked unconscious first, and the iron bar at her side was an obvious weapon. Suicide was ruled out; first as a bizarre way to choose, secondly because of the infrared; thirdly there was no suggestion of suicidal tendencies.

Jeremy was soon cleared of suspicion. His affair with Avelyn became widely known, but it seemed that Jan and Clare had been aware of it all along. He might have had motive, but he did not have the opportunity, having been with Marion in the counting room until just before Viktor called to say he was shutting the door. Marion recalled the beam coming on about half a minute afterwards, and Jeremy was back in the counting room soon after that. Lederle let him out within the week, but he missed the funeral.

"It was so sad," said Clare. "There were flowers everywhere, and everyone was so upset." Jeremy had managed to send a huge wreath, with a note that said quite simply,

"Avelyn - I love you - always - Jeremy"

It was just what she had always wanted to hear. Very decently, Jan had ensured that this one went into the grave with her body.

Jeremy could not forgive himself. It was all his fault. There were so many things he could have done, any one of which could have forestalled Avelyn's terrible death. He could have been living with her, or at least agreed immediately when she asked him to come round. When he changed his mind, he should have rung to say he was coming. If he had not left the note, she would have had no reason to go to CERN. If he had gone down to the floor with Bexler, she would have been saved. Maybe he should never have met her, flirted with her, made love. Certainly he could have been kinder while she was alive, taken her presents, flowers. Most stupidly he had never told her how much he loved her, and now it was too late. If only she were living now, he would tell her ten times a day. Avelyn, I love you, I love you, I love you. . . . . . I love you. If only . . . . if only . . . . . if only.

It was Clare, of course, and Simon and Julie. If it had not been for them, he would have gone with her as she wanted, and be living with her now. And she would not be dead. Most of all it was Simon and Julie that had held him back. So instead of feeling pleasure in his children, (their very existence should have been a source of joy), he came to resent their presence. It was not their fault, but indirectly just by being there, they had become part of the chain that led to this dreadful event. So bit-by-bit he found that he could no longer appreciate them. He tolerated them, but talked to them less and less. Wrapped up in his grief, he hardly talked to Clare at all.

On the scientific side there were other inquiries to be made. Why had there been a tritium alarm? What had happened to the apparatus? When the police and safety teams had finished their studies the group were at last allowed into the hall to look at the apparatus. What they saw was extraordinary. It looked as if some wild animal had been on the rampage. Could it have been Avelyn? The counters had been roughly pushed aside or smashed, cables were broken, the copper cylinder round the pressure vessel was on the floor and the container itself nowhere to be seen. There was a lot of radioactivity so they had to be careful.

"Look at this," said Chris. "The copper cylinder is on the floor, it's split open and partly melted! There must have been an explosion, and it was pretty damn hot!" Eventually Erik found part of the aluminium pressure vessel, largely reduced to a molten blob.

Enough data had been recorded in the computer before the bang to tell them what had happened. They had first got some results at low beam, then nothing for a while, and then a short burst at full beam. Chris managed to disentangle the data and his conclusions were startling. The X-rays, coming from neutron capture in the copper, had made a huge improvement, a factor of 2 at low intensity and much more at full beam. The number of fusions per JAV had gone up to about ninety million. It was an amazing figure.

They worked out the heat released, 300 watts. The liquid hydrogen would boil, the pressure would rocket so it was not surprising that the container had exploded.

"That would explain the tritium alarm," said Arthur. "But the main point is that catalysed fusion works. With a well designed system we could easily get a large positive energy balance."

"You mean more energy out than we need to make the JAVs in the first place."

"Absolutely."

"So JAV catalysed fusion really works," said Marion. "It's no longer just a theoretical prediction, and you don't need special detectors to see it. It produces real heat!

"Jeremy's dream," said Arthur. "We must go and tell him."

At this stage Jeremy was still in Saint Antoine, so they all went to give him the news and congratulate him. They cracked a bottle of champagne in prison and when he came out there was a group dinner and more celebrations, but somehow Avelyn's accident, if it was an accident, cast a pall of gloom over the party. Within a few weeks they had published a major paper on 'Javelin catalysed fusion' and showed that it would make a viable source of energy. That dramatic night had ushered in a new era of unlimited cheap power.

Meanwhile the police inquiries continued. Viktor's footprints had been identified in the snow, his fingerprints in the car, and hairs from her coat were found on his clothes. There was also his known tendency to harass Avelyn, and the long time he had spent away from the counting room. The case against Professor Bexler looked overwhelming.

At the trial the clinching evidence was the scratch on his face. Photographs were produced, and the traces of dried blood under Avelyn's fingernails were identified as Viktor's. His lawyer put forward the only plausible counter-hypothesis, that she had followed him into the experimental hall for some reason, interest perhaps, or to say something, and she had got trapped. But no one grasped the wonderful thermal properties of Avelyn's coat, so it made no sense. Also why should Bexler be tampering with the safety systems, and driving her car? It seemed more likely that he had set this up in advance, and either arranged to meet at the fatal spot or brought her there himself, dead or alive.

In spite of his fervent denials, Bexler was found guilty of murder. The judge castigated him for an exceptionally callous and disgusting offence, and sentenced him to 20 years in prison. Pale-faced and uncomprehending, he was led away amid jeers and boos, to atone for a crime he did not commit.

33 Fast forward

Everyone at CERN was excited by the results. Michel initiated a crash programme to make a prototype fusion machine which generated useful power. This would make CERN really famous. He called for a meeting in nine months time to review progress; and the engineers set to work. But it was not long before problems came to the surface.

Simon Steinmetz was one of CERN's top engineers, tall thin and quiet, trained in the prestigious university of Delft, he knew all the relevant physics and the engineering as well: everything he made always worked. He buttonholed Jeremy at lunch.

"Generating heat in liquid deuterium is completely useless. First of all with a few watts the deuterium will boil. The javelins won't stop in the gas and the reaction will end. Secondly you can't get useful energy from a cold source ...... thermodynamics will kill you."

Jeremy gasped. Thermodynamics! Something to do with heat and energy but he hadn't thought about it for a long time. "Oh, how come?"

"It's quite easy," said Simon. "Heat likes to flow from hot to cold. If you catch some of it on its way, you can get out useful energy. How much? It was all worked out by Carnot and the steam engine people in the eighteen hundreds. But liquid hydrogen is at -250 degrees. Generating heat there is useless: it has nowhere colder to go ...... so you can't get useful energy out of that. In fact you will use up lots of energy keeping the hydrogen cold."

"Oh dear! I thought we could boil the hydrogen and use the gas, like steam, to drive a turbine."

"No, you can't. Where would the gas go? You have to condense the steam after the turbine with a condenser, and that has to be colder. Remember all those massive cooling towers outside the power stations. In this case you would need something colder than liquid hydrogen ...... and you don't have that. It will never work."

"Thanks for the info! .... So .... we have to run it hot. Stop the javelins in hydrogen gas. High pressure gas. Then the fusions will make it hot and you can use that to drive the turbine." Simon nodded.

"That would be OK ..... if you can do it."

So now the story changed. A new paradigm! Would the catalysis work in a gas? It was not obvious. After one fusion the javelin would have to travel further before it picked up another deuterium or tritium; so fewer fusions before the JAV died. But it might work. Jeremy started a whole new set of measurements. No more liquid hydrogen, deuterium or tritium, but a new apparatus with high pressure gas. There were new safety problems. But the lab was pouring money into the work and he had lots of help.

Now he was famous. Invitations poured in, to visit, to speak, to write; and offers of jobs. But in spite of all this glory, and all this activity, Jeremy could not shake off his misery.

He buried himself in work. The quest for fusion had led to Avelyn's awful fate, so he wanted to make sure that it was worthwhile. The new particle was named after her; so by making sure the system worked he could in some small way atone for her death, make it seem a little less futile. He thought of nothing else, and gave even less time to his home and family.

Wives often have to slave and languish at home, while the husband interacts with the world. But when he finally hits the jackpot, she gets the payoff and all her sacrifices seem worthwhile. In this case, however, the promised land never arrived. Clare pleaded with him.

"This is so awful for Simon and Julie. You must get away from here, from the memories. Now you have arrived you can get another job, take a six-month break, a sabbatical, everyone will understand. Let's go somewhere different, Australia, California, Africa." But her suggestions were ignored.

For all the right reasons it was the family that had kept Jeremy and Avelyn apart, so now he was blaming them, and punishing them for her death. Clare stood it for several more months, but in the end she could take it no more.

"I am sorry Jeremy, but I am moving out. We are going to live with Jan. You don't seem to want us any more, and he needs me. We have become good friends over the last two years, and now he is all on his own. Also he loves the children, which is more than you can do. He plays with them, teaches them things. And they enjoy his little jokes. I won't need any of your money by the way. And I have found a Swiss lady for you, who will come in every day to do the cleaning."

So Jeremy stayed on by himself in the apartment. He was lonely, but he did not need company. His mind was still with Avelyn. He loved her now, in practice, more than when she was alive, made sure that there were always flowers on the grave, and visited the places where they had been happy together. He had not realised how happy he had been, until it all came to an end; and now he was trying to make amends.

All his efforts to resist her attraction and stay with his family now looked absurd. They did not want him any more, so why had he worried?

He could not believe that such a wonderful person had just been snuffed out. Somehow, somewhere, she must be living still, and in some way travelling forward. Sometime, somewhere, they would meet again.

A few people visited Bexler in prison. Whatever he had done, he was now suffering and desperately lonely. They took him books and journals and told him what was happening. A few hours of intelligent conversation spread over the week might keep him sane. One day at lunch Viktor's name was mentioned and Jeremy gathered that he was in poor shape. So the seed was sown and rather against his will the idea of a visit slowly germinated in his mind.

In any case he kept wondering about that fateful night. Like a gramophone stuck in track, he went over the same questions again and again. What had really happened? Why was Avelyn not in her apartment? She had called him only twenty minutes before. What was she doing at CERN? And above all, how did she get inside the concrete door? Did Bexler really intend to kill her? If so what was the point? In spite of all that aggressive egotism, he was not the murdering type. Killing her would not get him what he wanted. If the phenolphthalein had been a bit stronger, Jeremy could be the one in prison; accidentally of course. So was the whole thing unpremeditated, just a complex accident, that came from nowhere? If so, Viktor would know. Perhaps they were meeting secretly? With Avelyn you could never be really sure.

At first Jeremy hated Bexler, as an unscrupulous competitor and as the murderer of his dearest friend. But as time went on, with the old rivalry removed and in growing disbelief, he felt drawn to find out more.

Jan and Clare were now regularly inviting him to visit, have a meal and see Simon and Julie. They even went skiing together. No longer inhibited by domestic obstacles his conversations with Clare became more lively and interesting. One day he asked them what they really thought. For Jan it was just something that had happened; he had no idea why. Clare had never believed in the murder story. What good could it possibly do him? It must have been an accident, though how and why was a mystery. Just something inexplicable they had to live with. "Of course it's much worse for you!"

So in the end, with some trepidation, Jeremy found the address of the prison, the visiting hours, and drove there. It was in a depressing part of the city, with high brick walls, concrete yards and not a green leaf to be seen. He waited in the special visitor's room, sparsely furnished with no pictures on the walls, and then a door opened and Viktor came in. He looked thinner, haggard, haunted, but under it all happy to meet again. He took Jeremy's hand, more warmly and gently than before.

"At last you have come! I was hoping somehow that this would happen. That we would meet again. Stuck in here you have absolutely no control. It is terrible."

They looked at each other in silence for a while. Thoughts were whirling through Jeremy's brain, but he did not know what to say, where to begin. Viktor was the first to speak.

"The fusion's going well, I hear. Brilliantly in fact! It was a great idea, and I am so sorry not to be there to help you." Jeremy's mouth dropped open. This was a different Bexler. But there was more to come. "While you are here, and in case you do not come again, I . . . . . I would like to apologise. I . . . . I did not really grasp what I was doing; but looking back I realise that I was making your life difficult, trying to be the leader and get the glory. I see now that this was completely wrong. So . . . . I . . . . I only hope you can forgive me."

Jeremy gulped and said nothing. But Viktor went on. "From the very beginning I was a refugee. I had to make my mark, fight for recognition, scrabble my way up from nowhere. And the habit stuck. However far I got, I felt it was just a beginning, I still had to claw my way past the next challenge." He paused and looked across the table intently. "But now from this ghastly place, I can see it all quite clearly. I should have been more laid back, relaxed. Instead I put obstacles in your path. I can see it all now, and . . . . . well . . . . I just want to say I am sorry."

Jeremy nodded. But Viktor went on.

"Just in case you never come again, there is one thing more I want to say. About Avelyn, that is. I didn't touch her!"

"Then what on earth happened? I just can't figure it."

"Nor can I? How did she get stuck in the door? She was alive and well in the corridor when I went inside, and I never saw her again."

"What?"

No kidding. I didn't do anything to her . . . . . except talk."

"So what happened?"

"I have no idea. I went down to put the copper cylinder in place. I gather it worked brilliantly, by the way. And there was Avelyn. I assumed she was looking for you. We had a chat; then I went in to do the work. And when I came out she had gone."

"But where to?"

"She must have followed me into the hall. God knows why."

"And then she tried to get back when the door was shutting," cried Jeremy. "But why didn't it stop. That's the mystery."

"And that's why I am here. But I didn't do it, I didn't see her." Viktor put his head on the table and sobbed. After a while he sniffed, blew his nose, and added vehemently,

"I wish I had never set eyes on the girl - a stupid useless infatuation anyway."

A bell rang and a warder came in. The visit was over.

"I'll come again," said Jeremy, and he looked intently at Viktor as they shook hands, trying to read his thoughts. Was this the truth? The heat sensor in the door said it was a lie.

After that Jeremy started seeing Viktor regularly. His apology and obvious loneliness had somehow touched him. Whatever he had done in the past, and however odious he had been, he now appeared as someone who was suffering and needed support. Jeremy took him reports to read and papers, and discussed his latest projects. Viktor even made some intelligent suggestions, which were welcome. They gradually came to appreciate each other's qualities, and could talk as friends.

They did not speak of Avelyn again, but Jeremy kept wondering if her death had been an accident. He always came up against the same crucial fact. The door had continued to close, in spite of the heat sensors in the roof. And they always worked and they were working still. His apparatus was still in the same room, and again and again when he came through the door he tested the system. It was always the same.

34 Silver fox

At Christmas Jan and Clare took a chalet near Gstaad, and Jeremy was invited to join and ski with his children. It turned out to be a warm family occasion, with Jan always the gentleman accepting Jeremy without question. At altitude he always had lurid dreams, and usually they were about Avelyn. This time she stood naked by the wardrobe, got out the silver fox coat and slipped into it. She turned, giving him a long meaningful glance from those blue eyes and showing a flash of thigh and ginger tuft as she did up the buttons. Then they were outside holding hands in the moonlight, frolicking, and throwing snowballs. Jeremy caught up with her, and tried to slip a hand inside the coat.

"Go away, you're freezing!"

"Are we going to make love?"

"No, I just want to be with you."

"It's all very well for you, but I am perishing." He was wrapped up in all his ski gear with gloves and hat, but there was a wind blowing and it was bitterly cold.

"Not me, I am as warm as toast. The cold doesn't reach me at all. Come on, I'll give you a hug." She opened the coat and wrapped it round both of them, warm, soft and lovely.

He woke up with a start. The cold could not get in; and the heat could not get out. Oh Avelyn, why do you have to wear such beautiful clothes? He could imagine her squeezing through the gap, confident as all pretty women that the world will notice them and take care. But what if the heat detector could not see her? Poor Avelyn! If this was the answer he had to be sure.

Next morning Jeremy drove back to Geneva. He went straight to the Corraterie with its line of luxurious boutiques and found Dolfuss Migg et Cie. As he approached, the door was drawn open in front of him by a uniformed attendant. The shop was redolent with quiet opulence and the all-pervading smell of expensive furs. Still in his ski gear, Jeremy felt out of place, but the impeccably dressed manager inclined his head in smiling welcome.

"A silver fox coat? Of course. For a lady, sir? Or is it for yourself?" Jeremy was not sure, either would do.

"Er . . . . . can I just see what you have?" The flicker on the manager's face was barely perceptible, but the attendant at the door picked up the message and discretely slipped the latch, just in case.

Several fur coats were produced in various sizes. Jeremy picked one, a woman's. It was a beauty, just like Avelyn's, but being new smelled even better. The manager looked at the tag. "This one is 14,900 Swiss Francs. It is very beautiful and rare. We cannot get coats like this any more."

Money was not the question. But Jeremy did not really need to buy it. Could he rent it for a few days? The manager pursed his lips.

"This is a new coat, sir. If we hire it out, we could not really sell it afterwards."

"But I will pay you ten per cent."

"No," said the manager, "We cannot do it. It would detract from the image of our establishment."

What to do? Then Jeremy had an idea. "Do you have a model? Someone who could wear it for us? We just need to make some tests, heat insulating properties, that sort of thing. No, it will not be damaged in any way. You could supervise the whole thing. Yes, at CERN. Scientific measurements. It is quite important."

Well, yes. He did know a girl; they used her for shows sometimes. In the end they made a deal; to have the coat at CERN for the day, with model, would cost 1700 francs.

"She must have a fur hat, gloves, and bootees to match." That was not a problem. "I will telephone her, and we will arrange a date."

Jeremy went back to the lab, and made a few phone calls. Early next week they carried out the test. Duminy the head of security was there, and Chris and Marion. The model was a tall willowy blonde. She stripped down to her underwear with no apparent embarrassment, and got into the furs. She was much more nervous about standing inside the concrete passage.

"It won't hurt you," said Jeremy. "Now, Chris could you press the red button." The door started to grind inexorably towards her, and girl cried out.

"Do not move!" commanded Jeremy. "Chris, take your finger off the button."

"I have, and the door is still moving!"

"Right, press stop for God's sake! We don't want another victim on our hands." Natalie's face was white, but she was unharmed.

"OK, you can come out now. Take the coat off, and we will try again without."

They got her back inside, just in her bra and panties, and tried again. This time the door worked normally. Then they tried once more with the coat and the result was the same as before.

"Thank you," said Jeremy. "I think that's it. It is clear, there is no doubt about it."

"About what?" asked Duminy.

"It was an accident. She was not murdered. The heat sensor just did not work. It was an accident, and Bexler's not guilty. He is unjustly imprisoned."

It took some time for the message to sink into the ex-policeman's worthy brain. Jeremy, Chris and Marion, and eventually Duminy were all convinced. But now they had to convince the world, or at least the Swiss courts of justice. Jeremy phoned his division leader Hans. They got the director of administration and some other big names down to the floor and repeated the tests. Natalie was by now reasonably relaxed, and enjoying the limelight.

So Viktor's lawyers were drawn in, and the ponderous legal procedures began. Two weeks later, the tests were repeated in front of a battery of sworn officials, and before long Bexler was released. He spent a few months getting rehabilitated at CERN, but then went back to the States. His whole approach to physics had changed, and instead of the brash pushy entrepreneur, he became a wise helpful mentor and elder statesman. Jeremy did not see much of him in this period, but they got on well; and behind the scenes Viktor did everything he could to support the fusion projects.

Viktoria Water was eventually exposed as containing nothing special and the sales plummeted. But by then Bexler had sold his share and made a happy profit. As predicted he avoided prosecution; although he had duped the public he had cleverly kept within the letter of the law. The tins were filled from the tap, but the logo "Contains Heavy Water" was correct: normal water contains one part in 5000 of D_2O.

35 Tritium

Michel's great planning meeting to chart the future of catalysed fusion and usher in a new power source for the world took place in September. Other labs were racing for the same goal but he was determined that CERN should be the first. It was a small meeting for select leaders of industry who might fund the development. Sir John Harrison, a well-known nuclear physicist, Vice-Chancellor of Manchester University and leader of the CERN Council was in the chair.

Jeremy gave the first talk about the javelin and the basic physics of catalysed fusion. Marion described the new experiments. Jean-Marc explained how to make the krypton beam. Then the engineers unfolded their plans for a dedicated accelerator which would make millions of javelins, the hot hydrogen reaction vessel filled with deuterium and tritium, the turbo generators and how there would be enough energy to drive all this with plenty left over for the public. And an estimate of cost. It took up most of the day.

Finally it was Sir John's turn. He was a short, thickset man with a large head, long mottled grey hairs combed back, and he had a confident assured manner. People usually agreed with whatever he said; either because he was right, or because he was so convincing.

"First of all congratulations to Jeremy for discovering this new heavy, long-lived particle. Catalysed fusion has been a dream for many years, but you have shown that it really works. Congratulations also to Simon and his engineering colleagues who have devised what looks like a viable plan. After all this dedicated effort, I hesitate to raise a doubt .... but I do have a nagging worry. Can D - T fusion ever become a significant energy source: whether through catalysis as you propose or with a plasma machine such as the Tokamac, which is lavishly researched at the JET laboratory and other places? My question is, where will the tritium come from?"

Eyebrows were raised. Deuterium-tritium is the only thermonuclear reaction that works at temperatures low enough to be reached in the lab, and even that is almost impossible. It is the only possibility for catalysed fusion. At the moment you can buy tritium from the States; they have lots of it in store for their arsenal of H-bombs. No one at CERN was worrying about it. But Sir John was going on.

"Tritium does not exist in Nature. It has a half life of only 12 years, so whatever you make soon disappears. The Americans make tritium from lithium in nuclear reactors; lithium-6 captures a neutron and splits into an alpha particle (helium-4) and tritium (hydrogen-3). So we can get it from them or make our own in a nuclear power station. There is plenty of lithium around." Sighs of relief.

"But in the long term the idea is for fusion to replace nuclear power, based on uranium, with all its worries about radioactive nuclear waste. Anyhow the uranium will run out. So then where will you get your tritium?"

Michel was getting worried. He jumped up,

"Excuse me for interrupting, but we thought about that. The D - T fusion produces an alpha particle AND a neutron. In fact the neutron carries most of the energy and generates the heat as it is slowed down. So there are lots of neutrons coming out. Round the reactor we will put layers of lithium. The neutrons will be absorbed by the lithium, making more tritium, which we extract. It will be self-sustaining. So the process will really be fuelled by lithium and there's lots of that around."

"Yes, that is indeed the idea," said Sir John. "But it is far too optimistic. You can get some tritium that way, but not nearly enough. Here's the balance sheet," and he produced a slide.

D + T → He + n

"In each fusion you use up one atom of tritium and you get one spare neutron."

n + Li-6 → He + T

"And that neutron can be captured by lithium-6 and make one more atom of tritium. So you get your tritium back. In principle you can break even: you can replenish your stock of tritium as it is used up. But only just ..... only if there are no losses. But of course there are losses. Some of the neutrons will end up in other places. And anyway natural lithium is a mixture of isotopes, 92% is lithium-7 which will capture some of the neutrons, and give no tritium. So you will only get back a small amount of your tritium. Then you have to extract it from the lithium, purify it and so on. There is no way this can become a self-feeding process. It is a lemon ..... a very elaborate and sophisticated lemon ..... but a lemon all the same. This will never be a source of power for the world ..... and the same applies to the Tokamac which uses the DT reaction in plasma."

Sir John sat down. There was a stunned silence. For five minutes they just sat there ..... thinking ..... letting the news sink in. Would all this work be wasted? One or two hands were half raised; but then quickly withdrawn. Everyone was waiting for the DG to save the day. You could see that his mind was churning, but even Michel had nothing to say.

Finally Sir John rose to his feet again. "Well .... I think we are agreed. This has been an impressive initiative, an excellent study and I do congratulate you all. But there is no real point in taking it further. Let CERN get back now to its original charter .... fundamental research ..... and exploring the world of elementary particles."

That was the end of catalysed fusion.

36 Epilogue

Late one October evening a cacophony of cuckoos shredded the still night air of Bernex. Jeremy was living alone, though he saw quite a lot of Clare and the children. He rolled out of bed and groped his way along the corridor. The light had gone again; he must remember to buy some more bulbs at the supermarket. In the darkness he fumbled for the phone. Who could be calling at this time of night? Some cretin in the lab had got his wires crossed again.

"This is Professor Angstroem from the University of Lund," drawled the soft Swedish voice, molto andante, molto cantabile, e un poco lugubrioso. "I am speaking perhaps with Dr. Yeremy Partridge."

"Yes, indeed. Hullo Professor."

"Aah good. Aah yeas. I hope it is not too late for you at this time of the evening. Very well then. I have some information for you Dr. Partridge which I hope will be of interest. The Nobel committee for physics of the Swedish Academy of Sciences has been meeting today; in fact the meeting has just ended. I am asked to inform you that this year's Nobel Prize for Physics has been awarded to you Dr. Partridge for the discovery of the Javelin and Catalysed Fusion. May I be the first to congratulate you!"

Jeremy gulped. The whole enterprise had ended in failure. This would never be any use and never make energy for the world. But what could he say?

"Thank you Professor. Thank you so much, please thank the committee on my behalf."

It was fantastic, every scientist's dream. Telegrams poured in, congratulations from all over the world. It took him a month to answer them. The prizes would be awarded on December 10th, Alfred Nobel's birthday, and the celebrations would last for nearly a week. He could invite his friends and colleagues to go with him to Stockholm and his lady, of course, would have her expenses paid. If only the glorious Avelyn could be with him. She would have been the belle of the ball.

So who could he take? Clare deserved a break, as she had suffered while he worked, but in the circumstances it did not appeal. So many women, one imagines, would be available to participate in the Nobel ceremonies, but Jeremy could not think of a single one.

Until he thought of Juliet. What had happened to her, and how was she getting on in Paris? And would she be interested? He switched on the minitel and dialled into the French electronic telephone directory; and there she was, 'Eckerdovsky Juliet, danseuse'.

She remembered him all right, and was very chatty. By now Jeremy was more fluent in French. Yes, she had heard about Avelyn, it was in the papers, très triste. That scoundrel Bexler, it was totally unbelievable.

"Yes, I am still teaching the dancing. Always the same thing! Yes, all alone, except for Liliane of course. She is growing up fast, such a graceful girl with a Slavonic face, so like Ivan. Yes, life is going along."

"And you? Alone too! That is sad, I did not know. You should come and see me. We could visit the musées, theatres, I have contacts, we can get the tickets. Yes, I will show you around. A change of air. That is so important."

"I have something to tell you," said Jeremy. He mentioned the prize.

"Prix Nobel! C'est pas possible! Mon Dieu, how wonderful. I am so pleased. Congratulations . . . . ." She was so young, lively and vivacious, it all came through even on the phone. Jeremy hesitated; he did not know her very well. Then he took the plunge. Juliet did not understand at first, but once she grasped the message she was enthusiastic.

"Mon Dieu, to meet the King of Sweden, and all those famous people! Yes. Why not? For an old friend, and a friend of Ivan's. I would be delighted." Then she added,

"But before that, are we not meeting somewhere? The breaking of the ice, we are calling it? To get to know ourselves again a little. You should come to Paris for a few days, there are lots of hotel, and I will be your guide."

The divine Juliet. Memories were coming back. Jeremy felt a small glimmer of vitality and hope.

Stockholm in the winter was a magic city. Lots of happy people and the streets were full of glorious blondes. There was snow everywhere with sleighs drawn by reindeer running up and down. Father Christmas in one of them, full of presents with bells jingling. It was psychedelic, like a dream.

When the great day came Jeremy was sitting with Juliet in the front row of the ornate Royal Opera House in Stockholm, looking very elegant in his full evening dress. They had already met the other prize winners at the various parties, receptions and formal lectures that had filled the preceding week: all venerable scientists with multiple accomplishments, while Jeremy had only done one little thing.

His lecture would be tomorrow; and he did not know what to say. He could talk about the discovery and how the fusion worked in the lab. But he had to explain that it would never be useful. He should have refused the prize; but now it was too late. What could he say? What could he do? It was all so embarrassing. He was on the wrong train, going to the wrong place: but he couldn't get off.

Vivacious young Juliet had insisted on seeing everything and joining in every possible activity, rather more than he would normally have chosen; and she was an enthusiastic partner in bed. Luckily she was so seductive and he had managed to keep up. Now Jeremy felt tired, distinctly tired.

Actually he felt strange, different from usual. It was steaming hot in the Opera House and he was suffocating. This was a new shirt and the collar was too tight. For the last few mornings he had woken with a hangover and today it was worse; too many late nights and too much booze probably. Now his head was aching and it was hard to keep track of the ceremony. Juliet was holding his hand and saying something; he tried to reply but only managed a mumble.

Then the band struck up and a procession of dignatories in sumptuous robes filed onto the stage. After them came the king with his acolytes, calmly and seriously moving into their places. He was wearing medals of some sort and a bright diagonal sash. The music stopped and Jeremy heard a faint rumbling noise like a train in the distance. Did Stockholm have an underground? He listened to it slowly approaching, thrumming, louder and louder, until it was a roar and the whole building seemed to be shaking. There was a final deep woof, like the bark of a large dog right in his ear, and then everything went quiet.

On the stage he could vaguely see figures moving about, but his field of vision was somehow restricted. He seemed to be looking through a black tube at a small area straight ahead, but he could still scan left and right to see what was happening. Someone was making a boring speech. After that names were called out and the prize winners came forward in turn, but they were only a blur. The circle of light in which he could see was collapsing, getting smaller and smaller. His head throbbed so he shut his eyes and slumped down in the chair.

Then he heard his name being called by the usher and he knew that he must get up, walk up the steps and shake the king's hand. But he could not move. He tried to lift his hand to make a sign, but nothing happened. He could not move his arm nor his feet nor his head. There was a sound of running water like a river, or a lot of worried people murmuring to each other.

Juliet nudged him gently. "Jeremy . . . . Jeremy . . . . wake up." But it was useless; he could not move. All he could do was roll his eyes and that did no good because everything was black. He closed his eyes again and lay back in the chair. What was the point of it all anyway? Might as well give up. He drifted off to sleep.

Vaguely and very far away, Jeremy heard a voice calling. "Jeremy . . . . . Jeremy . . . . . wake up."

It was Avelyn's voice!

Avelyn! He woke with a start and rubbed his eyes. Where was he? This was not the Opera House. He was lying on a white sheet and lightly covered. It was cool. He was in a large airy room. There was a big window or door, wide open, and beyond that a garden full of shimmering colour and flooded with an intense brilliant light. Colourful birds were warbling ethereal tunes.

Avelyn was standing in the doorway in a diaphanous gown, surrounded by a halo of light.

"Jeremy . . . . . . Jeremy . . . . . . come on . . . . . come with me. It is so lovely here."

"Avelyn," he cried out in amazement. "Avelyn, are you OK?"

"Of course I'm OK. I've had a long swim and I feel wonderful ..... because I'm with you. This is paradise. Come, let's enjoy it together." She held out her arm and helped him to his feet.

"I've been waiting for you, for so long. But you were far far away."

He got up shakily moving towards the door.

"But Avelyn . . . . have. I . . . have I . . . . have I got the Nobel prize?"

She turned to him with a broad smile. "Not that I know of, darling. But you've got me! Isn't that better than any prize? And I am real and you are still half asleep. Feel me."

He held her close, still not knowing what was true and what was a dream. Then hand in hand they went out together into the garden. They were bathed in soft shimmering light and all around them the birds were singing their chorus of heavenly joy.

---------- o 0 o ---------

26205708R00152

Made in the USA
Lexington, KY
21 September 2013